W9-BNS-450

THE DISHONORABLE
MISS DELANCEY

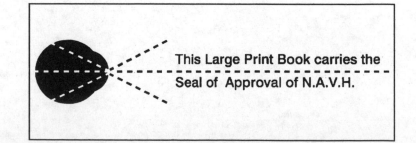

This Large Print Book carries the
Seal of Approval of N.A.V.H.

REGENCY BRIDES: A LEGACY OF GRACE

THE DISHONORABLE MISS DELANCEY

CAROLYN MILLER

THORNDIKE PRESS
A part of Gale, a Cengage Company

Farmington Hills, Mich • San Francisco • New York • Waterville, Maine
Meriden, Conn • Mason, Ohio • Chicago

LIBRARY OF CONGRESS CIP DATA ON FILE.
CATALOGUING IN PUBLICATION FOR THIS BOOK
IS AVAILABLE FROM THE LIBRARY OF CONGRESS

ISBN-13: 978-1-4328-4580-3 (hardcover)
ISBN-10: 1-4328-4580-2 (hardcover)

Published in 2018 by arrangement with Kregel Publications, a division of Kregel, Inc.

Printed in the United States of America
1 2 3 4 5 6 7 22 21 20 19 18

For my sister Roslyn.

*Thank you for sharing your
love of Georgette Heyer.*

Duke & Duchess of Salis

David Ellison ——— Grace
Reverend
      Edmund Danver ——— Patience

Nicholas Stamford ——— Lavinia
Seventh Earl of Hawkesbury Countess

George
Baronet

Phillip DeLancey ——— Frederica
Viscount Winpoole Viscountess

Richard   Clara

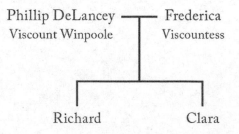

bury

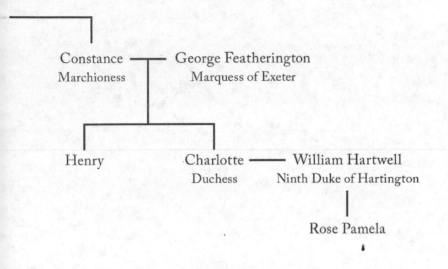

Constance — George Featherington
Marchioness   Marquess of Exeter

Henry   Charlotte — William Hartwell
             Duchess   Ninth Duke of Hartington

                        Rose Pamela

Kemsley family

Benjamin Richmond   David McPherson — Matilda   Theresa
                     Reverend   "Mattie"   "Tessa"

CHAPTER ONE

Brighton Cliffs, England
April 1815

The Honorable Clara DeLancey stood atop
the chalky cliffs. Above her, heavy clouds
menaced the moon, revealing then conceal-
ing the scene below. At her feet glowed the
lantern borrowed for tonight's escape, while
far beneath, the English Channel churned
white and deadly. Wind whipped clothes
around her body, tugging at her, like the
despair that had tugged for months, begging release.

Leaning forward into the night wind, only
half hoping it would retain its furious
strength, she closed her eyes and breathed
in the salty tang as sea spray spattered her
cheeks. Another breath. Another. She hadn't
felt this alive in weeks.

The wind grew louder, rushing in her
ears, a snarling, savage thing. How capri-
cious nature could be, how cruel; capable of

causing shipwrecks, yet also of sustaining life. How strange that something could be one day so admired, the next feared or despised. A broken laugh escaped. She, like nature, fell into the latter category.

A kaleidoscope of images raced through her mind. A handsome man. A beautiful lady. A ballroom filled with the expectations of the *ton.* A broken promise. Soul-sweeping shame.

The anger burned again, as if stoked by the very fires of Hades. How could he? She dragged in another breath. How could he reject her?

She opened her eyes. Peered down through the gloom to where specks of foam denoted the crashing waves of high tide. The wind continued its merciless grasp, teasing free her hair from the cloak's hood. Would the wind hold her should she step out? Did she even want it to? She leaned forward, farther still. The roaring surf grew louder, louder. Should she dare —

"Miss!"

She jumped. Pebbles scattered beneath her feet, upsetting her balance, and she was sliding, sliding, closer to the treacherous edge —

And in that moment, knew she did not want to die.

A scream erupted from her depths.

A firm hand grasped hers.

She clung desperately, as ebony locks lashed her face. Angry fire roared down her right arm until it felt like it would snap. She scrabbled frantically amid the rock and wispy tufts of grass for a handhold, tearing her left hand's nails and skin.

Slowly, slowly she was hefted to the cliff-top, the final tugging momentum surging her forward to collapse on the grassy verge. She dragged in air, heart pulsing faster than her fingers could ever play, and rubbed her right arm, so near to being wrenched off. She would never play piano again!

She'd nearly never played *anything* again.

Guilt streaked through her, twisting her insides. How dared she have been so fool-hardy? How dared her rescuer risk his life for her?

She glanced to where he lay gasping beside her, one hand over his face. An angel sent from the Almighty? No. Not unless the Almighty employed angels who looked like disreputable seafarers, dressed as this person was in a battered cocked hat and sealskin cloak. She inched away, pushing to her grazed hands and knees, wincing as she rose. She snatched her hair back, pulled the hood down nearly to her eyes. Perhaps he hadn't really seen her, would not recognize her and add further shame to her already impressive roll of dishonor.

"Miss?"

Angels didn't growl, did they? She peeked across. And they definitely wouldn't have a propensity for startlingly blue eyes capable of flailing a person with an angry glare.

"What the blazes did you think you were doing?" the most unangelic creature yelled, getting to his feet.

She scurried, wretchedly rabbitlike, away from the dim glow cast by the lantern. "Th-thank you." Her voice was too soft to be heard above the wind's roar. She tried again, slightly louder. "Thank you."

The man stood — sandy haired, taller and far broader than she'd first realized — and took a step toward her. "Thank you? That's all you have to say?"

What more could she say? She lifted her shoulder in a shrug.

He took another step toward her. "What on earth were you doing?"

She paced back. Lifted her chin. "Thank you for saving me" — her voice was now too high, too squeaky — "but I do not think I need tell you of my personal business."

"Tell of your personal — Miss, I'll have you know I just saved your life! You could have died. *I* could have died! What fool game were you playing at?"

Clara tugged the cloak closer as shivers rippled up her spine, through her limbs. How could she explain her moment of insanity? It wasn't a game, but life and death. Her eyes filled. Thank God the hood hid her features, offering small hope of recognition.

He studied her a moment, his fair hair gleaming in the moody moonlight, the hard contours of his face softening a smidgen. "Look, miss, I'm sorry for startling you. But you were standing so close." He shook his head. His frown returned. "What are you doing here at this time of night, anyway?"

She shook her head. Took a step away, inching closer to the path, not the cliff edge.

He snorted. "Meeting a lover, is that it?"

Another broken laugh released, sounding like the rasp of a dying bird. If only he knew. He was obviously not a member of the *ton* — otherwise he would most certainly both recognize her and know just how unlikely *that* scenario would be. She shook her head again.

"No?" His brows shot up, his gaze intently curious.

Clara retreated another pace. She had the feeling if she fled he'd simply chase her; if she spoke again, this illusion of anonymity might be pierced. Either could prove fatal. If she somehow returned home without either occurring, she might have a chance to slip into bed and pretend this was some kind of Gothic nightmare she would never dream again.

"Still nothing to say for yourself?" He gave a surprisingly warm chuckle. "Look, can I at least have your name? Or where you live? I'm sure there must be someone somewhere who cares about you."

Cared about her? Sadness rolled through her, certain and ceaseless as the waves pulsing below.

"Look, miss, I understand you might feel embarrassed, but I promise not to tell your parents." The wind began to shriek. "You do have parents, don't you?"

She took another step behind. He followed. What a bizarre clifftop dance in the moonlight this must seem to those angels tonight, those angels who had definitely *not* descended to assist her, electing as they had to watch the show like a poor man from Covent Garden's uppermost stalls. Why would God send angels to help her? He certainly didn't care.

Another step, another. When she judged enough paces met, she whispered another thank-you, then turned and fled into darkness.

Behind her, she heard, "Hey!" but she did not stop. Could not stop. Thank God Mother could not see her. Thank God Lady Osterley couldn't see her — any hope of regaining a reputation would surely be lost. Legs pumping, she picked up her skirts and ran faster, even faster, until another sound gave her pause. A short cry, then a thud. Her heart thumped. Surely he couldn't have fallen from the cliff? She glanced behind, saw a figure prostrate on the ground. So maybe the angels had decided to assist her after all. But delaying to check he was not hurt would eat into her escape and her chance to remain unknown. She picked up speed, panting, lungs burning. Anyone who saw her would think her a madwoman! A sob escaped. Anyone who knew her would think the same.

Eventually, with lungs fit to burst, her mouth tasting of metal and blood, pulse thundering in her ears, she recognized the path she'd walked daily this past fortnight had opened onto the lane linking Brighton to Rottingdean. She slowed, approaching the gentle crescent of near-new houses that formed Brighton's outermost limits. None of the brick-and-stucco terrace houses were, of course, large enough for her parents' satisfaction, but that mattered not; Lord and Lady Winpoole received few visitors these days. Besides, satisfaction played little part in her family's world anymore, what they could afford being of far greater importance.

She hurried past the central garden with its sad statue of the Regent — designed to win the builder acclaim but instead reaping disdain for its disproportions and now-missing right arm — carefully avoiding the gravel as she rushed to number ten. Fortunately, their elderly neighbors' lights were dim, but still she needed to moderate her frantic breathing to be as soundless as possible. A step up to the front door — remaining unlocked, thank God — a twist of the handle, and she was inside, had removed her shoes, was creeping up the stairs, careful to avoid the eighth and ninth steps which always creaked. A heart-pounding minute later she was in bed, her pelisse hung crookedly on the back of a chair, her cloak puddled on the floor, two more items she would need to remedy tomorrow morning.

Clara crooked an arm around her pillow, huddling into warmth as the clock downstairs struck midnight.

The witching hour. The hour of affliction. She closed her eyes, her escape still beating frantically in her chest, and begged the dreams to stay away.

Cursed hour? Cursed life.

No one would ever tell her different.

"Benjamin Richmond Kemsley!" His sister's eyes widened.

Ben stumbled to the fireplace, holding out his hands, wishing they would heat faster. He might have faced a thousand nights of icy furor on the open seas, but he'd never felt so chilled as he did tonight. He snuck a peek at his sister. Sure enough, her jaw still sagged.

Matilda closed it with a snap. "What on earth were you doing, racing out of here like that? And now, look at you! You seem to have faced Napoleon singlehanded!"

He fought the pang of regret at missing such a fight and nodded to Matilda's husband. The Reverend David McPherson possessed humility and meekness that often proved the perfect counterbalance for Matilda's volubility, volubility a trait all Ben's family seemed to possess.

A noise drew his attention to the drawing room door and the other member of the household, young Tessa, her red hair tousled as if she'd just woken from sleep. "Benjie!"

"Why aren't you in bed, little sister?"

"I heard noises." She frowned. "Why aren't *you* in bed?"

"Because I am not seventeen." He ruffled her hair, smiling as she protested this usual display of affection.

"What on . . ." Her blue eyes widened as she took in his appearance. "For heaven's sake!"

Humor faded as the events from earlier grew large in his mind again. Yes, he'd felt heaven's urgent call guiding his steps tonight. "Just that."

"What happened?" Matilda gestured him to sit, handing him a cup of steaming tea. "You had us worried."

"I . . ." Couldn't explain, really. How to say he'd felt a sudden urge to go to the clifftop, when it was nearing gale-like conditions outside? Couldn't. "I needed a walk."

"Tonight?"

He nodded to his sister, even as he exchanged glances with the reverend. He could perhaps share his suspicions with his brother-in-law, but not while Tessa was in the room.

Matilda scowled. She murmured something to Tessa. Whatever that was, it resulted in Tessa hugging him and whispering, "I'm glad you're safe" before she departed.

Leaving him with his not-to-be-so-easily-

18

placated sister. Her brows rose. "Well?"

He shrugged. "I was using Tessa's telescope, and I saw a light."

"A light?" She sighed. "Don't tell me you were off saving the world again?"

"All right. I won't."

She snorted, but it sounded more like a chuckle. "Why you think you need to rescue everyone and everything, I'll never know."

"Mattie," her husband murmured.

Ben studied her levelly, as a hundred raw memories surged through his soul. African skies, desperate children, shark-menaced waters, a life unsaved . . .

Pink tinged her cheeks. "Well, yes, there is that." She shook her head. "My brother, the rescuer."

"Not always," he muttered. He cleared away the emotion clogging his throat. "I saw a light atop the cliffs."

"What? Someone was out in this weather?"

"Aye."

"Who was it? Anyone we'd know?"

He slid David a look before meeting his sister's blue gaze. "I'm hardly acquainted with my new brother-in-law, let alone all the people of your acquaintance, dear sister."

The rose hue darkened but the intense

stare did not waver. "Why do you think they were there?"

"I don't know."

He thought about the girl. He did have a suspicion, but such an action was so drastic he barely dared form the thought, let alone speak such a thing aloud. What would cause someone to abandon all hope, ignore God's principles, and risk eternity?

The pain etched in his heart sharpened. He'd seen men give up, men in war, those flung into seas, men who'd succumbed as pain or blood leached all life from them. But he'd never known someone to yield who was healthy — and from the way she'd sprinted off, the firm body he'd so briefly held, the lass was certainly healthy.

"Ben?"

He glanced up, met their worried faces, worry he'd seen too often in the weeks since his return from the seas ringing Cape St. Francis. He smoothed his forehead free from scowl, forced his lips up. "What does a man need to do here to get another cup of tea?"

Mattie eyed him, then rose and exited the room.

The fire snapped, crackling warmth through the wee hours. Outside, the wind continued its weird moan. He pressed against the pain still throbbing in his knee. The absence of his sister might bring a hush to the room but never to the questions in his heart. Why had God allowed him to live? Was it for nights like these, when he just might have made a difference?

Matilda reentered the room carrying a fresh teapot and mug. She poured, he murmured thanks, and she resumed her seat. "Did you injure yourself?" She nodded to his dirt-stained leg. "You know the doctor wants you to be careful not to twist things again."

Too late for that. He batted away her worries with a genuine-enough-sounding laugh. "You worry too much, Mattie." He turned to his clergical brother-in-law. "I'm afraid you'll discover my sister has a tendency to overdo her gifts of compassion."

"One of the reasons I care for her so."

Ben smiled, pleased to hear his sister's soft sigh and see the pink filling her face. "You'll do well," he said to the new husband, garnering an answering grin and a mild "I hope so."

Mattie put her cup down with a clatter. "So you do not know who it was?"

He shook his head. "All I know is that she left that lantern." He gestured to the small tin lantern on the table beside the door.

"She?" His sister exchanged a glance with her husband. "Benjie has never been able to withstand helping a pretty maid in distress."

His smile dipped at her use of the long-familiar, long-despised nickname. "She wasn't pretty." Possibly untrue, but he'd barely been able to make out her features, shadowed as they were by that hood. All he knew was she possessed raven black hair and a high-pitched voice that suggested she was younger than her sweet, ripe form declared.

"Oh! A hag!" Matilda chuckled. "Perhaps she'll turn out to be a beautiful princess in disguise."

"I doubt it."

"How disappointing," Mattie said. "Well, heaven knows you need a wife. Perhaps we'll need to find this lady of mystery and learn her secrets."

Ben pushed his chair back, forced himself to rise without wincing. The poor wild creature he'd barely met tonight give up her secrets? "Good luck with that."

"We don't need luck," Mattie replied, an evil gleam in her eye. "We just need God."

He nodded, said his good-nights, and left to ascend the stairs to his bedchamber, his heart sinking. Experience chanted that

Matilda would not rest until the mystery lady was found.

CHAPTER TWO

The knock disturbed her dreams. Wild dreams. Frightening dreams of plummeting, plummeting to hungry rocks below. Clara woke with a gasp, breathing hard, yet striving for quiet as the knock came again and the maid immediately entered the room.

"Begging yer pardon, miss, but madam wants you downstairs."

A glance at the windows revealed sunlight peeking past the curtains. "What time is it?"

"Near noon, miss."

She sat up in a hurry. "I had no idea it was so late."

"You missed services today."

They missed services most Sundays. Why should today be any different?

Meg remained hovering near the doorway, as if unsure what to do. Clara fought the flicker of annoyance. Oh, to have a proper lady's maid again, one who knew to wait to be granted admittance, one who could fix hair as well as she could hold her tongue.

Meg moved half-heartedly towards the chair holding the abandoned pelisse.

"Please leave it. I'll deal with it later."

"Are you sure, miss?"

"Of course I'm sure."

The look of chagrin on the woman's face filtered regret through her heart, but Meg exited before Clara could apologize for her tone. Sighing, she pushed aside the bedcovers and moved to pull open the curtains. Other signs of her late-night exploits stared at her: the damp cloak, muddied shoes. She picked up the cloak, snapped it once, twice to get rid of the worst creases. Meg would doubtless have another word to Mother should further clothing be sent down for cleaning without reason. And Clara had possessed no reason to wear that cloak in days. No reason sufficient she could give her mother, anyway.

She dressed in a plain morning gown, then moved to the dressing table to attempt to bring order to her hair. Despite merciless tugging, dark strands refused to settle. Again the wish for the services of a proper maid arose, was smothered. Until one could be certain the servants' wages paid for their silence as well, Father had decreed no more staff were to be employed. Those few currently with them had served the family for years and kept their mouths shut from habit, if not loyalty.

The timber-framed oval glass revealed her reflection. Lank hair. Skin too pale. Light green eyes deeply shadowed underneath. Her nose and eyelashes were still good, but her chin seemed too pointy these days. And was that a spot? She peered closer, angling her neck to examine her chin. Groaned. Definitely a pimple. Though why should she care when nobody else would . . .

Her eyes filled. Shoulders slumped. How had it come to this? How had she, once the toast of London ballrooms, come to sitting in a cramped bedchamber in an ugly house on the farthermost outskirts of a once-popular resort town? Obsessing over a spot.

It didn't matter. None of it mattered. She herself apparently did not matter. Her value to her parents lay only in whom she might marry, and having failed to land the Earl of Hawkesbury as they'd so long wished — as she'd so long dreamed — their increasingly desperate attempts to fling her at any matrimonial prospect had diminished in both quantity and quality of would-be suitors. God knew — the world knew — at five-and-twenty she was a veritable old maid. Perhaps one day her parents would join her in giving up.

She shook her head at her foolishness, blinking away the moisture. Surrender was a concept her parents had never learned. Mother still seemed to believe the earl would "come to his senses," as she said, and divorce his wife to marry Clara, when any simpleton could see how devoted he was to Lavinia, Countess of Hawkesbury, gazing warmly at her as he'd never done with Clara. But still Mother persisted. That was the Winpoole way. After all, neither she nor Father had given up on Richard.

"Miss?"

Meg's call broke into her reverie. She pushed away from her memories, refusing to glance at the looking glass, and made her way downstairs to the room that served as both parlor and breakfast room.

"Is something wrong, Clara?" Mother asked, her brow knotted. "I cannot remember you sleeping this late."

"No. I'm just a little tired."

"Tired?" Father said, adjusting his newspaper with a snap and a frown. "You've barely stepped from the house in days."

Except at night.

"How can you be tired?"

"Oh, leave her be, Phillip," Mother said.

"All young ladies feel a little out of sorts at times."

"Well, it's been going on for months now." His dark eyes studied her, not without a trace of compassion, Clara thought. "I wish to know if there's even any point in sponsoring another season for you."

A season?

"Heaven knows the last however many have been a sad disappointment. What does it take for a young man to come up to scratch these days?"

"If only Hawkesbury —"

"Enough, Frederica! I do not want to hear your foolishness again. What's done is done and can't be undone, so I wish you'd stop this farcical nonsense and leave the poor man be."

"The poor man? After what he did to our dear girl?"

Shame quivered afresh as her parents continued their familiar battle. How could she have been so gullible as to believe the earl had ever truly cared? She'd been swept along on a tide of emotion, ably supported by both her mother and his, the dowager countess who could never forgive Lavinia's well-connected relatives for casting aspersions about the Hawkesbury family so many years ago. Her son's marriage to a woman

28

the dowager despised had made the marriage difficult, a fact Clara had seen with her own eyes, and something that continued to spark hope in Mother's breast, even if Clara could no longer share in her optimism — or wished to. There'd been something so tremendously affecting about how the earl's wife had received them last year, her grace in a time of sorrow as indisputable as it was unsettling. Clara had yet to reach a point of wishing him well, but she could no longer wish them ill.

"Well, what do you say to that?"

She looked between them. What had just been said? "I beg your pardon?"

Father coughed. "Perhaps there is no point in sending you again if you cannot be bothered listening when someone speaks. You really must try harder to act interested, my dear, if you want to land a husband."

"Yes, Father." They continued to gaze expectantly at her. "Oh, and I do wish to visit London again." Hope flickered within. Perhaps one of her old friends would be willing to receive her now. Anything had to be better than the infernal boredom of Brighton. A pleasure playground it might prove for those with sufficient funds and friends; a lonely outpost for those lacking either.

"We won't be able to go for a few more weeks. And I'm afraid we won't be able to attend every social function of note," Mother said with a sigh and a sideways glance at Father. "Cost, you know."

And a lack of invitations. Her fingers clenched. How long must she pay for her brother's sins?

"Never mind that," Father continued. "She'll get to the ones that matter. But I want you to put off this gloomy manner and find something of your sparkle. Men don't like a sour face, my girl."

Men didn't like her anyway, even when she hadn't been so wretched in heart. She pasted a smile to her lips. "Of course not."

"There! That's what I want to see. Now just act happy and all will be well. You'll see."

She kept the mask glued on as she nodded. Well, if Father wanted her to secure a husband and leave the shelf of unwed ladies, she'd be the best little actress he'd ever seen.

The organ's piping continued as they exited the church into sunshine. David, dressed in his clergical robes, greeted them as he did the other parishioners, with the warmth and candor of his sermon earlier. Tessa released Ben's arm and moved to talk with some other young ladies, their bright chatter suggesting a friendship of some standing. He studied the milling congregants, glad to finally get the chance to properly examine those attending. But still the lady who had haunted his dreams last night remained unseen.

Young ladies there were aplenty, no doubt due to Matilda's ease of manner, and unexceptionable family, but young ladies with midnight hair and flashing eyes were not to be found. Though perhaps a sermon on Leviticus was more inclined to induce dull eyes rather than flashing, regardless of the congregant's age or gender. He esteemed his brother-in-law but could not esteem the dry-as-a-desert address given today.

"Have you found her?"

He glanced down at Matilda, peering around like a small, blond robin. "Found whom?"

"Your mystery lady, of course. Don't pretend you were not looking."

"Then, no. I have not."

"Hmm. Well, perhaps she goes to St. Michael's. You might try there next time."

"Of course I won't go there, Mattie. I'll attend the service where my brother-in-law currently presides." Even if the sermons weren't to his taste. He glanced down, met the twinkle in her eyes.

"I will speak to him about the sermon topics. He feels he must follow the bishop's prescribed texts, but I think we both know if he does, the pews will empty faster than a sailor's bottle of rum."

A chuckle escaped. "I don't know if David will appreciate such candid opinions."

"Well I do know the bishop will not appreciate receiving fewer tithes than what's required." She eyed him, her gaze falling to his left leg. "How is it today? You seemed to be favoring the right on the way over."

He swallowed a sigh. She remained as observant as ever. "It works."

"But not as it ought. Don't you think you should have it seen to?"

"I told you before, Mattie. My knee is fine. I'm fine."

"No, you're not," she said bluntly. "I wish you'd have a grain of common sense and go back to your London man. You don't want to be a cripple before you're thirty."

But he *was* a cripple before the age of thirty. Mattie just refused to believe it. "Go talk to that older lady over there. She looks like she'd appreciate your advice."

She gave a sniff and marched away, leaving him to nod to those congregants who caught his eye and make small talk with those bold enough to speak with him. He thought he'd spoken long enough last Sunday about his time in Africa, but apparently not long enough for some of the men who wished to know more, before he finally steered their conversation to Napoleon's latest deeds.

Tessa soon returned, the remaining congregants dispersed, and they walked through the grassy churchyard, now abloom with bluebells and early buttercups. Such a contrast to the wild, uninhabited African shores where his desperate walk had only been cheered by the sparse and hardy white flowers that reminded him of tiny daisies. He shook off the memories, replying to Tessa's observations about the improved weather as he ought.

They passed the large residence of the parish rector, currently empty while he took extended leave in Ireland, his absence thus promoting David to the pulpit. The vicarage — a far more humble abode accorded the rector's assistant — lay a twisting street away. Ben's knee began paining again as he climbed the hill, forcing him to grit his teeth. If David and Mattie's cottage did not possess so excellent a view of the sea and the cliffs towards Rottingdean, he'd be tempted to find accommodation that was far easier to navigate. Not that he could afford it, or — he grinned — that Mattie would permit him. He stumbled at the doorway, glad his sisters were too engaged in conversation to notice. David eyed him, however. Ben shook his head at his brother-in-law's unspoken concern and collapsed into the sofa, from which he could see the shining sea.

As the sunlight bounced light across the glassy water, in stark contrast to last night's tumultuous waves, his thoughts drifted to Matilda's earlier words. He pressed against the throbbing in his knee. Perhaps he should see Dr. Townsend again. If he saw the old sawbones, he might also have opportunity to catch up with Burford and Lancaster. Perhaps he'd write and see if they were amenable to a visit. Perhaps a trip to London might not be such a bad idea, after all.

CHAPTER THREE

Two days later

Clara walked the half mile along Marine Parade into town, glad to escape Mother's worries which seemed to line each room like heavily papered-over walls, making their home feel ever smaller and even more restrictive. She'd abandoned her clifftop walks; they held no pleasure now. Who knew if that man might return, might recognize her? She shuddered. What if he did? What if she recognized him? Her heart raced. She dragged in a quiet breath, willing herself to calm, in case her companion noticed.

Meg's faded, fixed features suggested she remained oblivious as always. She trotted alongside, completing errands for Mother whilst supplying nominal chaperonage. Not that Clara needed a chaperone. At five-and-twenty she scarcely need worry about the propriety of such things. But Mother still did, so Clara did not argue, acquiescence the lesser of two evils.

Clara paused by the iron railings, not too close to where the bathing boxes waited, and shifted the books in her arms. The breeze, so much a part of Brighton life, had settled for moments of bad temper, puffing fiercely now and again, as if to remind pedestrians of its capability. She sucked in brine-laden air — cool, sharp, invigorating. Well she could understand why Dr. Russell had recommended the benefits of seaside visits in the middle of last century. Just breathing in the sea's freshness made her feel healthier, cleaner somehow. Almost like the cobwebs of her soul could be blown away; that possibility hung around the corner.

Which was ridiculous. As pretty as Brighton might be, out of season it was just another fishing village. It might host the Prince Regent's famous Marine Pavilion, but he was not due to arrive for several more months. And until he did, neither would the fashionable set, who so often took their cues from the King's heir, like bees buzzing around a rose. So Brighton would remain dull until he tired of London, which she supposed was not such a bad thing. Society-less Brighton held the advantage that nobody knew her. Nobody would gossip. Fewer people to judge. Society-less Brighton also held a disadvantage, however. Nobody might know her, but even after months of living here, neither did she know anyone.

A seagull wheeled solo in the sky, cawing high above a small fishing boat, as if eyeing a prize forever out of reach. A sudden ache swept through her, causing her breath to catch and heat to fill the back of her eyes.

"Miss?"

Clara broke from her reverie to glance at the maid, whose expression spoke of unutterable boredom. "Yes, Meg?"

"I might head to the market now, if you've no objection."

"No, of course. I must return these books to Donaldson's. I shan't imagine it will take very long." She eyed the maid steadily. "I imagine your errands will take considerably more time."

Meg blinked. "I . . . er, of course, miss."

"Then I will bid you good morning and see you at home."

"Yes, miss."

Clara hastened away before the maid could change her mind. Walking alone, even if it were only such a little way, felt so freeing. She crossed the Parade, hurrying past a draper's cart turning into Manchester

37

Street, walked along the Steyne, and entered the library.

The elegant building was quiet at this time of day, which meant she returned the borrowed books more efficiently than doing so at a more fashionable hour might allow. She moved past the lounge where the newspapers were kept, rushing to escape detection by the overly friendly Mr. Whitlam, a stout, gout-afflicted older gentleman who seemed to have taken up residence in the sofa by the window and made it his mission to speak to her whenever she visited the library. She ducked behind a large wooden bookcase. She might be lonely, and perhaps a tiny part of her still dreamed of finding a husband, but she was not that desperate! Rounding the corner she found the novels that formed the substance of her reading matter — and Mother's. Two young ladies stood perusing the shelves: one a blond, one a redhead.

"I don't know," the blond lady said, eyeing the book the younger held. "I'm not sure if it's quite appropriate." She glanced up, caught Clara's eye, and smiled. "Good morning."

Clara bobbed her head. "Good morning." How strange of this lady to speak to a stranger. She edged away, fixing her attention on the shelves. Miss Burney's novels always appealed, but had she not read all of them several times now? Surely Donaldson's could get more in.

"Excuse me."

Clara turned to see both ladies gazing at her, sisters if the wide blue gazes and matching features were any indication. The redhead's smile seemed more hesitant than the other's.

"I was wondering if you've ever read *Waverley.* I understand from my brother that it has some graphic battle scenes."

"I have not, although I have enjoyed some of Walter Scott's poems."

"Oh, I love *Marmion!*" the blond exclaimed. "I don't care what those critics say, I like a flawed hero. Makes him so much more believable, would you not agree?"

"Er . . ." Who *was* this strange lady? As for offering her opinion on flawed heroes . . . "I suppose so, yes."

"We know only too well that heroes can be flawed, don't we, Tessa?" She turned to the redhead, whose bright hair crackled with light as she nodded. "Some can hide their good hearts under a layer of tease."

Clara thought back to her rescuer three nights previous. "Or anger."

"Exactly so! Oh, you must excuse me."

The blond held out her hand. "My name is Mrs. McPherson, and this is my sister, Miss Kemsley."

Clara shook their hands. "Miss DeLancey."

"Well, Miss DeLancey, it's a pleasure to make your acquaintance. I wonder that we have not met before."

"I . . . that is, my family has only lived in Brighton for the past year or so."

"By all that is wonderful, so has mine! Well, more like six months, really. I moved here when I married." Mrs. McPherson smiled engagingly. "I previously lived with my brother in Kent, you see."

Clara nodded as if she really did see. Had she ever met such a firecracker of a lady? Mother would have a fit! Father would no doubt call Mrs. McPherson a vulgar mush-room. But something spurred her to stay and continue the unsought conversation. "Is that the brother who read *Waverley*?"

"George? No, I rather doubt he's read anything beyond a racing guide in years, the more's the pity. No, Benjie is the one who has always liked reading, which is fortunate when one spends so much time at sea, don't you agree?"

Benjie? What a peculiar name, like some-thing one might call a pup. He must be quite young, though somewhat precocious to be offering opinions on Scott's novels at such an age. Aware that both ladies were studying her curiously and awaiting her answer, she finally said, "I imagine it would be."

The blond chuckled, a warm sound that prodded recent memories, but before Clara could pinpoint which one, Mrs. McPherson said, "So Miss DeLancey, should we risk it?"

She had hooked a hand through her sister's arm and was moving slowly through the room, necessitating Clara to keep up.

"Risk what, exactly?" Clara said.

Mrs. McPherson held the book aloft. "Shall we endeavor to see if this novel be worth reading?"

"I suppose if you do not like it, you can offer it to your brother to read again. Provided he's not in school, of course."

"School?" The ladies shared a puzzled look.

So perhaps he was a little older? Oh, that's right — he was at sea. She offered a wry smile. Mrs. McPherson's brother was not the only one at sea, it seemed. Perhaps Father was right, and she really needed to pay more attention to what other people said. "The beauty of a circulating library is that one can always return a book unread if necessary. So borrow it, if you like."

"Do you like, Tessa?"

The redhead murmured in the affirmative.

"Then it is settled." Mrs. McPherson's smile broadened. She turned to the man at the circulation desk. Clara blinked. How had they arrived at the circulation desk? Did this extraordinary woman sweep all before her path?

Her business concluded, she turned back to Clara. "I do hope, Miss DeLancey, that you'll risk the other."

"What other?"

"And permit us to be friends."

Perhaps it was the frank gaze, or the sisters' open smiles. Perhaps it was because she felt she could not deny this indomitable force. Perhaps it was the yearning ache she'd felt before, or the tug she felt now. Whatever the reason, she could only give one answer.

"Yes."

Ben limped back to the vicarage. The letter he'd posted yesterday to Dr. Townsend couldn't be replied to soon enough. The throbbing in his knee had worsened this morning, a foolish wish to walk along the beach exacerbating the strain. Why didn't God heal him? Like all members of his family, save his older brother, he dared believe the promises of the Bible held true today as they had centuries before. Perhaps he'd used up all God's favor back on African shores.

He pushed through the French doors to the drawing room, catching his sisters' commentary to David in the next room. Mattie sounded excited. Even Tessa seemed more animated. Bracing himself for interrogation, he forced himself to walk normally, smile, and ease into the nearest chair.

"Benjie!"

"Hello, Matilda. How was your morning?"

"I was just telling David. Tessa and I visited the library today. Look what we got." She proffered a copy of *Waverley.*

"A good read, as I recall."

"And we met someone."

Ben raised a brow at his brother-in-law. "Should we be worried?"

Mattie laughed, stroking her husband's hand. "I think David would not be concerned, save for the salvation of her soul." Her attention returned to Ben. "You, however . . ."

He frowned at her. He did not need his sister's interference in his nonexistent

43

private life.

"She was so funny. Staring at me like she would a stuffed creature at Bullock's Museum."

"Sounds sensible. I suppose you hadn't been properly introduced?"

She sniffed. "This isn't London. Nobody cares for such things here."

"You might be surprised. Not everyone appreciates such informality."

"Like George?"

George. Their brother. Whose recent ascendancy to a distant cousin's baronetcy had led to a sudden interest in being correctly addressed, much to the amusement of his siblings.

"She was very nice," Tessa offered softly.

"Who? Oh, this lady you met. Does she have a name?"

"Miss DeLancey."

He frowned. Why did that name elicit a twinge of memory?

"Ben? Why do you look like that? Do you know her?"

"I vaguely recall the name," he admitted. It was possible that he had met her, once upon a time, when he was a different man in a very different world.

"Well, perhaps you'll get the chance to see if you do. I've invited her to call on us on

Friday."

"This Friday?"

"Yes." Her brow puckered. "Don't tell you won't be here."

He leaned back in his chair, his smile growing genuine. "Very well. I won't."

"Oh, but Benjie! She seems quite sweet and has a lovely smile."

"Be that as it may, I have no desire to meet her."

Mattie pouted. "How can you be so rude?"

"Surely you did not suggest I would be here."

"Of course not!"

"Then I don't see the problem. You'd do better to turn your matchmaking attentions to George. Heaven knows our brother will need help to find someone prepared to overlook his pride."

She laughed as if reluctant. "Very well. But you can't fault me for trying."

"I can't fault you for caring, that is true."

Blue eyes looked up at him. "You do need to marry one day, Benjie."

"One day, Mattie. Remember, I don't like to have my hand forced."

She grabbed his arm, squeezed gently. "I want you to be happy."

"I am happy."

Her brows lifted.

He glanced across at Tessa, whose expression matched Mattie's look of doubt, igniting a pang of conscience. Well, perhaps he'd never be as happy as before that fateful last voyage. But he was content. Mostly. And wasn't contentment close enough to happiness?

Matilda sighed. "Well, it doesn't matter how much you protest. I'm not convinced."

"That is your prerogative."

"But I am convinced of something." She tossed her blond head. "I feel certain you will meet Miss DeLancey one day soon."

And she stood and exited the room, leaving him wondering about her determined interest, and uneasy that her gift for being correct would be in evidence once again.

CHAPTER FOUR

The next day a note arrived, addressed to Clara, with an invitation to tea at the vicarage the upcoming Friday. The vicarage? Was Mrs. McPherson the wife of a church minister? Never would she have imagined such a thing! Weren't all ministers and their wives supposed to be incredibly staid and old-fashioned? Who could have imagined a vicar's wife to be so forward and friendly, let alone so frivolously daring as to be interested in novels?

When Mother learned of the invitation, she frowned. "I suppose one must attend if it is the vicar's wife who has invited you. But I cannot like it. How on earth did you meet?"

"At Donaldson's, Mother."

"Hmph. Perhaps you should not go to such places if you're to be accosted by all and sundry. Where was Meg?"

"Completing errands, I believe."

"Well" — Mother tapped the invitation — "I cannot attend. I have already accepted Lady Osterley's invitation to luncheon. Are you sure you'd rather not come with me? Reginald should be there."

Reason enough not to accompany her mother. The only person capable of duller conversation than Lady Osterley was her son. "Thank you, Mother, but I really feel I should accept Mrs. McPherson's invitation."

Mother sighed. "Then I suppose you should go. But only this once, mind. One visit should be sufficient to discharge any obligations."

"Thank you, Mother."

"Although I cannot but wonder, who is her family?" Her mother's forehead creased. "McPherson? I do not know any McPhersons, do you?"

Clara did now. She kept that thought behind her teeth and murmured, "I believe her maiden name is Kemsley."

Father looked up from his newspaper, a frown in his eyes. "Kemsley? Why do I remember that name?"

Another question she could not answer.

His frown grew more pronounced. "I do not want you spending time with someone unworthy. These are our sorts of people, are they not? You are a viscount's daughter after all. We need not associate with everyone who claims acquaintanceship."

How to explain the indefinable tugging in her heart to go? "They are everything that is respectable." Perhaps that was overstating things. "Mrs. McPherson was friendly, and Miss Kemsley seemed quite shy and sweet."

"But who introduced you?" Mother said, brow still puckered. "I do not understand."

"As you said, Mother, if she is the vicar's wife, it would be impolitic not to attend." She pushed to her feet, pushed out a smile. "I shall write and accept for Friday."

And before another word could be said, she escaped.

Friday

"Miss DeLancey, I cannot tell you what a pleasure it is to have your company today."

Clara smiled, murmuring something of her reciprocal feelings to Mrs. McPherson. The day had already proved surprising. The aged vicarage, though modestly proportioned and decorated, was positioned to capture views of both the sea and the chalky cliffs. Indeed, she could almost see where her home was, centering the Royal Crescent on Brighton's opposite boundary. She had met Mr. McPherson, the assistant to the rector of St. Nicholas's Church, whose mildness contrasted sharply with his vivacious wife, before he then had made his apologies and murmured something about visiting the infirm. Miss Kemsley, though somewhat diffident, had proved friendly when Clara asked for her opinion on the borrowed novel, saying it had not proved as terrifying as her brother initially suggested.

Clara had nodded. "It can be hard to trust another person's opinion on such matters, can it not? If someone gives fulsome praise one is bound to be disappointed, while another's negative review seems certain to ensure the novel will be enjoyed very much. One needs to be akin in mind and spirit to truly trust another's judgment."

"Oh, but I do trust Benjie," said Miss Kemsley. "Even if he is so much braver than I."

Such sisterly devotion to a younger brother was rather touching. Clara's smile faded. A pity she could no longer hold her own brother in such esteem.

The conversation flowed surprisingly easily, considering Clara had felt sure the matter of church attendance would arise. But no mention of spiritual matters had been made — their discussion of novels, fashions, and the attractions of London versus those of Brighton as innocuous as any other conversation she might have held.

"You possess a wonderfully fine view," she said, gazing through the large windows.

"Benjie recently gave me a spyglass," said Miss Kemsley. "Would you like to see it?"

"Oh! I thought your brother away at sea."

"Not anymore, poor thing." The redhead rose, murmuring something about retrieving the gift.

"Your brother lives with you?" Clara said.

Mrs. McPherson nodded. "For the moment, until he is more settled. Our eldest brother is not always the most easy of persons with whom to reside."

Clara must have inadvertently looked a question, for the vicar's wife continued.

"Our father died not so long ago, then George inherited a title. I believe he feels he must live up to being head of the family now, which means he's far less enjoyable company. I think Benjie prefers life near the sea to being stuck with George at Chatham Hall."

Clara offered a wry smile. How well she knew about being less-than-enjoyable company.

"Tell me, Miss DeLancey, do you like the sea? I have not tried sea-bathing yet — my husband has scruples about such things —

51

but it does look most invigorating."

"I'm afraid my parents share Mr. McPherson's scruples."

"A pity."

Miss Kemsley returned, holding the cylindrical object. "If you look through the small end, you can see the most marvelous distance away."

She showed Clara how to hold the spyglass, how to adjust certain knobs to gain sharper focus.

"How wonderful!" Clara exclaimed. She could see the sea-bathers, the small huts lining the shore, the bathing machines in the water, complete with sea-dippers, and — "Oh!" Cheeks heating, she lowered the spyglass. "I did not realize one would see *quite* so much."

"Benjie is always warning us not to look too closely. Some sights are better left unseen," Mrs. McPherson said, a twinkle in her eye. "I hope you were not grossly offended."

"I did not think such a portly fellow would be able to stay afloat, let alone feel the need to be invigorated *all* over." Clara shuddered, the image of the naked man refusing to go.

"Seawater is very buoyant, or so Benjie tells us. He says to swim in the ocean is a most marvelous experience."

"I would love to go sea-bathing," Miss Kemsley said almost wistfully. "Would you ever wish to try it, Miss DeLancey?"

"I —"

"Now, dearest, we must not bore Miss DeLancey. Why don't you tell our guest about your telescope?"

"Oh. Well, the spyglass can prove quite useful." Miss Kemsley leaned forward. "In fact, it was used just the other day to help someone in trouble."

"Really?"

The redhead nodded. "That night of the terrible winds. I would never wish to be outside on such a night, would you?"

Clara froze. No, surely not. The rescue must have involved a boat; that must be it.

Mrs. McPherson smiled. "There's no need to look alarmed, dear Miss DeLancey. All proved well in the end. Apparently the poor old dear didn't really mean to harm herself."

"Poor old dear?" Relief oozed through her chest. They referred to another incident, after all. Though how many people requiring rescue would be out on one of England's most stormy nights . . .

"Yes. Atop the cliffs. Poor dear. It seems to have been a near thing."

Oh, dear God! It *was* her incident they

referred to! But who? What connection did her rescuer have with the McPhersons? Would that she could ask — but surely that would only raise suspicions. She glanced around the room. Spied the small lantern she'd inadvertently left behind. Nausea slid through her stomach. She needed to leave before her rescuer returned. He might have thought he'd rescued an old lady — indignation heated her chest, surely she hadn't seemed so old! — but what if he recognized her?

"Miss DeLancey? Are you well? I'm sorry if discussion of such matters is distressing. Truth be told there are many who struggle, especially now, with so many men killed in war. It is little wonder some feel they have no resort but to harm themselves. It is why we established the Sailors and Soldiers' Hostel here in Brighton." Mrs. McPherson looked at her sister. "Tessa, take the glass away. I'm sure it must be time for more tea."

"Oh, but I . . ." What could she say? That she needed to leave before her mysterious rescuer visited again and possibly recognized her? Conscious that they continued to study her, Clara gulped, and said, "I'm sure I should return soon, and I would not wish to intrude on your time with your family."

"Never tell me you do not wish to meet

the hero?" Mrs. McPhersons's smile widened. "Most young ladies would."

"I am not like most young ladies," blurted Clara.

Mrs. McPherson laughed. "I knew I would like you. Never mind, Miss DeLancey. He will be out all day."

Relief made its presence felt again, and conversation over tea was almost enough to make her forget her earlier discomfort. Soon it was time to depart. Clara rose, aware of a strange reluctance. Well she understood why the ladies' young brother would wish to live with them. She had not experienced so warm and friendly an atmosphere in years.

"Thank you, Mrs. McPherson. I have enjoyed my time today."

"I'm so glad, for I have also. Oh, and please call me Matilda, seeing as we're to be such friends and all."

"And I prefer to be called Tessa," said her sister.

"Very well, Matilda, Tessa." Clara smiled, holding out her hand. "Please call me Clara. I do hope we might meet one day again soon."

Now would come the invitation to services, she felt sure.

But no.

A simple farewell and she was walking

along the path, exiting the gate, then heading along the street back to where she'd arranged to meet Meg near Donaldson's again.

She smiled to herself. What an extraordinary time. The vicar's wife and her sister seemed quite normal. If Mother were to overlook their frank ways — her skin heated again at the unfortunate incident with the spyglass — she might almost approve of such an acquaintanceship.

Chatham Hall . . . She would have to ask Father if he knew the place. From the way Matilda had spoken, it sounded like their family was well connected. If so, surely her parents would not begrudge her the only friends she had made in Brighton since their arrival months ago.

Her heart tugged again, in a twisting yearn for friendship. Brighton might be pretty, but it was a lonely place, generally filled with the old and the infirm. Strangely, she had not hankered overly for her London friends, those friends whose acquaintanceship had faltered after the trouble wrought by Richard. But these ladies, though they lacked a degree of sophistication, possessed an earthy warmth that something deep within her craved. Perhaps it might be worth persuading Father to attend services on

56

Sunday.

Lost in her musings, she rounded a corner, only to bump into a burly figure. "Oh, I beg your pardon!"

"The fault was mine entirely." A man whose tanned face and broad shoulders declared him something of a sportsman offered a small bow.

Her breath hitched. She backed away.

The sandy-colored hair reinforced the vague notion of recognition elicited by his voice.

He straightened, his open countenance eyeing her curiously, his gaze as blue as the heavens.

The man. Her rescuer. The person she suspected knew her secret and whom she desperately wished never to see again.

"Excuse me."

She turned and rushed back around the corner, hurrying into the sanctuary of Donaldson's, praying he lacked courage to follow.

Ben managed to limp the rest of the way home, his visit to Captain Braithwaite forgotten as his thoughts churned over the unexpected encounter. While never thinking himself a prize as far as ladies went, he'd never known any young lady to actually run

57

away from him before. And while he had no thought of marriage — what impecunious near cripple could? — to have two young ladies flee from him in the space of a week was a trifle disconcerting.

Pushing open the squeaking gate, he walked along the cockleshell-lined path and entered the cottage he currently called home, to find his sisters in the drawing room.

"Benjie? You're back! Oh, what a shame. You just missed her."

"Missed whom?"

"Miss DeLancey, remember? She came to tea and — Benjie? What is it? You look as though you've seen a ghost."

"No ghost." Just a pretty brunette with the most striking green eyes he'd ever seen. Striking green eyes that had widened in something akin to fear when she'd bumped into him, almost like she had seen a ghost. He frowned. Why did that thought prompt a quiver of remembrance?

He shook his head, trying to clear away his confusion, aware both his sisters were regarding him curiously. He cleared his throat. "Did you have a good time?"

"Oh, yes." Mattie's face brightened. "She was a little reserved to begin with but soon grew quite affable. Until . . ." She glanced at Tessa.

His youngest sister flushed to match her hair. "I showed her the spyglass you gave me."

"Let me guess," he chuckled. "She saw rather more than what she anticipated. Haven't I told you to be careful when the bathing machines are out?"

"I forgot."

He ruffled her hair. "Never mind. So apart from that you had a pleasant time?"

"Yes."

"Very pleasant." Mattie nodded. "I rather gained the impression she had not been out in company much in recent times, which I cannot but wonder at, seeing she's quite pretty and has been out in London, of all things."

"And so stylishly dressed," added Tessa.

Mattie's head tilted. "I wonder why she is not married. She must be my age."

His thoughts flashed to the young lady he'd collided with earlier. Was she married? She had no maid in attendance, so she probably was. He felt a tiny, strange pang of regret.

Mattie's brows rose. "What? No comments about spinsterhood? No jibes about last prayers?" She turned to Tessa. "Perhaps our brother is unwell."

Tessa's brow clouded. "How was Captain Braithwaite? Is he any better?"

His sister's concern drew his thoughts back to his earlier visit. "A little," he allowed.

"Poor man." She sighed. "He knows you do not blame him?"

"He knows." But one could know and still not believe. It had not mattered how many times he'd tried to reassure, still Braithwaite could not forgive himself for not providing Ben with a marine chronometer. Ben cringed again internally, remembering the tongue-lashing they had both received on their return. He would have preferred a whip on his back to the words that stung his soul and the invective Braithwaite had been subjected to. Ben knew the admiral's vehemence was compounded by grief and loss, and perhaps his dismissal was unfair, but the truth could not be denied. Ben *had* failed. Ben found comfort in knowing God had forgiven him, even if the admiral never could. Braithwaite didn't have that assurance.

"We must continue to pray for him."

Ben studied his youngest sister. Her interest in his colleague had not waned in past months. But recently turned seventeen, she was at an age of susceptibility in matters of the heart. It would not do for her to grow enamored of Braithwaite. He exchanged glances with Mattie.

She gave a little nod. "It is good to pray for all God's children, that is so. Ben, I've been thinking perhaps it is time for Tessa to visit our dear brother. Oh, don't make that face, dearest. George is not that starched and stuffy. And now he has the title, he should exert himself to think about someone other than himself."

"You *do* believe in miracles," he said.

"Of course I do," Mattie replied.

Her steady gaze bored reproach within his heart. Well he knew how long his sisters had prayed for him while he was lost. Well he knew it was their faith that had kept him alive. In moments of utter despair, he'd felt the comfort of a Presence he'd long known, a presence poor Braithwaite scarcely dared believe in. When all had seemed hopeless, God had shown Himself yet faithful. Ben's return to England had seemed a gift from God rewarding his sisters, who had never stopped believing, and proof that His mercy extended to the wretched and undeserving.

"I don't want to stay with George," murmured Tessa.

"Of course not, but with his money and title you could have a London season."

"I don't want a London season. You didn't have one, Mattie."

"But Father did not have the baronetcy then. Wouldn't you like to go to London and see the wonderful sights Clara was describing during her seasons?"

"Who?" Ben asked.

"Miss DeLancey."

He leaned back in his seat. "If this Miss DeLancey has not found matrimonial success with multiple seasons, perhaps Tessa should not be pushed into something she's no wish for."

Mattie frowned. "That sounds very unkind to poor Miss DeLancey, if you ask me."

"She cannot be so very poor if she's undergone multiple seasons. In fact, it's enough to make one wonder what is wrong with her."

"Benjamin!"

Tessa shook her glossy head. "I do not think I want to go."

"Ignore Ben. I'm sure it will prove better than you think, dearest."

"I do not like crowds and noise."

"Only because you have not experienced them much," Mattie said. "Even Brighton will get busy when the Prince Regent returns."

Tessa bit her lip, then murmured an

excuse and left the room.

"You should not tease her, Ben."

"And you should not push her."

"She needs to grow in confidence."

An image of the timid young lady he'd bumped into reasserted itself. He shook his head. Heaven forbid Tessa grow so insecure. "I suppose she won't learn to do so hiding under your shadow."

His sister's eyes flashed. "Nor yours."

"No."

"Which is why I think George, in his indifference, might be just the one to make her realize the need to assert herself."

"If his apathy doesn't kill her," he said. "He's so self-absorbed he does not notice anyone that does not benefit himself."

"This could prove beneficial for them both," Mattie nodded slowly.

"And you. David is a most accommodating host, but I do not think he bargained on gaining *quite* so many Kemsleys when he proposed."

"You know he loves Tessa as his own sister."

"And I'm sure like most newly married husbands he'd love our not being here, also." Ben fought a sigh. His idyll in Brighton might need to come to an end sooner than he'd planned.

"But, Benjie, I do not want to lose you again, not when it seems you've only just returned."

"You would not lose me. I'd only be in London."

"I forget sometimes how well you know London." Mattie pushed a lock of hair behind her ears. "You never met Miss DeLancey when you were in London before?"

Had he met Miss DeLancey on his one brief excursion into society? If so, she'd left no impression of any substance.

"That was five years ago, Mattie. A lot has happened since."

"Of course. I just wondered."

Perhaps Miss DeLancey wasn't the only one lacking the power of attraction, Ben thought wryly, his mind flicking back to the two ladies who had demonstrated this so ably this past week. Leaving him with this strange feeling of being stuck ashore, yet — more than ever — adrift on life's seas.

CHAPTER FIVE

"Darling Clara" — the earl's thick-fringed hazel eyes smiled at her lovingly — "would you do me the honor of becoming my wife?"

Glorious warmth filled her as she leaned closer, her smile matching his. "Yes."

She'd be a countess! Wife of the most handsome man imaginable! Married to a war hero, no less. A man — oh, such a man! — who shared her passion for so many things. A thousand images sang in her soul. The earl smiling tenderness at her. The earl dancing with her. The earl applauding her musicality. The earl sharing dinner with her family.

Coldness crept around the blanket. She squeezed her eyes shut even more, desperate to hold on to the last fragments of the dream. But it had disappeared as surely as morning fog in the heat of a rising sun.

The familiar ache rippled her heart. How could he have rejected her? How could he have preferred a countrified nobody to a viscount's daughter? She, who'd been accounted one of London's belles. She, who knew how to dress, knew the Peerage inside out, knew everything a lady of title and consequence must know. She could have given him children. She would have made him the perfect wife. It had been each of their mothers' dearest wish.

A tear slipped down her cheek. What was wrong with her?

Rejection swirled, pressing painfully against her soul, wisping ghostlike memories and imaginings.

The earl laughing warmly with his *wife.* The earl holding his *wife* close. The earl sharing a house, meals, a bed — his everything! — with the woman that should have been Clara.

How could he have smiled into her heart and then discarded her like she meant nothing?

Had she grown ugly? No man had dared approach her since. Was she simply unlovable? Her heart clenched. Would anybody even tell her if she was?

A sob throttled breath from her body. She rolled to her side, swiping at the tears as she stared at early dawn light seeping past the partially opened curtains. Why had he preferred Lavinia Ellison to her?

Lavinia. The new Countess of Hawkesbury. The woman she had hated for so long until it seemed Clara had a poisonous black hole for a heart and she'd forgotten how to live.

Lavinia. Whose unlooked-for graciousness last year had increased Clara's self-loathing. Shame had lapped at her soul for months, eroding the last vestiges of self-confidence. She had nothing; she *was* nothing. She could barely remember how to be around other people. Granted, Matilda and Tessa made it easier than most to pretend to be nice, but that was because they did not know her background. If they did, they would be sure to cut her as so many others had. Besides, she could not expect Mother to countenance her continued acquaintance with such ladies, kind though they may be.

The heaviness inside refused to leave. She could see the years rolling ahead of her much like the past two, years of loneliness and boredom, years of hopelessness and drear. Would she ever be freed to live again and laugh?

The dim light slowly took on a golden glow. She squinted. It must be Sunday. She counted back the days. Yes, today *was* Sunday. A day of rest.

She pushed herself upright, rubbing a hand over her bleary face.

A day when she felt a strange desire to accept Matilda's unspoken invitation and insist her parents accompany her to church.

"Well, Clara, I can't say your dragging us here is quite to my liking, but at least there appears to be some acquaintances worth our notice."

Mama's comment, whispered though it was, caused a sting of embarrassment. Not that other congregants were not talking, just that she wished Matilda's husband was not trying to deliver a sermon at the same time.

She fixed her attention to the front, forced herself to listen to his words. It took a while to focus, to keep her thoughts from wandering. God knew she didn't like to bother Him, but perhaps there might be something worth heeding in the vicar's address.

". . . so this is why our Lord said, 'He that is without sin among you, let him first cast a stone at her.' " Mr. McPherson glanced around the congregation. "Can any of us claim to be without sin?"

"Really! What a nerve some people have, asking such things!"

"Mother!" Clara whispered. "People will hear you."

"Let them hear! I have nothing of which to be ashamed."

Except, perhaps, last year's ill-advised trip to Hawkesbury House in Lincolnshire. That trip had proved extremely humiliating. The fortitude the new countess had displayed at a time of personal tragedy shone in marked contrast to the icy address of the earl, whose own mother had concocted the scheme designed to unravel the marital felicity of her son.

Shame crawled over her. In that moment, so much of her hatred of Lavinia had withered, the seething mass of emotion heating her chest waning under the weight of pity and mortification. To intrude at a time of grievous loss was unconscionable. Yet for the new countess to have borne their presence with so much dignity was unfathomable. What had made her behave in such a gracious way?

The rest of the service passed in a blur, the questions from the past demanding attention. Soon they were swept up in the tide of exiting worshippers, were shaking the minister's hand, were outside among the milling congregants, exchanging gossip under an ancient elm.

"Miss DeLancey!" Clara turned to see

Matilda hurrying towards them. "You came."

"As you see." Clara smiled and introduced her parents. "Mrs. McPherson is the lady I visited on Friday. Her husband delivered the address today."

Mother acknowledged Matilda's curtsy with the slightest of nods. "On her return Clara mentioned that you have a brother who resides at Chatham Hall. He is a baronet?"

"Yes."

The suspicion clouding Mother's face cleared a mite. "Well, that is something, I suppose."

"It is something, I suppose, if one considers such a thing to be worthy of notice."

"To be sure." Mother nodded, seemingly oblivious to the smile lurking in Matilda's eyes.

Clara spoke quickly, before her blunt-spoken new friend said something to jeopardize their amity. "Mother, I was hoping we might invite Mrs. McPherson and her sister to tea sometime soon."

"Oh! Well, I'm not sure —"

"Thank you, Miss DeLancey, but Tessa is to return to Kent very soon."

"There." Relief softened Mother's face. "What a shame."

"But perhaps Mrs. McPherson could still attend, if she is not too busy."

Matilda smiled. "Thank you. I'd be delighted."

Her smile warmed a corner in Clara's heart. Perhaps the way to have friends was to be friendly. Heaven knew she needed to do something other than isolating herself as had been her wont these past months. They arranged a day and time, before someone claimed Matilda's attention and the surge of congregation members separated them.

"Really, this is such a crush, one is almost reminded of a London ballroom," Mother complained. "One cannot imagine why so many feel the need to attend services on a Sunday."

"Which day would you prefer people to attend, Mother?"

"There is no need to be impertinent. Oh! *Dear* Lady Osterley!"

Clara moved to one side as her mother began conversing with one of Brighton's inveterate gossips. She smiled politely — it would never do to get on that lady's bad side — and returned her attention to the crowd. It seemed a veritable who's who of Brighton society attended the church of St. Nicholas.

Nicholas.

Her heart dipped, her thoughts returning to the earl. Nicholas Stamford, seventh Earl of Hawkesbury, love of her life.

Eyes burning, she jerked her reflections away.

Only to encounter the fixed gaze of the man she'd bumped into two days ago.

"You!"

The pretty lady blinked. Averted her eyes. Stepped a pace back, closer to the headstones littering the churchyard, as though preparing to flee again. Ben couldn't really blame her. He might have been raised a gentleman, but she'd be hard pressed to tell by his recent behavior.

He pushed past a couple of gossiping old biddies to where the brunette stood, green eyes the color of tropical seas widening at his approach. "You again."

Her gaze lowered. "I don't know —"

"Forgive me, but did we not meet on the Steyne two days ago?"

"Clara?" One of the ladies he'd abruptly pushed past eyed him with a frown. "Do you know this young man?"

"No, Mother."

"Young man, I do not know who you are, and neither, it appears, does my daughter."

Her daughter named Clara. A pretty name

for a pretty face. Ben swallowed. Nearly introduced himself as *captain* before recalling that title was gone forever. Mr. Kemsley sounded so very plain in comparison. He opened his mouth to speak when the hatchet-faced lady plucked the other's sleeve and said in a loud murmur, no doubt designed for him to hear, "Some young gentlemen these days are simply not what one could wish."

Heat crept up his neck, her words a sad echo of Jane's father, who'd forbidden Ben's suit all those years ago. Perhaps Lord Ponsonby had been right. He could never have borne such a prideful family, nor — truth be told — could they have borne him, when he'd returned a not-quite-whole man. He could only thank God that youthful infatuation had soon blown over, revealed to be little more than a newly promoted lieutenant's fanciful dream. Jane herself had quickly proved the depths of her feelings, marrying another but two months after Ben had returned to sea.

He glanced at the young lady, whose blush suggested she'd overheard and even felt a mite of pity for him. He jerked a nod, and walked stiffly away. So much for a letter of commendation from the Regent. His lip curled. What difference would placing pride in such things ever make?

"Kemsley!"

Ben turned. "Braithwaite! Forgive me. I did not expect to see you here."

"More fool you, then, seeing you invited me."

He grinned, shaking hands. "I'm glad you came."

Braithwaite nodded. "A tidy service. That brother-in-law of yours packs them in."

"David is a good preacher." He paused. "He preaches truth."

A wave of sadness washed over his friend's face. "I would like to believe, but . . ."

"But you still cannot let go of your doubts."

"How can a good God permit me to live? Answer me that."

"Braithwaite, did you not hear the message? None of us are blameless. Not one. The only perfect man to have lived is our Lord Himself. And even Jesus refused to pick up a stone."

As if Braithwaite had not listened, he shook his head and muttered, "But I'm the one who should have insisted a chronometer be used. And Miss York's life lost, and I am responsible . . ."

Ben bit back a sigh. What would it take for the man to forgive himself? Self-recrimination would eat at a man until all semblance of self-worth was gone. The only one who could heal was Jesus, but until a man chose to listen . . .

He clasped the other man's arm. "Remember that God loves you."

Braithwaite gave a mocking laugh. "Which is why I'm left in torment." His desperate eyes fixed on him. "Can we meet again this week?"

"Alas, no. I'm to take my sister to my brother in Kent."

"Tessa?"

Ben nodded and the light in Braithwaite's eyes faded. He should take issue with the man's familiar use of Tessa's name. Yes, taking his sister away from Brighton — and Braithwaite — might be necessary for all. "I shall be in London soon. I might write, and we could meet there, if that is suitable." He hesitated then added, "I plan on seeing Burford and Lancaster, too."

Braithwaite groaned. "Such a meeting would be torture."

"It need not be —"

"It must be."

Ben saw Tessa's red curls move towards them. "Forgive me. I must away." He clasped Braithwaite's hand. "You are in my prayers."

"I need to be," was the muttered response.

Ben forced a smile to his lips as he advanced on his sister, steering her gently to the side.

She peered past his shoulder. "Was that Captain Braithwaite?"

"He is a little busy." Wallowing in regret.

"Oh, I wanted to say goodbye." She sighed. "I wish we did not have to leave for Kent. I do not want to stay with George."

"It will be better than you think. Now, where is Mattie?"

"Oh, she's always busy talking." Her face brightened. "But I saw her speaking with Miss DeLancey. It was good to see her. I have not seen her here at services before."

Miss DeLancey he neither knew nor cared about, but he would like to know more about the pretty brunette named Clara.

He glanced back over his shoulder.

Green eyes met his.

His heart thudded. Clara was peeking back at him as the older lady shepherded her away.

CHAPTER SIX

The sounds of the pianoforte rang out through the drawing room. Clara finished the last run and lifted her hands. A little Mozart had always helped soothe away inner turmoil.

"Very nice, my dear," Mother said from the doorway. "It is good to hear you play again."

Clara smiled. Her sore arm had made practice challenging, but playing again had been necessary, if for no other reason than to clear her mind of the disquieting thoughts elicited by Sunday's encounter with that man again.

He had appeared far more handsome and gentlemanly than previous encounters had led her to believe possible, given his disconcerting gaze and uncouth manners. She couldn't help but admire his neat appearance, dressed as he was in a well-fitted coat of dark blue that had stretched across the broad width of his shoulders — no need for padding there! — and pantaloons that hinted of muscular strength, his cravat arranged with such precision that even Richard would approve. Mother had commented about the unknown man's forward manner, remarking disparagingly about his tanned face which indicated he spent too much time in the sun. Clara had kept her thoughts to herself: that the tan showed off the blue of his eyes to greater advantage, whilst his manners reminded her of Matilda's similarly free and easy way. She hoped, indeed almost dared to pray, that if they did meet again — when they met again, as Brighton's small number of year-round inhabitants strongly suggested they would — he would not remember their first time of meeting, atop the cliffs on a windy night.

"When does the vicar's wife come again?"

"Mother, you say his occupation like you think it something poisonous."

"And so it is. Harmful to our way of life."

To their pursuit of self-interest, perhaps. Clara kept her lips pressed together. Since hearing Mr. McPherson's sermon, she had felt an inner restlessness, a tugging in her spirit only music seemed to pacify. Though she rather doubted anything could ever truly heal her soul.

The doorbell tinkled.

Clara slid from the piano stool and moved to join her mother in the drawing room. From the hall came a murmur of voices, then the door opened, and Mrs. McPherson was announced.

As had occurred previously, Matilda's broad smile kindled Clara's smile in response, before she settled down to follow Mother's lead in the usual conversational niceties: the weather, mutual acquaintances, and news from London. Matilda must have passed Mother's silent test because tea was ordered.

By the time Meg arrived with the tea and a plate of currant scones, Mother was at her most conciliatory, even going so far as to enquire about Matilda's family home.

"I understand your family comes from Kent."

"Yes, my lady. We grew up not far from Chatham Hall, when Father's cousin had the baronetcy. Father died before inheriting, so it passed to my brother George two years ago."

"And your mother?"

"She died when we were very young."

"I'm sorry," Clara murmured.

"Yes, yes, of course." Mother said, offering their guest more tea. "And is your brother married?"

"Both my brothers are unmarried."

Clara swallowed a smile. Yes, because one of them was but a boy.

Mother sighed. "We thought Clara would have been wed by now, but life can take such cruel twists sometimes."

The internal smile fled.

"Very true, Lady Winpoole." Matilda's serious tone, her swift — pitying? — glance at Clara froze her insides. Had she heard something of Clara's pitiful past?

Fortunately, Mother seemed content with the damage so far inflicted and soon excused herself. Awkwardness filled the room in her wake. Should Clara explain? Should she refrain? Oh, what did it matter? Her story was one oft repeated in a hundred drawing rooms.

"Please forgive my mother's comments. She is still bitter. I was going to marry an earl, you see."

"Oh!" Matilda's eyes grew round. "Forgive me, I did not know."

Where had she been hiding the past two years? Surely the story of the Honorable Clara DeLancey's failed pursuit of the Earl of Hawkesbury was known to all and sundry! Or was she even more of a nonentity than she'd realized?

Matilda watched her carefully, biting her lip as if unsure what to say.

Which made two of them. Should she continue her explanations? Or had she said too much already? Something urged her to continue. Matilda McPherson was the first person in a long time to offer Clara friendship. And if she truly was uninformed, then at least Clara could present her side of the story without previous tattle tainting Matilda's perception.

"It was the Earl of Hawkesbury," she admitted.

"Oh! I have heard of him. Something of a good sportsman? And a hero in the war?"

She nodded. Try good at everything. He was even good at jilting. The bitterness slashed again.

"I remember now," Matilda said. "Did he not marry a year or so ago?"

Her head jerked.

"That must have been very hard." The sympathy in Matilda's eyes pricked heat in her own. "Had he proposed?"

"Yes. No." She swallowed. "It had been implied . . . it was always understood."

"But not by him if he married someone else."

"It was the dearest wish of our mothers."

"But not his own."

Heat crawled across her chest, strangling her voice to a raspy no.

"Oh, forgive me, Clara. I do not wish to offend you."

"I am not offended," she lied. This had been a mistake. She glanced at the tall case clock. How soon could she get rid of her visitor?

"I have upset you." Matilda sighed. "I am sorry. Mothers should wish for their children to be well situated, but they can be blind also, thinking something might be good when in actuality it can be the reverse."

How could marrying the earl have been anything but good? How could being laughed about, sneered at, whispered about in a hundred ballrooms ever be considered good?

"I see you do not believe me."

Clara willed a smile to her face. "I confess the past two years have not felt particularly good." As if compelled by a greater force, she murmured something of the failed schemes to win him back, something of her despair.

"Oh, my dear." Matilda's eyes grew shiny, as if she wished to cry.

The compassion forced Clara's gaze down, tugging at the last of her defenses. "I hated her — and him — those first months. Hated them!" She peeked up. "I suppose you think me evil for admitting such things."

"I think you honest, not evil."

Clara swiped at her eyes. Why was she admitting to such ill-feeling? Could Matilda even be trusted? But it felt as though a pond had burst its banks and nothing could gather the spilled emotion again. "Now I just hate myself, for spending so long caring for someone who could not care less." A sob hiccupped from her depths. Mortification stole across her. This was simply not how one made a friend, let alone kept one!

Before fresh shame choked her, she was being clasped in a hug. She stiffened. Matilda's arms only tightened. After a moment, Clara relaxed, too weak to resist, her pride shriveled under the weight of honesty and the burden of loneliness that had so long held sway.

She closed her eyes, felt Matilda stroke her hair as she imagined Mother might have done a score of years ago. How long since she'd felt affection from anyone? How long since she'd been comforted so? Her parents had been angry on her behalf, but never had that translated into tears as she'd seen in Matilda's eyes. Was the blow to their pride what had caused their anger? At times

it was hard to tell; they seemed angry with
her, too. Warmth and affection had never
been characteristics of her family. Perhaps
their love for her lay dormant, like a spring
bulb, under layers of duty and pride. She
preferred the honest emotion Matilda exhib-
ited now, even if she knew Mother would
die of shame should she return and see such
unseemly behavior.

Clara drew in a breath, caught a tang of
lavender as she eased from the hug. She
smoothed her hair, wiped underneath her
eyes, her cheeks hot with embarrassment.
"I'm sorry."

"You have nothing to apologize for. I'm
sure I would feel similarly in the same situation."

Her kindness wrapped around Clara's
cold heart like a thick blanket, impelling
her onwards. "I . . . I just feel so lost, like I
don't know who I am anymore."

There was a pause. "So who is Clara?"

"I beg your pardon?"

"Who are you? Really?"

Clara sat back, thinking. Who was she?
Daughter of a viscount? Someone whose
chief interests included the acquisition of
new clothes? Pleasure? Someone forever lost
in a dream that could never happen? The
earl had certainly moved on; wasn't it time

she did also?

"Will you truly allow one man's rejection to define the rest of your life?"

Clara laughed brokenly. "I rather think it is the sum total of all the men who have rejected me."

"God does not reject you, Clara."

The words washed around her heart, that infinitesimal tugging of past days growing stronger. "I don't know . . ."

"I do. I know that God loves you, that His plans for you are good."

Matilda's confident words instilled a mite of hope. Did God really notice her? Could the Creator of the universe really care about her?

"Perhaps this is a time for you to allow God to heal you, to show who He thinks you are."

Clara swallowed. "Perhaps."

"Now, did I hear someone playing the pianoforte when I arrived?"

The abrupt change in subject made her blink. "I . . . er, yes. I was playing."

Matilda smiled. "Then I'm sure part of God's plans involve your musical ability. You're really very good."

"Thank you." She bit back the prideful comment, about how she had once played and sung at some of London's finest salons.

Those days were long past.

Matilda's brow puckered, then cleared as she smiled. "Would you mind helping us by playing at the mission? Benjie, my brother, is keen to help the sailors and soldiers adversely affected by war." Her eyes twinkled. "Your music would ensure the men will be keen to attend."

"Oh. I . . ." How could she graciously refuse? But — a little part of her heart niggled — she did not want to refuse. Didn't she need to live differently than before? And it would provide her the chance to meet Matilda and Tessa's revered brother. "I . . . of course."

"Excellent!" Matilda pushed to her feet. Held out her hand. "Thank you so much for today. I hope you know that I will never breathe a word of your pain to anyone."

"I do," she said, surprised at the revelation. Somehow she knew she could trust her new friend implicitly, that the cords of friendship had only strengthened today. "Thank you for not condemning me."

"Ah, well, we've all done things we've been ashamed of. And if it's any help, I did not meet Mr. McPherson until people thought I was well and truly on the shelf. It just shows that good things are worth waiting for."

Clara's smile grew wry. Apparently she was waiting for someone very good indeed.

Chatham Hall, Kent

"But, George, don't you see? It will not do. If Tessa marries Braithwaite she'll forever be held hostage to his melancholy."

His brother eyed his own reflection in the glass, touching his recently rearranged neckcloth. "How the man can blame himself when *you* obviously do not, I cannot fathom."

Ben bit back his initial response. Bit back his second response also. There was a lot his dandified brother could not fathom, particularly anything demanding self-sacrifice. He strode to the windows over-looking a garden as green as he remembered the Ceylon trees to be. As for blaming himself for the shipwreck, that was something he'd come to terms with months ago. The wreck of the *Ansdruther* had been an unforeseen tragedy, one that possibly could have been averted through the use of Braith-waite's precious chronometer, but the winds and the waves had been so fierce there quite likely would have been loss of life even had they not been pushed onto the reef.

"Excuse me, sir?"

At the sound of the servant's interruption

and George's mumbled excuse, the tranquil vista of ordered trees and shrubbery blurred, replaced with the memories of that fateful voyage. Charged with returning soldiers and a few families back to England, he had been dismayed at the sudden change of weather as they rounded the southern tip of Africa. The swift gathering of clouds, ominous in their dark volume. The shrieking wind so hungry it swept stout men from their feet. The creaking then crack as a mast broke. The cruel scrape and splinter of wood on reef, a sound no sailor wanted to hear. The day his career — his world — crashed with an almighty boom.

Silver streaks had split the sky like wicked fingers stretching toward him. Around him screamed the terror of soldiers' loved ones, their cries gulped up by a voracious gale. The sea — so long his friend — had turned vicious.

The admiral's daughter, Miss Marianne York, dragged herself to the deck, her usual headstrong insouciance muted in the concern common to all on deck.

"Miss York, I'm afraid I need you to step back down."

"I have endured storms before, Captain Kemsley. My father —"

"Not on my ship, you haven't." Reckless,

foolish girl. "Please move below deck now."

"But —"

"Get below! Now!"

She made a face, flouncing off and disappearing below, freeing him to refocus on the turbulent seas.

God, help us! Fear fired grit within. Straining against the wind, he hefted the wheel with all his might. If she shifted a fraction more, they had a chance — a minute chance — but a chance nonetheless. Still the waves pounded them toward the shore.

"Captain!"

Ben strained to hear his lieutenant's words, snatched as they were by the wind. "What?"

"The hold!" Burford shouted. "She be filling fast! We need to abandon ship."

God, what do I do?

He glanced about. His men worked on, faces set hard against the terrible truth. He could bet his last guinea that, like him, none of them had experienced such a wicked night. Lancaster might boast of facing terrible squalls in the Caribbean, but even his face shone with fear.

Ben tightened his lips, struggling to still his own fears to hear the voice of the One who had saved him so many times before.

Reassurance came, a measure of peace. "Go."

Burford nodded before sliding off to warn the men. The flurry of activity on deck took on a new tempo as soldiers joined his men. Ben grimaced. Too many of them appeared underweight, emaciated by a sun and sickness so foreign. And then there were their women and children. He fought a groan. Straightened his shoulders. Addressed the assembled. "We need to put in to shore, but there's a reef trying to devour our ship. How many of you can swim?"

Half a dozen soldiers raised their hands. He knew his men all could.

"You will need to. The women and children must get in the lifeboat" — thank God they would all fit in one — "and the rest of you will need to grab whatever you can and kick to the shore. There's coral around here that will scrape and sting like the blazes, but keep going. You do not want to stop."

Because coral wasn't the only thing hungry for a man's body. Off these southern coastlines swam deadly predators.

The lifeboat had just been safely launched when the mast toppled with a final, fatal crack, flinging all still on deck into the raging seas.

He remembered the shock of water, being

smacked in the head by a barrel. Blurred vision. The frantic battle to stay afloat amid waves higher than a house, while avoiding the crush of crashing timbers. His moments of terror when his foot got trapped in a length of rope, wrenching his knee into uselessness.

He could hear the panicked cries, above which he could just make out the plash of oars. Until a huge wave dumped him. Choking on seawater, he sputtered, looked up. The storm had abated to steady rain, as storms so often did around this stretch of African coast. Quick to rise, quick to settle. He pulled ahead. Around him a dozen men clutched broken pieces of vessel, bobbing cork-like in the midnight sea.

A fearsome creak made him glance behind. The wreckage of the *Ansdruther* listed, then with a terrible groan, veered to the opposite side. The cannons below deck must have overbalanced. "Look out!"

His yell alerted Burford, who screamed at the men beside him. They paddled furiously out of the way before the giant mast crashed into the sea, only inches from where they'd been.

The movement sent a new wave, pulling at the lifeboat. Beside it, four sailors towed it toward shore, but it tipped sideways, releasing Miss York into the clutches of the sea.

Ben tugged corpulent old Major Dumfrey to a piece of wood, instructed him to hold tight, then duck-dived under the waves.

Where was she? Panic clawed his chest. He could not let the admiral's daughter drown. *Would* not let the admiral's daughter drown. *Lord, help —*

There!

Her white gown floated angel-like around her. He reached out a hand, snagging her dress, hoisting her with all his might to the surface.

"I've got you," he managed to sputter, hooking an arm around her chest as he began a desperate crawl to shore. The waves kept pushing him back. Muscles screaming, he gritted his teeth and plowed on. He would do this. He had to!

Coral nipped and stung his legs. Ahead, he could see men collapsing on the sands. Above the relentless hiss of rain and waves, he heard a scrape of wood and saw the ladies and children being plucked from the small boat and carried to shore.

He peered at the woman he held still. Her eyes were open, but she spoke nothing, terror keeping her quiet. A gash trickled blood on her forehead. At least she wasn't fighting him, not like some panicked people he'd witnessed.

His feet touched bottom, his knee screaming for rest.

"Captain!"

Hands hurried forward, releasing him from his burden.

He stumbled onto sand, gasping. He wasn't the young man he'd once been, but at nine-and-twenty he was still one of the youngest post captains His Majesty's Navy had ever seen.

He pushed to his feet, staggering a little as his knee buckled, to see the shore filled with the wet and bedraggled. "How many of us?"

Lancaster performed a head count. "All present and accounted for."

"Thank God." After issuing further instructions, he noticed his second lieutenant look behind him. Ben turned to see another desperate cause. The ship's surgeon looked up from Miss York's still form and shook his head. "I'm very sorry, sir."

Only then had the hollowness of his miracle begun to bite.

"I'm very sorry, sir."

The servant's apology followed George's return to the room. The scenes of distress faded; the garden reemerged. Ben swallowed. Shook his head. If only he could shake free of these memories.

He forced his thoughts back to the present and turned to his brother, his brother who had never understood him, who he feared never would. "Back to Tessa. Have you any thought for our sister's future?"

"I admit it has not been on my mind."

No surprise there. "Well, I would like you to give her some thought. I intend on visiting London again soon, then returning to Brighton, and I do not think Mattie needs her house filled with us anymore."

"McPherson too clutch-fisted is he?"

Ben clenched his fingers. Breathed to control his voice. "He's not clutch-fisted at all. Unlike some." He eyed his brother evenly.

George flushed. "I don't know what you imagine I can do with the girl."

"She *is* your sister. Get Aunt Adeline to come stay. But Tessa is your responsibility, now you are head of the family."

"But why can't you —"

"Because I do not think trying to launch our sister into a good marriage will be possible if she lives in a bachelor's establishment in such accommodations as I can afford."

George's mouth dropped open. "What do

you mean? Did you not receive a vast sum for your heroics?"

"The Prince Regent might have promised so, but I've yet to see a penny." He fought the rising tide of frustration. He did not want to depend upon a royal promise, but the money would come in very handy. He'd spent much of his previous prize money helping the widows of Smith and Anderson, who had survived the wreck only to succumb to malaria three weeks later. It did not seem right to him to have funds when his two crewmen had families in far greater need.

He forced his attention back to the issue at hand. "Besides, whatever I might have earned pales in comparison to your competency as baronet."

His older brother's eyes narrowed.

Ben restrained a sigh. Perhaps it was time to resort to emotional extortion. "Don't you love our sister, George?"

"Of course I do!"

"Then perhaps it's time to show it."

"But, but —"

"Oh, for goodness sake! Fine. Give me enough funds and I'll set up a house for her."

"You have nothing?" George's eyes goggled.

"I have but a few thousand," he corrected.

"But I thought —"

"I know what you thought! And I can see what you currently think, too."

"George doesn't want me?"

The small voice snapped his attention to the doorway. "Tessa!"

George's face mottled even more. "Tessa, my dear, of course I would be very happy to have you stay."

"I don't believe you." Her lips flattened, and she sent Ben an imploring look. "Please don't make me stay."

He dragged in a long breath. "I wish I had more to offer you. Perhaps once I am properly settled —"

"When will that be?" George said, his tone suggesting a sneer. "I imagine there are plenty of rich young ladies wishing to meet a hero."

If there were, he'd yet to meet any that caught his eye. An image of a pretty brunette flickered before him.

"Why do you always speak to him that way, George?" Tessa asked, looking between them. "It makes you sound not a little envious."

Ben shot his sister a grateful glance before smoothing his features into blandness as George glanced his way.

"I could not be envious of such an ill-dressed man even if my life depended on it."

Ben smothered a wry chuckle. "Let us hope it need never come to that."

His brother's forehead creased, and Ben used his momentary confusion to sweep Tessa from the room. A few minutes of hurried explanation and she was reconciled to staying for a week or two, at least. For all his hesitation, George still possessed a strong sense of family duty. Ben hoped.

"And I promise to take you to London soon."

"But not back to Brighton?"

He gave her an affectionate squeeze. "We should not wish to crowd poor Mattie and David, would we? They are but newly married."

She slowly nodded. "I hope I was not too troublesome."

"Troublesome? You? Never."

Tessa chuckled, and the tension abated, leaving him with a strange mix of assurance and unease. For much as he wished his sister to come live with him, she could not do so without a female companion to lend the chaperonage society considered proper. And he wasn't likely to find a lady prepared to overlook his limp and lack of fortune or title, as well as the inconvenience of a younger sister, beloved though she may be.

Such a lady would prove impossible to find.

His lips curved wryly. Unless his sisters begged God for yet another miracle for their poor brother, after all.

CHAPTER SEVEN

Brighton
One week later

Clara hurried along Marine Parade, the morning breeze tousling her hair, as the earlier argument continued harrying her spirits. She had thought helping Matilda with her request would prove beneficial, just had not anticipated her mother's response to be quite so hostile.

An hour ago, the footman had entered with the post on a silver salver, both footman and the formal presentation of mail two traditions her parents had yet to forego despite straitened circumstances. Mother had scanned the letters, her face lighting. "Oh! Richard writes at last."

Clara had fought back the prickle of irritation as her mother scanned the letter.

"He says he wishes to come for a visit."

"How wonderful," Clara said flatly, when it became clear Mother expected a response.

"It *will* be wonderful to see your brother again, so there is no need to take that tone, my dear."

On the contrary, there was every need. As if Clara's own humiliation was not enough, Richard's actions had proved the final straw, his misguided attempt to help resulting in a shame so deep even her parents' self-righteous anger could scarce explain it away.

She managed to maintain a polite facade as Mother murmured some more about poor Richard — conveniently forgetting, it seemed, that Richard was the reason their circumstances had been reduced so drastically in the past eighteen months.

When she had finally finished on the sad state of Richard and moved on to the next letter, Clara had managed to murmur something about needing to go into town again.

Mother had looked up from the letter she was reading. "My dear, surely you do not mean to return to that woman and her dreadful people again."

"Mother, Mrs. McPherson and her husband are simply trying to help those who are less fortunate. The men they help are not dreadful, but poor —"

"Yes, but they are men, my dear. Unfortunate, to be sure, but they are men! It cannot do your reputation any good to be known to be consorting with such as they."

Heat shot through her chest. "I am hardly consorting, Mother," she said stiffly.

"You misunderstand me, my dear."

Clara raised her brows. "Do I?"

Her mother sniffed. "I am simply concerned for you. What should happen if one should suddenly develop an interest with you? I will not stand for your reputation to be maligned."

"Mother, there is no chance of my reputation being sullied further. And to be honest, I quite enjoyed the opportunity to contribute my skills where they are appreciated."

"Well, I am sure that is so. How can they not? You are so skilled at the pianoforte." Mother tapped the letter. "But you are not to be thinking only of them. Dear Lady Asquith requests the pleasure of your company next month."

"I'm to go to London so soon?"

"Yes. Your godmother is having one of her musical evenings and particularly wishes you to be in attendance. I suppose your friend won't object if you're unable to assist for a few weeks?"

"I imagine not," Clara murmured.

"Very good. I shall write and tell Penelope we shall endeavor to arrive in the next fortnight or so. I imagine you will be needing new gowns and all." Mother had given a faint sigh. "We shall contrive something, I suppose."

Clara hurried along the path, across to the Steyne, mulling over her mother's words. A trip to London would involve more expense — futile expense, some would say. But this might be her last chance to find a man willing to make her an offer of marriage. Had her absence been prolonged enough for the whispers to abate? Surely people would be talking more about Napoleon's latest escapade. She smiled at herself. How self-absorbed was she to think people would think about her?

She turned the corner, up towards the small church hall where the McPhersons had begun holding weekly meetings for returned servicemen in a bid to boost the spirits of those who had fought and now were disabled or receiving the pittance of a pension Clara had never realized was so inadequate. How could a man — let alone a husband or father trying to provide for a family — possibly survive on less than ten pounds a year? Matilda's soberly shared information had made Clara's own problems seem very petty indeed.

When she'd questioned Matilda about her

reasons for helping, her friend had looked at her with no small measure of surprise. "Well, I suppose I am motivated by my brother."

The rich one? She must have looked her confusion, as Matilda had given a half smile. "I forget not everyone would be aware of my brother's efforts during the war. But it was particularly brought home when he returned and was made to realize the dire circumstances of those left behind. He was blessed in having funds enough to support himself, but not many were in that happy circumstance, so he has spent nearly all he has in helping those less fortunate. And more than that, is it not our duty, our responsibility as members of the church, to help those who are poor and struggling?" She'd nodded her head, saying adamantly, "We must do something."

How could Clara argue with that?

Truth be told, focusing on something other than herself and her own troubles was quite releasing. The sadness did not weigh so heavily. The dreams did not torment as much.

She pushed open the door to be greeted by the smell of cabbage soup and unwashed bodies. Thank goodness Mother was not here to be assailed by something so unrefined.

"Oh, good! You are here." Matilda hurried toward her. "We seem to have grown in numbers since you played for us last week."

She smiled. Thankfully Mother could not see the twinkle in the eyes of the vicar's wife.

Clara nodded to the ladies who were helping in the little makeshift kitchen area, moving to her position behind the battered pianoforte Matilda had convinced her husband to shift from their house to the hall. She positioned her music, peeked at the men, restrained a shudder, and began to play.

Slowly the scent of pain and grime faded as the intricate melodies possessed her attention. Music had always proved a panacea, a way of losing herself through the discipline and creativity such performance demanded. Much might be wrong in her world, but making music meant a little corner was as it should be. And while she might provide a measure of relief and distraction for those in attendance, the very songs she played soothed her own soul as well.

She glanced up from the pianoforte, pleasure stealing through her at the sight of bandaged men and those missing limbs closing their eyes and smiling. Each time she played, the men seemed to forget their worries for a moment. And yes, some might smile at her, but she took little notice. She was glad to smile back, even if Matilda said she best not encourage them to get too far above themselves. "For it is obvious you are a lady."

So perhaps Mother need not be *quite* so concerned.

After the soup was served, Matilda drew near, and Clara was finally able to mention her upcoming return to London.

Matilda's eyes brightened. "Oh, you must let me know, and I will write to Tessa, if you have no objection. Benjie has promised to take her for a visit, and I'm sure she'd like to see you again. She sounds quite lonely sometimes." She peered at Clara closely. "You would not be opposed to seeing Tessa? I need not mention your plans if you prefer."

"Of course I do not mind. Perhaps she might like to come to the musical evening Lady Asquith is hosting."

Matilda's eyes rounded. "Really? Oh, she would love that! Just fancy, a real lady."

She swallowed a smile. Apparently Matilda did not realize just how well connected Clara's family was. "If you let me know her direction, I shall write and let her know our place of residence in London."

"Thank you," said Matilda. "I'm sure it would do her a world of good to have opportunity to associate with those in the upper echelon of society. I gather from her letters that she will be very glad to escape my brother's company. George can be a little dull at the best of times."

"Will he not go into London with her?"

Matilda lifted a shoulder. "I cannot say. But from what Tessa writes, it seems she's extracted a promise from Benjie to accompany her." She smiled. "You may finally get the chance to meet him."

"Indeed." Clara ignored the twinkling smile and busied herself with rearranging the sheets of music. Really, Matilda's level of enthusiasm for Clara's encounter with this mysterious adored brother was quite absurd.

Yet why did she feel a flicker of interest at the upcoming encounter? He was too young to warrant any serious interest, wasn't he?

London

Ben subtly shifted his weight, trying to remember Dr. Townsend's instructions of three days ago: exercise in moderation, but when possible, rest and elevate, bandaging as necessary. Not that there had been much chance of rest these past days.

106

He glanced at his sister, eyeing the shelves of Hookham's circulating library with the practiced eye of a London matron three times her age. Anyone might think she was a seasoned debutante, and not a young woman on the cusp of entering polite society. Though perhaps that was the effect of their Aunt Adeline. Since their arrival, Ben had been dragged to most of London's bookstores, as well as a mantua-maker their aunt had promised would neither charge the earth nor take longer than absolutely necessary. The funds George had relinquished were adequate for their expenses — and for the gowns and fripperies their mother's sister deemed necessary. It had not taken long before both he and Tessa realized they'd been very blessed with their aunt offering both her chaperonage and her Curzon Street town house for accommodation.

Aunt Adeline's deceased husband had left her well provided for, and she was proving to be the ideal companion for Tessa, sharing both the elegant taste and geniality Ben recalled his mother possessing. Now out of widow's weeds, Aunt Addy was keen to revisit places she'd enjoyed in her own season so many years ago, though she had absented herself from today's excursion, due to a slight cold.

Tessa peered past a stack of books, meeting his gaze. "Do you mind if I get two?"

"Of course not." He wouldn't mind if she requested two dozen. It was worth it to see his timid sister coming out of her shell.

"I might also see if they have a copy of *Mansfield Park.*"

"Surely you couldn't prefer that to *Waverley*?" he teased.

She grinned.

A short time later, they were at the circulation desk. Tessa made her request, to which the elderly attendant instantly adopted a sorrowful look. "I'm sorry, miss, but that particular edition is out of stock. We are expecting a new delivery in the next week or so. Shall I ensure one is put aside for you?"

She glanced at Ben. He looked away, determined she would answer the gentleman herself. "Th-that would be good, th-thank you."

"Very well."

After leaving her name and direction, they exited the library onto Bond Street, the clatter of hooves on cobblestones and the fashionables strolling past near breathtaking in their contrast to the library's sedate surrounds. Tessa's hand tightened on Ben's arm, her eyes sparkling with pleasure. "I love London."

"It is exciting." He glanced down at her shining face, her enthusiasm so different from her usual reticence, and so different from the other young ladies whose expressions of hauteur suggested they either found London boring or had been well schooled to never show true emotion. Neither reason appealed to him. The young lady to appeal to his heart would need to be honest and sincere, neither hiding her emotions under the proverbial bushel, nor so quiet and diffident as to make him wonder if she could even feel. He wanted someone sweet, yet of spirit; perhaps not so forthright as Mattie, but not so quiet as Tessa. An image of the wild and desperate creature of the cliff filled his head. He batted it away. He did not want dull, but neither did he wish for desperate!

He steered a course past a flotilla of young gentlemen. As they passed, he heard not a few opinions on the attractiveness of his sister. Ben turned to see them still ogling her and sent them a scowl that had won him respect on many a ship.

Glancing up, he encountered another young exquisite, dressed to meet even the highest stickler's approval. The young man — he couldn't be more than four-and-twenty — met his gaze. Eyes widening, he raised his quizzing glass, then dropped it. "Kemsley?"

Ben stopped, raising a brow.

"Forgive me, but are you Captain Benjamin Kemsley of the *Ansdruther,* by any chance?"

"Yes."

The young gentleman stretched out a hand. "I thought I recognized your name back at Hookham's. What an honor to meet such a hero."

The tips of Ben's ears heated. "Good afternoon, Mr. —"

"The name is Featherington. But I am a Lord, not a mister, Captain Kemsley."

"And I'm a plain mister, not a captain anymore."

"Of course," murmured the young man, before stealing a glance at Tessa. His smile grew. "And you are Mrs. Kemsley? What a lucky fellow is our captain, indeed."

Tessa's cheeks pooled with color. "I am Miss Kemsley," she said, almost inaudibly.

Lord Featherington's face brightened. "Then I'm a lucky fellow." He peered at her novels, tied up with string. "I see you have *The Wanderer.* My sister enjoys Miss Burney's novels."

Ben studied him as the young man began

discussing books with his sister, whose eyes had rounded, as if seeing a marvelous exhibit from the Egyptian Hall. The young man was exceptionally well attired, he supposed, though a trifle too florid for his taste. He seemed quite the dandy. And a lord? What kind of lord? Clearly this was one expedition where they would have benefited from Aunt Adeline's superior insights into the peerage.

His gaze slid to his sister, her animation such as he had rarely seen. Clearly she found something about the young man appealing, though he doubted it was his possession of some sort of title. And clearly the young man found Tessa worth attention, though Ben hoped it was not simply an attempt to please him. These past months he'd encountered many quick to stoke the fires of egotism at the expense of reality. And Tessa's confidence was such a fragile thing, her soft heart and eagerness to please something to be handled delicately. Admittedly, she was in her best looks today; even Aunt Adeline agreed. Was this young man's reaction one Ben should come to expect when gentlemen met his sweet sister?

". . . the war." The gentleman smiled. "What do you think?"

Ben mentally scrambled for an answer.

Settled for an all-inclusive, "We all hope the war to be finally over soon."

"Yes, yes, of course." Lord Featherington's brow creased. "But do you miss being part of the action?"

Ben glanced at his sister. She was biting her lip, as if worried the discussion surrounding the trials and tribulations of his time fighting for his country was not to his taste.

Featherington seemed to notice this, as he bowed. "Forgive me. I do not wish to speak such things that would distress you, Miss Kemsley." The cherubic features seemed to soften. "I would never wish to distress *you,* Miss Kemsley."

Tessa's cheeks glowed.

Lord Featherington smiled, turned to Ben. "I know how untoward all this must seem, but I was wondering if you might be free to join me sometime at my club? I would like to speak with you about your time in Africa. I confess it has interested me enormously, ever since my cousin first mentioned your exploits."

Judging from the way he kept snatching glances at Tessa, Ben gathered conversation concerning his misadventures wasn't the only thing in which Featherington was enormously interested.

They arranged to meet at White's in two nights, at a time when George had promised to visit to escort Tessa and Aunt Adeline to an opera. That was an evening he could gladly forfeit. Screeching men and caterwauling ladies had never been his thing.

Upon their return, Tessa's gentle inquisition of their aunt led that lady to look at her in astonishment. "Oh, my dear! This is such an honor. You simply must foster the acquaintanceship. Do you not know who he is?"

Tessa's blank look no doubt echoed Ben's own bewilderment.

"Young Featherington is a viscount; his sister married last year to the Duke of Hartwell."

He blinked. Exchanged a sagged-jaw glance with his sister as his aunt continued.

"Lord Featherington is the heir to the Marquess of Exeter!"

CHAPTER EIGHT

Brighton
Two weeks later

"There is a visitor for you, Miss Clara. Mrs. McPherson."

Clara laid aside the embroidery, her spirits rising. "Thank you, Meg. Please show her in."

The maid disappeared, returning in less than a minute with Matilda. Clara welcomed her warmly. She had not realized just how lonely she had been until her attempts to assist at the hostel had been forbidden, thus curtailing her friendship with Mattie, save for Sunday services.

"Please tell Cook we'd like tea."

Meg curtsied. "Very good, miss."

Matilda settled herself on the blue-striped sofa with a smile. "Oh, I do like how you do that, acting the grand lady when it's only me."

How to explain she used to be considered

a lady, if not exactly grand? Easier not to. "You should not speak so about yourself, Matilda. You have no idea just how much I have longed for your company."

"Your mother will not relinquish?"

Clara said carefully, "I'm afraid she thinks I consort with those beneath my dignity."

Matilda's eyes flashed, her lips flattening in an obvious attempt to not insult her hostess with her true thoughts about Clara's banishment from helping at the shelter.

Good thing she had not repeated exactly what Mother had said. Matilda would probably storm out if she'd heard her good works denounced as pandering to the idle and lazy. Such comments coming from a woman who had rarely lifted a finger to help another creature, let alone those who had fought for their country, struck Clara as the height of ironic incivilities.

"How is the shelter going? I have missed it, you know."

"Oh, and you have been missed! Lieutenant Saunders asks after you every day."

Clara fought a smile. This was why Mother had been aghast and then refused Clara's involvement. She could hear Mother's horrified voice now, after that unfortunate episode following services ten days ago: "When the likes of a Lieutenant Saunders

115

takes it upon himself to aspire to a daughter of my lineage, well! Enough is enough! It simply will not do!"

"Give them my best," Clara said.

Meg returned, carrying a tray topped by tea things. After handing her guest a cup, Clara continued. "And how is Tessa?"

Matilda's face brightened. "I had a letter from her just this morning. Oh, she is having the most marvelous time! Aunt Adeline is proving to be a far better companion than I had hoped. It seems she has been busy not only instructing Tessa in the art of buying inexpensive materials but also has helped turn her out into the first style of fashion! I always knew Tessa to be a clever seamstress, but I did not realize our aunt would prove so adept also."

"That is fortunate," Clara murmured over the rim of her teacup.

"Isn't it?" Matilda took a bite of her cake, gave a sigh of satisfaction, and continued. "Tessa also writes that Benjie is becoming quite the toast of the town."

"Really?" How could a boy do such a thing?

"Yes! It seems they met quite a nice young man recently who introduced Ben to some others at a club. Apparently this young man is a viscount or some such thing. Oh!

Perhaps you know him?"

Perhaps he'd know her. Or at least know *of* her. Fighting the tremor of uncertainty, she asked, "Did she mention a name?"

Matilda's brow creased. "Give me a moment." She rummaged through her reticule and drew out a slightly crumpled letter. "Here!" She passed it over. "I'm sure she would not mind you reading it."

Clara scanned the childish loops and scrawl. Tessa's excitement nearly leapt from the page. She had lovely new gowns . . . had visited Bullock's new museum . . . Benjie had promised to take her to the theatre . . . there!

Her breath caught. No. It couldn't be.

"Clara? My dear? You look as if you've seen a ghost."

She lifted her head to meet her friend's gaze of concern. Of all the viscounts in the *ton* . . .

"Do you know him? Featherington, I think it is, now I recall."

Clara nodded. Oh yes, she knew him. A sick swirl churned through her insides. That piece of cream cake had been a bad idea.

"So what is he like? Is he eligible? Is he nice? Tessa certainly seems to think so."

Clara nodded again, handing back the letter without reading any further. "He is considered most eligible."

"Really?"

"His father is a marquess."

"No!" Matilda's eyes rounded into blue saucers. "Truly?"

"Yes." She swallowed. Braved a smile.

Matilda shook her head. "I'm sure nothing will come of it, Tessa is such a romantic after all, but just imagine! My little sister, a marchioness!" She chuckled. "I hope you'll be able to report more exactly on what is truly going on. For all her timidity, Tessa has a tendency to see everything through the most optimistic of imaginings, whereas Benjie can hardly be trusted to notice the really important things, let alone remember to write me about them. But then, he is male." She placed her cup back on the table. "I suppose I should be going. I know you must be busy with packing. You will write, won't you?"

"Of course."

"Now, here is Tessa's direction. I know she would be greatly appreciative if you could spare the time to see her for an hour or so."

Clara's smile grew genuine. "I can spare far more than an hour."

"Thank you. I am relieved to know that, as far as society goes, Aunt Adeline is up to snuff as Benjie might say, but I feel certain you would be better for helping Tessa navigate those social points dear Aunt Addy might not be quite so familiar with."

Things like never throwing yourself at a man who does not want you? Never letting society know you were the owner of a broken heart? Clara might not be the best at demonstrating such things, but oh, how she now knew of their importance.

"I almost forgot." Matilda tugged a small volume from her reticule and placed it on the tea table. "Something you might find valuable, when you have a moment."

"Thank you."

Her guest rose and moved close, surprising her with a hug. "Have a wonderful time in London."

The affection drew moisture to her eyes. She returned the clasp lightly. "Thank you. I will write."

"Good." Matilda shifted back, adjusted her hat. "Well, I'll be off. See you in a few weeks."

Clara waved farewell, and sank back on her seat. Emotions clashed within. Gladness at going to London had been tempered by the knowledge that Tessa's infatuation with Lord Featherington — and vice versa — would doubtless mean she might have close contact with a family who despised her. She gnawed her lip. How on earth could she avoid that?

"Well, well."

Her head snapped up. She spied the figure in the doorway. Breath escaped. "What are you doing here?"

"Come now, Clara. Is that any way to greet your favorite brother?"

Her only brother. Try as she might, she could not elicit the faintest stirring of enthusiasm for his return. "It is good to see you," she said in a voice much like she'd use to observe the sky was gray.

His eyes sparked. "I can only hope dearest *Mater* and *Pater* will be a little warmer in their welcome." Richard sank onto a seat, stretching out his long legs as if he owned the house. "Where are they, anyway?"

"Out."

"Obviously. But where?"

"They are visiting Lord and Lady Osterley, if you must know."

He yawned like a pampered cat. "Y'know, this animosity towards me grows a trifle dull. It is not as if it were I who caused you to hanker for that fool of an earl."

She pressed her lips firmly together, fighting the truth that begged release.

He laughed, eyeing her curiously. "So the

parents are out, and you are in." He glanced at the tea things, yet to be cleared away. "Who was that frumpy creature I passed on my way in?"

Surely he did not refer to dear Mattie? She stared at him coldly. "I do not know who you mean."

"Yes, you do." His eyes flickered. "I think you know exactly who I mean."

Her fingers clenched within her lap. If only her brother had not always been able to read her quite so well. "If you are referring to my visitor, her name is Mrs. McPherson. She is the vicar's wife and a dear friend."

"My, my. We have come down in the world."

"Says the man who has not dared show his face in polite society for over a year."

He had the courtesy to flush.

Satisfaction coursed through her. "Are you planning on staying?"

"For a little while." He lifted a nonchalant shoulder. "Who knows?"

With any luck, if he stayed while she went, he might be gone by the time she returned. She spread her skirts. "I go to London tomorrow."

"Really?" His voice, his eyes suggested everything of boredom. Had the past eighteen months changed him that much? "P'raps I'll come, too."

"I'll be staying some of the time with Lady Asquith. I cannot think she will be too pleased with your showing up unannounced."

"Who said anything about staying with her? No, I'd much rather stay at my club."

"I didn't realize they still let you in."

His teeth gleamed in a mocking smile. "Careful, Clara. You're showing your claws. Though why you have any right to show me claws I cannot fathom."

Again she struggled to withhold accusation. Again she failed. "Perhaps the scandal surrounding me would have been less if you had not behaved in such an ungentlemanly manner."

"You and I both know I did it to help you."

"Well it didn't help!"

"But neither did your public pining over blasted Hawkesbury. I do not think it fair for me to accept all the blame."

Because he didn't accept personal responsibility for anything. She pushed to her feet. Arguing with her brother had always proved a fruitless exercise. "Excuse me. I still have a great deal of packing."

"Of course you do."

His dismissive words, the hardness in his

gaze brought tears to her eyes as she hurried away. How had their once close relationship, the very one he referred to when he mentioned trying to help her so many months ago, transmogrified into something so tense and awful?

Another layer of heaviness settled around her shoulders as she made her way up the stairs. Her visitors today had made something abundantly clear. Her time in London would prove far more challenging than even she had once supposed.

London

Ben glanced around the opulent fittings of White's, the leather padded seating, the crystal drops shimmering from the chandelier above. Visiting with Burford and Lancaster yesterday in a quiet coffee house had been like finding an islet of sanity in a tempestuous sea. Never in his wildest dreams would Ben have imagined the level of interest in his story. The initial meeting with the viscount had resulted in a veritable storm of attention as the news filtered through the clubs. He'd dined at White's, been a guest at Boodle's, been treated to dinner at Watier's, been introduced to such illustrious personages as dukes and even Mr. Brummel, all the while sharing about his exploits in the sea on that last disastrous voyage off Africa's southern cape.

"Captain Kemsley, was it true you swam with sharks when you were wrecked?"

He nodded, glancing around the table at the men who kept peppering him with questions. No one seemed to believe the waters were warm in that part of the world in January, let alone shark-infested. Flying fish seemed as fantastical to his listeners as his account of his trek for help.

Ben took another sip of water, his memories surging like the tide to shore. The realization the morn following the storm that they were hemmed in by impassable cliffs. His decision two days later to risk no lives but his own in swimming back out into the sea until he finally found access across a low headland. He rubbed his knee, worsened by the long trudge across endless sand dunes, before finally, *finally* finding help at a remote village.

"I trust you do not mind sharing?"

Ben glanced at Lord Featherington, who had asked the question. "Not at all."

He didn't mind sharing, except he didn't especially like the stirring of memories best forgotten, nor that he felt this constant need to remind them he was not some great hero, that in fact it was God who had enabled so much of what had happened to come true.

He'd prayed, and God had miraculously untangled the ropes.

He'd prayed, and God had given him strength to reach Miss York, even if the waves had stolen her life.

He'd prayed, and God had sustained him on that march to find help, three days sun-scorched, foodless, his only water what he could lick from the dew-drenched blades of grass each morning. So many times he had wanted to give up, but the knowledge that so many desperate people for whom he was responsible remained helpless on a lonesome beach had kept him going. That, and God.

It was on his walk he'd rediscovered the Sustainer of life, found his faith reinvigorated. Otherwise he would have toppled over, his bones would now be crow-picked and sun-bleached, and he would be lamented by a few, not celebrated by so many. He had faced the impossible and survived. Thank God for His enabling.

"And you really didn't eat for three days?"

"Apart from a few shellfish on the beach, no."

There was a general cry of "Get the man another plate of beef!" which he declined with a smile. "Thank you, but I do not suffer hunger now."

How to turn the conversation to something of his faith? He did not wish to live in the past so much these days. "You know, I certainly could not have done it without God's sustaining power."

They drew back, faces nonplussed, as if he dared suggest something scandalous, like Napoleon might win this latest conflict enveloping Europe.

All except the Earl of Hawkesbury, whose interest in the welfare of returned soldiers had set him apart from others similarly titled. Lord Hawkesbury leaned in. "Sometimes it is only when we are at our lowest that we realize our need for Someone higher than ourselves."

Ben nodded, eyeing the tall man curiously. He was an ex-soldier; that much was obvious from his upright demeanor, the way others lost any hint of slouch when he walked through the door. His aunt had obligingly expounded upon Lord Featherington's friends and relations, so he knew Lord Hawkesbury was connected by marriage. What else had Aunt Addy said? The earl and his wife had suffered some kind of loss last year? No wonder he seemed to understand. Tragedy had a way of plumbing the depths of a man's character. But was he a believer, too?

Conversation veered to the Duke of Wellington and the situation in Belgium. Opinions were sought, offered, dismissed, scorned. The earl was appealed to, as a veteran of the Peninsular campaigns. His answers, weighted with grim experience, soon sobered the younger members of the gathering. Ben found another layer of respect for the viscount's cousin by marriage.

Later, when the others had left, save Lord Featherington and the earl, the conversation left Ben pleased to learn his initial guess had been correct. The earl shared Ben's grace-based faith: faith that recognized meritorious works could never match the work done by Jesus on the cross, faith ably demonstrated through practical works as those which the earl had tried to perform for those in his company left maimed or worse.

The earl met Ben's scrutiny with a small smile. "I make no claims for recognizing the needs for such assistance. It was not until I met my wife that I truly realized how important my actions could be."

"Lavinia is never backward in offering her opinions," murmured the viscount.

"Nor is she backward in offering her assistance," Hawkesbury said mildly.

Featherington flushed. "She is a very good woman, that is true."

The earl's smile hitched up a little farther to one side. "Tell me, Kemsley, do you object to ladies who perform good deeds?"

"Of course not. In fact, my sister is married to a clergyman."

"Really? My wife is the daughter of one. Imagine that."

Ben caught the earl's sardonic glint and turned to Tessa's would-be suitor. "I happen to know both my sisters are very suspicious of those who despise such things."

"Really?" The viscount's brows drew together. "I would hate for her — I mean, to be thought of as not caring about those who are less fortunate."

Ben bit back a smile as the earl nodded gravely. "To be regarded as selfish, a man who cares more for how one ties a neckcloth than his fellow man, why that would be something to abhor, would it not?"

The viscount turned to Ben. "Please tell me how I can help you to assist those men."

"Of course." Ben glanced at his pocket watch. "But it will have to be another time. I promised Tessa I would meet her at Hookham's."

Featherington's eyes rounded with hope.

He looked so much like a desperate pup Ben had no heart to deny him. He fought a sigh. "Perhaps we could discuss such matters on the way."

A short time later they were walking along Piccadilly, the hustle-bustle of traffic doing little to curb the young man's keen questions. Ben wondered again about Lord Featherington's notice of his sister. Clearly he would be expected to marry well, but to fix so much attention on someone with neither connections nor fortune to recommend her seemed foolhardy at best, destined for causing Tessa pain at worst.

They found Tessa and Aunt Addy deep in concentration, perusing the shelves. Any doubt about Tessa's partiality was instantly dismissed by the way her face lit at the sight of Ben's companion. He exchanged glances with his aunt and patiently waited until the two younger members of their party had exchanged conversation and promises to be at Lady Asquith's musical evening the following night.

"I cannot wait," Tessa confided. "I'm looking forward to seeing my friend perform."

"And I am looking forward to seeing you," the viscount said, smiling.

He bowed, exited, and after Tessa secured the book held for her, they continued home.

Ben frowned, trying to remember the details of tomorrow evening's invitation. Tessa had received the surprising invitation from her friend Miss DeLancey, hadn't she?

He wondered about this mysterious woman. What did she look like? Aunt Adeline had refrained from saying much, conscious of not wishing to taint Tessa's opinion, if the guarded look had been any clue. But even when he'd managed to ask her — font of societal knowledge — what news she had on the mysterious lady, she had merely shrugged.

"I believe there was something concerning a broken engagement."

Which induced pity, not distress, did it not?

She'd frowned. "I do recall hearing about some trouble with a brother. Very wild, they say. But I cannot recall exactly what it was. You must remember I was engaged with other matters at the time."

Like his uncle's ever-worsening illness.

He shook his head at himself. Why was he even bothering to listen to gossip about Miss DeLancey, anyway? Matilda seemed to regard her highly, and she was not exactly a fool when it came to measuring the worth of a person's character. And Tessa, though young and naive, had never said anything that might make him suspect anything out of the ordinary. Really, he should be ashamed of himself for even speculating on the young lady in question. Why, he was no better than the young bucks at White's earlier, gossiping around a table as if in possession of all the facts. But still, he could not but wonder a little about the young lady Matilda had been less than subtle about. Would she ever capture his attention so much as that mysterious clifftop girl? Would she look as striking as the brunette he'd bumped into in Brighton?

They rounded a corner.

He collided with a figure. The figure he'd just imagined: dark hair, pale green eyes, fair skin.

"You!"

She blinked. Her mouth fell open. She stepped back a pace.

"Clara!"

Tessa knew this girl?

Apparently so, for there was an exchange of smiles and hugs that left him confused — and not a little envious. He tamped down the feeling. Who was this girl who'd haunted his dreams?

Tessa turned to him, her smile as bright as her hair. "At last you get to meet."

Ben frowned; then when his sister refused

any further introduction, he introduced himself. "Good afternoon. I believe I have seen you before at church in Brighton. My name is Benjamin Kemsley."

He heard an intake of breath, which triggered another wisp of memory. When —

"Benjie?" she whispered.

His lips flattened as the green eyes slid to Tessa as if for confirmation. Nobody called him Benjie if he could help it; his sisters however seemed never to have understood that decree.

"And you are . . . ?" He put up his brows.

She moistened her bottom lip, drawing attention to its pink plumpness. Surely to kiss —

Stop! He gave himself a mental shake, realizing her nerves had still refused her answer. He felt his frown deepen. Why would anyone be nervous to give their name?

Tessa chuckled. "Oh, Ben. Stop scowling. Your face is enough to frighten a small child."

Or a beautiful young woman.

Tessa drew forth the young lady — Clara, was it? — and held out her hand. "Clara, meet my favorite brother. Benjie, this is the friend I was telling you about. This is Miss Clara DeLancey."

CHAPTER NINE

Him. The man on the clifftop. The man from the Steyne. The man she'd tried avoiding for so long. Matilda and Tessa's brother: the man who had saved her life.

Was that a flicker of remembrance in his eyes? Did he recognize her as the one who had behaved so foolishly on that wild night weeks ago? Nausea slid through her stomach. What should she do? What *could* she do? She couldn't very well avoid him now.

Clara shivered as he enveloped her hand in his. Just as he had that night so many weeks ago. Breath hitched. She swayed —

"Miss DeLancey!"

Warm hands on her elbow, her shoulders. Tessa's blue eyes clouded with concern. Soft murmurs of alarm came from the well-dressed older lady behind them.

Clara pushed iron into her spine, forced a smile onto her lips. "Forgive me. This heat, you know." She fanned herself as if hot, trying to ignore their lifted brows hinting of suspicion.

The older lady chuckled. "I'm sure my nephew does not mind the thought of young ladies swooning upon making his acquaintance."

Clara's cheeks heated to something she was sure approximated the flush spreading across Mr. Kemsley's face. Now she really *did* need to fan herself.

"Miss DeLancey? Clara?" Tessa still held her elbow, the tiny freckles dusted across her nose golden in the sunlight. A frown appeared between her eyes. "Please, let Benjie find you a hackney. You do not appear well."

Clara forced a laugh to her lips. "I am very sorry for worrying you, Tessa. There is nothing wrong with me but what a brisk walk cannot fix." A brisk walk preferably in the opposite direction of "Benjie" Kemsley. She slid him a glance. Surely he must suspect who she was by now.

He wore a frown much like he had minutes ago, his lips a flat line. Did he remember? Oh, she hoped not! Hadn't he thought that troubled person atop the cliff a poor, unfortunate elderly lady? Her heart twisted. Unfortunate she might be, and definitely poorer than before Richard had gambled away the Winpoole fortune, but elderly? Really?

Beside her Tessa and what must be her aunt were still murmuring about a hackney, but Clara could not drag her gaze away.

Now she studied him more closely she realized just how solid he appeared. The coat appeared molded to his shoulders. No wonder he'd been able to haul her up safely from the cliff edge — he looked like he had strength enough to haul an elephant from the seabed. But despite his strength, despite the square planes of his face, his watchful eyes held a look of something softer. They were lined with a dozen creases, as if he smiled a lot, or had undergone a painful trial not long ago.

"Clara?"

She startled. Turned to Tessa, a smile plastered on her face. "I'm sorry. I believe this is your aunt?"

"Oh! Of course." The knot between Tessa's pale brows smoothed away as she completed the introductions.

Clara curtsied. "Mrs. Harrow."

"Miss DeLancey." The older lady curtsied in response. "I understand my niece has you to thank for the invitation for tomorrow night?"

She nodded. "I'm sure Lady Asquith

would be pleased to have your company as well, if you so wish."

"Thank you. There is nothing I like more than to hear well-performed music. I understand from dear Theresa that you are an excellent musician."

The tension in her shoulders diminished. How nice to hear praise for a change. "I think she has overestimated my ability," she murmured.

"I'm sure the truth will be revealed tomorrow night."

The deeper voice drew her gaze back to Mr. Kemsley. "Were you planning on attending, sir?"

He shrugged. "I confess musical soirees hold little appeal."

"Oh, but Benjie, you must go!" cried Tessa. "You must be our escort. How else can we attend?"

The solidity of his face eased a fraction. "I thought you'd prefer young Featherington to escort you."

Lord Featherington? Clara's head grew woozy. Not him. Dear God, protect her from him. Protect her from his family's criticism.

"Clara?"

She squeezed Tessa's hand. "Please excuse me. I must return home. It was good to meet you." She nodded to Mrs. Harrow, half met Mr. Kemsley's eyes, before turning —

"Oh, Benjie will accompany you."

Clara closed her eyes momentarily. She turned to oh-so-helpful Tessa. "Thank you, but that will not be necessary."

"Of course it is necessary," Mrs. Harrow said. "Young ladies do not walk around London unescorted."

Clara tilted her chin, but kept her protest locked behind a tight smile.

The older lady's gaze remained steady, piercing, as if she knew some of Clara's secrets but had decided to ignore them in the interest of propriety. "My nephew will escort you. Won't you, Benjamin?"

"But of course," he muttered.

Clara's smile grew fixed. She nodded, curtsied again, and made her farewell amidst promises of seeing the two ladies on the following evening.

Mr. Kemsley asked her direction. She gave it, then handed over her packages at his request, before settling her hand on his forearm as they walked toward Wigmore Place.

Awkwardness refused her speech. He had said nothing, his silence as condemning as his frown suggested. Was he that shocked by her lack of escort? Her lip curled. Perhaps he was worried that being seen in her company might taint him . . .

A carriage passed them. A flower seller hawked her wares. "Flowers for the missus?"

Clara cringed, but Mr. Kemsley only shook his head.

What could she say? She had no wish to speak and possibly reveal herself. She had no wish to even be in his company, despite the tug within insisting he held a burly kind of appeal. She supposed she should be more grateful to the man who had saved her life, but what if he exposed her? She was already a laughingstock in so many of society's circles. Lady Asquith's musicale was supposed to be a safe place, a refuge where she could recover some social standing. How could Tessa think of inviting Featherington of all people? She shuddered.

"Miss DeLancey?"

She stumbled to a halt. Peered up at him. His sandy brows had pushed together.

"You do not appear well. Should I call a hackney?"

Resentment at his comment on her appearance warred with reluctant appreciation for his consideration. A hackney would mean she could return more quickly and he could be freed from his obligation that much sooner. "Thank you," she murmured.

He looked at her sharply, studying her for a long moment, before raising his hand for a passing cab driver to stop. Two minutes later she was at the front door of the nondescript house her father had rented.

"Thank you, Mr. Kemsley." He nodded, passed back her packages. "I am . . . I'm sorry you were obliged to go so far out of your way."

"It was no trouble."

She doubted that. She had seen him pay the cabdriver, seen the battered leather pouch in which he kept his coin. She hoped he did not feel too badly used. "I . . . I hope Tessa and your aunt enjoy tomorrow night."

"But not me?"

Her mouth dried. She swallowed. "I thought you did not care for such things."

"So you wish me not to attend?"

The blue of his eyes seemed to hold a magnetic quality. She could not look away. "I . . . I do not wish you . . . *not* to attend, sir."

His brow creased, then smoothed, as something like a smile pulled at one corner of his mouth. "You are a mystery, are you not, Miss DeLancey?"

Fortunately, the door opened, preventing her reply. She hurried a curtsy and hastened

139

inside, up the stairs to where her bedroom overlooked the street.

Sure enough, he stood there still, gazing at the house, the frown she'd come to associate with him firmly returned. He stood a moment longer, then turned, swished his hat through the air, descended the steps, and strode from view.

Her heart thudded. Had he recognized her? Remembered that dreadful night? It would only be a matter of time until he did. Oh, what could she do?

Asquith House, Park Lane

A night amongst toffs and the pretentious was not his usual idea of fun, but Tessa and Aunt Adeline had left no room for his backing out. He'd been surprised at their enthusiasm and not a little dismayed at the excitement twinging his chest. The boy who'd dreamed of visiting different lands across a moonlit sea eager to attend Lady Asquith's soiree? The boy who'd hated anything stuffy and formal keen to pretend he had enough musical nous to hold his own amongst those who knew an oboe from a clarinet?

Ben shook his head at himself. He was a fool to pretend his desire to be here was anything but a wish to see the intriguing Miss DeLancey again.

He peered past a large lady whose gaudy headdress contained a dozen ostrich feathers. He knew precisely how many for he'd counted them during the insufferable wailings of the previous performer, a lady of high title but less certain pitch, according to Aunt Addy's whispers. Due to an unfortunate crush of vehicles on Piccadilly, they'd arrived a little late and been relegated to the last row. While Tessa and Aunt Addy had been disappointed not to see Miss DeLancey, he couldn't help but be glad for the chance to gather his composure, to harken back to the days when he recalled how a gentleman behaved at such events, during his one foray into the upper class years ago. Around him sat the *ton* of London society; he was loathe to embarrass his relatives with anything less than gentlemanly manners and demeanor.

The master of ceremonies introduced the next performer. Ben clapped automatically — not too loud, but not so soft as many of the namby-pamby men around here seemed content to do. His hands were not used to being encased in softest kid; his fingers still bore the callouses of career and cares.

His peripheral vision caught the sight of Viscount Featherington, whose bored expression as he glanced behind immediately brightened as he encountered Ben. He lifted his brow, as if to ask if Tessa were in attendance, to which Ben responded with a small nod. Featherington grinned, then turned back to face the front, seemingly as eager as Ben was for the interval to be proclaimed.

Another song, sung in Italian, which Ben could never hope to understand. His neckcloth grew tighter; his coat pulled harder. The navy coat of superfine Aunt Addy had insisted he wear felt like bands of steel encompassing him. He tried to subtly roll his shoulders and release the prickling tension. Couldn't. Sweat dribbled down his back. How warm did Lord Asquith heat this place, anyway?

Finally interval was announced, to a collective sigh of relief from the back half of the audience. Viscount Featherington appeared, and after an exchange of bows and curtsies, turned to Tessa with a smile.

"I'm very glad you came. I confess I thought I'd expire on the spot if I had to endure another ear-piercing shriek from that last lady. A musical genius? I ask you!" He exhaled. "I was sorry to miss you earlier. I saved you a seat, but then Lord and Lady Pennicooke insisted on sitting there, along with their daughter." His nose wrinkled. "I cannot but think of cabbage whenever I see Anne."

Tessa blinked. "Cabbage?"

"I know," Featherington continued, his gaze growing tender. "But when I see another young lady, all I can think of are stars and fire, and turquoise beauty, and pearls that cannot do justice to so fair a face."

Ben frowned as Tessa's cheeks grew rosy, before Aunt Addy directed her attentions elsewhere. Were such things truly what young ladies wished to hear? Wait — did Featherington truly mean them? Surely a viscount — an heir to a marquess, no less! — would need to look higher than Tessa if his intentions were honorable.

As if sensing his thoughts, Featherington looked at him. "Is something wrong, Kemsley?"

"It depends, my lord," he replied in a low voice, angling his body so Tessa could neither see nor hear him, "on whether your flattery towards my sister stems from noble intentions or not. I would not have Tessa hurt by thinking more of your meaning than you do."

"I . . . I hope she takes my meaning exactly as I intend."

"As you intend?" Ben's brows rose.

"I find her exquisitely charming."

Ben glanced between them. "Really?"

"Yes, really." The viscount studied her, a tender light in his eyes, before returning his attention to Ben with a grin. "You need not fear my attentions to your sister. Perhaps we should find someone for you to fix your attention on. I wonder — no. I wouldn't wish you Anne Pennicooke; that is a measure far too hard even for someone who dared believe me of nefarious intent." He continued glancing around before his gazed grew fixed, his mien hardened. "I might have known she would be here tonight." He gave a dismissive snort. "Such a desperate creature. I suppose her godmother's soiree the only invite she could wangle these days. They say she's desperate for a husband."

Ben frowned. He did not like Featherington's description of some poor young lady; it felt too close to how Mattie might have once been described.

The viscount leaned in, "Quiet, here she comes." He bowed stiffly, and then said in a louder voice, "Miss DeLancey."

Ben's breath caught. Featherington referred to her? He met her emerald eyes and quickly bowed. How could this glorious creature be denigrated in such a way?

He straightened, found the pale cheeks

had flushed rosy red, as she glanced between him and the viscount. Had she heard his mean-spirited remarks? Why had Featherington's comments been so unkind? Perhaps Ben should let her know he did not share the viscount's opinion. He opened his mouth to compliment her on her gown —

"Oh, Clara!" Tessa hurried to her side. "I'm so sorry we missed you before. Tell me we have not missed your performance."

"No. I am yet to perform."

Featherington looked between them. "You know each other?"

Tessa gave an artless smile. "Of course! It's due to Miss DeLancey's kindness that I'm even here tonight. We've become friends, you see."

"Friends?" The viscount's expression took on something approaching a sneer.

"In Brighton," Miss DeLancey said softly. Her gaze met Ben's before falling away.

Featherington offered an arm to Tessa. "Hope you don't mind, Kemsley, but I feel the need for a little liquid refreshment, as does your sister, I believe."

Tessa only waited the briefest moment for a nod from Ben before traipsing off with her suitor. Her suitor? Perhaps a better alternative to poor Braithwaite, but surely the viscount's father would have a say in the suitability of any prospective daughter-in-law. His smile of politeness fell. And when the marquess discovered just how little Tessa would bring in terms of title or dowry, he was sure to put an end to any romance between them.

He dragged his attention away, only to encounter Miss DeLancey's uncertain look. Aunt Adeline was chatting to a dowager nearby. It was left to him to attempt to smooth the waters. "Miss DeLancey?"

Her eyes seemed shaded with sadness; her mottled cheeks spoke of embarrassment.

Compassion twisted within. "My sister has been looking forward to hearing you perform."

She nodded, bit her lip. Her gaze skittered away.

He stepped closer. "Miss DeLancey?"

She glanced up. Her eyes were shining with tears.

He moved to shelter her from the perusal of the curious. Frustration burned within. What was he supposed to say? Clearly the viscount had some kind of grudge against her. But what was it that could make her cry?

"Clara?" A thin querulous voice was immediately followed by a thin, fussy-looking woman.

Recognition tugged at him. Of course; she was the mother he'd had the misfortune to encounter after services.

Lady Winpoole's elaborate coiffure turned to him, her mouth turning down in dislike. "Who is this person, Clara?"

Defensiveness rose within. He tamped it down. Offered a small bow. "Benjamin Kemsley, at your service."

"Hmph," she sniffed. "I hardly think you would ever prove of service to me."

Heated words rose, then fell as he noticed her daughter's anxious expression, the way she bit her bottom lip.

"Please excuse me." He offered a bow to them both and moved to join the queue lining up for liquid refreshments. He now understood why some men found such things necessary.

"Kemsley!"

Another of the gentlemen from White's hailed him, and they began a discussion of Napoleon's tactics that lasted right up until the bell tinkled to announce the recommencement of the program. He resumed his seat, apprehensive when he discovered Tessa now sat next to the viscount in front. When questioned, Aunt Addy said she had given permission, so he could scarcely argue. But was encouraging such a futile connection wise? Wouldn't it just lead to aching hearts?

Consumed as he was with his sister's plight, Ben barely heard the first performer. Only the sound of applause jerked his attention to the fore.

The master of ceremonies rose. "And now, may I encourage you to acknowledge our next performer, Miss DeLancey."

The applause was much muted, dimmed as it were by the murmurs filling the room. He saw how her cheeks paled, then grew rosy, the way her chin lifted as if summoning courage. Clearly she knew her name was being whispered about in a manner less than complimentary. He frowned. But what were people saying?

She settled at the pianoforte, glanced up once, with almost a scared look, then began to play.

Ben shifted in his seat, ostensibly to get more comfortable, but actually to eavesdrop on the talkative couple in front.

"Shameless! . . . poor thing . . . earl, you know . . . Richard . . . gambling debts . . . ran away!"

The words raced around his heart as the music intensified. How could they malign an innocent lady? His indignation was soothed somewhat by the excellence of the musicianship. Compared to some of the others, her playing seemed flawless, the piece sounding far more technically demanding than any he had heard before. He leaned back against his seat, pleasure filling his senses. While she might have manners that made Tessa seem bold, she also possessed far more skill than he could have imagined. Emotion seemed to roar through her fingertips, demandingly, pleadingly, until the audience's murmured conversations quieted to respectful awe. He smiled, glad she'd had the chance to show her critics she could not be silenced.

And when she finished, he sat a little higher, gladness stealing through him as she looked up and caught his eye.

He smiled wider, and she ducked her head.

Leaving him wondering all the more about the Miss Clara DeLancey who had long ago snagged his attention.

CHAPTER TEN

The scent of the half-dozen floral tributes filling the entryway teased Clara's senses, reviving memories of years past when she had been considered one of the most eligible young ladies on the market. She lifted a posy, breathed in the sweetness, and read the card. Her spirits dipped as she recognized her godmother's handwriting. She rifled quickly through the other tributes; they were more of the same. People who remembered her, but few from those under fifty, and none from any her parents might deem eligible suitors.

She tried to be pleased, to focus on the positive, to be glad for the thoughtfulness of so many after last night's performance. But the lack of interest from any and all eligible young gentlemen showed just how shallow and fickle some men's attentions could be. Hadn't the Earl of Hawkesbury trained her to mistrust men's motives? Her memories flicked back to the time he'd asked her to request Lady Asquith to invite Lavinia Ellison to play at one of her evenings. Until then she'd felt quite sure of his affection. Afterward, she'd known herself to be nothing but a romantic fool, something only further confirmed when Richard's gambling debts had forced Father to dip into a substantial portion of the dowry to which she'd been entitled, resulting in the loss of all other suitors as quickly as the news spread amongst the *ton.* Believe a man who said he loved her? Good thing such weak emotions were stamped out of her now.

"Ah, my dear." Clara turned to see Mother descending the stairs. "It is good to see a return of pretty tributes, is it not?"

"Yes."

Mother picked up the cards, glancing at them before returning them to the silver salver. "I think last night went off quite well. I do hope it will help relaunch you back into society. We must ensure you get invited to the Seftons' ball."

Clara's smile stiffened.

"The Asquiths were very kind to ensure so many of the better families were in attendance, but I could not help but wonder if some of their invites had gone astray." A pleat appeared between her brows. "There did not seem to be quite as many young men as I had hoped, and as for that Mrs. Harrow creature, I cannot fathom how she could be in attendance, when so many of better lineage were not."

"She is the aunt of my friend Tessa."

Mother waved a hand as she led the way to the drawing room. "Oh, I know it is unfortunate, and these things cannot be helped, but I do not understand why such persons have not sent a card of thanks for the privilege of attending last night." She sniffed. "I do wish you enjoyed the company of some of the young ladies you used to know, those who know what is expected of them."

Such as who? she longed to say, but didn't. The only girl she'd ever really counted as friend, Harriet Winchester, had married and moved to the wilds of Scotland two seasons ago. She had few other friends. Perhaps she really *was* unlikeable.

Her self-examination was cut short by the arrival of Father. He greeted them, enquired briefly about how they had slept, then shook out a freshly ironed newspaper and began to read. Outside, cloud shadows rippled dimness through the room.

Mother frowned, darker than anything to be glimpsed from the drawing room window. "I do not think I like your continuing this acquaintance, Clara. I cannot foresee any advantage from these people."

"Must we only speak with people who offer us advantage?"

"Well, I agree it is very kind of you to want to help the girl further her social aspirations, but I cannot think it does your credit any good. Especially at a time when we are doing our best to redeem it."

Clara swallowed emotion, her protest dying upon her lips.

"Frederica, now really." Father lowered the newspaper, glanced between Clara and her mother. "I think your words are a little harsh. The family is not exactly nobodies, are they?"

This last was said with a glance at Clara, prompting her to murmur, "Tessa is the sister of a baronet."

Father nodded, his brows rising as he glanced back at Mother, as if to say, see?

"Yes, but only a baronet!" Mother's face creased as if she were in pain.

"A baronetcy is hardly to be sneezed at."

Should she point out she'd never met the baronet? That Tessa herself held far more social cachet as the object of attention from the heir to a marquess? Though perhaps refraining from mentioning the Exeter —

153

and thus Hawkesbury — connection was the wiser course of action.

Mother sighed. "I had envisaged so much more for our girl."

"You can envisage all you like, but it cannot change the fact that there needs to be some degree of interest from the opposite party. No, Frederica, I know you do not like me to say it, but our girl is hardly a simpleton. If Hawkesbury had not played her false and given rise to speculation, then perhaps she might have snared an earl. But the fact remains he did not offer, and we must find someone who will suit."

Mother's small hands clenched and unclenched. "Perhaps if you were to exert yourself a little more in this quest, then we might not be feeling like this."

"Of course." He folded his newspaper. "I might be a mere husband and a father, but I can tell you that any red-blooded man will not be searching for a wife at an Asquith musicale." He made a movement reminiscent of a shudder. "She'd be far better off playing to a different strength, like her riding." He glanced out the window. "Pity those clouds look like rain."

"The ability to ride well is hardly the kind of activity a young man requires when searching for a wife."

"Nonsense! It shows she is healthy, and spirited, and not one of those dull young misses too frightened to go outside."

"Really, Phillip. You speak as though she is a horse!"

Their quarrel was cut short by the knock and entrance of a footman. He glanced apologetically at Mother before saying, "A Mrs. Harrow, a Miss Kemsley, and a Mr. Kemsley to see you, my lord."

Father glanced between them. "I gather this visit is chiefly for your sake, Clara. Shall we agree to be in?"

"Yes, please," she murmured, fighting a frisson of excitement as the footman withdrew.

Mother frowned. "Do they have no idea about paying social visits?"

"But weren't you just complaining about how they had not sent anything?" Clara murmured. "Surely being paid the honor of a call in person is to be valued more highly than a posy of flowers delivered by a servant."

"It depends on the flowers — oh, *dear* Mrs. Harrow, how delightful to see you again, and so soon."

The elder of their female visitors flushed. "I trust it is not inconvenient."

"No, no," Mother oozed. "We are quite at

our leisure, aren't we, Clara?"

"Quite." Clara turned to Tessa, smiling as warmly as she knew how. "I hope you enjoyed last night?"

"Oh, how could we not? Lady Asquith was a very generous hostess, and I felt so very privileged to be in such company."

Clara sneaked a peek at Mother, pleased to see she appeared not a little mollified by this ingenuous speech.

Mother bestowed upon Tessa one of her more gracious nods. "Penelope has been a friend of mine since girlhood. I'm sure she'd be gratified to learn of your appreciation."

Mrs. Harrow nodded. "We sent her a card and posy this morning."

Clara's smile broadened, and she resisted the urge to look at how her parent was taking this admission of social nous. "Would you care to stay for tea?"

"Oh, we could never presume," said Mrs. Harrow.

Tessa nodded. "Fifteen minutes only, Benjie said, else we'll overstay our welcome."

"Did he?" Mother said, studying him curiously, as if finally seeing him for the first time, before issuing instructions for tea.

Clara finally permitted herself to look at the male guest, the only gentleman whose words last night had flickered an ember of interest. He seemed uncomfortable in the gold-toned drawing room, his height and breadth making the delicate furnishings seem a little too small and fragile, leading her to wonder how long the chair he'd stuffed himself into would bear his weight. His expression was polite, yet closed, as if he'd been well trained in not displaying boredom with social engagements not to his liking. But the keenness of his eyes, the way his lips quirked at prosy comments, were suggestive of a quick mind and a fast decision maker. Had he made a decision about her? Did he remember her yet? What did he think of her? Her cheeks heated. Of her family, that was all.

His blue eyes bent to her. She glanced away, murmured something inconsequential to Mrs. Harrow about the weather.

Reprieve was supplied by the entrance of the footman bearing a loaded tray, as if Cook had been ready with such offerings, had indeed been looking for an opportunity to show off her culinary creativity.

"Kemsley." Father said, once the cups had been distributed. "Now I remember. I've been trying to recall for several weeks now how I knew your name. Any relation to that sea captain responsible for the incident off Africa a few months ago?"

Mr. Kemsley cleared his throat. "If you mean the *Ansdruther,* then yes. I am he."

"Ah." Father nodded, a pleased smile on his face. "Well! It is an honor to have you in our house for tea."

Clara watched as the sunburned face reddened. The spark of appeal prompted by his kindness last night kindled into deeper interest. What was so remarkable that her father seemed to approve of this bluff, blunt-spoken man?

Ben had never seen the point of tea parties. They seemed but weak excuses for ladies to engage in polite fencing around matters of gossip and fashion that held zero interest for him, while drinking tepid, tasteless tea and eating the barest amount that only scraped the sides of his hunger.

That was until today.

This tea must have been imported from Ceylon, for it bore all the flavorsome qualities he remembered from his time on that isle. If he were to close his eyes, he could almost imagine himself there — save for the inanities of his hostess, whose icy sneer at their arrival had gradually thawed as she apparently realized they weren't quite the savages she'd obviously imagined. The viscount's attitude he had yet to determine;

neither could he definitively interpret the daughter. He'd thought he'd caught a flicker of interest in her eyes upon his entry, but she gave little away, had spent much of their visit not looking in his direction.

He took a bite of the large slice of cake, the crumbs of goodness filling his mouth, sliding down his throat. Upon being offered a second piece, he was forced to revise his earlier opinion of his hostess. For all her snobbishness, she seemed aware that a healthy young man's appetite was not the same as a gently bred young lady.

"I hope we'll have the pleasure of hearing you play again sometime when you return to Brighton, Miss DeLancey," Tessa said.

Miss DeLancey murmured something noncommittal, but he caught the glance she slid at her mother, as if seeking her approval. Lady Winpoole's stiff countenance did not alter a jot.

"Would you tell us something of your last voyage?" Lord Winpoole asked.

Ben fought a sigh. Would his life be forever shaped by events on the other side of the world? Glancing at the room's other inhabitants, he caught the flare of something that could be interest in Miss DeLancey's green eyes.

"I'm not sure if the ladies would be that

keen —"

"Oh, stop being modest. I'm sure they'd be fascinated by your adventures."

He glanced again at his host's daughter. Definitely interested, judging from the tilted head and intent gaze. He nodded, and set himself to answer. "We were travelling from Ceylon to England. I was the captain of the *Ansdruther,* an East Indiaman, charged with returning soldiers and a few families back to Portsmouth. During a fierce gale we hit a reef, just off Cape St. Francis, and the boat began to break up."

The memories rushed in anew. The great wall of water, a huge black mass rolling towards them. The desperation. The cries and shouts. He swallowed, forced himself to complete the story. "I thank God that despite the encroaching darkness and the furies of the waves, we were able to reach shore without loss of life, save one soul."

He heard a quiet exhale from the young brunette opposite. He looked up; her gaze was fixed on him, soft with something that looked like sympathy.

"We spent the next two nights watching the ship slowly break apart, trying to salvage what we could, while different men searched for ways to scale the cliffs and try to find help." He gave a small smile. "There was no way. It required going back into the sea. Fortunately the storm had passed so the sea wasn't nearly so rough as before. And the sharks weren't there, either. Not visible, anyway."

Miss DeLancey's eyes widened, her gasp identical to one emitted by her mother.

"So you went back into the sea?" his host asked.

Ben shrugged. "I had good lieutenants and knew they could keep order. I also knew I was the strongest swimmer, so I remained the best chance of finding help. Which I eventually did."

"After swimming for a day then walking five more, so the newspaper reports said."

"It was only three days walking," Ben said, his gaze lowered to his boots. "The southern cape is remote, but not completely devoid of human habitation."

"What an ordeal," Miss DeLancey murmured.

"It was an experience I'm not keen to repeat, although I do remain extremely thankful for God's protection throughout."

"You were very lucky," the viscountess said, wide-eyed. "The luck of the gods!"

"Not lucky, and any protection was not from any so-called gods. There were many prayers being prayed throughout, and only one God to whom they were addressed."

She looked slightly abashed, covering it by offering him another piece of cake, as if feeding him more now might go some way to helping him forget the pangs of starvation.

As if obeying a silent summons, Clara refilled his cup, her fingers accidentally brushing his as she passed it to him.

Fire rushed up his arm. Awareness filled his senses. He sought to hide such feelings by having another bite of cake, washing it down with tea.

Conscious their eyes remained on him, he sought for a way to turn the conversation, but it seemed his hosts were not content to move on.

The viscount frowned. "And the people remaining behind?"

A sigh rumbled from his inner depths. "My only regret is that I did not return as quickly as I had hoped. I was tired —"

"You would have been exhausted!" Tessa interrupted.

He shot her a grateful smile and continued. "I needed some time to recover, and it took a while for the villagers to understand me. By the time I got back, some of the injured soldiers had died."

"How awful!"

The sympathy pooling in Miss DeLancey's eyes clogged his throat. He swallowed, wishing he had not begun to tell the tale that now threatened to unman him. He needed to change the subject, and fast.

Ben gestured to the cake. "Please pass on my compliments to your cook. This is one of the most tasty I've had the pleasure of eating." He slid a look at Tessa. "Do not tell Mattie I said that."

Tessa giggled, as his hostess nodded, murmuring something appropriately gracious. So he hadn't appeared too uncouth then. Encouraged, he addressed his hostess once again.

"I must confess, Lady Winpoole, that most opportunities of this nature seem more fitting for a man of a wasp-like appetite than one more used to hearty eating."

"Oh!"

Her startled look suggested he wasn't gaining ground in her favor regarding his manner; rather, losing it. He smiled somewhat desperately, and sailed on. "I gather your generosity comes from having experience of a son." He glanced between his hostess and her daughter. "I seem to recall something about a brother."

"Richard," the viscount said, frowning.

"Richard, yes. I remember." Barely, but if

it helped win him favor. "Where is he these days?"

He glanced between the stony faces, as the room's atmosphere immediately chilled. And realized their visit must conclude, any hope of winning favor sunk as deep as the wreck he'd just described.

CHAPTER ELEVEN

Time spent in London reminded Clara of different things. Like how she used to love performing. How much she enjoyed opportunities to wear fine clothes. And how much she enjoyed riding in Hyde Park.

"Come on, Blackie," she urged her hack. It was too early in the morning for many of the *ton* to be out and about. Therefore it was safe to ride faster than decorum demanded, which meant she was free to give the horse its head. Free to enjoy the trees and flowers, quivering scented color in an early June breeze. Free to thank God her brother had yet to show up as he'd threatened. *Dear* Richard. She hoped it proved just another of those things he said to worry her.

She turned into Rotten Row, nudging her mount to pick up speed. For a moment escape felt possible, that if she only kept riding she might leave her past behind. If only —

"Miss!"

Clara glanced behind her at Button, the groom, desperately flailing his steed to keep up. She slowed to a more decorous pace. If only societal expectations did not constrain one so. She sighed, patting her mount's glossy mane. It would not do for a poor horse to bear the brunt of her need to escape the demons in her mind.

They rounded the curve. She looked up. Recognized a large black stallion — and its owner.

Her heart panged. It was too late to turn around now. Any opportunity to alter course would be so obvious as to raise speculation. But would he think she'd come deliberately to spy on him? That she'd come with the wish to relive past encounters? Bile rose; she swallowed it. There was no escape. Perhaps if she slowed a little — but no. He had neared. Had glanced up.

"Miss DeLancey." The surprise in Lord Hawkesbury's face quickly melded into something akin to revulsion.

Her heart panged even more. "My lord."

The words tasted bitter in her mouth. He would never be hers. He'd made that only too clear last year when Mother's machinations had led them to a visit to Hawkesbury House during a time of tragedy for the earl and his wife. Precisely what the dowager countess had hoped to accomplish by issuing such an invitation she did not want to know. Precisely what her mother had hoped might come by their acceptance Clara had some idea. She was sure Mother had not meant to be spiteful, but being there, conscious of the earl's obvious fury, conscious her presence was deemed by Lavinia's family members to be the utmost in insults, made her wish they had never set foot in the carriage that took them north to Lincolnshire.

Man and horse rushed past her in a blur of black and speed, leaving nothing but a sense of loss. He would never be hers. He despised her. Her eyes filled. He probably felt she was responsible for suggesting the idea to the dowager in the first place. It was done. He was gone. That time was done.

Blinking against the burn in her eyes, she fixed her attention at the oaks that proclaimed Hyde Park Corner. Her chin lifted a fraction. She would need to show him she did not care. Show everyone — especially Mother — that all thought of the Earl of Hawkesbury was long gone.

Even if it felt as though a hook had been

placed in her heart that would never be extracted.

Her hack's hooves thundered along the grass and sand. The scent of horse mingled with summer blossom as a prayer lifted in her heart. *Lord, help me forget him.*

A snippet from the devotional book Matilda had lent her rose again. Something about forgiveness requiring one to pray blessing over her enemies. While she wouldn't exactly count the earl as her enemy — even though he might consider Clara an enemy — she could see the advice as something powerful. To wish good for someone who had hurt you surely required something from God, as opposed to natural inclination. When that person seemed to have used you, manipulated you for their personal advantage, then to not only forgive but also to pray blessing on them would surely require something of the divine.

But wasn't that just what Lavinia had done?

She wheeled the hack around, continued along the park perimeter, then veered closer to a path that led to the Serpentine. The water sparkled under sunny skies, a few ducks paddled, others squabbled on the water's edge. She'd never really thought about how the earl's wife might feel towards her, until that moment last year when Lavinia had descended the stairs of Hawkesbury House a few days after the loss of her child and extended a wan-faced welcome that had shamed Clara. Yet there had been nothing false about it. Instead, the earl's wife seemed to possess a natural grace, offering kindness to someone who'd been unkind even whilst undergoing personal tragedy. Her heart panged anew. No wonder the earl had preferred Lavinia to herself. Clara would never be able to show such graciousness to someone who had hurt her.

"Miss Clara?"

She glanced over her shoulder. Lost in her thoughts she'd forgotten the groom. She reined in. "What is it, Button?"

He heaved out a red-faced breath. "You were travelling a mite fast for my peace of mind," he said with a gasp. "I don't think your mother would be happy to know you're out here like this."

"I'm sure you're right."

He studied her with a suspicious air. "Then might I suggest we slow down to something more appropriate?"

"By all means."

She forced her steed to slow to the walking pace deemed more ladylike. The surge of emotion in her heart slowed also, as she thought on that reading. Should she pray for God to bless the earl and Lavinia? She didn't want to. And it still didn't seem fair that he'd ill-treated her in such a way, making her believe his actions were leading to a permanent attachment. It would *never* be fair. But how long could she keep carrying this aching hurt inside? Could praying blessings on them really release her from this heavy feeling of unforgiveness?

Clara glanced about her. Button trotted sedately several paces behind, as both he and her parents preferred. Nobody else was near; nobody to see her behave in a most peculiar manner. She drew in a breath of warm grass-scented air. "God?"

She swallowed. Pressed on. "I forgive him. I forgive her. Help —" She swallowed again, forced herself to speak through the bile rising in her throat. "Help them in their marriage. Please bless them." Her heart writhed. "Please bless them with a child. Amen."

The prayer fell from her lips like she'd spat out poison. But inside . . .

Inside, it seemed like something hard in her heart had cracked. Amid the hurt and clashing emotion stole a sweet softness, like the slow unfurling of forgiveness in her soul.

She glanced up at the soft blue of sky. Could God hear her better out here? It certainly felt so. "Thank You."

A twitter of birds rose as one from the branches of a large elm. She watched them swirl and sweep through the sky, their movements graceful and majestic. As though they were putting on a show just for her.

"Miss Clara?" Button drew alongside.

She kept her gaze fixed upwards. "They are beautiful, are they not?"

"Very nice, miss. But are you sure you wish to be here? I thought I heard you say something before."

"You probably did," she agreed mildly.

He frowned, rubbing his chin as if not sure how to take her. A flash of amusement cut through the dregs of the earlier heavy emotion. Yes, perhaps these days she was not quite the rigid, self-centered young miss he had always known her to be. If only she had behaved a little kinder, perhaps the earl —

No! She swallowed. Gritted her teeth. *Lord, bless him.* When that didn't seem to be strong enough, she muttered, "Bless him!"

"Pardon, miss? Did you say something?"

She turned to the groom. Found a smile. "Nothing to worry about."

When he continued to search her with an anxious air, she said, her smile now genuine,

"God bless you, Button, for being so obliging these many years."

His widened eyes creased as he chuckled. "I gets paid to be obliging, miss."

She laughed, and the sound seemed to chase away more of the cobwebs in her soul. So she wheeled her hack towards Wigmore Place, and home.

Somerset House

Ben glanced around the principal chamber of Somerset House. The yellow walls were heavily lined with paintings, from floor to eaves, the position of each portrait or landscape seemingly designed more to ensure a maximum number of paintings on display than from any real finesse or desire to align according to subject matter. Not that he was any expert on art. The room bustled with the knowledgeable and the novice, those loudly proclaiming their artistic pedigree and those content to gawk, occasionally murmuring something about the colors and whether the images portrayed were lifelike or not. He most definitely fell into the latter category today.

"Ah, Captain Kemsley."

Ben turned, encountering the puffy, self-important features of old Lord Babcock, the latest and most elderly of Tessa's admirers. Fighting to maintain a pleasant de-meanor, he bowed. "Good afternoon, my lord."

"Tell me, is that rather lovely younger sister of yours here by any chance?"

"By any chance?" Ben's smile thinned. "I was under the impression you thought her attendance today something of a certainty, given you were privy to the conversation after services on Sunday when such an ar-rangement was made."

"I . . . er . . ." The older gentleman looked nonplussed. "Well, now I do recall Miss Kemsley saying something of it to her friend."

"I rather thought you might," Ben glanced away, saw Tessa talking with Miss DeLancey. Tessa's friend seemed a little brighter today, her face animated, her gown as elegant as he'd come to expect.

He turned back to see Lord Babcock had followed his gaze, and was now frowning. The baron met his gaze with a loud har-rumph. "In fine looks, I see."

"Yes." Both young ladies were.

The baron gave another loud clearing of his throat. "A word to the wise, my boy. Young ladies like your sister should not be permitted to spend too much time with those around whom scandal clings. You might wish to steer her clear of such tittle-tattle."

Ben raised his brows, not bothering to hide his dislike anymore. "Thank you for your concern, but my sister —"

"Your sister is not the problem, can I say," Lord Babcock tapped the side of his bulbous nose.

Coldness seeped through his chest. "Excuse me, my lord."

"Of course, Captain."

An exchange of bows later and Ben was stalking across the room, trying to stifle the desire to smack the self-satisfied glint from the older man's eyes. How dare he insinuate Miss DeLancey was anything but honorable?

By the time he reached the two young ladies, they had been joined by yet another admirer, a Mr. Dubois, if memory served. They exchanged greetings before the dark-haired young man said, eyes fixed on Tessa, "Do you not think the pictures most fine, ladies?"

Tessa did not answer. Miss DeLancey murmured, "Wonderfully fine."

Ben clenched his fists.

"And you, Captain Kemsley?"

"Mr. Kemsley," he growled.

"Ah, yes. I wonder what you think of this

fine picture." He pointed to a ship in flames.

"I think it quite apparent the artist never stepped aboard an Indiaman in his life."

"Really?"

"If he had seen such a ship, he would not have painted it missing a mast, nor would he have ignorant people call it fine when it is obviously a fabrication."

"Benjie!" Tessa whispered, her horror-struck expression making him aware of his *faux pas,* and the blushes of both Miss DeLancey and Mr. Dubois.

"If you'll excuse me," the latter said, moving away stiffly.

Ben swallowed bile and glanced at Miss DeLancey to make his apologies, but she'd turned to study a picture of a small rural scene.

"That was too bad of you!" Tessa murmured.

"Come now, surely you do not care what that jackanapes thinks. I noticed you barely looked at him, let alone spoke to him."

"That does not give you the liberty of speaking so rudely."

"Would you rather get rid of your unwanted suitors yourself, then?"

A reluctant smile flashed. "I think I prefer your assistance."

Ben crossed his arms. So perhaps his

forthrightness wasn't considered entirely inane.

Wading through the social mores had proved difficult at times. After the debacle at the Winpoole residence, Ben had received a severe scolding from his aunt and sister, the likes of which reminded him of a dressing down he had once received from his first captain. His relief when Tessa had secured her friend's company today, following a brief conversation after services last Sunday, had been considerable. He was thankful Miss DeLancey had not severed his sister's friendship — though he wondered how many more gentlemen seeking Tessa's favor he might need to navigate away.

"Ah, there you are!"

That voice, the light suffusing his sister's face, could only mean one thing.

Ben turned and bowed. "Lord Featherington."

"Forgive me, but I could not wait a second more." He turned to Tessa and began speaking of an outing to take place in a few days' time.

Ben noticed how Miss DeLancey had seemed to freeze before shrinking back, as if wary of receiving the viscount's notice. He frowned.

"Benjie?" Tessa laid a hand on his arm,

looking up at him with a puzzled expression. "What is it? Do you not like the sound of Lord Featherington's scheme?"

Ben shook his head, turning to the viscount. "I must beg your pardon. I was distracted for a moment."

"Not surprising in a room like this. If it didn't seem as though half of London were here, then these paintings would be enough to get your attention."

Ben swallowed a smile. "I rather think that is the artists' intention."

"Mebbe." Featherington gave a good-natured shrug. "Well, I cannot say I've ever cared overly for such things. My brother-in-law likes his pictures though, has some rather nice views of Venice in the breakfast room, as I recall. But for me, I'd much rather be outside than in. I say, did you see that rather striking painting of a burning ship?"

Ben opened his mouth to speak but Tessa jumped in. "He did, and he doesn't like it. Says it's not true to life."

"Well, I guess a captain should know. Shall we say eleven on Friday, then?"

"I . . . I shall have to speak with Aunt Addy."

"Of course. Well, I'll be off. Got an engagement at Manton's. I like to think I'm quite a good shot, but Hartington — Charlotte's husband, y'know — most unassuming man imaginable, but an incredibly good shot. I'll need to better mine if I'm to visit Northamptonshire for the hunt in October. Must be able to hit a wafer or three!"

Ben nodded politely, though he barely knew of what the young man spoke. Hartington he knew to be the duke recently married to Lord Featherington's sister, but *wafers*? He scarcely knew what to say to men of leisure, his life rather one of toil and command, and much preferred the honest reckonings of men who understood him, like Burford and Lancaster. While in past weeks he'd been invited by several gentlemen to various pleasure jaunts, he'd found the visits a challenge. He couldn't participate in conversations about aristocrats he'd never met, nor engage in activities that strained his knee, and he'd little liking for gossip. Whenever talk of his exploits arose, he'd turn the conversation by introducing the topic of shelters and helps for the returning soldiers. This at least made his time feel somewhat more gainfully employed.

The viscount talked on, his farewell to Tessa taking an inordinate amount of time. Perhaps Ben being adrift in London wasn't completely futile. It had provided opportunity to safeguard his sister from some of the more determined suitors who had found her too much at liberty to answer their every invitation to a drive through Hyde Park, or the theatre, or another of those dreadful musicales that seemed so popular.

With a bow and a flourish, the viscount finally disappeared. Perhaps he liked Tessa's ability to listen as much as her fair face.

"Clara?"

The brunette turned from her perusal of the art lining the walls of Somerset House. He ignored the strange pang as her gaze flicked past him to settle on Tessa. "Yes?"

"Have you ever been to the Tower?"

"I don't believe so, no."

"Wonderful! Do you think your parents would permit you to attend? Lord Featherington has invited us for an excursion on Friday. He must have overheard my wish to visit last week. He is all that is thoughtful, is he not?"

"Indeed." Miss DeLancey's voice sounded strained.

"So, will you come? Benjie mentioned recently he would like to visit, and although some of the history sounds most gory, I confess I would still like to see it."

"I . . . I am sure I am busy that day. I am sorry."

"Oh! But it would not be the same without you."

"The viscount did not invite me, Tessa, so I hardly think it will matter if I do not attend."

"You are far too modest! I, for one, would miss your company immensely."

"You are very kind, but I cannot think the viscount would like it."

"Well if he objects to you, then I object to him."

"I *really* think —"

"And Benjie would like you to come, too." Tessa turned to him. "Wouldn't you?"

He swallowed, aware of the skeptical expression in Miss DeLancey's eyes that made his answer suddenly important. What could he say? There was no possible polite answer, save, "Of course."

Miss DeLancey studied him for a moment as she bit her lip.

Remorse for his careless words earlier surged again. "Miss DeLancey, we would truly value your company."

She blinked and ducked her head. "I would not wish to intrude on your plans."

"Our plans these days seem quite fluid. Tessa needs only mention the barest scrap-

180

ing of an idea and one of her besotted swains instantly gets up a notion to carry out her every wish. Why, one fellow thought she might like to see the tightrope walker at Vauxhall Gardens, then had the nerve to create a fuss when he'd ordered an elaborate picnic for an evening that proved impossible to attend due to a prior engagement. Soft-hearted Tessa here then felt so sorry for the chap that she nearly had us all going to the man's excursion to Astley's Amphitheatre to see the horse ballet."

Her smile peeked out. "You seem much put upon."

"I *am* much put upon," he said. "Thank you for understanding."

"You're welcome," she said, meeting his gaze with a look of conspiracy, even as Tessa protested.

For a moment, he was trapped in the shimmering depths of that gaze. Her eyes reminded him of the water near the Seychelles, a beautiful garland of isles off the coast of Africa. His ship had once moored there for repairs, and he and his crew had spent a magical week eating fruits and fish from the tropics whilst swimming in a warm blue-green sea, so unlike Britain's cold waters. One day he'd managed to escape the crew to go exploring, and whilst on the lookout for snakes and scorpions, he'd stumbled across a stream wending through the rainforest. Under a canopy of palms and ferns, he'd jumped into the clearest water he'd ever seen, water he could see through to the sandy depths, water that tasted as clear and fresh as anything fallen from the heavens. Her eyes reminded him of that: clear, fresh brightness, whose depths he wanted to —

"Benjie?"

His sister studied him with a strange smile on her face.

"Yes?"

Her smile broadened. "I just wondered why you were staring at Miss DeLancey for so long."

He fought the fire climbing up his neck, heat he was sure matched the color painting Clara's cheeks. "I beg your pardon," he muttered before moving across to pretend interest in a rather vividly painted picture of a sinking Portuguese man-of-war. He frowned. The rigging lines were wrong. Clearly the artist had never —

"Benjie?" A small hand curled into his arm. He met Tessa's repentant gaze. "I'm sorry."

"It is not kind to tease your friend," he said in a low voice.

"No." She peeked over to where Clara's fixed study of a still life of fruit cascading from an epergne made him wonder if she was using the time to recover from embarrassment, too. His sister's attention returned to him. "I did not think you would mind being teased, however. Why is that, I wonder."

He shook his head, working to keep his voice from being overheard. "Do not think that just because you have found success in London society that a similar feat is possible for me. I am not someone the parents of well-bred young ladies will ever deem marriage material. Considering I have little in the way of either income or prospects, I will think myself fortunate if a lady of lesser social standing than even us will consider my proposal. I certainly cannot aspire to a viscount's daughter."

A pucker appeared in her forehead. "But you think Lord Featherington will offer for me?"

"I don't know. I certainly hope so, for your sake, otherwise he's been making a monkey of himself these past weeks. But I would think a marquess of the king's realm would have quite a lot to say about such a match, so I pray you will not pin all your hopes on him."

She bit her lip, her downcast expression making him wish he could drag his words in again. But it was best she knew the truth, wasn't it? Best she learned that dreams did not always come true, no matter how many pretty words might be spoken, or even how many prayers were offered. Just because someone prayed did not mean God would answer the way one imagined. God's will still prevailed.

He gently squeezed her hand, steering her back to where Aunt Adeline was chatting with Lord Beevers, the young buck whose invitation to the exhibition had revealed him far more cognizant of art than any of his guests could pretend.

Lord Beevers appeared to notice them, if the way his eyes brightened and how he broke off his conversation with Aunt Addy were any indication. "Miss Kemsley! I trust you have enjoyed yourself today?"

After being assured that she had, and expressing hope for another excursion in the not-too-distant future, Lord Beevers was summoned by a man requesting his opinion on a rather large landscape, and they were released.

Aunt Addy sighed. "Thank goodness. I don't know why you thought yourself suddenly enamored of art, Theresa, but I trust the next young man will have sense enough to be able to converse on something else. I now know far more about the preparation of canvases before painting than I ever had wish to know."

Tessa gave a soft giggle. "Thank you, Aunt Addy. I knew I could rely on you."

"My sister the schemer," Ben said, with a glance at Clara.

The lady smiled, and once again he felt a surge of camaraderie, a surge of affection, swiftly chased by the galling knowledge that attractive as he found her, his words to Tessa earlier were only too true. His smile faded, and he glanced away. He could not afford to mislead her, could not afford to stir up feelings — neither hers nor his — with no hope of satisfaction.

For how could a humble sailor ever hope to win a viscount's daughter?

CHAPTER TWELVE

"Well!"

Father's exclamation drew Clara's attention at the breakfast table. "What is it, Father?"

He lowered the newspaper. "It appears Napoleon has been routed on the eastern flank, and he's concentrating a great deal of resources in the west. Wellington better be ready."

"Where is he situated, Father?"

"Could be anywhere now," he said, tapping the newspaper. "These reports are days old."

"Do you think Wellington will succeed?"

"He does not have much choice, my dear." A rare smile cracked his face. "I must say it is good to see you take an interest in things other than fashion, or the latest *on-dit*. Too many young ladies these days have no interest in anything beyond what immediately affects them. Mind, best not to let your mother hear such talk."

"Of course not, Father."

They shared a smile of understanding.

She lowered her gaze and sipped her tea, thinking back to the visit two days ago to Somerset House. Despite Tessa and her aunt's misgivings that the excursion to the Royal Academy's exhibition might prove dull, Clara had enjoyed examining the array of paintings. She'd never laid claim to being an art connoisseur, but the experience had reminded her of how things used to be. She'd even seen a number of acquaintances there, people who had smiled and not sniggered and turned away. And then that moment when she'd encountered Mr. Kemsley's intent gaze, a gaze so full of warmth, evoking a feeling of perfect connection, her heart fluttered again at the recollection. Surely Tessa's brother did not hold her in admiration.

She smiled at her vain imaginings. She would *not* go down that road again.

"Clara?"

She glanced up, met the bemusement in her father's eyes. "Yes, Father?"

"You seem happier these days."

"I feel happier these days," she allowed. With her now daily practice of turning thoughts of loss into prayers of blessing, she felt nearly better, that were she to encounter the earl and his wife, she could greet them without feeling a niggle of discontent. Her smile twisted. Well, maybe not *just* yet.

"I'm glad. Whatever it is that is making you so, keep doing it."

"I will."

"Good."

"Good?" Mother's peevish voice preceded her entry to the room. "What on earth is good?"

Clara studied her in surprise. Her mother, known to be as fastidious as any lady who considered herself a pattern study for society, appeared to have dressed in a hurry. Her wrapper was awry, her mobcap skewed. She was holding a letter. She frowned at Clara, shaking the letter. "Can you tell me the meaning of this, miss?"

Amusement at her mother's absurd request faded at the anger in her eyes. "I'm sure I cannot."

"Nobody can, Frederica," said Father, "until you deign to tell us what the letter contains."

"Very well! Read it! Read the latest gossip about your daughter."

The breakfast she'd just consumed slid uneasily through her stomach. "Mother, I assure you —"

Her words faltered as her mother held up a hand. Father finished reading the letter, his brow creasing. "I'm sure Lady Pennicooke misjudged things." He handed the letter to Clara, his expression wry. "It wouldn't be the first time that good lady has displayed imperfect understanding."

"If you mean to imply that Amelia is less than honest, I simply cannot agree!"

As her parents continued bickering, Clara scanned the sheet of spidery writing. Her heart wrenched. How could someone misconstrue such an innocent visit? She glanced up. "She is wrong. I visited the art exhibition with Miss Kemsley and her aunt. I had no knowledge her brother would be there. I would never behave in a manner to draw such censure."

Her heart panged. She'd had no certainty Tessa would be accompanied by the handsome captain, it was true, but she'd had a fairly firm suspicion that he would escort his sister as he had on so many other outings.

Mother snatched the letter back, rereading it with a moan. "Amelia says she has it on the very good word of someone else —"

"Who remains conveniently nameless," Clara murmured.

"Who nevertheless assures her that the

Honorable Miss DeLancey was behaving in a most indecorous manner with a young gentleman well known in naval circles. There" — she flung the letter down in the middle of the table — "can you deny it?"

"Mother, I promise I did nothing to warrant such spite. Nothing at all." Save exchange glances a trifle too long with said naval gentleman. Her cheeks heated.

"It sounds like a lot of silly nonsense, if you ask me," said Father, calmly finishing his sausages and eggs. "I've always held that Pennicooke woman to be amongst the silliest of our acquaintances."

"Phillip! You cannot speak so."

"I just did," he parried, *sotto voce,* with another exchange of glances with Clara.

Fortunately, Mother was too busy being upset to hear her husband's aside. "What nerve!"

"You mean writing such dross, then sending it, when she calls herself your friend?" said Father.

"No!" Mother's cheeks grew blotchy. "Calling this Mr. Kemsley a gentleman!"

Clara knew herself to be unwise in venturing comment but could not refrain. "He is the brother of a baronet."

"And a famous captain heralded by the Prince," Father said.

"Yes, well he may have once been a famous captain lauded to the ends of the earth for all we know, but I ask you, who are his people? What are his prospects? I can't but think him a good deal purse-pinched. No" — she shook her head decidedly — "I'll not have my daughter throwing herself away on a man who can scarcely be considered a gentleman, much less fit to manage my only daughter's future in the manner to which she is accustomed."

Clara placed her fork to her plate with a deliberate clatter. "Mother, I think this a gross exaggeration. I assure you I do not hold the least whit of affection for him."

The snap in her mother's eyes dimmed to something approaching sorrow. "You still hold a candle for the earl, do you?"

"No!" Clara tempered her tone with a gritted, "No, I do not."

"Well, I can see by that reaction someone is still a little upset," Mother said with a sniff.

Clara clamped her lips together. Apparently there would be no convincing her mother.

"You are sure you do not hold a *tendre* for this man?"

"Oh, leave her be, Frederica. If she wishes to encourage the fantasies of a heroic sea

191

captain, who are we to stop her?"

Mother gasped. "You would truly allow your daughter to be pursued by someone of his class?"

"She said it herself: she does not care for him."

"But Amelia said —"

"Amelia is a pea-goose, and the sooner you stop listening to her gossip the better. Now, Clara, I gather from your apparel that you are going out today."

"Yes." She had previously informed them both, but as usual, they had forgotten. "To visit the Tower."

"Not with that captain, I hope. I do not wish for further rumors about you racing around our friends."

"One has to wonder why such people might be considered friends if they indulge in rumor-mongering about us."

"Oh, Phillip! You are impossible!"

No, he was logical, Clara thought, a smile tugging at her lips.

"Well?" Mother said, turning back to Clara. "Is he?"

Tessa had said he would be. If she admitted that, Mother was sure to ban her attendance. But she couldn't lie. Clara swallowed. "I believe so."

"In that case, you cannot go."

"But I have promised."

"You shall have nothing more to do with that captain, do you understand me?"

Father banged his fist on the table. The crockery and cutlery rattled. "Frederica, you are being ridiculous. Do you really believe our daughter would forget her rank and become entangled with such a man?"

"She's already been inveigled into indiscreet behavior by that family," her mother muttered.

"Enough!" Father turned to Clara, his eyes filled with frustration. "You gave your word, so you must go today. But I trust you will take heed to yourself and your family's reputation. We cannot afford more idle speculation."

"Of course, Father."

"And after today, I do not think it wise for you to accept further invitations. Your mother might be forced to her smelling salts, and I cannot have that, you understand?"

She nodded meekly. After Richard's disgrace, Mother had retreated to her bedchamber for almost a month. It was only the promise of removal to a discreet abode in rural Sussex that had lured her to taste fresh air once again. Twelve weeks later, her mother's complaints about the draftiness and dampness of the Sussex estate combined with complaints about a lack of company had led to their reestablishment in Brighton, in a house far more appropriate for a family in much-reduced circumstances. Clearly, it was best to avoid triggering repetition. Who knew where they might be forced to remove to next time?

Mother rose from the table with a sniff, refusing to look at Clara as she exited. Clara drew an internal sigh of relief, the departure reducing concern that she might succumb to maternal pressure to remain, and forgo a final outing with the Kemsleys.

Clara rose from her seat, kissed her father on the cheek, and ventured to the hall, where she gave instruction for Meg to bring her blue pelisse, bonnet, and reticule while she waited in the drawing room for Tessa's arrival. Avoiding Mother was probably the most prudent course of action she could take right now. She perched on a gold-striped settee, thinking over all Father had said.

Perhaps he was right. She had better take heed to herself and guard her heart, her emotions, and their reputation. The dishonorable Miss DeLancey was not an appellation she wished to incite.

Something had changed.

Ben glanced at the brunette, who had scarcely said a word all day. While polite, the animation Clara possessed at the art exhibition was gone, and her conversation — what little there was — was directed only to Tessa or his aunt. All through the treasure room, the Royal Menagerie, the visit to the Bloody Tower's sad rooms of poor prisoners mysteriously disappeared — through it all, Miss DeLancey had scarcely looked at him. What had happened?

He exchanged a glance with Tessa, whose small shrug indicated her confusion about their near-silent guest. Fortunately, Lord Featherington's presence had kept matters rolling, his virtual ignoring of Miss DeLancey seemingly reciprocated.

Ben tucked Tessa's hand on his arm and strolled along the battlements. "Is Miss DeLancey unwell?"

"I don't know. She seems a little sad."

"Has Aunt Addy learned anything?"

"She says not." Tessa sighed.

"Shall I distract Featherington while you see if you can get her to admit what is wrong?"

"I don't know how much good it will do, but yes, if you don't mind."

Ben spent the next quarter hour discussing with the viscount the latest news from Belgium concerning the Duke of Wellington's activities. Apparently the Duchess of Richmond's ball had been disrupted by the news of Napoleon's rapid approach. Officers who had been dancing one hour had scurried the next to the front line, some still in their ball clothes. It was a very near thing.

As Featherington continued discoursing, Ben's insides knotted and gnarled. How he wished to still be involved. How he wished he knew with certainty what the viscount's intentions were towards his sister. He glanced across to where Tessa and his aunt were talking at Miss DeLancey. Talking *at*, for it seemed she still barely responded. His fingers clenched. Had something been said? Why did he care? He shouldn't care. She should be as nothing to him.

He frowned. She had seemed most keen to avoid his company today, avoiding his gaze, moving aside when he drew near, barely speaking to him. To test his theory, he descended the rough-hewn steps and made his way to her side. "Miss DeLancey, are you enjoying yourself today?"

She nodded, turning away, but not before

he caught the sheen of tears.

He followed her gaze, watching the muddy water of the Thames swirl and eddy below them. The tension between them felt tangible, heavy. What could he say to break such a mood?

Aunt Addy joined them, her glance and pursed lips at the brunette beside him speaking volumes about their lack of success in learning what was wrong.

As though his aunt had enquired of him, he began to point out ships of interest, coupled with a few stories about his time on different crews. Gradually he sensed the young lady beside him begin to relax. He dared to peek at her. Soft afternoon light shone on her face, revealing an almost wistful expression. It was all he could do not to touch her hand, to remind her that they were alive and this day was worth living.

But he could not do that. He could not allow himself to become imprisoned by those eyes and that smile. He could not — dared not — permit these feelings in his heart to develop any further.

As if sensing their need for something to gaze upon, the sun shifted behind a cloud, then reemerged to filter golden light through the arched stone windows atop the White Tower. The stone seemed gilded in the sun, the drama and bloodthirsty history forgotten, like a fairy-tale castle come alive.

"It is beautiful, do you not agree, Miss DeLancey? Like something from a dream."

"A dream," she murmured. "Yes. It has been a dream."

And the look on her face and that in her eyes when she finally met his gaze filled him with a sad and desperate certainty.

Their times of golden adventures had come to an end.

CHAPTER THIRTEEN

The Seftons' ballroom glistened and gleamed with the cream of London society all wearing their smartest attire and their most impenetrable, smiling facades. Clara followed in the wake of Lord and Lady Asquith, wearing her own best gown, courtesy of her godmother, and her own veneer of half-smiling indifference. For at this, her first real ball in a year among those considered her social equals, she was not going to let anyone see just how nervous she felt. Her time in London had led up to tonight. This ball, whose ostensible objective was to celebrate Wellington's defeat of the French menace once and for all, held an underlying purpose, the same as any occasion when young ladies could dance with young men: opportunity to mingle with marriageable material.

Behind her, she could hear her parents murmuring hellos to long unvisited acquaintances. Mother had been unsure about attending, her concern about the possible reception given Clara fading when she considered what possible reception might be her own. It had only been Father's most strenuous efforts that had made Mother don her best silk gown and ruby necklace and venture to Arlington Street. The evening at the Seftons was not to Clara's liking, but her parents had decided during the carriage ride they would not permit anyone to treat them in a manner less than what their rank deserved. So Clara had determined to be poised, to be gracious, to give nobody the impression she had ever held so much as the tiniest little candle for a certain earl.

Clara nodded to Miss Pennicooke, whose mother had proved one of Mother's false friends. Anne's eyes flickered down Clara's gown, as if unsure what to think. Clara knew herself to have dressed out of mode for most unmarried ladies, but the whites and creams deemed essential for the freshly come out had never suited her. Lady Asquith's gift of a claret gown had seemed somewhat shocking at first. But the color was muted by the embroidered lace overdress gathered under the bust, and the sleeves were cut so beautifully, she could not but be pleased. Even Father had said how well she looked, and she herself thought she had never looked better. Half smile fixed in place, she met Anne's widened gaze, gave her another cool nod, and walked to where the chaperones sat.

She glanced around the room. Eyes met hers, looked away, before conversations began behind fluttering fans. Her chin tilted, her smile grew strained. She would not let them see how excruciating she found this.

Lady Asquith turned, eyeing Clara with a smile of satisfaction. "Dear girl, that color makes you look positively resplendent! Now, shall we see if we can find you a partner?"

Clara nodded, heart writhing as her godmother sent her husband to find someone. Once upon a time she'd needed no one to find her a partner; young men had simply come flocking. Now she was five-and-twenty, virtually dowry-less, and plagued by scandal. Her looks were all she had to entice some man to come up to scratch, as Father so inelegantly put it.

Her search around the room continued. Were any of her old acquaintances here? Both Lady Asquith and Mother had felt sure they would be, her godmother's discreet enquiries leading her to confirm that Harriet Guthrie *née* Winchester was expected to be in attendance.

Finally Lord Asquith returned, trailed by a gentleman of unassuming mien with whom she was unacquainted. Lord Asquith performed the introductions, and she took Mr. Molyneux's hand and joined a nearby set that was forming. Mr. Molyneux was not a tall man, and both his demeanor and dearth of conversation suggested he had been coerced into dancing with her. Her attempt to engage him in conversation had so far been met with monosyllabic replies.

"Do you enjoy dancing?"

"No."

Her misgivings gave way to amusement. "Then one must wonder why you attend a ball?"

"Really?"

His raised brow speared a quiver of embarrassment through her. Still she attempted to push aside the hurt, and smile like she remembered. "Do you not think the musicians wonderfully fine?"

He'd glanced at her, then up to the minstrel's gallery. "Fine, I'll grant you, but hardly so wonderful as to deserve nonsensical praise."

Anger at his churlishness streamed hot across her chest. When next they had opportunity to speak, she summoned up the sweetest smile she could find. "Have you a headache, sir?"

"What?"

"I am not used to partners so inclined to be displeased. I'm surprised the Seftons invited you."

He smiled nastily. "William Sefton is my cousin."

Her insides froze. The music drew to a close, but still her mouth continued to speak words that refused restraint. "Then I am sorry."

"So you should be, Miss —"

"For him."

Ignoring his gasp, she tilted her chin and left the dance floor.

Lady Asquith frowned as she drew near. "What is it, my dear?"

Clara told her in an undertone, eliciting her godmother's sigh. "I am afraid he's always thought of himself more highly than he ought. But he has a tongue when he chooses to use it. I think our best bet is to find Lady Sefton and get in her good graces."

She rose, sailing through the press of people with ease, while Clara trailed in her wake, attempting to keep her head high. They found Lady Sefton near the door, fanning herself as if exhausted from her hours of welcoming her guests.

The two ladies exchanged air kisses and a little conversation before Lady Sefton turned to Clara. "Miss DeLancey." Her gaze traced down Clara's gown, not uncritically, before meeting Clara's gaze with a smile. "I must say, not everyone could wear that color, but you most certainly should."

For the first time that evening Clara's smile became genuine. "Thank you, Lady Sefton." She motioned to a nearby footman. "Would you like me to procure you a drink?"

"Oh! That is very thoughtful of you, my dear. It is rather warm, with such a crush of people." This was said with a complacent smile, so as to suggest a crush was exactly what she had hoped and envisaged.

Clara hurried to the footman, returning with a glass of champagne for her hostess, who accepted it with a smile of thanks.

"Have you been dancing?"

"Yes, my lady. I was dancing with your husband's cousin, and I'm afraid I might have made something of a *faux pas.*"

"Oh dear! I cannot imagine poor Bertie causing anyone to do that." She trilled with laughter. "Now there is no need to look like that, dear girl. Bertie thoroughly disapproves of me and dear William, so you can

204

be sure we won't take any of his venom to heart."

The relief seeping into her chest at her hostess's earlier words drained away. "Venom?"

"Don't mind him. I never do. Sometimes we need to merely hold our heads higher when the gossipmongers feast. For what are we but to provide amusement for our friends?"

Her words cut deep. Clara soon returned to her seat, watching the dancing with her smile firmly pinned in place, but only with half an eye. Was that truly the way of the *ton*? Where were the genuine friendships she'd sensed possible with people like Matilda and Tessa? They weren't opposed to teasing, but underlying that was always a feeling of genuine affection. Did concern for riches and rank squeeze out desire for warmer emotions?

Of course, Tessa wasn't here tonight, her lack of rank naturally precluding her from such an event. And even if she were, Tessa was sure to not want to speak to her after that horrid trip to the Tower last week, whose horrors through history had only further dampened Clara's day. Her heart writhed. Knowing the excursion was the last time she would be permitted to spend time with Tessa and family, knowing she should do nothing to encourage Mr. Kemsley nor to encourage the wisps of affection in her own heart, she'd acted so cold and aloof she would completely understand if they wished to sever all acquaintanceship. She would write a letter of explanation — as soon as she figured out what to say.

Across the room her gaze met Harriet's, her friend from their first season. Clara smiled, but the dancing soon blocked her from view. Resigned to sitting out another dance, she perched on her seat, waving her ostrich-skin fan slowly, hoping to assuage the heat in the room. She watched the nearby dancers: the Duke of Hartington and his new wife; the scandalous Lady Harkness dancing with the rakish and much younger Lord Carmichael; Mr. Molyneux, whose glare in her direction made her smile harder while she shivered inside.

"Miss DeLancey?"

Clara looked up. "Harriet! How good to see you!"

"And you." She studied Clara's gown. "You look most dashing, I must say."

"Thank you. As do you." She admired Harriet's blue silk gown before saying, "It has seemed an age since we've met."

Twin spots of color appeared high on her

cheeks. "I — that is, Mama would not, you know, after the trouble . . ."

Clara's smile grew brittle. "Of course she would not. I completely understand." Her own mother would have been none too keen for Clara to maintain friendship with a young lady tainted by scandal. She pushed aside the hurt, patted the seat beside her. "Come, let us have a good catch up."

Harriet perched on the edge. "I'm afraid I have not very long. Mr. Molyneux solicited my hand for the next dance. He has quite an air about him, wouldn't you say?"

"Quite."

"And of course he's Lord Sefton's cousin, so it will not do to keep him waiting."

"No, indeed."

After exchanging a few reminiscences, their conversation languished. Clara fought to keep her smile, her spirits from slipping. Had lack of society numbed her conversational skills so much?

"Oh, look," Harriet said, with an air of relief, "here comes dearest Mariah! You remember, we all came out together. She married Lord Ashbolt a year or so ago and has grown terribly stout, but she's still a good sort to know the latest scandal."

"Wonderful," Clara said flatly.

Harriet waved, drawing Mariah Ashbolt

to their side. After an exchange of curtsies and awkward remembrances, her two friends launched into a discussion of the matrimonial prospects of a number of the young ladies present tonight, coupling observations on their gowns with tidbits about their persons that ranged from inane to cruel. As Clara listened to such conde-scension — gossip she was well aware she would have once participated in, before becoming the star feature — she realized anew how little she shared in common with these ladies.

The music ended, releasing her from the stultifying chatter and artificial expressions of goodwill, as the two young ladies she'd once considered friends returned to their posts where their next partners collected them. Clara's heart ached. Not once had they asked after her, how she had coped these past months, even though she'd en-quired about them. Had she truly once been so self-absorbed to not venture to ask after another?

"Clara?"

Lord Asquith's voice broke from her reverie. She forced a smile to her lips. "Yes, sir?"

He held out a hand. "I believe this next dance must be mine."

"I believe it must be. Thank you."

Her eyes filled, and she followed him blindly into the fray. Around her, gentlemen danced with ladies they had chosen, presumably not been forced into dancing with through coercion or pity. Was she so very pitiable that nobody save those manipulated by her godmother were willing to dance with her?

She performed the steps mechanically, clapping hands, pirouetting, turning to the right then left. Her smile felt like it might be crushed, probably under Lord Asquith's feet — he was no dancer. But his kindness welled further emotion in her eyes, in her throat. She blinked away the burn, swallowed the pride. Lord Asquith need not know his kind actions felt as shaming as sackcloth and ashes. She smiled at him, he beamed back, and she turned her head away. Then froze.

Heat suffused her cheeks. She was bumped from one side, had to drag her gaze away, before hurrying to catch up to where the movements of the dance had taken the others in their set. Had anyone noticed this latest gaffe? She wished to groan, to collapse in a heap as Mother had after learning of Richard's indiscretions, but she could not. Too many eyes were watching, too many lips would murmur.

The Earl of Hawkesbury, face set like stone, moved past her, his arm around his wife as if protecting her from such a contaminant as Clara. Another bump suggested that her distraction had not gone unnoticed, and she forced herself to focus blindly on the remaining maneuvers of the dance. The music came to an end, Lord Asquith returned her to her seat, she thanked him and sat down.

Clara drew in a breath, waving her fan, thankful the exertions of the dance gave some excuse for her hot cheeks. She had thought herself well in hand, but seeing him, seeing his wife, she still could not fully hide her reaction. She drew in another shuddery breath. When would this pain end? It was as though a string was attached between them and tugged at her while he remained immune. He had not even looked at her! Accepting a glass of lemonade from a passing footman, she reflected further. Perhaps the prayers for blessing him were working, because the sting had been less potent than usual. Perhaps she was the only one who had noticed . . .

Lady Asquith leaned across, speaking behind her fluttering fan. "I saw what happened."

So that hope was futile.

"You must not let him see he still affects you. Hold your chin high, flirt with someone else, preferably higher ranked."

So when the only man available and more highly ranked than the earl requested her to stand up with him, she gritted her teeth and accepted. Arthritic Lord Broughton — whose quest for a wife younger than his own children had long been the talk of many a society household, and had nearly overtaken her own family's proclivity for inducing gossip — was little more than a lecher, eyeing the low neck of her gown with a practiced eye, holding her hand and touching her waist far longer — and far higher — than propriety deemed necessary. But she held her head high, smiled as if it didn't hurt, and performed the movements as she had a dozen times before.

The number of ladies in attendance exceeded the gentlemen present, precluding Clara a partner for the supper dance. She followed her parents and the Asquiths to the supper room, managed to eat while maintaining the smiling facade, maintaining the illusion before excusing herself to visit the ladies' withdrawing room.

Relief cascaded through her. Finally her smile could drop, she need not pretend —

"Miss DeLancey."

She blinked. Swallowed. Dredged up a smile and curtsy. "Lady Hawkesbury."

"Tonight has been quite a crush, don't you agree?"

"Y-yes." She studied the dainty countess before her, her gown, her coppery-blond curls piled on top of her head — everything *à la mode.* How could she have ever mocked Lavinia?

"Miss DeLancey?"

The gray eyes studied her. Was that compassion in her eyes? Her heart twisted. "Yes?"

The countess offered a sweet smile. "I suspect you may think me gauche, but I will confess to being glad we do not need to attend such entertainments too often. I still find these things a little overwhelming."

"And overwhelmingly artificial."

"Yes." The earl's wife's eyes glinted as she nodded.

Such understanding elicited a trickle of warmth towards Lavinia, quickly followed by shame at how she had treated her in the past. Clara swallowed, remembering the last awful time they had met. "I hope you are well now?"

Lavinia stilled, her eyes sparkling with something now more akin to sorrow.

"Thank you." After a moment she continued, "I am trying to leave the past behind, to remember God's plans are good."

The moment stretched between them. Emotion tumbled within her heart. How could any of this be considered good? She swallowed. "It is not always easy, leaving the past."

"No." Lavinia studied her, before holding out her hand. "I have been praying for you."

Tears burned Clara's eyes as she clasped her hand. She swallowed, murmured, "I have been praying for you, also."

The gray eyes widened slightly, before a charming smile filled Lavinia's features. "Thank you."

A lump formed in Clara's throat. She sensed opportunity in this moment. She had to say this, now. "I . . . I am sorry for" — she swallowed — "for how I have treated you." And the earl, she added silently.

"The past has passed, would you not agree?"

"You . . . you forgive me?"

"How can I, imperfect that I am, hold unforgiveness when we've all been forgiven so much by One so perfect?" Her smile returned, gentle. "My mother told me long ago: Forgiveness sets us free."

Clara nodded, her emotions clashing with

the awkwardness of knowing others saw them, would no doubt be gossiping about the strange encounter. She released her hand, wished the earl's wife well, stammered an excuse about needing to speak with Lady Asquith, and scurried away. Finding her godmother engaged in conversation, she swerved to hide behind a pillar where she would not be spotted by Lavinia. How bizarre an encounter! Never had she imagined such goodwill to one so long despised. Perhaps they might never be friends, but it no longer seemed — to Clara, at least — that they were foes.

". . . the *very* dishonorable Richard DeLancey."

What? Clara peered over a shoulder, where one of the dowagers continued speaking to another chaperone about her brother. A large potted fern hid her from view. She shrank against the wall as the ladies continued.

"I cannot see how they can show up here, pretending all is well. What about the money? And the poor sister? She has so little to offer now without that dowry. Have you seen her tonight? Poor dear, her looks appear to be fading fast. And wearing scarlet!"

"A scarlet woman, if you ask me," said the other.

Clara writhed. Really? People thought that of her?

"Is it any wonder she's resorted to the likes of that Kemsley man? What? You have not heard of him? Did something heroic near Africa, I believe, was supposed to receive a great deal of prize money from the Prince Regent for his efforts, but didn't. You know what Prinny is like. If he doesn't do something straight away, he'll just as likely say he never intended it to happen. Takes a pet about the most absurd things. Did you hear about the theatre manager's daughter? Apparently she has a child Prinny refuses to recognize . . ."

Their voices faded away. The hammering in her chest dropped a fraction. When she judged herself sufficiently composed, she returned to the ballroom, smiling brightly, trying to catch the eye of anyone who might wish to dance with her, thus showing the spiteful cats just how wrong they had been.

And then it happened. In an attempt to escape the beady eyes across the ballroom, she lifted her gaze and met the cool hazel eyes of Lord Hawkesbury. His lip curled with scorn. Her insides chilled. All her good intentions drained away.

Fortunately, a gentleman came to her rescue, and she'd agreed to dance before realizing it was the ancient Lord Broughton again. Somehow, through tear-blinded eyes, she managed to stumble around the ballroom, before he released her early, sending her tripping into the next set of dancers. Cheeks afire with mortification, she rushed to find Lady Asquith, who took one look at her before beckoning her husband and Clara's parents, and taking them home.

There were no bouquets the following day.

There were many tears and recriminations.

For the ball, of which such high hopes had been fostered, had proved yet another spectacular failure.

CHAPTER FOURTEEN

"I cannot believe it!"

Ben glanced up from the newspaper; Wellington's narrow victory against Napoleon's forces had filled columns for days. "Cannot believe what?"

Tessa's bottom lip grew pronounced, in the manner it had since she was a young girl whenever she was upset. She held out a letter. "Clara. She writes to say she's returned to Brighton."

He snatched up the letter, read the perfect copperplate ream of regrets. Clara was sorry . . . family concerns drew her home . . . hoped Tessa continued to enjoy her time . . .

"I don't understand. One minute she was so warm and affable, the next it was like she had no wish to know me."

"You cannot take this personally," Ben said, patting her hand. "Remember not everyone's actions need revolve around you."

She chuckled, drawing her hand away, even as she mock glared. "You are quite abominable, sometimes."

"I know," he said meekly, eliciting, as he'd hoped, another spurt of laughter from her.

"At least Lord Featherington hasn't abandoned us."

"No." His mood dipped. The viscount's attentions had yet to wane, which only served to increase Tessa's hopes and his own misgivings. It couldn't end well, could it? He believed in miracles, but surely she'd be deemed a poor match for a future marquess. But how to dissuade his sister without causing further upset? He'd mentioned his concern to Aunt Addy, but she had only waved off his fears with an assurance that neither heart was fully engaged.

Ben was not so sure. There were moments when he'd seen a special light in Tessa's eyes he'd never witnessed before. And even for the viscount, a kind of softening wonder in his expression when he gazed upon Tessa suggested she was some form of heaven-sent creature. Ben could not like it, could not trust it. Tessa, twelve years Ben's junior, to be thinking of marriage? He settled back in his chair, eyeing his breakfast with disfavor.

The dining-room door opened, admitting Aunt Adeline in a state that could only be described as agitated. He pushed to his feet but she waved him back down, clutching a letter in her hand, saying with a distracted air, "Oh, my dears. Have you received one, too?"

"A letter from Clara?" Tessa said. "Oh, Aunt, it is just too bad of her."

"Clara? What's this about Clara?"

"She's returned to Brighton." Tessa thrust the letter towards her. "She gave a host of trumped-up excuses, but I think she does not wish to see us anymore."

"No, no. You must not think that, Theresa. She is a sweet girl, I am sure, though rather at the mercy of those society-obsessed parents."

She cast Ben a swift look which gave him pause. What could Lord and Lady Winpoole have against them? Was it something against him? He gripped his coffee cup more firmly.

Aunt Addy continued. "I have had a letter also. From your brother, of all people."

"George?"

"He is the only brother you have, is he not, Benjamin? He writes to say he intends to come to London and stay a few days."

"Why?"

"That is a mystery his letter does little to elucidate. He merely states that he intends to visit us on the twenty-seventh. And today is the twenty-sixth!"

"Typical George," Ben muttered. "Never thinking of anyone but himself."

"Well, he did at least write to inform me."

"Inform you, yes. Not request permission."

"Hmm. Well, I suppose as baronet he might not feel permission necessary."

"I don't like it," said Tessa. "First Clara goes, then George comes. He'll spoil everything."

Ben picked up his coffee cup, eyeing the two ladies sitting across the table. "He must have some reason for coming. He rarely comes to town, so it must signify something of import."

"I wonder what it can be," Tessa said, eyes rounding. "Do you think he is unwell?"

"No," he scoffed. "George was in the pink of health only two weeks ago. He's probably here for some fancy London tailor to fix him up with expensive, baronet-worthy clothes."

Aunt Addy nodded. "Perhaps that is it, for a baronet must be seen to dress appropriately."

"And he's never one to wish to appear less than appropriate."

"Now, now. That is not worthy of you, Benjamin, dear, even if it might be true."

Ben and Tessa exchanged small grins.

"No," Aunt Addy continued complacently, "I'm sure whatever brings your brother here will be nothing to cause alarm. Of that, you can rest assured."

The next day, they learned that Aunt Addy's complacency was ill founded.

No sooner had George stepped in the door and shooed out the servants than his reason for visiting became plain. "I bring you most excellent news." Ben and Tessa exchanged glances as their brother harrumphed self-importantly. "I have met someone."

"What?" Tessa's eyes widened before quickly glancing at Ben like a startled doe.

Ben offered her a quick nod of reassurance and said, "Well, we all meet people nearly every day —"

George made an impatient noise. "She is to be my wife."

"What?" Ben and Tessa said in unison.

"My dear boy," said Aunt Addy, fanning herself, "I suppose this is wonderful news."

"Of course it is," George said. "She is the

most wonderful girl."

"I'm sure she is," continued their aunt, as Ben and Tessa continued staring, stupefied. "Who is she?"

"She is all that is lovely, and sweet, and kind . . ."

"That's something to be thankful for," Ben muttered in an aside to Tessa.

George shot him a nasty look. "And while she might not have an enormous fortune, she is respectably situated. Her uncle was in the army. I thought you might find that interesting, Benjamin."

"Because I am naturally interested in anything with the slightest whiff of the military, I suppose?"

"Yes," George said, ever unable to detect the slightest whiff of irony. "She has brown hair, plays the harp excessively well, and always dresses to a nicety —"

"Imagine that."

Aunt Addy shot Ben a quelling look over Tessa's smothered giggles. "This list of virtues is all well and good, but are we to ever find out the paragon's name?"

A dreamy look filled George's face. "Her name is Miss Windsor. Miss Amelia Windsor."

Ben exchanged another look with his sister. Never had sober, sensible George appeared less staid. Still, he should make an effort. "Congratulations."

"Amelia is a pretty name," Tessa offered.

"A pretty name for a beautiful girl," George stated.

Ben worked to iron out his smile. "And Windsor is a pretty last name."

"Yes — what?" George peered suspiciously at him. "Well, it won't be Windsor for long. That is why I am here."

"What do you mean? How soon do you plan to marry?"

"As soon as she gets her trousseau organized." He sat higher in his chair. "I plan to take her back to Chatham with me as my wife."

Ben blinked. "What? No, you can't mean to marry so quickly. Why, you must have only just met her. We've certainly never heard anything of her before."

"I'll have you know that I first met her six months ago, when you were lost in Africa," he said looking at Ben, before turning to Tessa, "and you were in Brighton with our sister."

"Why didn't you introduce us to her a month ago?"

"She was away visiting relatives in Hampshire. But don't worry, you'll get the chance to meet her soon. She's coming here to dine with us tomorrow night."

Aunt Addy gasped. "You did not say anything of *that* in your letter."

"Didn't I? Well, I'm sure it will not be any imposition. Not when we're all to be family. Oh, her parents will be coming also."

"Of course they would be," Ben muttered, glancing at Aunt Addy as she strove to overcome her shock at her nephew's high-handedness. Typical George, thinking of no one but himself. In a louder voice, he said, "Have you a plan for the menu as well, George, or is this to be left to our dear aunt's discretion?"

"Oh, Aunt Addy can manage, can't you? Near anything will be fine. But the colonel has a liking for turtle soup, and something of a sweet tooth, while his wife cannot eat anything made with flour —"

"Nothing made with flour?" Aunt Addy looked like she might faint.

"And your bride-to-be?" Ben said. "What special preferences might she be wishing to impose on our poor aunt here?"

George's eyes narrowed. "My Amelia has no special preferences."

"Amazing."

George cleared his throat. "You seem to forget, Benjamin, that I am the head of the family and as such am expected to be accorded some level of respect."

Ben gritted out a smile. "And you seem to forget, George, that this is Aunt Addy's house, and you cannot expect to blast in here and start ordering people around."

"I don't like that tone you use."

"The feeling is reciprocated."

"Gentlemen!" Aunt Addy said, spine ramrod straight. "I refuse to allow my house to become akin to a brawling tavern. Benjamin, I appreciate your concern, but I am well able to conduct my own battles. George, much as it is a pleasure to see you again, I'm afraid I will be unable to host your betrothed tomorrow night, as we have a prior engagement."

They did? Tessa's raised brows suggested she felt as much surprise as he did.

"Oh, but what could be more important than meeting my Amelia?" George complained. "Surely you can cancel whatever it is and —"

"I'm afraid that is quite out of the question. George, I feel it my duty to say that I cannot fathom how my brother managed to raise a son quite so self-centered as to not be aware of how his actions impose upon others. I received your letter but yesterday, and nowhere in it was there anything to suggest I might be forced to provide a dinner for people I have yet to meet. Are you always this inconsiderate of others?"

Yes, Ben said silently, a twist of gladness stealing through him as his brother reddened.

"But Aunt Addy —"

"Please do not interrupt me, George," their aunt continued, as if she hadn't just done the same. "Now, I might be persuaded to host your betrothed and her family one evening, but I will not be providing anything like a turtle dinner." She eyed him. "That is, unless you plan on paying for the turtles?"

"Oh, but —"

"I thought as much. Well, if you cannot have the decency to even ask properly, perhaps it shall prove impossible for me to help you, after all."

"But Aunt Addy, surely as the head of the family —"

"You are not the head of *my* family, and until you start behaving with a little more decorum, I shall be quite unwilling to give respect where it is obviously undeserved." She rose from her seat, smiled at Tessa. "Now, Theresa, shall we finish our shopping? Or would you prefer to stay and catch up with your brother here?"

Tessa instantly shot up. "I'd prefer to go

226

with you, ma'am."

"Very well." With a gracious nod, Aunt Addy exited the room, an obviously awed Tessa following.

George turned to Ben, a heavy scowl lining his face. "This was not the reception I had hoped to receive."

"I imagine it wasn't."

George shook his head. "I don't remember Aunt Adeline being quite so spirited. It is obvious living alone since our uncle's death has not been good for her."

"I disagree."

"Of course you would," George muttered.

"I think she's an absolute treasure." Ben smiled, murmured an excuse, and hurried to catch up to his fellow escapees.

CHAPTER FIFTEEN

After such a spectacular failure at the ball, it was no surprise Clara's parents insisted on an immediate return to Brighton. Although expensive, Brighton did not quite warrant London prices, and with the Prince Regent soon in attendance, Brighton would once again resume its seasonal merry-making as the *ton* followed the heir to the throne on holiday.

For two days after their return she'd followed Mother's lead and huddled in bed, regrets and self-recrimination warring with headaches and chills. After two days of darkened rooms and darker thoughts, she finally shook off her lethargy and descended to join her father for breakfast. His disappointment in her London season was less palpable than her mother's, but she felt it all the same in the averted glances, the sentences left unfinished, the pursed lips as he began to speak, then ceased.

No doubt he was as much disappointed for her as in her. Unless a miracle occurred, she would be an old maid now. Five-and-twenty, without prospects, without fortune. No wonder he felt sorry. If she had an ounce of emotion remaining, she'd feel extremely sorry, too.

The door opened, and a footman appeared bearing a silver salver containing the morning post. Father sifted through them before offering Clara a letter.

She grasped it, surprised at the unfamiliar handwriting. She slit it open and unfolded the paper to see that it came from Tessa, who was still in London. Relief crept through her. So apparently her flight from London and their company had been forgiven. She scanned through the news — new ball gowns, a visit to Hyde Park with the viscount, the attentions from other suitors — before reading of Tessa's good wishes for Clara and the hope that they would meet again soon. A hastily added postscript gave her pause.

"We received the greatest of surprises today. My brother has announced his engagement to a Miss Windsor! We were never so astonished in all our lives. Aunt Addy says it is very poor form for him to have hidden such an understanding from the family, and I agree."

Her throat constricted. Mr. Kemsley, engaged? She shook her head, trying to shake away the tears. Had she lost all senses? Was she so lost in self-delusion she could no longer recognize truth? She thought she had detected tenderness towards her, only to discover he must have long preferred another. She exhaled sharply.

"Clara?"

She glanced up to where her father watched her. Forced her hand to stop trembling. Managed a smile. "It is a letter from Tessa."

"I thought we told you to have nothing to do with that family!"

"Her brother is engaged."

"Mr. Kemsley?"

She nodded.

"Really? I thought —" He coughed. Yes, she had thought that also. "To whom is he engaged?"

"A Miss Windsor."

"Windsor? I do not recall any Windsors, do you?"

She offered a bland look, unwilling to answer. She recalled a Miss Windsor, a rather beige nonentity of dull appearance and duller conversation if memory served her right. A spark of the old indignation crossed her chest. How could he prefer that type of person to her?

"Well!" He sat back in his seat, watching her carefully. "I trust this is good news."

"Of course it is. How can it not be?" She held his gaze for long seconds, willing him to believe her, willing her smile to look natural.

"Well, I'm not altogether sure I understand, but I know your mother will be relieved."

"Yes." She couldn't do this anymore. Her ability to pretend, to be the actress her father seemed to wish, was dying by the minute. Her gaze dropped to the glass vase of buttercups centering the table. "Father, would it be very lowering of me to marry beneath our rank?"

"Marry beneath you? Of course you won't need to do that."

"Father, there is no 'of course' about it. No man has expressed interest in me in years, there was scarcely a man who would stand up with me at the Seftons' ball who did not have to be dragged to do so."

"Nonsense," he said, in an uncertain voice that was hardly encouraging.

"It is not nonsense, Father. I am five-and-twenty, with little likelihood of any offers of marriage. I'm sorry to be such a disappointment, but there it is."

"You will never be a disappointment to me, my dear."

Her vision blurred. She blinked, drew in a shaky breath. "I know you do not feel the same as Mother, that you consider all people born of God as equal."

"Well, yes, but —"

She hurried on. "If a gentleman ranked lower than I should make an offer, I wish you and Mother would not consider it completely impossible, please."

"Of course." Silence stretched between them for another long moment. "Had this Kemsley fellow touched your heart?"

"No." She thought of his good humor, the way his eyes crinkled when he saw her, that sense of unanimity she'd thought they shared, that funny fluttering heated sensation when she'd accidentally touched his hand. She swallowed. "Perhaps a little. A *very* little."

At her Father's sigh she peeked up. "I was afraid of this."

"There is nothing to be concerned about. I am quite well." Her smile was about to crack. She needed, desperately needed, to change the subject. She motioned to the correspondence stacked before her father. "Anything interesting?"

"Nothing to interest you. Oh, there's

something from Richard, finally. He writes that he's in Ireland."

He gave a look that said they both knew very well that Richard's tales could scarcely be considered true. He had not stayed after his surprise visit earlier, so he might possibly be in Ireland. But he probably just wished them to inform his creditors of such things to ease their pressuring him to repay.

"I trust he's enjoying himself."

"You know your brother."

They exchanged another look, heavy with understanding. Richard be denied pleasure? The sun would sooner stop shining.

After breakfast, the day dragged interminably. She busied herself with writing letters to Tessa, asking for her congratulations to be passed on to her brother, writing to thank Lady Asquith, even writing to Harriet. The rest of the time was spent practicing her pianoforte, reading some more of Matilda's book of devotions loaned all those weeks ago, anything — everything — to distract from the pain circling her heart.

After an early dinner she finally managed to escape, having pleaded a headache as an excuse to retire early. But instead of retiring to her room, she ventured outside, where a strange buttery light suffused everything with golden charm.

She studied the sky. The past few nights had provided sunsets of extraordinary color, so Father had said. For all its soft-hued beauty here in the garden, she imagined it would look all the more spectacular over the sea. Being careful to remain unobserved, she followed the well-worn track to the top of the cliff. It held little temptation now, although the ever-present wind still tugged at her skirts. She sank down, wrapped her arms around her knees in a most unladylike manner, and looked out across the gold-lit sea to the horizon.

What would it be like to go into the unknown? To travel the seven seas as Mr. Kemsley had done, following the sun by day and the stars at night? She supposed he would do that with his wife now. Her heart panged; she shook her head. She was being ridiculous! She only felt this way because . . . because it would be nice to travel! To be unknown, save to those she chose to make herself known to.

What would it be like to explore exotic lands as he had? To see strange creatures such as those kangaroos locked up at the Tower's menagerie, but living as they ought, roaming free in their wild homeland? What would it be like to eat peculiar and spicy things? Unlike the scarcely palatable repast they'd had for dinner tonight, more bland than a nursery meal.

The breeze tugged at her pins, teasing her hair free to whip across her face. She winced, pushed heavy locks aside, focused back on the horizon.

She was a fool to think on him. A fool to think on any man. They were all as fallible as each other. Even Father had not been immune, digging deep into her dowry to keep their household afloat. Could anyone be trusted?

A whisper begged her to look up.

The sky held a myriad of color: deep violet melding into pink above a hazy orange, before the tint of soft green immediately above the horizon. The air seemed to hold a special, almost eerie quality. She shivered. The colors mingled, blurring to create a sky so wondrous God Himself must be the master artist at work.

She drew in a deep breath, one of which her long-ago singing master would be proud, and exhaled.

God.

She had not thought on Him much in past days. But now she remembered more on what that little book of verses had said, more of what Matilda had spoken, and Lavinia.

Forget the past. Forgive. Live.

"God, I need Your help."

The wind ruffled her hair, almost like her father's hand had ruffled her hair when she was a child. Like she'd seen Mr. Kemsley do with Tessa, affection evident in his easy smile as much as his action.

Somehow the tangle of knots that had existed in her heart for weeks loosened a fraction. She took another deep breath and released.

The heavens stretched more magnificently. There, far in the distance, gleamed a tiny star, diamond-like amid an ever-moving kaleidoscope of color. Her breath caught. How perfectly lovely . . .

For several long minutes she gazed in simple awe, conscious of nothing but an easing in her soul. The universe was so big; she herself so small. But in this moment, the depth and breadth and weight of the beauty above gave a kind of reassurance, almost like God was giving the display for her benefit. Her worries slowly dimmed, dulling to a faint echo as she drank in the beauty, the soft pinks so similar to the gown Lavinia had worn to the Seftons' ball last week . . .

Her heart panged as a wave of loneliness crashed against her newfound calm. Why had so few men wished to dance with her?

Was she so very unappealing? What was wrong with —

No.

Clara sucked in another lung-expanding breath and slowly let it go. Did she really need a husband in order to be happy? Society certainly thought so. Mother definitely believed so. But what if she never found a man willing to love her?

Tears pricked. "Lord, what do I do?"

The rasping breeze hushed into stillness. A tendril of something that felt like peace curled softly within. Perhaps God didn't need her to do anything — except trust Him.

Was Lavinia correct in attributing goodness to God's plans? Matilda seemed to believe that also. Could Clara really trust Him?

"Do You really love me, God?"

The sun's gleaming seemed to gild the sea anew as the peace inside magnified. The peace within and the beauty without seemed to be singing a resounding yes.

She drew in another deep breath, then exhaled.

God loved her.

God *loved* her.

God loved *her*.

Clara's eyes grew wet even as she smiled.

Assurance solidified. The breeze toyed with her hair as her ponderings continued.

If God loved her, then it followed that He would have good things for her, things that would bring her hope. Her smile widened as she wiped away the dampness on her cheeks. Perhaps she did not need to worry about whether she could find a man to love her; perhaps God's love could be enough.

Tightness eased in her shoulders. Hope thudded in her heart, the steady reassuring beat underlining a confidence unlike anything she had experienced before. She need not trust in her own abilities or looks or fortune anymore. God's love and His goodness meant she would trust Him with her future, rather than valuing such things as she had trusted in the past.

And she did not want to wallow in the old anymore. She did not want to be the shallow Clara of her past, the vain, mean-spirited girl whose friends were as quick to talk behind her back as she'd once been to talk behind theirs. She could *not* be that girl again.

"Lord, please help me change."

Her words were swallowed in the wind. Had she even been heard? Or was God ignoring her, too?

But — no. If she was to change, these

negative thoughts had to change also. God couldn't be ignoring her, not with this heavenly light show, more spectacular than any display at Vauxhall Gardens. God must care. God *did* care.

A soft kind of certainty coiled within. Her spirits lightened, lifted. Just as the sky transformed from azure to the rosiest of pinks, she too could change — would change — with God's help. He loved her. He had good plans for her. Conviction firmed further.

She would let go of self-pity, let go of the past, allow God to bring her into the new.

The new. The unknown. The far horizon.

She studied the ocean's smudging violet as another thought bubbled into remembrance.

What had Matilda said weeks ago? Who was Clara?

Someone who cared about the latest fashion? Someone who lived for herself? Who cared for music? Someone who cared for others? She was five-and-twenty. Who did she want to be? Who could she be?

The vaguest stirrings of an idea slowly unfurled, gradually taking shape. She drew in a brine-laden breath. Society would frown on her; her parents would not understand. And how on earth could she do it?

A smile tugged at her lips. Perhaps she could not do it. But with heaven's enabling . . .

Who was Clara?

A tremor of excitement flickered within. Her chin lifted. She knew exactly where to start. Father's words earlier had only confirmed it.

She would start by once again offering her services to Matilda, playing at the Sailors and Soldiers' Hostel as soon as possible.

London

"And here she is!"

George's dramatic interruption to afternoon tea jerked their attention to the door. Ben rose to his feet as a small brunette entered the room. Fine-featured, but lacking the soft prettiness one normally expected from the ladies who caught George's eye, she could scarcely be called handsome, let alone the glorious, beauteous creature their brother's description had led them to expect. She appeared shy, barely meeting his glance or responding to his bow or Tessa and Aunt Addy's murmured greetings except with an awkward curtsy.

George drew her hand over his arm, patting it tenderly, the love light clearly seen in his besotted eyes. "You mustn't mind them, my love." He performed the introductions, concluding with, "My younger brother, Benjamin Kemsley."

Trust George to reinforce his elder-brother status. Ben bowed again. "Good afternoon, Miss Windsor."

She curtsied and finally met his gaze, curiosity in her pale blue eyes. "Are you *the* Benjamin Kemsley?"

He chuckled. "Well, I am certainly *a* Benjamin Kemsley. I cannot be certain how many of us are in existence in the world."

Her cheeks flushed, and for a moment he could see why his brother might describe Miss Windsor as pretty. "I mean, the captain of the *Ansdruther*?"

"I am he." He looked an enquiry. She gave a small smile.

"I am acquainted with one of the soldiers you helped rescue. A Major Dumfrey."

"Really?" said George, with a frown.

"He is . . . was, my uncle."

"Was?" Ben asked.

"He died three months ago from influenza. My parents were most relieved to have him returned to England before he passed away."

"I am very sorry for your loss." He inclined his head.

He peeked up, noted George's frown, as if

his brother was unenthused to see his shy betrothed apparently eager to speak to his little brother. To soothe any ruffled feelings, he said, "My brother has been singing your praises, Miss Windsor. His heart seems ensnared most completely."

"Ensnared?" George sputtered. "I do not like to hear you describe my intended in such terms."

"It was not your intended whose heart I described."

George eyed him narrowly, before grasping Miss Windsor's arm and gently turning her to face Tessa and Aunt Addy. "Theresa, I trust you will be able to make dearest Amelia feel welcome as a new sister."

"Of course." Tessa shot Ben a worried look over George's shoulder before smiling kindly at Miss Windsor.

Through the course of conversation, they came to learn that Miss Windsor's parents wished to call upon them the following afternoon, that George would be dining with them tonight — this said with a tight smile at Aunt Addy — and that they hoped to have the pleasure of meeting all of George's family in the not-too-distant future.

"Are they planning on visiting Brighton, then?" asked Tessa.

"Why on earth would they wish to do that?" George demanded.

Ben restrained a sigh. He had no wish to inflict George and company upon what refuge he had found in Brighton. "Surely you don't expect a vicar to be able to drop his responsibilities at a moment's notice?" he said. "Or had you forgotten Matilda is married to a clergyman?"

George muttered something under his breath, before saying to Miss Windsor, "Perhaps your parents might be persuadable to a short stay, dearest?"

His dearest blushed again and murmured something about her parents not having made any fixed plans as yet.

"Brighton tends to fill up quickly whenever the Regent is in town," Aunt Addy said. "You might want to ensure they investigate letting a place as soon as possible," she continued, oblivious to Ben's silent protests about encouraging their brother to stay.

By the time she finally rose to leave, Miss Windsor had impressed upon Ben that she was as eager to please her parents as she was her betrothed and her family-to-be. George finally escorted her from the premises, their brother's company immediately exchanged for Lord Featherington's daily visit.

Aunt Addy sank back with a sigh. "Well! Such an insipid little creature I never saw."

The viscount looked between them. "Was that the drab, brown dab of a thing I passed on my entry? With a fair gentleman who looked rather more pleased with himself than he ought?"

"That would be George," Tessa said with a giggle.

"With his intended," their aunt added.

"Well!" Lord Featherington's brows shot up. "Rather a surprise, I gather?"

"It is something of a shock to us all," Ben admitted.

"She's certainly not in the style of your young lady, O heroic one," he said, with a sidelong look at Ben.

"My young lady?"

"Yes." The viscount's eyes glinted. "Apparently Miss DeLancey —"

"She's not my young lady," Ben muttered.

"You are sure?"

"Yes!"

"If you say so." The viscount's sardonic look spoke volumes of his doubt. "Anyway, apparently she caused something of a to-do the other night at the Seftons'."

"In what way?" Aunt Addy asked, preventing Ben from the necessity of doing so.

"While most young ladies wear white, she

wore a red gown — quite scandalous!" He chuckled. "Then she had a set-to with Lady Hawkesbury, then stumbled into several dancers before racing out! The whisper I've heard is that people thought she might be drunk."

Ben clenched his fingers. "That is ridiculous."

"Drunk? What an abominable thing to suggest!" Tessa looked the outrage Ben felt.

"Pray, don't bite my head off, dear one." The viscount shrugged. "But they say it may explain why the family's left London."

"Poor thing! I'm sure there is explanation for all of that." Aunt Addy said. "I do not like gossip, you know."

"None of us do," the viscount said comfortably. "Now, enough about her. What's this about your brother? Does he plan to marry soon?"

Tessa filled him in about George's plans to introduce Amelia to her sister.

Ben eyed his aunt. "How you could virtually invite them to visit Brighton, I don't know."

"My dear boy, what would you have me do? I cannot help matters if George wishes to see Matilda. Such a plan has nothing to do with me."

"But it will us," said Tessa. "Oh, Benjie,

what should we do? I don't mind her very much, in fact I am sure she is all that is pleasant, although it is a little difficult to know when she appears so shy."

His lips curled to one side. "I imagine she is not the first young lady whose diffidence hides a charming personality."

"Oh." Her cheeks tinted. She peeked at the viscount, whose look of admiration seemed nearly as besotted as that worn by George only minutes earlier.

His heart panged. Now with George's news, if Featherington did indeed come up to scratch and make Tessa an offer, Ben would be the only Kemsley left unwed.

Should he make more of an effort to secure a bride? He was nine-and-twenty, and if not exactly fit, he was at least healthy, what many would consider in the prime of life. But more than that, he was conscious of a feeling of something akin to . . . loneliness.

He shook his head. If his siblings all married, he would be alone. He felt sure they would all be happy to have him stay — with the obvious exception of George, though Amelia might persuade him. But was that enough? Could he be satisfied with being the brother, being an uncle, watching from the outside as other people's lives blossomed in ways he'd always vaguely imagined might one day exist for him? Did he not wish to be a husband, to be a father?

A twinge knotted his chest. He swallowed, forcing his thoughts away from places that would only lead to frustration. He *did* want more. He studied his sister, light suffusing her face. She smiled at Featherington as he continued to engage her in hushed conversation.

His siblings seemed to have a kind of radiance about them these days. In the time he'd spent with Mattie and David, he'd noticed the newlyweds seemed to possess a joy that lit from within, a peace that eased the ebb and flow of ordinary life. Should he seek to find someone who could partner with him through life's journey, someone with whom growing old would be a blessing?

What was the alternative? Growing older and more crippled and more sour — alone?

He shook his head, biting back a bitter laugh. It was not that he had never found young ladies attractive. Heaven knew he had felt the stirrings of attraction to Miss DeLancey when she'd been here, despite knowing nothing could ever come of it with their situations in life so vastly different. He stifled fresh frustration. The timing had

never been right. He had been too young —
Lord Ponsonby proved correct — then off
at sea, then rising through the ranks to be
made a captain, then under contractual
obligation to His Majesty until that last
disastrous voyage.

The timing was still not right. And unless
he was paid what he was due, the timing
would never be right.

"Benjamin?"

He started, glancing up from his rumina-
tions to see three pairs of eyes fixed on him.
"I beg your pardon. I was not attending."

"You were attending something if that
scowl is any indication," Tessa said.

"Forgive me." He plastered a smile on his
face. "Better?"

"Much." Tessa gestured to her suitor.
"Lord Featherington was saying he intends
on visiting Brighton soon and has taken a
house on the Steyne."

"Really?" He eyed the other man. Perhaps
it was time to finally force his intentions out
into the open. "Is attending Brighton a
regular practice of yours?"

"It was," the viscount said. "I feel it is
about time it was reinstated."

"Because you enjoy the seaside?"

"Brighton has many attractions." This was
said with a sidelong look at Tessa that raised

Ben's internal warning flags faster than the sharpest midshipman.

"Are your parents planning on visiting Brighton also?"

"My mother wishes to spend time with my sister, up at Hartwell Abbey in Northamptonshire, but I'm not sure if Hartington is so keen." He made a wry face. "My parents have a spot in Devon that we usually try to visit every year. Didn't last year, what with Charlotte getting married and all, so I imagine they'll be quite keen to get there this year."

"And you will go, too?"

"That depends." He glanced at Tessa again, like a love-struck swain.

"On what?" Ben persisted ruthlessly.

The viscount's blue eyes snapped back to Ben's, a faint flush overspreading his cheeks. "Forgive me. I fear I have overstayed my welcome."

"Oh, but you haven't!"

"Theresa," said their aunt, "I am sure the viscount has many responsibilities requiring his attention."

Lord Featherington rose, made his bows, promised Tessa he would call again soon, and exited.

"That was unkind of you," Tessa frowned at Ben.

"Perhaps a *little* less aggression next time, Benjamin," Aunt Addy murmured.

"Tessa, I am concerned for you."

"If you're so concerned, why did you chase him away?" She rose, flouncing out the door.

Leaving Ben to exchange glances with his aunt, and filling him with all the more determination to learn just how far the viscount was willing to pursue his sister.

CHAPTER SIXTEEN

Tessa's upset had not diminished the next day. When the viscount still had not visited by late afternoon, leaving them to the mercy of their only visitors of the day — George, the unassuming Amelia, and her parents, whose visit had accompanied an invitation to dinner that evening impossible to refuse — Tessa's discontent was scowled all over her face.

His sister's unhappiness seemed contagious, judging by the crease in Aunt Addy's forehead. "Really, Theresa, I would have thought you could be a little more circumspect."

Tessa only looked away, flicking through the pages of Ackermann's Repository before tossing it on the satinwood side table.

"Tessa, I am sorry you are upset with me, but I cannot be sorry for feeling a measure of caution." Ben gentled his voice as she crossed her arms, "I wish to know his intentions."

"But you are not the head of the family."

"No. The head of the family is too busy seeing to his own happiness to have any care of the responsibilities due others."

"You're just jealous."

"Of George? I assure you, I envy him nothing, save the respect you seem to feel owing him simply for being born first."

She hmphed, and looked away.

Aunt Addy cleared her throat. "Benjamin is right, Theresa. It is not usual for a young man of Lord Featherington's background to pursue a young lady lacking the consequence to which his family is accustomed."

"His sister married a duke, Tessa."

"I know that!" she snapped. "And his mother is the daughter of a duke, and his father is a marquess, and we are nothing but the cousins of a baronet."

"The siblings of a baronet, now," Aunt Addy said. "Be that as it may, surely you can see it is wise to ascertain what his intentions are."

"Does he wish to marry you?" Ben asked bluntly.

"Benjie! How can you ask me that?"

"I ask you because I see how he looks at you, because he plans on taking a house in

Brighton in an apparent wish to be near you, because he is here nearly every day. Now tell me I have no right to be concerned about the welfare of my little sister!"

Her bottom lip trembled. "He has been a gentleman."

"But has he spoken with you of marriage?"

A quick jerk of her head indicated no.

"Have you met his family?"

Another shake of the head.

"Then how can it be anything but a passing fancy of his? I'm sorry, I know you do not wish me to say such things, but can you not see? If his pursuit of you is not intended to lead to marriage, then his intention cannot but make me apprehensive."

"Make us both apprehensive," Aunt Addy murmured, nodding.

Ben shifted to sit beside Tessa, her bright hair tumbling forward to hide her downcast face. "We love you. We wish you to be happy, to marry someone who will treat you the way you deserve. And you do not deserve to be strung along while he decides if he's courageous enough to even introduce you to his family."

A drop of water slipped from her face to stain her gown.

His heart twisted. In moments like this,

he really wished George would take his head-of-the-family duty seriously. Ben wrapped an arm around her shoulders and squeezed gently. "I can speak to him if you like."

She gave a shuddery breath, shook her head no. "Perhaps . . . perhaps he should meet George. George might know what to do."

Annoyance coiled within, smothering his earlier wish. Why did people always seek his brother's opinion above his own?

"I think that a very good idea," said their aunt. "It's about time George started treating some of his responsibilities as he ought. The least he can do is to meet your young man so we can ascertain whether he really is your young man or just someone living in a fool's paradise."

Tessa nodded, her golden-red curls gleaming dully in the late afternoon light.

He hugged her closer. "I'm sorry, Tessa."

She sighed. "No, I suppose you are right. I always knew it was too good to be true."

"It doesn't mean it's over. But it might be wise to not encourage him quite so much."

"You . . . think it better I make him wonder about my affection."

"I suppose so, yes."

"Like you do about Clara?"

Ben straightened. "I beg your pardon?"

She turned to eye him, her gaze level. "You think we did not notice? You always seemed to brighten when she was around; you were always looking at her when you thought yourself unobserved."

His neck heated. "I did not."

She laughed mockingly. "Oh, yes you did. And yet you have the nerve to accuse me of aiming above myself when she is a viscount's daughter?"

Frustration stole through his chest, quiet and cold. "She is a viscount's daughter whom I may have thought I admired at one stage, but there is one significant difference. She is not here, neither has she indicated any interest in me by any stretch of the imagination."

"You sound as though you wish she had."

He shrugged, helpless against his sister's uncanny discernment. "And what would be the point? I cannot offer her anything resembling a secure future, not even a house."

"You wish you could, though."

A chuckle escaped despite himself. "Thank you for exposing my private concerns to our aunt here."

"Oh, I saw it, too," said Aunt Addy.

He strove for a blank visage, even as he

cringed inside. "I trust I have not given Miss DeLancey the wrong impression," he said stiffly.

"That I cannot say," his aunt said, in a far from reassuring manner.

"But if you did not, that is probably a good thing if Lord Featherington is to be believed," Tessa said.

He felt as though he were being led into a trap, yet could not stop himself from asking, "Why?"

"That to-do the other night at the Seftons' ball? A Mr. Molyneux is making the most wild allegations, that she was quite rude to him." Tessa's blue eyes widened. "I told Lord Featherington not to be ridiculous, but you know what else he said to me yesterday?" She leaned closer. "He said Miss DeLancey had once been scandalously in love with the Earl of Hawkesbury."

"No!" Aunt Addy said, interest gleaming in her eyes.

"Oh, yes. Apparently they were almost engaged!"

Jealousy slid across Ben's heart. He was a fool to have hoped Miss DeLancey had any thought of him. With an earl as a previous suitor, no wonder her parents did not wish their daughter to hobnob with mere gentry.

"I have to wonder how someone can be

considered almost engaged," Tessa mused. "Surely a man either proposes or he doesn't."

Both ladies turned expectantly to him. "I cannot speak to the matter."

"But worth thinking on, perhaps," said Aunt Addy, a twinkle in her eye, "should one ever wish to do so."

He narrowed his gaze at her, which only caused both ladies to laugh.

To change the focus, he cleared his throat in a manner that had afforded respect on not a few vessels under his command. "For someone who says he does not gossip, it's surprising just how much Lord Featherington chooses to pass on."

Tessa's brow creased. "Do you not like him?"

"I cannot say with any degree of certainty. I have noticed, however, that sometimes he says one thing, such as claim to dislike gossip, but appears to do the opposite."

"I do not think you are being very fair."

Again, they were at their impasse. Ben with his doubts, Tessa with her defense.

God, give me wisdom.

He sucked in a breath, swallowed his pride. "Tessa, I think you might be right. Perhaps we should talk to George tonight."

She nodded, leaving him feeling a mixture

of relief that his attempt at conciliation had met with success, and frustration that his brother would win again.

"You cannot be serious!" George's look of incredulity had scarcely shifted since his arrival this morning, when Ben, Aunt Addy, and Tessa had mentioned something of the viscount's attentions these past weeks. "The heir to the Marquess of Exeter?"

They nodded, heads bobbing in unison like marionettes on a string.

"Tessa, you could be a marchioness!" He looked at Ben. "Our sister, a marchioness!"

"Yes, but George —"

"I don't see what the problem is. How can you possibly object?"

"He has said nothing to give the slightest indication of permanent attachment. Nothing to indicate his intentions." Ben eyed his brother. "She has no dowry to speak of. Nothing that would attract a gentleman seeking a wife."

"You do our sister a great disservice, I must say!" George said, bristling.

"I speak the facts plainly. Tessa knows that." He gave her an apologetic look.

"And her portion is not exactly nothing. She will receive one thousand pounds when she marries."

Ben released a low whistle. "Well, I can hardly conceive a marquess rejecting that sum of money, can you?"

"Sarcasm does not become you, Benjamin," Aunt Addy said, a reproving look in her eye.

"Neither does not living in reality," he muttered. In a louder voice he said, "Perhaps if George were to meet the viscount —"

"Oh, yes, George! Please do," Tessa beseeched, hands clasped.

"George might be able to ascertain his intentions better than we have managed so far," Ben concluded. Appeal to his brother's pride, appeal to his brother's sense of superiority. "Seeing as he is the head of the family."

George puffed up, peacock-like. "Well, yes, I imagine he would wish to listen to me, seeing as I am responsible for you, Theresa." The pride suffusing his face softened as he gave their sister a benevolent, almost fatherly look. "When would suit the viscount?"

"He . . . he attends White's, I believe."

"White's?" George frowned. "I believe that to be something of a betting parlor."

"It also has quite a nice dining room," Ben said.

"Be that as it may, I cannot approve a man who gambles," George said, eyeing Tessa sternly.

She flung a worried, almost pleading look at Ben. Well they both knew of the viscount's propensity for a flutter. While Ben did not like it, he was in no position to object. Besides, the viscount could well afford to.

He shot her a half smile of understanding, before addressing George once more. "Perhaps White's would not be the ideal location. One needs to be a member, after all."

"Spoken like someone who wished to be a member and failed," George sneered.

Ben adjusted the sleeve of his coat. "Actually, I have attended more than once, and while I can recommend the steak as quite good, the pretension is greater, so I have no appetite to become a member, I assure you."

Tessa nodded. "He's gone to White's as the guest of Lord Featherington and Lord Hawkesbury. He's been four times now!"

"Five," he said, in as meek a manner as possible.

Just as he suspected, his brother's eyes bulged with a mix of surprise and irritation. "Well! I gather there is a lot to be said for acting like a hero." George's eyes narrowed. "Has the Regent paid you anything yet?"

"No."

"Hmm. Pity, but not unexpected. You know what a spendthrift he is." He drew himself up, as if wishing to put aside an unpleasant interlude. "But talking about our profligate Prince is hardly of concern now. I shall send Lord Featherington a note requesting an interview, and we shall see what comes of it." He directed a thin smile toward their sister. "I trust you will neither encourage nor discourage the gentleman, Theresa. Remember, it behooves you to act modestly and not give him the idea you are anything but an innocent young maid."

"But she is an innocent young maid!" Ben interjected.

George sniffed. "I would remind you, Benjamin, that as head of the family, my opinions . . ."

Ben ignored the rest of his brother's rambling self-adulation, muttering an excuse as he left the room. Trusting Tessa's future to their brother was going to require some serious amount of prayer.

Brighton
"And how was London, Miss DeLancey?" Lady Osterley said.

"Pleasant enough," Clara said, her forced smile at this unwanted visit to the Osterley mansion beginning to falter.

261

Lady Osterley sniffed. "Well, I suppose one can afford to be cavalier when one has had several seasons."

Clara swallowed the sting. Perhaps her ladyship wasn't quite so harmless as she'd previously imagined. She lifted her chin. "I have had several seasons now, it is true."

Lady Osterley blinked.

Beside her, Mother visibly wilted. "Clara, dearest, perhaps you should have some more tea. It is most delicious, I must say —"

"It is delicious tea," Clara said, happy to comply with her mother's unvoiced wish for amity.

Lady Osterley favored Clara with a slight curling in the corner of her lips, no doubt meant to represent a smile. "I like to think I serve my guests nothing but the best."

"Your pride serves you well," Mother said.

Well, her pride served her, Clara thought, hiding her smile behind her freshly refilled teacup. In all their interactions over the past year, she'd noticed that Lady Osterley did little that did not draw attention to her own self-importance or reflect her vaulting ambitions for her son.

"Where is Reginald?" Clara enquired. "I am surprised not to see him today." As he'd been every other time, gazing at her like a moonling, his conversation as stilted and awkward as a newborn foal's first steps.

"He will be disappointed not to have seen you, my dear, and gratified to know you enquired after him," Lady Osterley said with a sigh. "He had some previous business and could not get away. Most unfortunate," she said, with a triumphant air that suggested the opposite.

Clara studied her. Had something been whispered to the Osterleys about her sad experiences at the Seftons' ball? A twinge of regret streaked through her, followed by fresh determination. Did she really care for the opinions of such shallow people, whose interest in her extended only so far as her lineage? The Osterleys might possess an almost equally ancient name, but they were as venal as all those who'd once sought her for the dowry she was supposed to have brought to a marriage — the dowry Richard had gambled away. The Osterleys had clung on longer than most, perhaps believing they would somehow see its return, but it appeared that they, too, had given up on her.

Strangely, the thought such people considered her unmarriageable did not sting the way it would have once. She'd read this morning in the Psalms about God's love and His promise to take care of her regardless of circumstances. She did not need to impress these people, nor to play their games.

Seemingly aware of her perusal, Lady Osterley left off her quiet conversation with Clara's mother to offer Clara another thin smile. "I confess I heard something of your exploits in London from my dear niece, Lady Ashbolt."

"I wondered if that were so," Clara said, with a sweet smile.

Lady Osterley looked nonplussed for a moment before gathering her venom for another thrust. "It seems your conduct at the Seftons' ball was much talked about."

"And still continues to be," Clara said, her smile not shifting.

"Yes, well . . . Hmm."

Clara glanced at Mother, whose face had abandoned its customary cool politeness to something approaching despair. Her conscience panged. Whilst Clara might care little for Lady Osterley's pretensions, Mother still did, and the knowledge that her daughter was considered so scandalous by so many was anathema to her.

"Mother, shall we go soon? Tea has been very pleasant, but we still have another call to make, remember?"

"Another call?" Mother said, frown creasing her brow, as Clara eyed her steadily. "Oh, yes. Well, thank you, dear Lady Osterley. Your hospitality knows no bounds."

"Thank you, Lady Winpoole. It has been a pleasure, as always."

They rose, and after a surfeit of insincere expressions of gratification, finally departed, with Lady Osterley's caution ringing in their ears.

"You are always welcome, Frederica. And you, too, Clara. Pray do not forget to let us know when next you wish to visit."

Clara offered her arm to her mother as they walked along Marine Parade back to their house, the destination of their next call. She blocked out her mother's grumblings about Clara's conduct and the falsities of their hostess, conscious of one certainty: the next time they called, Lady Osterley would be certain to ensure poor, dimwitted Reginald be kept far away from the terrible man-chaser that was Clara.

She began to laugh.

CHAPTER SEVENTEEN

In the end, George's letter produced a response not entirely to everyone's satisfaction, save perhaps Tessa's. The viscount replied, deigning to visit Aunt Addy's house in Curzon Street for the interview on Thursday next, on the proviso that Ben would also be in attendance. Whilst Ben was happy to attend, George was not so pleased, seemingly fearful his status as head of the family was under threat.

Thursday morning arrived, the viscount was announced, he entered the drawing room, made polite enquiry about the ladies of the house, and after a brief exchange of such politenesses, so it began.

"Thank you for coming, my lord," George said.

"Not at all." The viscount, flicking open a golden snuff box, offered it around.

George's brow knit. The taking of snuff was almost as abhorrent as the vice of gambling. Leaning forward in the belligerent manner of a French *barque,* he fired the first shot. "My younger brother has expressed some level of concern about our sister's reputation."

The viscount's gaze flicked to Ben, the pleasant expression sliding away to something harder. "Oh, he has, has he?"

Ben smiled, aiming for a conciliatory pose. "Come now, my lord. My concerns are nothing new to you. You are aware I have only the interests of my sister at heart."

"As do I," said George, shooting Ben a displeased look.

"Your sister is . . . lovely," the viscount said.

"But do you think her lovely enough to marry?"

Lord Featherington sat back as George gasped at Ben's forthrightness. But he had no wish to play games. No wish to continue this frustrating dance of dalliance. "My lord?" Ben prompted, brows raised.

"I . . . er, I confess I had no thought of matrimony at this time."

"Really?" Ben said, as George grew slack-jawed. "You surprise me."

The sarcasm was not lost on the viscount, whose cheeks reddened.

"May I ask your intentions towards my sister?"

"You've asked me that before," Lord Featherington muttered.

"And you have failed to provide a satisfactory answer."

Their guest's lips flattened in an ominous line.

After a show of clearing his throat, George said, "Please forgive my brother, my lord. Benjamin, perhaps you should leave the questions to me. Especially as I am responsible for Theresa's well-being, after all."

Ben gestured for George to continue, his unflinching gaze refusing to leave Lord Featherington's face.

"My lord, please understand we all appreciate the attention you have paid my sweet little sister. Your notice has permitted entrée to levels of society we had dared not presume."

Ben folded his arms, watching his brother, whose smug face declared his lie — George had never *not* dared presume such things.

"But she is so young, you see. Only seventeen. And if your attentions continue, then she is at risk of not attracting the attention of a gentleman who *will* offer for her."

The viscount's jaw tightened. A muscle ticked in his cheek, beating in and out.

Finally, after what seemed an age, the viscount spoke. "I wish your sister no ill."

"Of course not." George gave a desperate, wheezy chuckle. "We would never think such a thing."

Featherington turned to Ben, an eyebrow lifting.

Ben shook his head. "I never thought you capable of harm. Just carelessness with her reputation."

"Many thanks."

So apparently the viscount could appreciate the subtleties of irony, as well.

There was another long, uncomfortable pause, as they watched the viscount play with his snuff box, variously opening then snapping shut the lid. Finally he sighed. "I would not have her —" He shook his head. "I could not hope to —"

"To convince your father of the suitability of the match?"

Ben looked at George with surprise. Perhaps his brother was more shrewd than he'd given him credit for.

The viscount looked a little shame-faced. "It is not my father, but my mother. She is always on about family honor. She would never countenance —" He stopped.

"Such an opportunistic young lady as my sister?" George said, something like anger

269

hardening his voice.

Featherington shook his head. "I know Tessa is as far from opportunistic as the moon from the sun."

"Just remember that when you are surrounded by those deemed more worthy simply because they have more money or titles than my sister," George snapped.

The viscount blanched. "I never meant to hurt her." He glanced at Ben. "Please believe me."

"Tessa is young," he replied. "She is not without friends. She has faith to comfort her."

The viscount swallowed.

Ben noted the action with a grim sense of satisfaction. Yet another way their match was unequal. Tessa possessed a childlike faith so strong in trust, while her swain seemed to regard their beliefs as something quaint, a product of their rural upbringing. His comments to that effect, and his sporadic church attendance, had not gone unnoticed or uncommented upon, either.

"I wish . . ." Featherington shook his head again.

George and Ben waited, unwilling to say anything that might hinder the viscount from offering the apology honor demanded from his conduct towards Tessa.

He glanced away, studying the glass-fronted satinwood armoire as if its contents fascinated. When he turned back, his expression was cool, inscrutable.

"I suppose it is for the best," the viscount said, eyeing Ben in an unfriendly manner. "I cannot in all good conscience align myself with a family who chooses to associate with one that has maligned mine."

"I beg your pardon?"

The viscount lifted a shoulder. "That young lady you were so often seen with. Miss DeLancey? She has scarcely been backward in her interest in my cousin's husband, even after he was a married man."

Heat writhed through his chest. "You are mistaken."

"Am I? Just ask anyone about her. She even had the nerve to confront Lavinia at the Seftons' ball."

No. He refused to believe it. Not shy, sweet Clara. She would never behave in a less than decorous manner. And as for still caring for the Earl of Hawkesbury . . . Had Ben misread her? Hadn't she shown interest in him?

"I can see you don't know her for who she truly is," their guest jeered. "Both she and her brother are corrupt."

"What about her brother?" George asked,

271

puzzlement knitting his brow.

A dark look crossed the viscount's face. "If ever I see that fiend it will be far too soon. He's a blackguard, blackhearted like his sister —"

"Please do not speak of her that way," Ben said in a low voice.

"I'll speak of her however I choose!" Lord Featherington said, angry sparks shooting from his usually mild eyes.

"Yes, but what's this about her brother?" George persisted.

"He's a thief, as well as a villain. It's said he gambled away nearly fifteen thousand pounds at one sitting at Watier's, betting that Hartington's child would be a boy."

"Fifteen thousand pounds!" George paled as though he might faint.

"Not quite fifteen. He'd gambled plenty before that. But the loss was still the same. Stupid fool. It was a girl, of course. Rose. A sweet little thing," he added, with a sudden smile. "Hartington later married my sister, you know."

George blinked. "The Duchess of Hartington?"

"Yes. Charlotte has done well for herself." He glanced at Ben, his expression hardening again. "But your Miss DeLancey has not."

It was pointless to argue the true nature of his non-relationship with Clara, so he kept quiet.

"The Winpoole debt had to be paid from somewhere, so the dowry it was." He made an expression of distaste. "How unfortunate for her that it wasn't tied up and unable to be touched as everyone expected. I suppose you're extremely disappointed."

Ben clenched his hands, yet met his gaze evenly. "I have no right to be disappointed."

"No?"

"I would never wish to be a man who considers it the wife's role to bring financial stability to a marriage."

"No? Well, you're the only one!"

Ben shrugged, glancing at George, who looked suddenly abashed. Well, well. Perhaps George did not share his scruples, and the beauty he saw in Miss Windsor had more to do with the handsome marriage settlements her father would pay than with any physical attraction. He shook his head at his cynicism.

The viscount snorted. "I will not attempt to argue with you but will say only this: if you choose to stay associated with that family I can have nothing more to do with your sister."

Anger pushed Ben to his feet. "Then you

have said all you can say, and I must ask you to leave."

"But I am the —" George protested weakly.

"Head of the family, yes we know." Ben said, eyes not leaving the viscount's flushed face. "I am disappointed, my lord, that your scruples do not allow you to overcome your past prejudice. I know Tessa will be grievously disappointed, but I should not wish her to align herself with someone so petty-minded, who would allow gossip to dictate her choice of friends."

"Very well." The viscount rose, offered a stiff bow. "Please convey my regards to your sister and aunt. I regret I am unable to take formal leave of them."

Ben dipped his chin in response. George murmured something of obligation, and their guest was gone.

His brother stared at him open-mouthed. "I did not figure him to be quite so, quite so . . ."

"Much a dandy?"

He shook his head. "Quite so irresolute. I felt sure he would fight for her more."

"Which says something about his character, does it not?"

"I suppose." George's face took on a thoughtful cast.

Ben hoped his brother would finally see reason. He would have preferred the encounter to not grow ugly, but perhaps it was better for the truth to be made plain about the viscount's lack of character. Want of character was like scurvy, an insidious disease that rotted a man's body as sure as a lack of principles could destroy an otherwise charming man.

Poor Tessa. He couldn't help but now feel a sense of relief, but how would she cope?

His hands fisted as the viscount's words swam around his brain. Featherington's ultimatum might have exposed his personal failings, but he'd also exposed further truth and, in the process, had flicked Ben on the raw.

Ben *had* wished for something more with Miss DeLancey. It was pointless denying it any longer. Such a desire had only clarified with the surge of jealousy he'd felt upon hearing her name coupled with Lord Hawkesbury's. Poor lass. He knew the ache of unrequited affection.

His hands fisted, then released. He shook his head, working to sort truth from the eddies of deceit. But still, the thought of Miss DeLancey bailing up the countess did not sit right. She always seemed so meek to him. Brittle, yes. Aloof, most certainly. But she was not the first person to encase her emotions with a facade far different from internal truth. He refused to believe her capable of such an action.

The door burst open and Tessa flew in, glancing around, her face alight. "Where is he?"

Ben captured her hands, held them tight, forcing her to still, to look at him. "He has gone."

"What? Without speaking to me?" Her face clouded, before lighting again. "Has he gone to speak with his father?" Her eyes shone. "Oh! Is he getting a special license?"

He swallowed. This would prove harder than he'd thought. "He is not."

"Then . . . where is he? Why did he not wish to speak with me?"

Ben exchanged a glance with George, but for once the self-proclaimed head of the family seemed reticent about the duties of his role. Ben swallowed. "I think he would have liked to speak with you," he allowed.

"But you would not let him." Her eyes filled with tears. "I always knew you did not like him!"

"Dearest Tessa, you know that is not true."

"I cannot believe it!" Tessa cried, prying her hands free to hit him on the chest. "How could you do such a thing?" she sobbed. "I thought you cared about my happiness."

"I do," Ben said, trying to capture her flailing arms and failing. "Please, Tessa, don't be angry with me."

One small hand reached up. A nail scratched his cheek. He winced.

"Oh!" Tessa covered her mouth with a hand. "I'm sorry."

"It's nothing," he said, accepting the handkerchief George offered with muttered thanks. He pressed the cloth to his cheek for a few seconds. Removed it to see the bright stain of blood.

"Oh, Benjie!"

He forced himself to smile. "Just another scar to add to the collection."

Her bottom lip quivered. A tear traced her cheek.

"I shouldn't worry," said George. "You'll probably think he deserves it once you hear what he said."

"What did you say?" Tessa demanded, all sign of remorse gone.

George continued, "Featherington said he wanted Ben to give up his association with Miss DeLancey, whoever she is."

"She was never mine to give up," Ben gritted out.

"Lord Featherington said that?" Tessa

looked between them, eyes wide with disbelief.

"Yes."

"How dare he?" Something like disgust crossed her face. "I thought him more honorable than that." Her bottom lip trembled again, only this time it seemed no anger was left to check it. Her face crumpled, she shuddered, and her shoulders convulsed piteously.

Ben drew her to his chest, felt her tears soak through his shirt. His throat burned, his compassion flayed ragged and raw, like the back of a deserter under whips. "I'm sorry, Tessa."

He refused to meet his brother's glare, conscious in this moment of wanting nothing more than to provide some comfort for his sister's despair. And he wrapped her closer — with his arms, and in his prayers.

CHAPTER EIGHTEEN

Brighton
Late July

The grounds of St. Nicholas were abuzz with conversation. The congregation had grown sizable in recent weeks, with an influx of visitors from London, here for the summer months by the sea. Clara wandered past pockets of gossip concerning the latest exploits of the Prince Regent and his extended family as she searched for Matilda.

"Oh, yes, apparently he wants the Pavilion transformed into some sort of temple! A Hindustani design, so I'm led to believe. Oh, yes, my husband had it from the Chamberlain, Lord Houghton himself. Can't say I care for such things myself, but you know Prinny's never been one to do things by halves . . ."

". . . the Queen and the poor Princess, a sad thing, indeed. But is it any wonder, when she's pursued by a rogue like that soldier? But he won a medal, so I suppose he cannot be all bad. Frightfully handsome they say, and possesses a good seat on a horse . . ."

". . . Imagine, wearing red to the Seftons'! I ask you!"

Clara froze. She recognized that voice, the topic of that conversation. She glanced over her shoulder, saw Lady Osterley bend her head towards her cronies. "I won't deny my Reginald was quite miffed, but I told him that a lady of her advanced years cannot afford to be so very choosy."

Clara smiled wryly to herself, casting aside the sting to appreciate the absurdity. Did Lady Osterley mean that as an insult to Clara or her own son?

Her gaze met Lady Osterley's widening one. Clara's smile broadened. "Good morning, my lady."

"Miss DeLancey. I did not see you there."

"So I gathered. How is dear Reginald? Please send him my best regards."

The older lady's face darkened to a shade of puce sure to be unhealthy. Clara sketched a curtsy and moved on, working to not allow the barbs of the ladies' hostility to hook her heart. What was it Matilda had said? To pray blessings over her enemies? *Heavenly Father, please help Lady Osterley find happi-*

ness. And Reginald, too. And help me not to allow her poison to infect me.

"Clara! Oh, there you are."

"Matilda!" They hugged. "I was looking for you."

The brightness in her friend's face faded. "And I you. Oh, I've so much to tell you." She glanced over her shoulder. "I'm sure nobody would miss me, and if so, well, too bad. I simply must speak to someone or else burst. Can you spare a moment?"

"Of course."

Matilda laid a hand on Clara's arm, drawing her to a slightly less busy corner, near where the stone bell tower jutted.

Clara eyed her friend, whose wan look gave cause for concern. "Matilda? You do not seem well. What is it?"

Matilda's eyes filled. "It's poor Tessa. I received a letter from her yesterday. She writes that the viscount has called things off."

"Oh! Poor thing. I imagine she is devastated."

Matilda nodded miserably. "They're planning on returning here in the next few days."

"Of course." Clara bit her lip. She would not ask. She would *not* ask . . .

"Benjie and George are coming, too."

A flicker of joy, then she remembered. She

281

willed her emotions back to neutral. He would be as nothing to her, just as Lord Hawkesbury was.

"He'll be bringing his intended, too." Clara's heart gave another traitorous jolt. "He wants us to meet her." Matilda muttered, "Thinks it only befitting his status as head of the family."

"Pardon?"

"Oh, never mind. But I do hope I might rely on you to help Tessa through this difficult time."

"But of course. Anything I can do, please ask."

Matilda nodded, her countenance lightening a little. "I knew I could rely on you. You are a true friend."

Clara's eyes filled. Nobody had ever said such a thing to her before. She blinked away the emotion as an elderly parishioner summoned Matilda.

"Ah, Clara, at last." Mother's disgruntled voice reached her. "Are you ready? I have no wish to rush you, but I cannot stay a second longer. Would you believe that awful Lady Osterley had the nerve to give me the cut direct? Cut *me*?"

Clara swallowed a throb of guilt. Matilda might believe her a true friend, but Clara's actions had proved rather less than that of a loving daughter. "Are you sure she simply did not see you?"

"Of course she saw me! How could she not?" Mother gestured to her Sunday finery, a somewhat brighter than usual arrangement of pink that had required all of Clara's tact to assure still looked appropriate for one of her Mother's years. Her face closed in consternation. "I cannot believe I ever gave that woman the time of day. How dare she, a trumped up little nobody from the back of Romney's Marsh, have the nerve to snub me, whose lineage can be traced back to Charles the First? I ask you!"

Clara patted her arm. "Never mind her. I am sure it is a misunderstanding that will be resolved later."

"I have no wish to resolve things with her. She is as one dead to me."

Her mother's histrionics were nothing new. Clara offered a guilt-tinged smile. "Then shall we depart?"

"Yes. Call the carriage at once, if you please. I cannot abide breathing the same air as her."

Good thing Lady Osterley was as one dead to Mother, Clara thought wryly, as they threaded through the dispersing crowds.

"Miss DeLancey?"

She turned. Met the dark gaze of a tall, handsome older gentleman. She raised a brow.

He bowed. "Forgive me, we have not been properly introduced, I know. I am —"

"Lord Houghton?" Mother moved beside her, hand outstretched. "How are you?"

He bent over her hand, looking up with a smile. "Frederica. It's been too long."

"Far too long," Mother said, with an expression not dissimilar to that of a cat eyeing a bowl of cream. She gave a trill of laughter, her attitude a million miles away from what she'd expressed only seconds ago. "Tell me, what can the Prince Regent's Chamberlain want with my daughter?"

Clara blinked. "You serve the Prince Regent?"

He nodded. "When His Highness is in attendance at the Pavilion."

"Oh!" she said, impressed.

He smiled, quite a pleasant smile for someone who must be nearer Father's age than her mother's. It made him seem much younger. "And that is what brings me to wish to speak with you. But not here, not now," he said glancing around at the curious eyes and ears turned their way. "Perhaps I might be permitted to call upon you tomorrow?"

"O-of course," she stammered.

"We should be delighted, my lord," Mother said gleefully.

With another bow and a smile, he departed, leaving them clutching his card in wonder, before their carriage was called, and Mother dragged her past Lady Osterley, whose expression was everything Clara felt sure Mother had hoped it would be.

What did Lord Houghton wish with her?

Next day

"Ladies, please forgive my enigmatic approach yesterday. I had no wish to embarrass or alarm you."

"Oh, Lord Houghton, please. We barely gave the matter a second thought, did we, Clara?" Mother said, with a stern eye, as if they had not spent the whole of yesterday and this morning in avid speculation.

"No, Mother," she said dutifully, aware their guest held amusement in his expression.

"I'm so glad," he said. "As I mentioned yesterday, I have a request that is certainly not meant to alarm you."

Clara swallowed. "A request?"

"Yes." He eyed her directly. "Miss DeLancey, your name was drawn to my attention recently when you were in London."

Her cheeks heated. "I see."

"Yes. Lady Sefton mentioned you."

Clara exchanged a look of horror with her mother. Oh, no!

"She mentioned she had been speaking with Lady Asquith —"

"She had?"

He chuckled. "Yes. Your godmother, I believe? Apparently your performance was quite the talk of the night."

She froze. Which performance did he refer to? Her musical performance, or her dramatic flight from society the night of the ball?

His warm chuckle came again. "There is no need to look so worried, my dear. I mention it simply because the Prince Regent is always a fan of musical talent."

Oh, her musical performance. The tightness in her shoulders relaxed, then resumed. Please God he hadn't heard about the other!

"I had hopes of persuading you to attend an evening at the Pavilion in the not-too-distant future when he is next entertaining."

What? Clara could only stare.

Mother, on the other hand . . . "The Prince wants my Clara to play for him?" She gave a screech of joy. "Oh, the heavens are smiling at last! I knew one day we would see justice."

Lord Houghton cleared his throat, as if to hide the laughter his eyes revealed as they turned to her. "I trust that is affirmation you will attend?"

"Of course she will," said Mother. "Oh, could anything occur more wonderful? Oh, *dear* Lord Houghton, please convey our immense gratitude to His Highness. Oh, and tell us if there is a particular piece he prefers? And what is his favorite color? It would not do for Clara to dress in something of which he is not particularly fond. Oh, and when do you think this most auspicious event may be?"

"Anything, any color, and Friday of next week," he said, ticking off his fingers. "I will, of course, be sending you an invitation."

"Oh, thank you, my lord. You are too kind."

Mother's gratitude saw him to the door and saw her floating through the remainder of the day. Lord Houghton's card was placed in the most prominent position on the silver salver atop the hallstand, right where their surprisingly high number of other visitors that day would be sure to notice. For to each visitor, even Lady Osterley — whom Mother had decided was not so very dead to her after all — Mother had

287

crowed of Clara's good fortune, determinedly riding across any turn in conversation, taking her moment of glory for all its
worth.

Clara sat quietly, answering enquiries
more from habit than from real interest, as
the morning's visitor and his extraordinary
news had near numbed her to all else.
Could it really be true that, far from being
a social pariah, she would now be somewhat
celebrated? And while she was certain many
other young ladies had been invited over
the years, neither she nor any of Mother's
visitors seemed to know of one either so
young or so lacking in title. Daughter of a
viscount she might be, but few unattached
ladies considered mere Honorables received
such honor. Their visitors were vocal in their
comments and nearly unanimous in their
approval. She smiled. Perhaps she would
not be considered quite so dishonorable,
after all.

"Oh, she must wear blue!"

"He likes Haydn."

"He hates anything that reminds him of
that Fitzclarence woman."

"He prefers young ladies to wear white."

"Are you invited to dinner?"

"You will be able to tell us all about those
heathenish refurbishments!"

Even Lady Osterley had seemed more humbled than hostile. "Oh, I remember when I was invited to the Pavilion, back when my poor husband was alive, God rest his soul. Such an odd sort of place —"

"Yes, well, you weren't invited to perform, were you, Lady Osterley?" Mother said, a nasty glint in her eye. "Besides, we are not talking about things dating from so many years ago, but things that matter today."

Unsurprisingly, Lady Osterley soon felt it time to take her leave. Even less surprisingly, Mother made no attempt to stop her.

When the door had firmly closed behind her, Mother had snapped her fan open, as if needing to cool down after all the hot air. "How that woman can have the nerve to come here as if she had not treated me in an abysmal manner yesterday, I do not know."

"We do not always behave in the manner in which we ought," Clara felt it necessary to say. Lady Osterley's visit had made it plain that it was Clara's words that had induced her ladyship to treat Mother in such a rude fashion. That knowledge had kept her from making few comments of any kind in that lady's presence.

Mother simply shrugged away excuses,

before turning with mouth agape. "Oh my dear!"

"What is it?"

"We shall simply have to get you a new gown! Oh, however will we afford it?"

"We do not need to, Mother. Lady Sefton commented on how well I looked in the red gown at her ball. I could simply wear that again."

"No, no, *no*! That will never do. We must get you a new one. Oh, I'm sure your father will not mind."

"Her father will not mind what?" said a deeper voice.

"Oh! You're back at last! Oh, darling husband, our Clara has received news of the highest honor! You will never guess!"

"That she has been asked to play at the Pavilion?" he said, a twinkle in his eye.

"Oh, you guessed!" Mother said, her face falling.

"I had it from at least three people on my way here. You did not think such news would remain secret for long, did you?"

"I suppose not," Mother said, with a return to her self-satisfaction.

"And I suppose this good news must lead to the purchase of new fripperies and furbelows for my clever daughter?" He turned to Clara with a smile. "You have made us very proud, my dear."

She swallowed the lump in her throat. "Thank you, Father. I just hope I will not disappoint you."

"Of course you won't disappoint us," Mother said. "Not when you're going to be practicing every day until your moment arrives. And especially not when you'll be wearing whatever the finest mantua-maker in Brighton can make you," she slid a look at Father, who offered a slow nod of approval.

"There! See? You will be wonderful, I assure you."

Their faith in her instilled confidence in herself, and she went to bed that night filled with visions of gowns and music and hope, beneath which swirled the knowledge that such an event might prove her last chance to find a husband who finally met with her parents' approval.

"She has what?"

Matilda's face lit with a big smile, her most genuine since their arrival in Brighton this morning. "Clara has been invited to play at the Pavilion. She goes Friday next week, so the invitation said. I saw it yesterday," she said smugly.

"How wonderful for her," Tessa said, her

face brightening for the first time in over a sennight. "I'm glad *somebody* has good news in her life."

This last was said with a look at Ben that left him in no doubt as to whom she still blamed for her present misfortune. Since their disastrous last meeting, nothing further had passed between the viscount and any of the Kemsley connection. Word was that Featherington had left London to head north to spend time at Hawkesbury House, to be followed by a stint in Northampton-shire with his sister. Ben could only pray that the viscount's time away would resolve matters and help him see clearer direction for his future.

To his own mind, Ben couldn't help but be glad they'd returned south, to put even more miles between Tessa and her lost *paramour*. Even if it did come with the added burden of a brother, and the challenge of seeing the ever-intriguing Miss DeLancey again. And now this news about the Regent, exciting as it was, proved just how far out of reach she remained.

"So," George said ponderously, looking between Mattie, Tessa, and Ben. "So this Miss DeLancey to whom you refer is the infamous Miss DeLancey we've heard so much about?"

"I don't know about infamous," Mattie bristled.

"Then clearly you have not been privy to the information we have received."

Before Ben could stop him, George started detailing some of Miss DeLancey's notoriety the viscount had shared during that last interview.

Mattie simply looked at him. "Is that it?"

"Well, yes," George blustered. "Should there be more?"

"I wouldn't know, and I shouldn't care to hear it if there was."

"Well! I never —"

"Oh, stop it George. You've told me nothing but malicious gossip, and nothing that poor Clara did not tell me herself."

"She told you?" Ben couldn't help asking.

She gazed at him, the speculation in her eyes causing his neckcloth to feel uncommonly tight. "She did. And I admit I quite understood her viewpoint."

"Yes, well, I imagine if you only heard her side of things then you would feel that way."

"George, be quiet!"

At Mattie's snapped comment, George's mouth fell open, then closed, making him look far more fishlike than baronet.

"If you must insist on imposing your company on my husband and myself, then may I ask that you refrain from acting out all of your usual pomposity."

Tessa caught Ben's eye, her amusement plain to see. He smiled. He could not be unhappy with his brother's plight at the mercy of their sharp-tongued sister, not when it brought light to Tessa's eyes.

George scowled at him. "Of course you would find her atrocious manners amusing. But then, you've always been her favorite."

Only because I don't behave like a pretentious bufflehead, he thought, but didn't say.

"George," Mattie continued, as if speaking to a very young child, "I understand you do not like people to have opinions not your own, but please do not try to press your ill-informed ideas upon us."

"Ill-informed?"

"How would you know what account is correct if you have not spoken to the parties concerned? Have you even met Clara or Lady Hawkesbury? No? Well, how can you know for sure what was said? Believing such things without real proof is hardly the act of a gentleman. And one can hardly think Lord Featherington to be unbiased in such a matter, can one? Especially when it concerns his cousin, and he's just been held to account by the brothers of the young lady he was interested in, which resulted unfavorably for him." She looked thoughtfully at Tessa. "I cannot help but wonder if his reaction to such things a trifle malicious."

Tessa flushed.

"Now Matilda, as the head of this family I must insist —" His words broke off at Matilda's peal of laughter.

She gasped, hands on her knees. "Oh, Aunt Addy wrote you'd taken to referring to yourself in that way, but I had no idea!" She gurgled again. "Oh, George, if you only knew what you sounded like!"

For the first time in Ben's memory, George looked a trifle uncertain. "I don't know what you mean."

"You! Your posturing knows no bounds! May I remind you that you are not head of my family? That responsibility falls to my husband. Remember him? You came to our wedding eight months ago, as I recall."

"David, yes, of course."

"Well then, your opinion about my conduct or my friends must remain simply that: opinion. You have no right to insist upon anything as far as I'm concerned. On the other hand, your assertions concerning being head of the family might matter a little more with Benjie and Tessa . . ."

She smiled a toothy grin that made Ben think the viscount not the only one capable of malicious behavior.

"Having captained my own ship for some years now, I confess I don't feel in particular need of George's guardianship," Ben murmured.

Tessa and Mattie gave smothered giggles.

George grew red. "I still cannot like this family's association with someone who is known to have been in the thick of such rumor and speculation, especially when it may unduly affect the expectations of our own family."

This last was said with a sidelong look at Ben, prompting his hands to clench. "Your scruples do you merit."

George seemed to miss his sarcastic tone. "It was Amelia's parents, actually," George said, inspecting his fingernails.

"I see." Mattie eyed George firmly. "Well, perhaps you can inform Amelia's parents that if the heir to the throne can have no objection to being in Clara's company, neither can they object to her being in ours."

"Amen," said Tessa.

"Bravo," said Ben.

And George found it necessary to soon leave.

CHAPTER NINETEEN

The door banged open. Clara glanced up from the battered pianoforte, her music stilling for an infinitesimal moment before her breath released and she resumed playing. The anticipation thrumming in her veins all week was not due chiefly to the invitation to play at the Pavilion. As exciting as that was, as busy as her days had become through a myriad of shopping expeditions, visits to the mantua-maker, and music practice, each night her dreams made her freshly aware that her nerves were due mainly to one thing: seeing Mr. Kemsley.

She had not dared think of him much in recent weeks, had shoved away each sly thought of him, determining to think on things other than the man who had almost entangled her heart, the man who had so quickly found himself a bride. Fortunately Matilda had been too busy with other matters to mention such things again. And

Clara had not dared speak of him to Mattie, sure her friend would have teased and carried on in a way that Clara would not have been able to have borne it. But she was conscious now, every time she walked the street, entered Donaldson's library, heard the front door open, that one day she would see him again and would have to pretend everything was perfectly well.

Which it *was*, she told herself, gritting her teeth as yet another broken sailor in stained and tattered clothes lined up for soup. As Mattie ladled out a fresh batch, Clara continued to play while resuming her contemplation.

She was playing at the sailors and soldiers' shelter for the first time in weeks. Upon mentioning her desire to become involved again, Mother had insisted — among threats of swoons — that she cease, but Clara had been equally adamant she wished to help. So while Mother was having her own fittings for a gown — Father's generosity extending to new outfits for all — Clara had managed to creep undetected from the house to the hall and offer her services to a surprised Matilda. Ever short of volunteers, Mattie had not hesitated — nor questioned her — all the while murmuring apology that she could not bring Tessa to the shelter, as she was far too young to be exposed to such things. "And really, neither should you, seeing as you're a fine lady and all."

"Not so very fine," Clara had demurred with a smile.

"Fine enough for the Regent." Mattie's eyes twinkled. "Oh, I am sorry I cannot introduce George to you as yet. But I will as soon as Amelia arrives."

"Is she still in London then?"

"Yes. My brother has been finding it something of a challenge to find appropriate accommodation for Amelia and her parents — apparently they're sticklers for a certain degree of elegance. When he learned we could only accommodate Tessa and Benjie, George was not best impressed. But then he saw the modest way in which we live, and I think he was relieved."

"But surely your brother should take care of Amelia's family?"

"And so he is."

"I mean your brother Benjamin."

Matilda had looked at her in a puzzled way before a destitute sailor had interrupted.

It had proved most confusing.

Clara shook her head again, refocusing on the task at hand. She should probably only stay for another quarter hour, half hour at most. If Mother were to discover that Clara preferred performing for charity than practicing for the Prince, she might never live it down.

"Miss?"

She glanced up. Jumped. How long had that man been standing there? She offered a small smile. "I beg your pardon."

The large man jerked a nod, eyeing her in a way she found a trifle disturbing. "Ye got a proper smile or is that the best ye can do?"

Her chin lifted, her eyes narrowing. "I beg your pardon?"

He chuckled, revealing a set of very stained teeth. "Ye seem to be doing that a lot, begging me pardon and all."

She ceased playing, eyeing him coldly. "You have your soup. It is best eaten when hot."

"Ooh, listen to ye, all hoity-toity. What are ye then, a duchess come to hobnob with the riffraff? Seen all ye wanted, or do ye want to see some more?"

The nerves from earlier took on another layer, prickling her skin. Really, the man was standing too close. Her nose wrinkled, and a wave of nausea threatened. How long since the man had had a bath? She glanced around the room. Where was Matilda? Where was Mr. McPherson? Where were the other volunteers?

The man chuckled again, taking a step closer to the table separating the dining area from where she sat. "Ye looking fer the others? I got 'em outside. Poor Braithwaite got in another stoush and is outside being fixed up good and proper. Ain't nobody here but me and me mates." He jerked a thumb behind him.

Clara looked at the grimy faces he indicated. They met her gaze boldly before turning attention back to their bowls. Not one of them seemed cut from the cloth of a gentleman. She swallowed. "I will scream if necessary."

"Scream? Whatever would ye need to do that fer?" Quick as a wink he was behind the table, advancing slowly.

She rose, bumping back the stool as she clutched the music sheets to her chest like a foolish child. "Sir, I —"

"Sir, is it?" She could feel his stale, hot breath on her. She refused to wince. "A minute ago ye were looking at us like scum and now it's sir, is it?"

Clara shook her head. "You're mistaken. I might have been looking at you, but I was not thinking of you. I was thinking of somebody quite different."

"Course ye were," he sneered. "Plenty of

people see us and never think, do they? Why should ye be any different, even if ye are pretending to care?"

"Wilson!"

The name cut through the room, taut as a whip.

The hair on the back of her neck rose.

She recognized that voice. She recognized that figure striding through the room.

Her mouth dried, the sheets of music slipped from her grasp and landed on the floor with a hiss.

"Miss DeLancey?"

Ben rushed toward her. She seemed so pale, almost trembling, as if the man he'd elbowed past had hurt her. He wrapped a brotherly arm around her shoulders and escorted her to a seat, all the while glaring at the man who'd frightened her so. There was a reason he was not in favor of gently bred ladies involving themselves in such activities.

"Miss DeLancey?"

She dragged in a breath and glanced up at him. Her face was so close he only had to shift his head forward a little and he would finally know the taste of her lips.

As if sensing his thoughts, she jolted and tugged away. "Mr. Kemsley."

302

"The very same."

No trace of a smile crossed her face. "I . . . I did not know you would be here."

"Apparently neither did our friend Wilson."

"He is not my friend." She shuddered.

He frowned, searching her face for the truth. "Did he hurt you?"

"No. No! He did not. I was just . . . alarmed. He seemed a little threatening."

"I'm not surprised. He is not exactly a small man."

"Neither are you."

Her glance met his, then shied away, leaving him with a slow curl of pleasure unfurling in his stomach. What was she not saying — that she felt safe with him? It was ridiculous, he knew, but the thought brought him no small amount of gladness. "I think it probably best to return you home."

"Oh, but I —" She stopped, biting her lip.

Again he felt the tug of attraction. What would her kiss feel like? He knew she smelled sweet, that she was all that was desirable. He stifled a groan. Had absence made him so foolish? How could he ever keep these feelings at bay?

He moved away, offered his hand to help her rise. "Your mother would not be pleased to learn what has happened."

Her cheeks tinted to rose. "No."

"Then we will go."

He helped her into her pelisse and escorted her from the small hall, tossing off an excuse to Mattie when she ran up to find out what was the matter.

They moved through the churchyard. How could anyone think Miss DeLancey all that the viscount had accused her of being? She was modest; anyone could tell that. Indeed, at times she seemed quite shy. How could such a genteel young lady be considered so lacking in propriety that she would set her cap at a married man? Surely that kind of woman would not deign to play for those unfortunates attending David and Mattie's hostel for sailors and soldiers?

Her steps were quick; he matched them. It was enough to make him wonder in what other ways they might be suited. Foolishness, of course — a viscount's daughter must remain forever out of reach, even if by some miracle the Regent paid his vow. But was it that harmful to dream?

He glanced at her, walking beside him, the breeze teasing strands of hair loose from her bonnet. She seemed more determined than he remembered, more at ease within herself, even if Wilson's actions had caused a moment's fright. Not that he blamed the man. She was pretty, with a figure a godly man fought not to dream about. And talented, as the music he'd heard in London attested. At times he'd even thought she shared his sense of humor. His lips curved. He welcomed her quickness in following his lead without any of the arguing Mattie would offer. Yet despite this submissiveness, Miss DeLancey must hold more spunk than he'd realized, if she was so willing to perform for the poor and thus defy societal decrees — and most likely her mother.

They turned the corner of the Steyne and hurried along Marine Parade. She kept her head down, as if fearful of recognition. He tried not to let it bother him that it may be because she might not wish to be seen in his company. Probably it was because she simply did not want it reported back to her parents just where she had been. That had to be it. Didn't it?

"Miss DeLancey?"

She glanced up at him, those green eyes he found so entrancing now more filled with light than ever. "Yes?"

"You —" He swallowed. He wanted to say something about her beauty, something about how he'd be happy to have her on his arm for the rest of his days, something about how he knew such a sweet, modest young lady should not be the subject of the scandalous speculation as found in London. He settled for, "You have been missed."

She blushed. "I . . . I understand poor Tessa has not had an easy time of it."

"No. She will be pleased to see you again, though." As I am, he added silently.

They passed on a few more steps. He found himself wishing the Royal Crescent was even farther. Walking on a sunny summer's day in the sea air with a pretty lady on his arm made him wish the walk was ten times as long.

"How is" — she breathed deeply — "Miss Amelia?"

"Amelia? I wouldn't know."

She stopped. Glanced up at him, a frown in her eyes. "You wouldn't know? That is hardly right."

"I beg your pardon?"

"How can a man have so little regard for his betrothed?" She drew her arm from his.

"His betrothed?" He frowned. "Forgive me, I do not take your meaning. I did not think you had met George yet."

"Your brother?"

"Yes."

"No, I have not met him."

"Then how can you think him so careless of Amelia's feelings?" He grinned. "I assure you, he takes the utmost care of maintaining her and her parents' sensibilities in the manner to which they are accustomed."

She blinked. "Amelia is George's betrothed?"

"Yes. Why, you didn't think she could be mine, did you?"

Her cheeks deepened in hue, but before he could study this fascinating development, she had hurried off, leaving him to catch up.

"You did think that, didn't you?"

"Matilda never mentioned which brother was engaged."

"And you thought it me."

She said nothing, but neither did she need to. It was written all over her face.

"Let me assure you, my dear Miss DeLancey, that Miss Amelia Windsor is not the type of young lady to engage either my interest or my heart."

"I'm sure I have not the least idea why you are telling me such things."

"No? I'm sure I have not the least idea why I feel you must be told."

She peeked up at him then. He smiled, biting back a laugh as she quickly turned away and resumed walking.

"I can only say that I am partial to brunettes, especially those with hair as dark as ebony."

He caught the way she bit her bottom lip. Did she still not take his meaning? He hurried to add, "Especially a brunette with the most intriguing green eyes I've ever seen."

"You . . . you should not say such things, sir."

"Probably not," he agreed. "But I find myself quite unable to cease from doing so."

She shook her head. "You are a tease." She turned to ascend the step to her door.

He stilled her with a gentle hand. "I am serious."

"Then you are unwise."

Her eyes caught his, reminding him of starlit seas, of tropical lagoons, of jade carvings he'd seen in the Far East. His heart snagged afresh. He swallowed. "Perhaps I am unwise, Miss DeLancey, but I find I must tell you one more thing."

She took a step back. Clutched a tall iron spike as if needing support. "What is that?"

"I think you are beautiful."

She gasped, turned paler still, then turned and hurried inside.

Leaving him ruing his folly, ruing his haste, but unable to forget the joy, the rightness, of feeling her tucked under his arm. Or her scent. Or her lips.

He strode through the park, down to the clifftop, and faced the sea. He glanced over his shoulder back at the house, in time to see a curtain flick back into place. Had she been watching him?

He hoped she might look on him favorably. He wished he had something more than a heroic past to offer her. For she felt so right beside him, her voice, her scent, her kindness, all that was intriguing. He wanted to know her more, to push past the reserve and understand why she kept him at an arm's length, why she seemed to care that he was not attached, to learn what went on in that pretty little head. He smiled, remembering her modesty as she backed away from him, as if unable to believe his words, her steps faltering, her face pale . . .

Wait.

His skin prickled.

He stopped. Paused. Turned around to eye the freshly shrouded window.

Had he once met Miss DeLancey atop a wild and stormy cliff?

CHAPTER TWENTY

What had he meant? Clara placed cool hands on hot cheeks and watched the captain stride away along Marine Parade. Surely he had to be joking. He could not think her so much as pretty, let alone beautiful. Hadn't Richard always made fun of her too-pale eyes and her too-dark hair? He had always said the combination of dark eyebrows, pale skin, and green eyes made her look witchlike. Certainly not beautiful.

She watched as Mr. Kemsley turned once more, eyeing the window as if he knew she was there. She drew back. Did he know she watched him still? Did he know she could look at no other when he was around?

Her heart thumped. Blood rushed in her ears. He was not engaged!

Joy-filled warmth saturated her chest. He was free! All the thoughts she'd once entertained toward him, all the flutterings of hope and attraction, could be dusted off and encouraged to live once more. Couldn't they?

Or was she like poor Tessa, indulging in dreams that might come to nothing — again?

She glanced across at the dressing table, adorned with the gloves and hair accoutrements deemed suitable for her night at the Pavilion. Mother had not been reticent in her hopes that Clara might still find a suitable match from among those who frequented the Regent's soirees. Precisely which princely acquaintance Mother wished Clara to attract was a mystery, and would doubtless remain so until they learned who else had received an invitation — Father said a summons — to appear at the Pavilion.

Clara swallowed. She liked Mr. Kemsley more than anyone else she'd met in such a long time. His humor appealed as much as his forthright manners, his care for his sisters as much as his blunt good looks. He was certainly gentlemanly enough, even if he lacked the title of his brother or possessed much in the way of finances to provide. But was that enough? Mother would say no, as would Father, even though he understood now how a man's fortune could be affected by circumstances not of his own making.

Her pulse picked up in pace. How could Mr. Kemsley say she was beautiful and gaze at her lips as though he wished to kiss her if he did not have serious intentions?

She pressed two fingers to her lips. What would it feel like to be kissed? How would she even know what to do, when — if — the time came? Was she supposed to close her eyes? Touch his cheek? Sigh something? Her parents but rarely demonstrated affection. Perhaps she should watch Matilda a little more closely and observe how she interacted with her husband. Though it was difficult to imagine the meek and mild vicar holding his wife in a bone-crushing embrace —

"Clara!" She jumped. Spun around. Met her mother's flinty gaze. "What on earth are you doing?"

Her hand dropped to her side. "I . . . I was just thinking." Heaven forbid Mother ask just what she had been thinking about.

Her mother scowled as if she knew just what Clara had been so focused on. "Is it true that you were seen by Lady Osterley walking with a man not less than half an hour ago?"

Clara thought through what had just been said, working to disentangle the truth. "I cannot say with any degree of certainty what

Lady Osterley might have seen in recent times."

"Clara!"

She lifted her chin. "If you mean to ask if Mr. Kemsley walked beside me whilst I returned home, then that is true."

"Clara!"

"Yes, Mother?"

"Oh!" Her mother's face screwed tight in consternation. "I do not like to be informed by anyone of your misdemeanors, and especially not by that woman."

"It is most unfortunate, given her propensity for doing so."

"Do not speak to me in such a manner."

"But, Mother, if I had walked home alone, surely that would give just as great a cause for concern."

"What I want to know is why you were out to begin with! You told me you were staying at home."

"I went to see Matilda."

"That woman!"

"Yes." Clara swallowed the protest. "Her brother did me a kind service of escorting me home, thus protecting my reputation."

"You were seen to be looking at each other in a most particular way."

"Really?" Fierce joy erupted within. So she hadn't just imagined it! She fought a smile, working to smooth her countenance to disinterest. "Is that what she said? Well, we both know that woman to be a trouble-maker, don't we? Not everything she says can be relied upon. I'd think it best not to listen to whatever she may say. Now, how did your visit at the mantua-maker's go?"

Thus distracted, Mother soon regained her amiability. But, Clara thought with misgiving, for how long?

The following day, Clara and her mother were surprised by a group of visitors in the drawing room. Barely had Mother begrudgingly permitted Meg to advise they were at home — and thus receiving visitors — then the door had opened once more to admit Matilda's family.

"Clara!"

Before she knew it, she was enveloped in a hug. She tentatively wrapped her arms around Tessa. Hugs had never been the pattern in her family. "You have been in my prayers and thoughts," she murmured.

"Oh, thank you." Tessa's clasp intensified.

Clara peeked over her shoulder to see her mother's expression of horror. She held her friend longer. Poor girl. She understood only too well what it was to have your heart broken by a careless man. "It will get better, one day," she whispered. "I promise."

Tessa shuddered.

Clara pulled back. "It feels an age since I saw you." She glanced at the others, her heart racing as her gaze skimmed past Mr. Kemsley to land on the gentleman and young lady beside him. This must be the brother and his intended. She nodded. "Good morning."

Matilda performed the introductions. The baronet seemed not unimpressed by her father's title, although his manner seemed a little stiff and overly formal. She gathered he and Miss Amelia Windsor had heard something of her story, judging from the way they glanced at each other. Miss Windsor she found a little unprepossessing, a little too eager to please, as if she had finally found a gentleman willing to propose and daren't do a thing to make him wish to cry off.

Sympathy stirred within. How well she knew that desperate desire to impress, to hide her true thoughts in the hope the man she loved might continue to think well of her. She lowered her gaze, shame curdling the edges of her soul, remembering the girl who had blatantly praised everything about the earl as "wonderfully fine."

Sir George cleared his throat. "Miss

DeLancey, I understand that you have been honored with an invitation to play for the Prince Regent next week."

"I will be one of many, no doubt."

"Oh, my dear," said Mother, before breaking into an extended monologue as to why Clara was the most perfect candidate for such an evening, that indeed, the Prince Regent was the one who would be honored, as Clara's great talent . . .

His throat was cleared again. Tessa and Matilda's smiles suggested this was not an unusual way of his to capture attention. "Your maternal affection does you great credit, my lady, but I am sure Miss DeLancey understands just what an honor this is."

"Thank you, Sir George," Clara murmured. "I assure you I am made aware of this almost hourly."

She caught the flicker of amusement crossing Mr. Kemsley's features, laughter mirrored in the faces of his sisters, before they, too, resumed their masks of polite indifference as Sir George delivered a near homily espousing his preference for the conventional and staid.

After the quarter hour deemed suitable for such visits concluded, their guests left, but not before Clara managed to whisper to

Tessa the hope of talking privately soon.

Tessa's eyes lit. "I would like that more than anything!"

"Perhaps after services on Sunday? I could meet you, and we could walk along the beach."

"Oh, yes!"

So it was arranged, and Clara returned to soothe her mother's ruffled sensibilities about being preyed upon by social climbing nobodies from the back of nowhere.

And to quiet the disappointment within, and the questions of why Mr. Kemsley had barely looked at or spoken to her at all.

Two days later

The Sunday service was still on her mind as Clara hurried along Marine Parade, trailed by an unwilling Meg. Her parents took the notion of a day of rest literally, so escaping the house had not been problematic. Meg was used to having half Sundays off, so Clara foresaw little trouble in getting rid of her once she had provided an element of propriety and escorted Clara to the shore.

The service had been about forgiveness, the sermon preached by Matilda's husband causing Clara to look into her heart and cringe. How much resentment had she kept in her heart over the years? Whilst she may have recently released the pain over the earl and Lavinia, still she held on to so much more. Some people, like Matilda and Mr. Kemsley, seemed immune to resentment; slights seemed to roll off their backs like water droplets from an oilskin parasol. But Clara, like her mother, seemed made of different stuff, and slights and offenses had always left a permanent stain on her soul, like rain-spotted silk. She wanted to change. Knew she *needed* to change. So in the prayer time after the preaching, she'd asked God to help her once again.

Later, while the congregation milled around, she'd managed to escape her parents for a brief moment to speak with Tessa and thus arrange more precisely the time and destination for their private meeting. Afterward she'd encountered Lady Osterley's hard gaze, but instead of feeling anxiety as she usually had, today she'd felt more free, so free she'd even smiled a genuine smile at her, which had taken that lady by surprise as she'd blinked, blushed, then turned away. Perhaps forgiveness was linked to choosing to be kind to one's enemies. Or perhaps it was simply realizing that each person had their own struggles and challenges, and one could choose to treat them with a hard heart or with compassion. Having realized for herself just how much unmerited favor she'd been shown — by Lavinia, by Lady Sefton, by Matilda, by God Himself! — surely it behooved her to show some of that grace to others.

Smiling to herself, Clara continued her walk. The day was sunny, the waves were glistening, her heart felt lighter than it had in years. She was going to play for the Prince Regent! Excitement rippled within. She had chosen her piece; something technically challenging yet well within her range. Her new gown from Madame Sabine — Brighton's finest mantua-maker — was to be delivered tomorrow, ready for any final alterations. Everything felt in readiness. Everything felt full of possibility. Even the fact Mr. Kemsley was in town —

No. She tamped down *that* overly exuberant thought. She would not stir up feelings for a man her parents would never approve. Had he a title or some money, they might be persuadable, but he had neither, so although she now believed God could do miracles, she highly doubted He would care to waste another one on her.

They arrived at the steps to the beach, where Clara dismissed the maid, whose look of speculation demanded Clara's rather forceful, "Oh, look, there is Tessa waiting

319

for me. Thank you, Meg. Enjoy the rest of your day."

"Very good, miss," Meg muttered, before disappearing.

Clara hurried down the steps, stretching out her hands. "Tessa."

"Oh, Clara! However did you get away?"

She explained, and Tessa nodded, gesturing to an indistinct figure down the far end of the beach. "Benjie is my escort, but he understands I wished to have a private word with you, and he did not wish to intrude."

Clara swallowed. "That is very thoughtful."

"He *is* very thoughtful."

They walked along the beach, the thousands of tiny stones and sea-washed pebbles making their progression slow at times as pieces landed in their slippers, requiring frequent stops to shake them out. As they walked they talked, Tessa sharing a little about her disappointment with the viscount, before going on to say, somewhat shamefacedly, something of what he had said concerning Miss DeLancey's own situation.

"But I knew you didn't feel the same way anymore, so I realized that even if you had once felt that way about Lord Hawkesbury, somehow you had managed to overcome such feelings." Tessa's eyes shimmered with unspent tears. "I want to know how, because I cannot seem to shake this feeling. It feels like he is a part of me, living here," she said, clutching at her breast.

Tessa's tears forced her to leave aside the intriguing question of just how Tessa knew Clara no longer cared for the earl — had she seen something? Had Mr. Kemsley said something? — to focus on the matter at hand. She placed her shawl on the ground and they sat on it, shoulders touching.

"I did not handle things very well," she admitted finally. "For a long, long time I was eaten with envy, eaten up with hatred for Lord Hawkesbury and for Lavinia, for I was convinced he had used me to make her jealous. In truth I was so full of pride I did not realize for the longest time that he'd cared for her months before circumstances made me think he cared for me. His mother and mine were friends from years ago and had orchestrated a union without consulting either of us. I'd had a few seasons and thought the earl better than any gentleman I'd come across but had reckoned without him. Loving someone who does not love you in return is a very hard thing to overcome."

She swallowed. Should she dare be this honest? Oh, why not? She sensed Tessa would respond more to the whole truth than just a partial truth. "When they got married, Lord Featherington was correct, I did not act appropriately and embarrassed myself and the Hawkesburys too many times to remember. That was part of what I apologized to Lady Hawkesbury about at the Seftons'."

"I knew it must be that!" Tessa cried. "I did not believe you could be arguing with her."

"But" — Clara swallowed again — "it was not difficult for others to believe, because I . . . I have not been very kind in the past."

"Well, you are kind now, and that's all that matters."

Clara's eyes burned. How sweet was this girl? "You did not know me well before. Back before I knew the hope God offers, I had" — she swallowed again — "I had reached the point when I wondered if there was any point in living."

She heard Tessa's soft gasp.

"I used to take walks along the top of the cliffs and imagine what it would be like to fall. Would anyone miss me? Would the earl be sorry? I realize now just how prideful and selfish was my thinking, but when I was trapped within myself I could barely see, much less care, about anyone else and how my actions might affect them."

Tessa clasped her hand, giving Clara courage to continue. "When I was at my blackest, I took a walk on a wild and windy night. I had a game I used to play, where I would lean into the wind and feel its power hold me upright. That night I got too close to the edge." Tessa's hand tightened on hers. "Fortunately I was rescued, and in that moment of falling I knew I did not wish to die. Not like that, not before I'd ever really lived."

"Someone rescued you?"

Should she admit the identity of her rescuer? Wouldn't it just make Tessa see romance and roses, when such a thing would not benefit either of them? Better let him remain a mystery. She nodded. "A man. I wondered if he might be a fisherman from around here." It wasn't a lie. She had wondered that before she knew. Better change the subject, quickly.

"My point is, I despaired because of an absence of hope. I did not realize then just how much God loves us and that His love means we can have hope. It was not long afterward that I met you and Mattie, and through attending services and reading the Bible, I found real hope again. Hope that was not dependent on my circumstances or whether a man loved me or not, but hope that rested on the promises that God loves me regardless of my situation. And if I know that God loves me, if I really know that, then how can I let despair overcome me again?"

She peeked across. Tessa's red-gold head was bowed, as if in serious thought.

Clara gently squeezed her hand again. "My feelings for the earl disappeared in time. Absence helped, along with praying for God to bless him and his wife and for their marriage to succeed. Praying blessings over those I once considered my enemies seems to have lightened my heart no end."

"You think I should pray for the viscount?"

"Pray for him and his family, and ask God to take away those feelings which are not beneficial, to help you treat him as you would your brother, if that be what God intends."

Tessa sighed. "The problem is, my brother and I are quite close."

Clara caught her glimmering smile. Her heart thumped. "I gather you refer to Mr. Kemsley."

"Benjie, yes. George, no. I think it difficult for anyone to get close to him. I wonder how Amelia managed it."

Clara could not answer.

Tessa turned to her, a speculative look in her eye. "So your feelings for the earl have quite passed?"

"Yes."

"That's good, for I would hate to think —" The younger girl smiled.

"Hate to think what, Tessa?"

A shadow fell across them. Clara squinted up, the sun's bright glare making it impossible to see. She peered a moment longer, before her heart thudded wildly. "Mr. Kemsley!"

Ben caught her pinked cheeks before he bowed. "Miss DeLancey, Tessa. I trust you have enjoyed your talk?"

The two ladies looked at each other, sharing a smile that made him wish he knew their secrets. He had his suspicions, but how he prayed Miss DeLancey might one day trust him enough to see him a fit recipient for her confidence.

"Talking with Clara has helped me enormously," Tessa finally said.

"I'm glad," he said, words softly echoed by Miss DeLancey.

She looked at him, then ducked her gaze as if embarrassed. His heart hammered. Was she as disconcerted by his presence as he was by hers?

325

"I am sorry to intrude, but as it's been nearly an hour, I thought it best to interrupt before your absence is noted."

"Oh, you are right." Miss DeLancey looked around. He bent to retrieve her slippers and handed them to her. Her blush deepening in hue, she murmured a thank-you and slipped them on without a word.

Tessa eyed him defensively. "We were warm, and the stones kept getting in."

"I said nothing."

"You *looked* something," she said, her suspicious pose sliding into a smirk.

Now he needed to hide the heat he could feel crawling up his neck. He extended a hand, helped up his sister, before reaching for Miss DeLancey's hand.

Her gaze finally met his, her eyes lit with an emotion he could not discern. The hand she gave him was small, delicate, making him wish to hold hers even longer. Once she was on her feet, he refused to let go, pressing his thumb to her gloved palm a moment longer. "Thank you, Miss DeLancey." He nodded toward Tessa, staring at the glassy sea, and continued quietly, "Your kindness is appreciated."

The green eyes widened, then blinked. "You . . . you are welcome." She drew her hand away, waiting as he collected her shawl and presented it to her. "Thank you, sir."

Again, another moment lit with magic flashed between them. She seemed to shimmer with muted joy, with golden possibility, her concern for his sister making her appear even more lovely to him, more serene, more mature somehow. Something jolted inside, the features he had long admired altering fractionally, as if finally providing recognition of the one person he'd waited to meet all his life. His pulse drummed loudly. Perhaps it was just the sparkle of sea, or the heat of the day, but all he wanted was to sail the high seas into the sunset with her.

They walked back to the steps carved in the cliffs, and he helped them both ascend. Not a word passed between them as they turned to walk toward the Royal Crescent; it was as if they'd strolled this way a hundred times before, and nothing needed to be said.

Tessa held his left arm, Miss DeLancey held his right. A sense of contentment washed through him. This was right, was good. All was exactly as it ought —

"Miss DeLancey?"

An older lady accompanied by a foppish young man stopped before them, peering between the three of them. Beside him, he felt Miss DeLancey's hand tighten, before she slipped it from his forearm and curtsied.

"Lady Osterley, Lord Osterley."

"I must confess to no small element of surprise at seeing you out this afternoon."

"It is a lovely day," Clara said. "Much too nice to spend indoors, which must be why you are taking advantage of it, as well."

"Hmph." The lady eyed him speculatively, prompting Miss DeLancey to perform the introductions.

"May I present Mr. and Miss Kemsley."

"Kemsley? I seem to have heard that name before."

"You probably have," Clara continued. "Mr. Kemsley captained the *Ansdruther,* you might recall." His arm tingled as she returned to rest her hand there and squeezed gently. "He is considered quite the hero."

She smiled up at him, her eyes lit with gladness, and something — dare he hope? — akin to pride. Suddenly he felt a hundred feet tall, stronger, like he could brave an ocean for her, swim the Channel if she so desired, her smile warming the weary corners of his heart.

The sound of a cleared throat brought his attention back to the gaping pedestrians. Ben offered them a bow. "Forgive me. We must return. No doubt Miss DeLancey requires her rest before her performance at the Pavilion later this week."

A murmur of goodbyes and they were again on their way.

Tessa squeezed his arm. "You managed her very well, Benjie. I do not think she quite knew what to make of you."

"I seem to have that effect sometimes."

Beside him, he heard a smothered giggle from Clara. He looked a question at her; she simply smiled and glanced away.

Upon finally reaching her door they exchanged farewells, and he was able to offer his best wishes for the performance. "I am sure you will dazzle them appropriately."

"Thank you. I fear I've dazzled inappropriately quite long enough, so I hope you are right."

He laughed, caught her smile, before the door shut between them.

As they returned to West Street, he noticed Tessa's pleased expression. "So your time together was beneficial?"

"Oh yes! Clara is so kind, was so open."

Curiosity burned within. He would not ask. He would remain the gentleman.

"I know she would not mind me telling you this, but —"

"Tessa, no —"

"But she is *completely* over the earl. The to-do with Lady Hawkesbury that Lord Featherington was so adamant about was nothing more than Clara apologizing and the countess offering friendship."

Something eased within his heart. "I am glad to hear it."

"I thought you might be," she said complacently.

He stopped. "What does that mean?"

"Oh, Benjie! It means, when are you finally going to admit your feelings towards her?"

"I have no feelings," he lied.

She snorted.

"Tessa."

"Please, Benjie? For your sake, as well as hers. You are so well suited, both so kind to others, sharing faith, and a sense of humor. And you cannot deny that you find her attractive." She giggled. "Oh, don't look so embarrassed! Just tell me, what will it take for you to make her an offer?"

He shook his head. "I cannot."

"Because you have little in the way of finances? But surely you can speak to the Prince Regent. He is newly arrived, is he not? It should not be so very hard."

"It is not that easy. Besides, it is not only a lack of finances to which her parents would object."

"You mean you lack a title."

"Yes," he gritted out.

She sighed. "I wish you'd been born first. If you had the baronetcy, then maybe they would see sense. And I'd much rather Clara as a sister-in-law than Amelia. I'm sure Amelia is virtuous and all, but she's not particularly forthcoming. She'd never be so honest as to tell me about —" She clapped a hand to her mouth, looking at him with wide eyes. "I nearly told you."

"I gathered as much," he said, smiling.

She frowned a little. "She'd most certainly not want me to mention that."

He wouldn't ask. He clenched his teeth. He would *not.*

They turned the corner into the Steyne and strolled past the Marine Pavilion, already showing signs building work had commenced. They ambled through the lush gardens, past the Dome, the spectacular Moorish structure seemingly more suitable for an oriental temple of worship than for stabling for horses, adorned with fanciful minarets and glass. Little wonder the Prince Regent wanted a magnificent summer palace to match his horse accommodation.

Ben glanced down at Tessa, a study in concentration, biting her lower lip. She peeked up at him. "You remember that very windy night in April when you were out? When you came back, I heard you and Mattie talking."

He ruffled her bright hair. "I knew you had big ears."

She shook her head. "You saved someone, didn't you? Someone on a cliff."

Despite the sunshine, coldness stole over him.

"You led her to believe it was an old lady you saved."

"It was a dark, wild night," he said cautiously. "I could not see clearly."

"It wasn't an old lady, was it?"

He paused a long moment, his heart hammering within him. "I believe not, no."

They turned around the corner. Crossed into King.

"In fact, the lady is quite pretty, isn't she?"

"I think so, yes." He didn't have to ask how she knew. They'd just escorted her home.

Tessa shook her head. "How could she —"

"She was desperate."

"She's better now." Tessa looked at him directly.

He swallowed. "Yes, I know."

And thinking on all that remained unspoken, they returned home.

CHAPTER TWENTY-ONE

Friday arrived, clear and bright. Following Mother's advice, Clara had forgone a final practice to avoid straining her voice, eaten a light repast — for one never knew what nourishment might be on offer, let alone at what time — and succumbed to the efforts of the hairdresser and Meg, who'd helped her dress, before descending the stairs to the carriage hired for the evening.

Clara caught a glimpse of her reflection in the hall mirror and paused. Was that really her? How long had it been since she felt so beautiful? The muted red of her gown seemed to enhance her coloring; the coral beads at her throat modest, yet of the highest quality. She touched her hair. The hairdresser hired for the evening had done wonders, twirling and braiding her hair into a Grecian style.

"Clara?"

She hurried to join her parents in the carriage, settling her skirts on the seat, smoothing her cream gloves around the elbow, admiring again her gown's ruched silk sleeves that perfectly matched the elegantly trimmed low bodice and hemline. It was not excessively adorned — Father's finances could only stretch so far, after all — but Madame Sabine knew how to best flatter a lady's figure, and Clara couldn't help feel a trace of wistfulness that Mr. Kemsley would not see her look so well.

As the carriage rolled along Marine Parade, nerves tapped within her, her pulse a hurried patter in her veins. She held her reticule tightly. What would tonight hold?

"Now, there is no need to be nervous, my dear. Just remember, the Prince holds great fondness for music, which naturally extends to those who are able to execute music well. You only need to play as well as you have in the past, and you will succeed most admirably."

"I will try."

Her mother nodded, eyeing her as light flickered from the oil lamps lining the road. "I must say, you are in your best looks tonight, my dear."

"Thank you, Mother." She savored the compliment. Mother's praise was hard won.

"Now just remember to smile, and flatter

the Prince. It never does for one to return a compliment too slowly."

"Yes, Mother."

Clara exchanged amused looks with her father, whose contribution to tonight had consisted chiefly of financing their gowns. His interest lay more in seeing the Pavilion, whose interiors were said to be a spectacle worth admission as much as any tourist destination such as London's Tower.

The carriage turned into the Steyne, then rounded a corner into a long graveled drive, then slowed as they joined the queue of carriages. The footman descended, was now opening the door. Father exited first, then Mother, then Clara.

A swirl of evening air lifted the scent of roses and lilies from the gardens. Ahead of her, in the porte cochere, a scarlet-clad footman stood at the double doors, waving them to follow the other guests up the shallow steps and inside.

She paused on the threshold, eyes widening in wonder.

The reception room was octagonal in shape, with a ceiling plastered to resemble the sumptuous interior of a tent. A painted Chinese-style glass lantern hung from the ceiling, emitting a soft glow to the peach-blossom walls. Scattered around the sides were several chairs, also of Oriental design. Conscious of those behind her, she hurried forward, joining her parents as they presented the gilt-edged, engraved card of invitation. If this was merely the entrance chamber, what exotic decadence lay beyond?

They passed into the next room, painted a cool shade of green. Her breath caught. Panels of serpents and dragons adorned the walls, giving the room a muted though somewhat menacing feel. She noted a grand piano in the corner. Was this where she was meant to play?

Clara murmured the question to her mother, who shushed her, with a whispered, "I believe we are to go farther."

Go farther? She took a deep breath and followed the footmen.

"Ladies and gentlemen, the Long Gallery."

She gasped.

The restrained palette of the previous room had given way to an explosion of color, the room richly decorated in reds and gold. The Oriental influence was all the more clearly seen, with tasseled lanterns competing for attention with life-size figures of Mandarin-robed men. The walls were papered in a delicate design of bamboo and birds, while large urns and a great painted central chandelier added to the ambience. The room seemed to stretch forever, until one of the end doors was opened, and the illusion revealed to be one made by the strategic placement of mirrors.

"It is fantastic!" she murmured to Father.

"It is certainly not in any way restrained," he muttered.

Similar comments could be heard from the clutches of guests around them.

"Marvelous!"

"Astounding."

"Bizarre."

"Most un-English."

Clara smiled. The latter comment sounded like something she imagined Tessa's brother George might say; he'd made his disapproval of the unorthodox quite plain during his visit. She wondered what Mr. Kemsley would make of it.

For herself, she wasn't sure if she liked such dazzling decoration. It almost hurt her senses. She supposed it was designed to overwhelm, but the excess of the bizarre and the garish drew the gaze too quickly, not allowing time to peruse at leisure, and left her feeling somewhat unsettled.

She glanced around at the other guests. She recognized no one; her parents recognized few more. It seemed the Prince Regent's guest list comprised not just the aristocracy, but also those who, for whatever reason, had piqued his interest.

Finally a figure she did recognize made her smile with relief. "Lord Houghton!"

"Ah, Miss DeLancey." He bowed and greeted her parents. "I am so glad you are here. Tell me, what do you think of the place?"

What could she say? "It is certainly magnificent."

"Enough to make you faint? Some ladies have, you know."

Should a building really make one faint? Such a thing certainly did not seem hospitable.

"There will be refreshments soon. The Prince will be along shortly. He's in the Saloon." He smiled. "Perhaps I might be able to show it to you one of these days."

She nodded, her thoughts awhirl in confusion. Wasn't she only here for one visit? Surely any further visit would be dependent on how well tonight's performance went. The blood pulsing in her ears rushed even faster.

Lord Houghton moved away, and footmen began bringing around trays of filled glasses. Clara sought the lemonade, certain the punch would not be conducive for the clear head she needed in order to perform at her best. After what seemed an age, when her legs were growing weary, the end doors were finally opened, and another footman strode forth. He murmured something to Lord Houghton, who turned to address the guests.

"Ladies and gentlemen, may I request that you accompany me to the Yellow Drawing Room."

The guests moved, their murmurings displaying the excitement Clara felt. Her moment was nearly arrived. They were herded, sheeplike, into a bright golden room, again dressed in fanciful chinoiserie fashion, with lanterns hung from plaster dragons, and white-and-golden furniture. Patterns of interlocked circles hung between green-and-gold silk drapes. Although not as visually demanding as the Long Gallery, there was still quite enough to draw the senses and make her long for a chair. A fainting miss she'd never thought herself, but the Pavilion certainly made her weak at the knees.

A door to the left opened, and at once the assembled company bowed. A most magnificently attired man drew near, his girth and regal countenance proclaiming him to be their host, the Prince Regent.

Clara gave her deepest curtsy, harkening back to the days of her presentation to his mother, Queen Charlotte.

The Prince drew closer, closer, his murmurs of welcome accompanying Lord Houghton's hushed words of introduction. Still she held her curtsy. Her left leg felt like it might start wobbling when finally she spied a pair of gilded shoes. Her breath caught as she heard her parents introduced. Now it was her turn.

"And this is the Honorable Miss DeLancey. She is here to play at Lady Sefton's behest."

"And one must do whatever that good lady commands, mustn't one? Rise child, you look as though you might topple over any moment."

Clara pushed herself upright, and met a merry pair of rather protuberant blue eyes.

Those eyes opened a little wider. "Well, you are a pretty thing, aren't you?"

She smiled despite her nerves. What was she to say to such a comment? "Thank you, Your Highness."

"Oh, don't thank me. Thank Lady Sefton and Lord Houghton here; he's the one who thinks you should be here. Now, tell me, is it pianoforte only, or do you sing as well?"

She swallowed. "I have come prepared for either, Your Highness."

"Good, good. Well, there's no need to look so nervous, my dear. I shall not eat you."

"I am glad, for I fear I would not taste so very well."

He laughed, a great booming sound that made heads turn their direction and her cheeks heat even more. His smile crinkled his eyes. "Well, I look forward to hearing you play. Anything you need, talk to Houghton here. Oh, and I hope you won't take offense if I should feel it necessary to join in. I am rather fond of a good song, you know."

"Of course, Your Highness."

"Good, good."

He moved on to greet the next guest, and Mother pulled her close, saying with shining eyes, "Oh, my dear! You seem to have taken his fancy, his *particular* fancy. He has not exchanged more than a dozen words with anyone else."

Clara eyed her mother sternly. "Mother, please do not think more of it than you ought. I am here to play music, not to provide any other type of entertainment."

"Clara!"

Mother's whisper carried around the room. Clara caught sight of her scarlet cheeks in the looking glass opposite, cheeks which nearly matched the color of her gown. She turned away, studying the intricately patterned Brussels carpet. Finally, when it seemed she could not stand any longer, the Prince finished making his rounds of greetings and chose a chair at the center and front of the room, and the assembly was finally permitted to sit.

Lord Houghton rose and outlined the order of proceedings. A number of others had been selected to play, mostly pianoforte, though the large harp waiting suggested musicians accomplished to play that also. Clara was announced the fourth name of seven, giving her several performances to learn the correct protocol — whilst giving her several performances to grow all the more nervous.

Finally Lady Mansfield finished her sonata and it was Clara's turn. Her hands were shaking, and she forced a wobbly smile as her parents wished her well, patting her arm as she moved past. She walked to the rosewood grand pianoforte, bobbed a curtsy to the future king, and sat down on the brass-inlaid stool.

Nerves thrummed within and without. She cast a quick look at the gathered assembly. Apart from her parents and the Prince, who were leaning forward, as if in anticipation, the others sat with expressions of hauteur, expressions with which she was all too familiar. Some of them seemed to sneer, as if to say, who is this young person? Others eyed her more knowingly, as if aware of her reputation. She swallowed. Attempted a smile. Turned back to the piano. Lifted her hands.

Lord God, help me. Use me for Your purpose.

And she began to play.

The rich tone of the piano seemed to roll through her fingertips. She completed a run, felt her shoulders relax, the very movement giving ease within. She may never have played in front of royalty before, but this, *this* she had done so often she could almost do so in her sleep. And she opened her mouth and sang.

An hour later, she was once again being congratulated, the Prince's smile and clasping of her hands all the signal needed to show she had succeeded far beyond her mother's highest expectations. Lord Houghton only confirmed it as he drew near, smile stretching across his face.

"My dear Miss DeLancey! What a hit you have made! The Regent just told me he has scarcely heard such talent in one so young.

He trusts you can be persuaded to come again?"

"Oh!" She glanced at her parents, nodding enthusiastically. "Yes, of course."

"Wonderful! We're having a little soiree here next Friday. I trust you'll be free to attend?"

"If we weren't we soon would be," gushed her mother, her smile as bright and broad as Clara had ever seen.

"Wonderful. We're expecting quite a few; tonight was rather more intimate." His glance lingered on Clara. Her skin prickled. His smile widened. "I trust you will not mind performing for a larger audience?"

"N-not at all."

"Good. I imagine there will be a few more of your acquaintances here. The Seftons, of course, the Asquiths, the Exeters, and the like."

"The Marquess of Exeter?"

Lord Houghton waved a careless hand. "One of them at least. Could be the son? I cannot recall."

Could she? Dare she? Nervousness quivered through her. Surely if she . . .

"Lord Houghton" — she licked her bottom lip — "I wonder if I might ask you something."

Her parents were distracted, being congratulated by Lady Mansfield and congratulating her in return. When Lord Houghton nodded, she moved a little aside to avoid being overheard. "I know this is awfully untoward, but I wondered if the Regent would mind if I were to have a friend accompany me next week?"

"Is she young and pretty?"

She blinked. Nodded.

"Then of course he would not mind." He leaned close. "He only minds when they're old and hag-like. Much harder to flirt with, then."

She managed to nod, smile, and thank him, before remembering snippets of an overheard conversation. "Oh!"

"Something else I can help you with?" He raised a brow. "Perhaps further advice on which music the Regent particularly favors?"

She gave him her best smile. "No, thank you. But I do appreciate your thoughtfulness. I'm sure you help so many people in so many different ways."

"Another favor's price cancelled by flattery. What else can I do for you, Miss DeLancey?"

"My friend would probably feel more comfortable in the company of her brother."

"I see. And whom might this brother be?"

She told him.

He eyed her curiously, before saying slowly, "I will see what I can do."

"Thank you, Lord Houghton." She beamed at him.

He studied her a moment longer before nodding again and taking his leave. She watched him walk away, hope humming in her heart. Perhaps her appearance tonight was mere practice for the real performance to be held next week.

CHAPTER TWENTY-TWO

"How was it? Was it extremely magnificent? Did the Prince talk to you? What is he like?"

Clara looked around at the eager faces. The Sunday service seemed but the precursor to their reporting of the night before last. Mother's loud account of the night had surrounded her with eager listeners. Clara's gaze settled on Tessa. "Have you not seen him before?"

"Never. But I'm told he can be most gracious when he likes somebody."

Somehow Clara's gaze strayed to Mr. Kemsley. His expression, unlike the others, was grave, as if he disagreed with the general verdict. Her heart panged, remembering what those ladies had said at the Sefton ball. Of course he would feel so, if it were true the Prince had not fulfilled his promise of reward. She forced her gaze to lower, to listen as the others praised the Regent's magnanimity.

"Of course, he wasn't so very kind to all those mistresses, leaving them with all those children."

"Perhaps his morals should not be discussed in front of Theresa," George said, with a warning frown.

"That's right, George," his youngest sister said. "Continue in your assumption that I am completely unaware of anything."

Clara bit her lip. Somehow she had to let Tessa know that Lord Featherington would be in Brighton soon. Good heavens; he might be in town now! He did not seem the type to mind travelling on Sunday.

"Miss DeLancey?"

She spun around. Smiled. "Lord Houghton! How lovely to see you again."

"And you."

As they exchanged bow and curtsy, she noticed Mr. Kemsley eyeing the Chamberlain with a frown. She smiled to herself. Just wait until Lord Houghton revealed what she hoped he was about to say.

The older man glanced at her friends, his gaze resting on Tessa a moment before Clara remembered herself and performed the introductions. He nodded to Matilda, George, and Amelia, before smiling at Tessa again. It was hardly to be wondered at, for really, Tessa looked the perfect picture of sweet innocence, Clara thought.

"Miss Kemsley?"

"Yes, my lord?"

"Meeting you today has proved most propitious." He held out a small envelope to a collective gasp. "His Highness, the Prince Regent requests your company at an evening party this coming Friday night."

"My company?" Tessa paled.

"Her company?" George frowned.

"Yes." Lord Houghton turned to Mr. Kemsley and proffered a second envelope. "And yours also, Captain Kemsley."

"Mine?" Sandy eyebrows shot almost to his hairline.

"His?" George demanded.

"Yes," said Lord Houghton, offering Clara a small smile before turning to thread his way through the crowd.

"What?" George said, snatching the envelope from Tessa's hand. "I cannot believe the Prince . . ." His frown grew more pronounced as he read the invitation. "I don't understand! Why should Tessa of all people be invited to the Pavilion?"

Matilda met Clara's gaze, her brow furrowed. "I have heard Prinny likes to flirt with pretty ladies. Did you encounter anything of the like?"

Clara could not help but notice Mr.

Kemsley's head rise at that. She kept her gaze firmly fixed on Matilda. "He was all that was kind and gracious."

Mattie still seemed worried. "But I cannot like it. She is so young, and it will be quite overwhelming. Did you have any idea of such an honor?"

Clara could not admit to the truth. Admit she'd practically begged their invitations? No. "I'm sure it must be some consolation for Mr. Kemsley to have also been invited."

"I'm afraid I do not understand this, either," he said, frowning. "He has ignored my letters for months, then to receive a summons to the Pavilion? It seems most peculiar."

"I cannot fathom how they could invite you when the person who by all rights should have been invited was me," complained George.

"Perhaps the Prince wishes to recognize your brother's heroism, Sir George," Clara murmured.

He eyed her narrowly but did not speak.

Tessa had gone from white to pink to white again. Clara moved closer to hold her hand. "If it's any comfort, I shall be attending also."

"Oh, you will?" Tessa said, eyes huge. "Oh, that makes me feel so much better!"

"But where would we get the right attire?" Mattie wrung her hands. "We cannot send Tessa dressed in anything less than appropriate!"

Clara looked directly at George. "I imagine the head of the family would not wish for his sister to be so disgraced?"

He cleared his throat. "I . . . er . . ."

"I thought as much," she smiled sweetly. "If you like, I can take Tessa with me tomorrow to Madame Sabine, who I assure you is quite the best modiste to be found. She will be sure to know exactly how best to dress such a beautiful young lady."

"But the cost!" he spluttered. "She will cost a small fortune!"

"Is that not what you possess?" Clara tilted her head, working to ignore Matilda's barely smothered laughter. "I assure you, none of the ladies I saw on Friday evening wore anything less than their best. And I assure you their best was never what might be called . . . provincial."

"But . . . but —"

"Then it's settled." Clara patted Tessa on the shoulder. "I will come to collect you tomorrow at ten. You need not worry, for Madame Sabine is a sweet dear, even if she does pretend to be French." She glanced at Mr. Kemsley and held out her hand. "I trust you will not risk offending the future King of England by refusing to attend?"

His face still held traces of confusion, but he grasped her hand warmly. "I don't know what to say. I suspect some sort of trickery, but I dare not speculate as to the source."

She forced herself to meet his gaze. "Probably wisest not to."

He nodded; a twinkle appeared in his eye, then disappeared. He leaned closer, still holding her hand. "Would you be so kind as to advise *me* on what attire I should wear?"

"I'm sure that is a question best put to the head of the family."

And amid a chorus of laughter, she made her exit and was gone.

"Is it true?" Mother demanded, when they arrived home.

"Is what true, Mother?"

"That the Kemsley chit is also going to the Pavilion next Friday?"

"She received an invitation, so I gather it must be."

Mother frowned. "This did not have anything to do with your speaking to Lord Houghton last Friday did it?"

"Me?" Clara opened her eyes wide. "Surely you do not suppose the Prince Regent would take notice of an insignificant person like myself?"

"It just seems a trifle strange that one moment you are speaking to Lord Houghton, and the next moment two people who would normally escape Royal notice are being invited to such a select assembly."

"I hardly think it will be select, Mother. You saw the people last Friday. Many ordinary Misses and Misters were there. I imagine this will be much the same. Besides, you cannot forget that Mr. Kemsley was hardly unknown to the Prince. After all, wasn't he mentioned by name by the Prince in all those newspaper accounts long ago?"

"Well, yes, but —"

"I understand the Regent made rather grand promises about rewarding his heroic deed, do you not recall?"

Her father, to whom this appeal was made, nodded. "I believe so."

Clara turned back to her mother. "I hope the Prince will see fit to finally reward him for saving all those people's lives."

"Well, he does deserve something, I suppose."

"I should rather think he does." Clara took a breath and continued. "Did you know he spent a great deal of his prize money in helping the wounded and the families of those sailors under his command who died?"

"I . . . no. I did not."

"Surely such a generous-hearted individual deserves some sort of recompense, especially when the Prince has declared he would do so."

Father sat up a little straighter, placed his newspaper down. "Now you mention it, I don't think he received any compensation, did he?"

"Matilda says not, which I think a real shame."

"You seem to take an untoward interest in the welfare of this young man, Clara."

"I only wish for what is right, that justice may be served."

"Do you?"

Mother's straight look brought heat to her cheeks. "I am sorry, Mother, if you would prefer me to find him unattractive, but I cannot find him so. He has always behaved in a manner most gentlemanly, and I would not have you think that because his people are not titled as ours that he is somehow to be considered less worthy. Surely you would not prefer us to be aligned with people of lesser values, such as the Osterleys, even if their lineage might be considered more socially acceptable?"

Mother shuddered. "I find I cannot abide that woman."

"Surely character is more important than one's breeding?"

"Yes . . . but one's breeding is supposed to bring about good character."

"Like Richard?"

Her mother blanched.

The words had slipped out before she thought, but really, what argument could there be in the face of her brother's scandalous actions? Bred from aristocracy, sent to the best schools, surrounded by wealth and luxury, still he had chosen to turn to gambling and theft to support his lifestyle.

"I am sorry if you do not wish me to speak of him, but his actions have reflected badly on us all. I cannot wish for you to think ill of a person whose actions have only brought help to so many."

"You talk as if you know this Captain Kemsley well. How do we know —"

"He saved my life."

"What?" Mother sank into a chair, eyes agog. "What do you mean?"

"I mean he saved my life. He stopped me from falling from a cliff several months ago."

"What? Why have we not heard of this until now?" Father growled.

"Because I was too embarrassed. At first I

did not think he recognized me, and as I did not want to bring it to his attention, I thought it best to leave such things forgotten."

"Forgotten? To forget that someone saved your life?" Mother fanned herself. "What on earth were you doing that he needed to save your life?"

"I . . ." Clara's cheeks heated. No need to tell them all. "I was standing too close to the edge and started to slip, and he caught me before I fell."

"Oh my dear!" Mother paled even more, as though she might faint. "Oh, I think I need my smelling salts."

Clara rushed to collect them from her mother's room. When she returned, her parents were talking quietly. They looked up as she entered, their faces matched pictures of worry and dismay.

"We cannot like it, Clara. We cannot like that you have kept this from us all this time."

"I am sorry."

"Neither can we like that we have been in this young man's debt and treated him less than we ought."

A tremor of hope lit within. Her parents' endorsement had hardly been what she'd been after when she'd first proposed Mr. Kemsley's invitation to the Pavilion. She'd merely wanted to see if it was possible for further restitution for him. "I am sure that if you are pleasant to him, then he will understand you do not hold him in contempt."

"Hold him in contempt? Surely he would not have thought so!"

"Social climbing nobodies from the back of nowhere?" Clara said, with a raised brow.

"Well, we never said that to his face!" Mother declared.

"I never said it at all," Father said.

"Please, I would like you to regard him for his own sake. And if you can come to appreciate his many good qualities as so many other people have, that would make me very happy."

Mother's look grew piercing. "Do you have feelings for this young man, Clara?"

Did she? It was pointless to lie. "I esteem him. I think him one of the finest young gentlemen I have ever come to know."

"That sounds more like affirmation than anything else." Her mother released a whinnying breath. "I suppose we shall have to get to know him."

"Thank you, Mother," Clara said, rushing to envelop her in a hug.

"Oh, my dear!"

But soon she felt her mother's arms surround her, and she rested her head against her mother's thin shoulder, reflecting this was the first time since she was a child she had felt her mother's affection in such a tangible way.

"Please, no more talk of Richard," her mother whispered. "Your father cannot bear that his only son turned out to be so weak."

"But one day, Mother, you know his sins will be discovered. There will be no escape for us, then."

Her mother sighed. "Just a little longer, that's all I ask."

Clara hugged her closer. Her mother could hope all she liked, but something told her that Richard, forever master of his own destiny, would once again take little notice of those around him, those with whom justice demanded he make restitution.

Ben adjusted the telescope, gazing out across the rooftops and roads to where the Channel glistened and gleamed beyond, a promise of cool refreshing for those brave enough to venture in. His heart snagged. It had been too long. Perhaps he should revisit those waters — though not as those in Brighton seemed to prefer, in one of those namby-pamby bathing boxes. No, give him the shore, and the waves, and the chance to dive like the seals he'd seen off the Cape of Good Hope. Back when he'd dreamed he might one day rise to commodore status. Back when his knee worked, and his prospects seemed sure.

How he wished his time as captain had not ended. He swallowed regret. But if he had not, he would not be here, forging closer bonds with his siblings. And he would not have found such a fine young lady to occupy his dreams. And he would certainly not have been invited to the Marine Pavilion as a guest of the future king.

A smile tugged at his lips. He did not know exactly why he'd been so honored with an invitation to the Prince Regent's gala. Only knew that his brother was livid, his sister panic-stricken, and his own emotions ranged between bewilderment and anticipation at the thought of spending the evening with the Honorable Clara De-Lancey. Really, it seemed nothing short of a dream, a delightful dream, where he could once again be the hero and save the fair maiden. Except this time, he had the strangest feeling the fair maiden was the one rescuing him.

The door to the cottage swung open, and Tessa swept in, her grin illuminating her face as much as George's deep scowl darkened his.

His brother collapsed heavily into a chair. "I cannot believe that woman."

"Which woman?" Mattie asked from her corner, placing her sewing down.

"Miss Clara DeLancey, that's who!"

"I believe she should be more correctly referred to as a young lady," Mattie chided.

"I don't care what she should be called. I know a word for her, and it's one that should not be repeated —"

"Enough!"

George caught Ben's narrowed gaze, sighed. "I forgot she has some hold over you."

"She has no hold over me, but I still take issue with you referring to her in that way."

"George," Tessa said, "I don't know how you can cast such aspersions. Clara was everything that was wonderful: so kind, so helpful."

"Yes, I know she was so kind and helpful. Kindly pointing out the most expensive fabrics, and so helpful in insisting it all had to be ready by Thursday at the latest, all for the special premium Madame Thingamy was so helpful in adding to the cost."

"I'm sure Tessa will look wonderful," said Mattie.

"I know I will," said Tessa complacently.

Ben bit back a grin as his brother covered his face with his hands. "I do not know what's come over you! What happened to modesty? Why can't you be content with less?"

"But you heard Madame. She said the clothes I wore were positively provincial! Surely you did not imagine my best ball gown appropriate for the Prince. It was made in Kent!"

Ben snickered. Mattie smiled. George groaned. "I wish you would take your lead from dear Amelia, and be satisfied with something less expensive."

"But I do not want to look a frump."

George's cheeks mottled. "Are you saying my Amelia is a frump?"

"I was not the one to just do so."

"Now, look here —"

"I am sorry, George, but I would rather take fashion advice from someone who is always elegant, and often one of the best dressed in the room. Why wouldn't I listen to Clara," Tessa continued, "especially when she has been to the Pavilion and been counted a success, and you have not even gone there?"

The head of the family growled something and stalked from the room. Ben finally released his pent-up laughter. "That was too bad of you, Tessa. You know he will act like a bear for the rest of the week."

"Are you sure choosing such expensive attire was completely necessary?" asked Mattie worriedly. "What if George refuses to pay?"

Tessa laughed. "Oh, Clara knows all the tricks. She told him Madame Sabine required a deposit of half the final sum immediately, with the balance to be paid on delivery. Of course, everybody knows that dressmakers are scarcely in a position to demand those kinds of arrangements, and often must survive on IOUs for months, but George obviously does not know as much as he thinks he does."

Mattie smiled. "So you really will be the belle of the ball?"

"Oh, Mattie! The gown is more magnificent than I could have dreamed! I feel like a princess in it! I know you thought me vainglorious earlier, but truly, when I looked at my reflection, with the color and my hair done the way Clara managed, I could scarcely recognize myself."

"Clara seems something of a fairy godmother," Mattie said.

"I'd rather her be something else," Tessa said, with a sideways look at Ben that made the tips of his ears heat. "Oh, and you know what else she did?"

"What?"

Tessa's face took on an unearthly glow. "She told me . . . the Exeters would be there."

"The Exeters?" Mattie asked.

"Lord Featherington's family."

"Oh!" Mattie sat back in her chair, exchanging glances with Ben. Suddenly the reason for their sister's transformation was most plain. If Tessa could be seen in her best possible light, in the presence of the most highly ranked member of the kingdom, surely any claim she'd laid on their son's heart would be deemed slightly more acceptable.

"Clara did this," Mattie said slowly. "She must have spoken to the Prince."

"Or at least that Houghton fellow." Ben's stomach tightened with unease. He had not cared for the way that man had looked at Clara, nor for that matter the way he'd gazed at Tessa, as though the two young ladies Ben cared most about in all the world were nothing but delicacies designed for consumption. He shook his head, faking a smile until Tessa had floated from the room.

He drew his chair closer to Mattie's. "Houghton seemed the sort of man who might expect something in return for a favor."

"Do you think so?" Mattie bit her lip. "I'm sure Clara would not have thought such a thing."

"She would not, but he . . ." He shook his head. "I cannot judge the man. I do not know him after all. But I cannot like the way he looked at her."

"At Tessa?"

Mattie's sharp gaze brought the heat to his cheeks again. "At both of them."

"Then isn't it good that Clara managed to get you included in said invitation?"

She'd done that for him. Somehow managed to inveigle an invitation for him, giving him opportunity perhaps to finally speak to the Prince Regent about that reward he'd once promised. "Yes. She is . . ."

"Considerate? Talented? Kindhearted? Lovely?"

"All of that." And beyond his touch. His spirits dipped.

"You shall have to be on your guard, though."

"Of course."

He gritted his teeth. He would certainly be on his guard — to protect both his sister and the young lady who'd laid claim to his heart from the Prince whose reputation as a

Lothario had long been known throughout
England.

CHAPTER TWENTY-THREE

Never had he imagined himself in such a venue. Ben glanced around the pale green antechamber into which they'd been waved after handing their invitations to a little man at the door. They had joined a long line waiting to be received by the Regent, giving Tessa and himself — and every other guest — plenty of time to be astounded by their surroundings.

The vestibule held a dragon and serpent motif, with the scaly creatures carved in wood panels and depicted on banners the same green as the wall.

The line surged forward, permitting view of the Chinese gallery, and the Prince Regent who stood near its doors, ready to welcome his guests as they entered. Ben eyed him as they waited. Magnificently attired, his girth was as impressive as the dazzling decor surrounding them. He swallowed, forcing down unaccustomed nerves.

Would the Regent listen? Would he even remember?

They drew a few steps closer. His heartbeat hammered loudly, like an ironmonger forging chains. Ben glanced at Tessa, whose open-mouthed countenance betrayed the wonder she felt. The Long Gallery, decorated in garish crimson and gold, was some strange concoction of Moorish and Chinese, like someone had seen a tracing of a Chinese temple and tried to emulate it here. It certainly bore little resemblance to what he remembered from his trips to the East — nothing seemed especially authentic. Yet put together, in this higgledy-piggledy mishmash of design, it somehow seemed to work.

A throat was cleared nearby. Ben gave their names to the servant, who announced them, and they were ushered into the presence of the Regent.

Tessa immediately sank into the deep curtsy painstakingly taught her by Clara, while Ben proffered a bow he hoped worthy.

"Mr. Kemsley. Oh, and Miss Kemsley. What a lovely addition you shall make to our party tonight, my dear."

The light filling the Regent's eye as he looked over Tessa appreciatively made Ben's heart sink a little. Before he could say another word the Regent had turned to the next guest, and they were forced to pass into the gallery proper.

He fought frustration. The Prince had given no sign of recognition at his name. And if it could be determined from the crowds, any chance of a private word had just been and gone.

Tessa squeezed his arm. "Do not worry. I'm sure there will be opportunity later. You are not so very forgettable, after all."

He hoped not, anyway. "You, at least, made an impression."

Ben wrestled with unease. Surely the Prince could have no design on Tessa. As for Lord Featherington . . . Would he indeed attend? And if so, what could Ben say after that last painful interview? He rather doubted the young viscount would even remember holding a candle for Tessa, which would no doubt devastate her, as evidenced by her excitement about seeing him again. But if Featherington had not forgotten her, if his character proved firm, then perhaps there was a chance. Ben muttered a prayer for her. If tonight brought about securing his sister's happiness, then dealing with his own disappointed hopes would be that much easier to bear.

Around them milled what seemed like hundreds of people, yet he was still to find the dark head that had lent wings to his feet and haste to his dress. He tamped down his impatience; she would be here soon. And in the time spent waiting, he would try to approximate the cool hauteur of these people so his gaucheness did not appear so marked.

He refrained from tugging at his coat sleeves or checking that his neckcloth remained neatly tied. While Tessa's gown was all that was lovely, he'd needed to resort to his old coat, and trust that new silk breeches and waistcoat would suffice. He'd never considered himself a vain man, but among such splendor, he couldn't help but wish to look well, as much for his sister's sake as for the honorable young lady he wished to impress.

Chinese banners and trophies were interspersed with bamboo couches that lined the walls. He nudged his sister, nodded to a tall pair of blue-and-white vases, two spots of calm amid the riot of bright colors. "Do you think Mattie should redecorate?"

Tessa lifted her face to his, her eyes huge. "It is amazing."

"I rather think that is the idea."

She glanced up, emitted another soft gasp. "Look!"

Halfway up the wall, a canopy carved to resemble the roofline of a Chinese pagoda curved gracefully to end in a row of bells. Above that, a series of painted windows, lit from without. And directly above them, an enormous lantern, suspended from a painted-glass ceiling. "Very Oriental."

"You do not like it?" she said in a whisper.

"I cannot say it accords to my taste."

She shook her head. "I do not know what to make of it, except" — her brow wrinkled — "it does not seem right that he should spend so much on this when he has not bothered to give you what you are due."

"Hush," he said. "We are not here for that."

"No?" Tessa arched an eyebrow in a way that made her seem suddenly so much more knowing than a seventeen-year-old had any right to be.

Or perhaps that was simply the effect of the gown she was wearing. Ben smiled at her, barely able to see his baby sister in the beautiful young lady before him. Dressed in the palest of sea greens, and with her hair intricately coiled atop her head and with her shining face, she made all the other ladies present seem either overly fussy or too plain. Her youth and beauty shone like a beacon in the sea of people, and he'd noticed more than one man put up his quizzing glass to eye her with an appreciative smile.

Conscious she still watched him, he drew her close again. "I think we both know why we are here."

As her cheeks tinted pink, Ben heard a muttered oath behind him, "Dashed fine pretty girl!"

Glancing over his shoulder, Ben spied an older gentleman, whose coat of many medals suggested he'd seen action in not a few wars. He was eyeing Tessa like a bulldog might eye a prime leg of lamb. Ben cleared his throat, causing the gentleman to turn his attention to him.

"Yes? What?" He peered closer. "Say, don't I know you?"

Ben bowed. "Benjamin Kemsley, at your service, sir."

The older man coughed, studying Ben with a frown between his eyes. "Not the captain?"

"Of the *Ansdruther,* yes."

"Ho, ho! Look!" The man gestured to some others. "Heathcote, Vincent, come here!"

Within a short space of time Ben was surrounded by people demanding to know if the legendary walk as reported in the papers were true. The older gentleman, whose name turned out to be Palmer, had somehow made him the recipient of as much fervent interest as any of the Regent's exotic decorations. Ben drew Tessa to his side, and before he knew it, she too was being peppered with enquiries about his time, and invitations to dinners and teas and all manner of excursions.

Every so often he scanned the crowd, searching for the viscount or the claret-colored gown Tessa had intimated would be Miss DeLancey's attire tonight. He found himself bracing, straining to hear each time a name was announced. Talk and color swirled around him, forcing him to pay attention to dull bores when he'd rather watch the door. He was half listening to an account of a Mediterranean voyage gone wrong when Tessa grasped his arm. "There she is!"

Ben followed his sister's pointed finger. The crowd surged, then parted again, and he saw her. Smiling at the Regent. Turning her beautifully coiffed head. Spying them. Her features lighting.

His heart thudded painfully as she drew near. Dressed in a burgundy a shade darker than the red ornamenting the room, a color that made her skin seem fairer, her eyes more luminous, and her hair lustrous as sable, she appeared perfectly regal, as if born to live in such a place. Uncertainty twisted within. What right did he have to wish for her to be his? "Miss DeLancey." He bowed.

"Clara!" Tessa hugged her. Envy spiked. How he wished to have that right. "Oh, Clara, this is everything most wonderful!"

"I'm so glad. You look so very lovely."

Tessa sighed. "Oh, I *feel* so very lovely. You cannot know how grateful I am."

The green eyes flashed with amusement as they turned to him. "You have met the Regent, then?"

"I have."

"But he didn't seem to remember Benjie," Tessa said. "Which is not very good of him, is it?"

The eyes flashed again but with something other than amusement. She placed a hand on his arm. "There is time yet."

He covered her hand with his own. "I know."

For a moment the whirl of gaiety and excess seemed to fade as they gazed at each other. Desire strained within him, pushing against his chest like a caged beast. If only there was a way to show himself worthy. What could he do to remind the Prince? What could he do to show Clara's society-obsessed parents that he would do anything to protect her?

As if summoned by his thought, Lord and Lady Winpoole appeared. The viscount eyed Ben's hand atop Clara's, forcing his release. "Good evening, my lord, my lady." He bowed.

"Mr. Kemsley. Miss Kemsley."

"Good evening," Tessa curtsied, blushing.

The viscount nodded, his mouth bending upwards slightly. He drew his daughter away before moving with his stiff-backed wife as the crowd moved toward a central set of doors. Ben watched him move away in disbelief. Had that been — well, if not exactly approval — acceptance, at least? Might his suit be deemed satisfactory, one day?

He drew his sister's arm through his as they joined the procession. Beside him, he could sense Tessa's agitation as she searched for Lord Featherington's fair head. Perhaps Clara had been misinformed; perhaps he would not be here, after all.

They entered through mirrored doors into the Saloon, decorated in blue, lilac, and gold. Again the influence of the Far East was evident in the painted panels of Chinese scenes and the tasseled lanterns hanging from the ceiling, painted the palest blue with drifting clouds to resemble the sky. A richly gilded cabinet, however, contained hints of Indian influence, with its carved arch of shells and lotus blossoms, and mirrored backing reflecting urns of ormolu and brass. It was, once again, so very ostentatious.

Footmen mingled, offering refreshments. Ben plucked two glasses from a tray and offered one to Tessa. She took a sip, made a face, then said, "I don't think that was lemonade."

Ben sipped it cautiously. Sourness tingled on his tongue. "No." He held out his hand to retrieve her glass, but her face had paled and she was looking past his shoulder.

He turned just as she whispered, "He's here."

Viscount Featherington paused in the doorway, simply dressed in plain black that would do Mr. Brummel justice. Two haughty looking personages, with such similar coloring and features they could only be his parents, strode forward before melting into the crowd. Lord Featherington cast a bored glance around the room, before his gaze chanced upon them. He blinked. For a moment his jaw sagged, then was closed with a snap. Seconds later he was at their side, casting Ben a cursory greeting before turning his attention fully on Tessa.

"My dearest!"

The joy in his eyes coupled with Tessa's rapturous look bade Ben turn away, only to encounter Miss DeLancey's soft smile of pleasure from across the room. She met his eyes, blushed, and half turned away. In six quick strides he was at her side. "You knew."

"I hoped." She bit her lip.

"What is it?"

"I trust you do not disapprove?"

He chuckled. "A man would have to be blind to not see his affection. I believe absence has not impaired his feelings."

"And if his parents can be brought to realize that also, perhaps there is some hope."

So she *had* arranged this. Fresh appreciation for her kindness welled within. "You are wonderful."

She shook her head slightly. "I wish only to make amends. I . . . I know he cried off because of . . . of my association with you all."

He reached to gently clasp her hand. "You are wonderful."

She smiled at him; a little smile that soon bloomed across her face.

His chest glowed. In this weird clash of cultures, where gently bred English sat surrounded by Oriental flamboyance, somehow it did not seem so very strange to be holding a viscount's daughter's hand, as if the realm of fantasy could actually be made real.

A gong drew their attention to the front of the room where Lord Houghton held up a hand for quiet. "Ladies and gentlemen, if you would follow me, I assure you we shall be enchanted by the talents of some wonderful musicians, including our most excellent and esteemed host."

The company filtered into the next chamber, a room painted gold, complete with flying dragons clutching tasseled lanterns in their feet. In one corner a gleaming pianoforte stood near a small group of musicians, their instruments and music poised.

Ben turned to Miss DeLancey. "Will you be performing tonight?"

"I believe so, but nothing has been said so far."

He was about to offer assurance that she would most definitely be asked soon, when her parents returned, gesturing for their daughter to join them. Ben bowed and found his sister already seated next to the viscount. He only had time to take his seat beside her, in the row behind the Winpooles, when the Regent moved to the front of the room amid loud applause. He turned to the musicians, murmured something, and without further ado they commenced to play, and he began to sing.

Ben had never considered himself an expert on musicianship, but he thought the Regent's singing voice quite fine. The copious clapping when he finished suggested the audience agreed — or at least were not prepared to offend their host and future king. This led to an encore performance, before the Prince bowed and waved a hand at their ovation.

"Thank you, thank you. So kind. Now, perhaps I can ask some others to exhibit?" The Regent called forth a young lady to accompany him on the pianoforte as he sang. Her performance was pretty, but Ben paid more attention to the way in which Miss DeLancey's fingers were clenching and unclenching. She was nervous, poor thing. He shot up a prayer for her to have peace.

The music concluded, applause renewed, and the Regent helped the lady back to her seat.

"And now, I believe," the Regent scanned the seated audience members, before his eyes alighted on Ben. For a moment he held the gaze, an almost curious look on his face, before his eyes slid to Clara in the row ahead. "Ah, Miss DeLancey. Would you grace us, please?"

She murmured an affirmative, gifting Ben

a shy smile as she rose. A moment's conference with the Regent, which resulted in his raised brow and nod, and then she was sitting at the instrument as the Prince announced the song. "One of my favorites, which I hope you shall all enjoy."

Ben settled back in his seat, anticipation beating his chest as she began to play. The notes rippled smoothly as her fingertips danced across the keys. The tension banding his chest eased. Of Clara's musical ability there could be no doubt. The Prince once more began to sing, only this time his tenor was accompanied by Clara's higher, sweeter tones, their voices blending beautifully well.

When the music finished, the clapping was much louder and sustained. Ben clapped louder and longer than most, enough to draw her father's attention and look of speculation. But he did not care. He only wished he might show the entire world exactly how he felt.

Clara sank back into her seat with a sigh of relief. Her most public part of tonight's proceedings might be over, but there was still so much to do. The futures of Tessa and Mr. Kemsley depended on her.

Her mother patted her hand, and they

listened to the remaining performances. When they finished, and footmen arrived with trays of filled glasses, she was surrounded with well-wishers, including Tessa and her viscount.

"Oh, Clara, you were wonderful!" Tessa exclaimed. "I was telling Lord Featherington how you were responsible for my being here tonight."

Lord Featherington rubbed at the back of his neck. "Never in my wildest dreams . . . I am in your debt, Miss DeLancey."

"Not at all."

"I trust" — he swallowed — "I hope you will be so good as to overlook some of my . . . less discreet comments in the past."

"They shall remain in the past, my lord."

"Thank you," he said, offering her a small, but genuine-looking smile.

A knot in her heart loosened. "It may interest you to learn, sir, that I have found myself the recipient of your cousin's forgiveness, and now realize just how powerful that can be."

His smile grew. "And it may interest you, Miss DeLancey, to learn that I have been challenged by Lavinia about the very same. I find I cannot hold a grudge when she refuses to."

"She believes in showing grace to the undeserving."

"And in doing so follows our Savior's example."

Tessa looked up at him quickly, her eyes wide. "You believe?"

"I find I cannot ignore truth."

"Oh!"

Her beaming smile brought an ache to Clara's heart. She turned away. She did not wish to be thinking of herself, but oh . . . if only she were free to gaze adoringly at the man she loved.

Loved.

She peeked up. Mr. Kemsley was listening patiently to an elderly gentleman with a swath of medals across his chest. She lowered her gaze; she would not wish him to be embarrassed. But she could not deny the hot tumult that swirled within whenever he drew near. The way her insides clenched whenever she caught his scent, a delectable blend of salt and spice and some indefinable masculine essence all his own.

His strength seemed to pass into her, his confidence seemed to make her more so, the very excellence of his qualities compelling her to wish to be more like him in generosity and kindness. And he was so brave! And *so* forbearing. How had he coped with her awkwardness, her family's rudeness for so long? If only she could show him what he meant to her —

"Miss DeLancey?"

"Oh, Lord Houghton." At his quick gesture she hurried to his side. "Did the Regent mention I wished to speak to him? I am sorry to bother him, but I so wished to have a word."

"Of course." His expression remained bland. "Please come this way."

She looked an apology to Tessa, but the young woman was caught up in meeting the viscount's parents, their gracious smiles looking more genuine than usual. It was probably best they did not associate Tessa with Clara. Their son might have learned the power of forgiveness, but she rather doubted the marchioness would forgive her any time soon.

Her parents were likewise engaged, chatting with Lady Sefton, while Mr. Kemsley she could no longer see at all. But still, that would not matter. Just one quick word, and she would be back. It was not as if anything could be seen as untoward. The Regent was old enough to be her father, after all.

Lord Houghton led the way into another room, a far quieter chamber. Here were none of the garish decorations of the other rooms; instead it seemed a place where one could recover from the exotic excess. He gestured to a bronze-colored settee, designed with shells and nautical themes, and she lowered onto it gratefully. "Shall I fetch you a glass of something? I'm sure you must be parched."

She did suddenly feel thirsty. The rooms remained quite warm. "Yes, thank you. That would be greatly appreciated."

She perched on the edge of the settee, looking around, breathing slowly to calm the rapid beating of her heart. This was certainly not usual, but when else would she have opportunity? When else would he?

Lord Houghton returned holding a glass, which he offered, and she accepted, and drank.

A peculiar light-headedness came over her. She stared at the glass. "What was that?"

He smiled, and came toward her. "Just a glass of punch. It might have had a special additional ingredient."

"Might have had?" His face seemed to leer at her. She blinked. He'd assumed his usual bland expression.

"Miss DeLancey, do you know how lovely you look tonight?"

"I . . . er," She placed a hand to her forehead. Why did she feel so ill? "I beg your pardon?"

"You look so very charming. Quite the best-looking lady here tonight, even allowing for your sweet companion. I confess, I had thought her more to my taste, but realized she seemed quite attached to another. But you on the other hand . . ."

His words made no sense. "What do you mean?"

". . . afraid the Regent is so busy . . ." He drew nearer still. "What is it, Miss DeLancey? You don't seem terribly well. Perhaps you should lie down."

Before she knew it, he had pressed her back onto the settee, was smiling down at her most peculiarly. She closed her eyes against the sight, tried to think. What had he just said? Her eyes flew open. "What do you mean the Regent is too busy? Then why am I here? I don't underst—"

"He's such an important man, my dear. And I was sure anything you wished to say to him was something I could assist in. And I'd much prefer to be the one to assist you."

The look in his eyes. No . . .

"Surely you must know that I do not issue favors without expecting some reward in return?" He chuckled and lowered himself to sit beside her. Close beside her. Far, far too close.

"My lord —"

"Hush, now, Clara. I trust I may call you Clara? After all, we're going to be such good friends. And after tonight, when your father realizes we must wed, I shall call you Clara as often as I like. Now close your eyes, that's a good girl. This won't hurt a mite —"

"No!" She tried to sit up, but he pushed her back down. All strength seemed to have abandoned her; her bones felt like liquid. "Please sir, get off me." Why did her tongue feel so thick? Why did her words seem to be slurring? Wait, why was his face looming over hers? "No!"

She felt the hot, sour stench of his breath on her face. A large meaty hand pawed at her gown. She tried to scratch him, to push him off, but he was too heavy, too insistent. From somewhere deep within she felt a scream arise. Who cared what people might come in? She'd caused enough scandal in her life, hadn't she? One more breach in propriety would matter less than if Lord Houghton had his way with her. A desperate prayer escaped. *Lord, help me!* His lips were on her neck; her skin was crawling, her stomach heaving. "Get off me!" she gasped and turned away.

And saw the door had opened. A little part of her died. The man she'd hoped to marry

held blackness in his face and contempt in
his eyes.

CHAPTER TWENTY-FOUR

Anger, thick and terrible, swarmed over him like spewing lava.

"You heard the lady. Get off." In a dozen strides he was beside them. Had grasped the fiend's collar. Hauled him to his feet. "How dare you?"

"Release me, you fool. Can't you see she was begging for my attention?"

"She was begging for something else quite entirely. As for you . . ." He hefted a solid fist and thumped him in the jaw. A cracking sound echoed through the room; then Lord Houghton was sliding off the settee, knees crumpling, until his head landed on the floor with a satisfying thud.

Clara was by this stage sitting upright, trembling, her face a mask of terror. Ben felt the rage surge anew. "Did he . . . did he —"

Her eyes were wide, unfocused. A dread-filled moment later she shook her head.

"Thank God," he breathed and sank down beside her and pulled her close. He felt her freeze, then slowly relax, and rest her head on his shoulder as her breath juddered in and out. He carefully wrapped both arms around her, drawing her closer still. He would not take advantage as that scoundrel had, but he would do his utmost to comfort her, as he'd comforted Tessa, and even Mattie when she'd been a girl.

Blood still rushed in his ears; she was sure to hear his heart threatening to flee his chest. His heart — that wished to run away with hers. A weak smile escaped. How fanciful this place made him. But he had to help her regain a sense of decorum before the door opened and others spied them. He cringed. How on earth could he explain this to her father? Worse, to the Regent?

His lips grazed her hair, and he marveled at the softness, at the scent, a clean combination that reminded him of roses and heather. She fit so snugly in his arms, he could tilt her head back, could kiss her —

"What is the meaning of this?"

Before he could remove his arms, Clara's father was walking toward them, the heavy scowl on his face doubtless echoing the one Ben himself had worn when he'd entered earlier.

"I demand to know at once what you are doing here —" He stopped, gazed at the motionless figure on the floor, then at his daughter. The hard expression seemed to soften a fraction. "Clara?"

She wobbled to her father, hugging him as he patted her awkwardly on the back. His face when next he looked toward Ben held fury, a trace of white around the mouth. Ben rose, eyeing him, thankful he could reassure the man with a small shake of his head. The situation could have been so very much worse.

"I assure you, sir, I took no liberties," Ben said quietly. "I came in, much as you did, and found him," he nudged Lord Houghton with a toe, "trying to take advantage, and Clara — I mean, your daughter — doing her best to escape. I fear he had her at a disadvantage, though. I rather think he might have given her a drugged drink."

"Clara? Is this true?"

She looked up at her father, her face piteous as she nodded. "I did . . . I did not know. I thought he was going to get the Regent."

Her father gave her a hard look. "Tell me you did not wish for *his* attentions?"

"No. No! Of course not! I just wished . . . that is . . ." She shot Ben a pleading look.

"You wanted to speak to him on my behalf," he guessed. At her nod, he took a step toward her before checking himself. "You did not need to, my dear. I could never wish for an interview with him if it came at such a cost."

Her eyes filled with tears that spilled, trickling down her cheeks. His heart wrenched, and he wished violently for the right to hold her in his arms, but her father held her still, looking like a man prepared to throw himself before a cannon rather than let another man touch her.

"I don't understand," Lord Winpoole muttered. "Why would she speak to the Regent?"

A throat being cleared drew their attention to the doorway. Ben's throat constricted as the Prince walked into the room, a frown upon his face. "Forgive the interruption, but I cannot help but be interested when I hear my name being bandied about." He looked between them, saw the blotchiness of Clara's face, and eyed Ben thoughtfully. "Somehow, sir, I did not suspect —"

He stopped, his gaze dropping to the prone figure on the floor. He lifted his quizzing glass, and then let it fall. "Well, I'll be." A mild oath fell from his lips. "Houghton, in the petticoat line?" He sighed, his gaze hard and steady as he faced Ben. "I suppose this to be an affair of honor."

"Yes, sir."

The Regent sighed again, turning to Clara. "Come, my child. I suppose you've had quite a shock, but surely it is not worth all these tears? I trust nothing has been irretrievably damaged?"

This last was said with a hooked brow and knowing gaze. A wave of revulsion passed through Ben.

Clara either missed the insinuation or chose to ignore it, as she drew herself up to face the Regent squarely. "F-forgive me, sir, but I am unaccustomed to being attacked."

"Especially by someone in your employ," her father muttered, with a narrowed gaze.

The Regent's face grew a little pink. "My dear girl, I do not understand what you were doing with him in the first place. I cannot think he dragged you in here. I do not recall hearing any screams."

"I wished to speak with you, remember?"

"Clara!" her father said in agonized tones.

She pressed on, eyes fixed on the Prince. "I . . . I thought he would fetch you —"

"My dear, I'm hardly one either willing or able to be fetched, as you so obligingly put it. I had not entirely forgotten our little tête-à-tête prior to our exquisite performance."

Ben's heart wrenched as she blushed to a hue to match her gown. "I am sorry, sir. I meant no disrespect."

"Yes, well, I begin to see," the Regent said. "Houghton has hardly been a man to let opportunity pass him by. It all begins to make sense."

Clara bit her lip. If it was possible, her cheeks had colored even more deeply.

"It may surprise you, but I had not disregarded your request. When Lord Heathcote thought he saw a scarlet-clad young lady enter my chambers here, I was surprised, but not unwilling to learn what you wished to say."

Ben stepped forward. "Sir, I —"

The Regent held up a hand. "I wish to hear my songbird speak."

Clara's chest drew up as she dragged in an audible breath. "Sir, it concerns Mr. Kemsley here."

"It does?" The Regent turned toward Ben and held up his quizzing glass, revealing a grossly magnified eye. "I am simply agog."

"Sir," she continued, "forgive me, but do you not recognize him?"

"Clara, please," Ben began, stopping as the Regent's frown grew more pronounced.

"Clara, is it?" He eyed Ben with curiosity. "This grows more interesting by the minute." He waved to her. "Please continue, my dear. I simply cannot fathom what might be so important that it's worth this contretemps. I haven't been so diverted in ages, and I assure you, I know very well how to be diverted."

Ben caught her quick glance, the way she swallowed, the slight lift of her chin. With a steadying voice she continued. "Mr. Kemsley may not have told you he was a captain in your father's navy."

"Captain, you say?" The bright blue eyes turned to him. "Made post?"

"Yes, sir. I was captain of the *Ansdruther.*"

There was a pause, then a blink of recognition, the Prince Regent's face lighting. "I remember! You are the man who saved all those people. Well, I *am* pleased to meet you."

Ben swallowed the retort. Willed his face to assume pleasantness. "And I you, sir."

"Well, this is something. Thank you, Miss DeLancey, for drawing this to my attention, although why it could not have been said out there amongst my other guests I do not know. Now, forgive me, I have been absent long enough. No one likes an absent host after all." He made a move as if to go.

Clara shot Ben a frantic look. He shook his head to dissuade her, but she ignored him and ran after the Regent. "Your Highness?"

"Yes, my dear?" he said, with a trace of impatience.

"Sir, forgive me, it is just," she swallowed, "it is just that when reports of Captain Kemsley's heroism reached England, it was reported that you wished to reward him."

"What?" the Regent turned back to him. "Is this true?"

Ben swallowed, inclined his head. "I was not in England at the time, sir, but my sisters kept the newspapers where such things were reported."

"Really?" The Regent seemed to hover, obviously torn between continuing this conversation and wishing to return to his guests.

Ben stepped forward. "Perhaps, sir, it might be better to continue this conversation when you are not otherwise engaged?"

Relief streaked across the Prince's features. "Yes, yes. A very good idea. You must speak to my secretary —"

He paused, eyed the man still lying on the carpet and sighed. "Hmm. Perhaps not. You appear to have told him what you thought already."

Ben could only incline his head and wait.

"One punch?"

He glanced up, met the Regent's shrewd gaze. "Yes."

"I thought as much. Ever done much boxing?"

"A little, sir."

"I pride myself on being one of Jackson's premier students. Well, I *was*, you know. Ever faced him?"

"I have not had the pleasure," Ben said. Or the means.

"Hmm. Well, I used to be quite the sportsman." He patted Clara's father on the shoulder. "Winpoole here knows, don't you? I once rode my horse from London to Brighton and back in ten hours. Ten hours! Can you believe it?"

What was Ben supposed to say? That looking at the Prince's girth now it was hard to believe him to have ever been anything of a horseman, let alone able to accomplish such a feat?

The Prince chuckled. "I see I shall have to bore you with more stories. I'm having a dinner on Tuesday. You must come, Captain Kemsley; and you, too," he said to Clara's father. "Gentlemen only, my dear," he said to Clara, "but I insist you attend later for the evening fireworks. Perhaps you could play again, too."

"Of course, sir," Ben managed, echoing

the viscount's affirmation.

"I will give the matter some thought. You might wish to bring those clippings, although I'm sure my secretary —" He stopped. Sighed again, examining his nails. "The trouble is, he's been such a good secretary."

Though not a good man. A hempen cravat would be too good — Ben swallowed the surge of hatred toward the unconscious man.

The viscount stepped forward. "I should not wish to be forced to call out a man who assaulted my daughter's honor."

"No, no, of course not." The Prince waved a careless hand. "We will talk more, but first I must return to my guests. They have been kept waiting quite long enough." His face lit. "And we are to have fireworks! You know I simply adore fireworks."

Except when they occurred between a guest and his secretary in his chambers, apparently.

"Now, if you'll excuse me?" And the Prince took his estimable presence from the room.

Clara seemed to slump. "I am so sorry." She peeked up at Ben. "I thought he would see reason and would give you your dues." She glanced at her father. "I had no wish for all . . . for all this."

"Clara," Ben began, "all is not lost. And you must not blame yourself —"

"She most certainly should!" Lord Winpoole snapped. "What did you think you were doing, trysting with the Regent of all people? I do not know what to think!"

She blanched and swayed.

Ben hurried toward her but was checked by her father. "As for you, young man, what possessed you to think you should encourage my daughter to speak on your behalf? I would have thought you a man of more courage than that!"

Ben's retort was cut short by Clara's pleading look, as she placed a hand on her father's arm. "Father, please, he did not know."

"I would never wish a lady to speak on my behalf," Ben said stiffly.

"And yet you stood there, letting her do all the talking for you, just now, didn't you?"

"He could scarcely contradict the Prince's request, could he? Father, Mr. Kemsley rescued me from Lord Houghton. You should be weak with gratitude, as I am." Her voice had grown shaky. "It was horrible!"

"There, there, my girl" — he patted her awkwardly — "no need for tears." He met

Ben's gaze atop Clara's head. "I suppose I am obliged to you, again."

Again? Had she told her father about that clifftop encounter? "You must believe, sir, that I would never permit your daughter to be harmed if I could at all prevent it."

The older man shuffled uncomfortably. "Yes, well." He harrumphed. "Good, then. Now, we best get back. Your mother will be frantic for you, my dear."

Clara put a hand to her head. "I do not feel quite able to face all those people, Father."

"Oh." Frowning, the viscount looked at her, then up at Ben. "Is it too much of an imposition to request you stay with Clara while I find my wife? I cannot imagine we will be staying for any fireworks tonight."

"Of course, sir. I only ask that if you see my sister, you might request her to join us? She was with Lord Featherington and I suspect she may be quite as anxious as your wife as to our whereabouts."

Clara seemed to draw herself up. "I'm making too much trouble. I will come."

"Well . . ." The viscount seemed undecided.

"Sir, I will escort Miss DeLancey back. We will rejoin you shortly."

"Thank you. Much obliged." And the

viscount exited.

Ben turned to see Clara visibly wilt. He wrapped an arm around her shoulders.

"I'm so sorry," she repeated, eyes awash with sorrow. "I've burdened you enough, and now Tessa —"

"Forget Tessa. I'm sure she's having a good time. I only hope she's managed to thoroughly convince the marquess and marchioness of her merits."

"She's such a sweet girl, I'm sure they cannot fail to see that."

"Sweetness is a quality that can never pass unnoticed."

Her gaze lowered.

He tipped up her chin. "What is it?"

"I have never been considered terribly sweet," she whispered. "I'm afraid I've made too many people think I'm simply terrible."

"I suspect you're simply fishing for compliments, now." He smiled.

"Mr. Kemsley —"

"Please, call me Ben."

She shook her head. "Mr. Kemsley, you do not know —"

"On the contrary, sweet Clara, I do know, and I know there is no sweeter girl I wish to kiss than you, right now."

Her eyes widened. "Sir!"

"But I will not, not after what has happened, and not if you don't wish it."

"But I —" Her cheeks flushed. She touched them. "Oh, it's so warm in here."

He agreed. But it had nothing to do with how the Prince preferred to heat his rooms. "We should return."

Sliding his arm from their embrace, he offered it for her to lean on, exultation dancing in his heart. She wanted his kiss; propriety had merely refused to let her confess such a thing. He placed his other hand on hers and gently squeezed, and her eyes met his again, the green fire still shadowed.

They passed back into the whirl of color, able to join the general movement to the doors from where the Regent's voice could be heard, "Quickly! The fireworks are almost at time!"

He scanned the room, relief washing through him as Tessa met his gaze. Her face lit, she leaned up to murmur something to Lord Featherington, whose arm she clutched, before leaving him to weave through the guests still trying to attain the gardens.

"Ben! Wherever have you been?" Her brow puckered as she glanced at Clara. "Hello, Clara. You were missed. Lady Sefton was asking about you."

"I . . . I was taken unwell."

"You poor thing. That must be why you look so pale. Good thing Benjie is so strong, isn't it? No wonder you must lean on him."

His neck burned as Clara dropped his arm. "Tessa."

She turned to him, her overly innocent blue eyes now alive with excitement. "Oh, Ben, you'll never guess! Henry introduced me to his parents!"

"Henry, is it?"

"Yes. Oh, and you'll never know this: I am to have tea with the marchioness on Monday. Imagine! Me, having tea with a marchioness!" She fanned her face with two hands. "I hardly know what to think!"

"I'm so pleased for you, Tessa," Clara murmured.

"Henry is so very kind. He was telling me about his time with his cousin and sister up north. It seems he's found deeper purpose now that he believes as we do. He told me not a day went by that he did not regret leaving me without a word. He seems quite changed."

This was said with a half-pleading, half-defiant glance at Ben that made him swallow a smile and murmur something about arranging a more civil interview with the viscount soon.

"Oh, I am so happy!" She drew both of

Clara's hands into her own. "I cannot thank you enough, dearest, sweetest Clara. You have been so very good to me. I was telling Henry about how you have helped me with tonight —"

"I hope you didn't tell him how you were invited."

"A little credit, please. Believe it or not, sometimes I know when to speak and when best not to."

"Then you are well on the way to being able to hold your own in having tea with a marchioness," Clara said, with a strained smile.

"Do I hear my mother being referred to?" Lord Featherington joined them. "I hope you don't mind that I've rather stolen your sister's attention tonight," he said to Ben. "Thing is, she's proved rather popular here, and I thought it best to make my intentions plain."

Ben hooked a brow. The viscount flushed but held his gaze steadily. Well, then. He gave a tiny nod. "I do not mind. Thank you for being so assiduous in your attentions."

"Thing is, my mother has rather taken to her. Thinks her the best-dressed person here, barring herself of course. She's always pleased to see someone with natural taste."

Tessa grabbed Clara's hand. "See? You

must help me. I cannot have her know just how simply I am usually attired."

"I'm sure she'd still be able to see your natural grace and charm even if dressed like a pauper."

Lord Featherington coughed. "A charming thought, Miss DeLancey, and 'tis kind of you to say, but I rather doubt it. Mama is something of a stickler for fashion. But never mind." Before another word could be said, he'd tucked Tessa's arm under his and they walked away.

Ben turned to Clara, who by now had regained all poise from earlier in the evening. "Do you feel a little better now?"

"A little better, yes, thank you." Her smile faded. "I do not know what I would have done if you had not come in —"

"Please, don't think on it anymore. Houghton is a scoundrel and a man whom you need never deal with again."

"But the Prince wished me to return on Tuesday. What if he is here?"

He clasped her hand. "Then I will be here to protect you."

How he wished he could always promise to do so. They stared at each other a moment longer, until he became aware that her parents were approaching. He released her hand, stepped back a pace. "Once again,

I thank you for what you've done for me and for my sister. I can but pray for both circumstances to resolve as God sees fit."

"Clara?" Her mother approached, looking between them with a piercing stare. "Are you quite well? Your father has told me you were taken ill."

"I . . ." Clara coughed, her eyes beseeching, as Lord Winpoole met him in a level gaze.

He did not like to lie, but he also preferred avoiding unnecessary trouble. "Miss DeLancey is feeling better, ma'am. She was just now talking to my sister, who was most grateful for your daughter's assistance in several matters."

"Really?" She frowned, glancing between him and Clara.

He refused to take offense. "Your daughter is most magnanimous in her thoughtfulness towards others. My family is deeply appreciative."

"Well, er, good, then." She gave him a puzzled look before peering at her daughter. "Clara? You seem a little peaky. Do you wish to see the fireworks or shall we go home? I confess I have something of the headache and have no inclination to stay if you do not desire it, but I'm prepared to stay if you want."

"I would much prefer to go home," Clara murmured.

"Good," her mother said, with a relieved smile. "For really, I could not bear to stay a moment longer. These things can get quite tiresome, although I will admit that it was quite nice to hear so many people singing your praises. Lady Sefton was quite impressed . . ."

As she ushered Clara away, Ben caught a quick glimpse of Clara's eyes before she was turned determinedly to the exit.

Which left him standing with Lord Winpoole. The viscount shuffled his feet, glancing away, before finally holding out a hand. "I suppose I must thank you."

Ben shook it. "I meant what I said, sir."

The viscount released his hand and looked down.

"I will do my utmost to protect her, all her days," Ben swallowed, "if you were to so honor me with the privilege."

"I gathered you . . . cared for her, but . . ."

Ben's heart grew taut. Here it came.

Lord Winpoole shook his head. "But what can you offer her? She has little dowry, I'm afraid to say, and by all accounts neither have you much money. And you've no title. I won't deny that you have more character than some, but character won't feed or

405

house my daughter."

The hope stirred up from earlier was drifting away. "I hope the Prince will recall his promise of restitution when we meet again."

"Prinny? He'll be lucky to remember he invited us for Tuesday, let alone that you wished to remind him of any obligations he's obviously long forgotten. No, I'm sorry Kemsley, but as a father who must ensure his only daughter makes the most advantageous match available, I cannot encourage you to entertain any hope."

"But sir —"

"Good evening to you."

Something akin to despair coiled inside him as the viscount turned to follow his wife and daughter.

Cold reality had blown hope far away.

CHAPTER TWENTY-FIVE

Tuesday

Clara huddled on her bed, snatches of memory from the past few days running through her head. Her sense of victory last Friday after her performance, when she'd met the eyes of society and known herself to be esteemed once more — victory that had quickly slid into utter fear amid the lecherous gropings of Lord Houghton. Her shame when discovered by Mr. Kemsley, a feeling that melded into extreme gratitude and reassurance, knowing she was cared for by someone as capable of knocking down her enemy as praying for her. For a few minutes, she'd allowed herself to believe that in his tenderness she'd find a future, that she could be loved for being who she was, that he'd meant those words about her sweetness, even as she doubted him. Surely that look in his eye was not prideful deception, nor the way he'd gazed upon her mouth, nor his words about a kiss.

Her eyes filled. She blinked the tears back. Was it better to blink or let them fall? She could not afford red eyes tonight, but neither did she want them to look puffy. Oh, why was she so concerned anyway? What could any of it matter?

But it did, and she allowed her thoughts to wander back to that moment of tender refuge. That he cared for her, she knew. Or had thought she'd known. He had made it plain that evening, but upon their next meeting after services on Sunday, she had not been so sure. He had scarce looked upon her, much less spoken to her. After their previous time together, where she'd thought such intimacy had been exchanged with scarcely a touch, his aloofness had hurt in a way she'd not imagined possible since the earl's rejection so long ago.

Had she done something to upset him? Perhaps, upon reflection, he'd realized she was not so sweet as he avowed, and he believed her actions wanton, like Father had implied. Her throat constricted. She took in a shuddery breath. Had she thoroughly spoiled things between them? Would her actions from years ago forever haunt her?

She turned, careful not to disturb the elaborate coiffure the hairdresser had labored over for hours. At least Tessa was not displeased with Clara. Her brother — indeed, both brothers — might have reservations, but Tessa seemed desirous of continuing the relationship, especially in light of her interview with Lady Exeter. "Oh, tell me Clara. What must I do? What should I wear? You must advise me!"

Clara had promised to lend her assistance, and Tessa and Matilda's morning visit yesterday had left Tessa arrayed in one of Clara's near-new London gowns, a creamy muslin overlaid with tiny rosebuds. It was most appropriate for a girl of Tessa's years and now, neatly altered by Matilda's nimble fingers, looked as though made for her.

Their return visit later that evening had gone well, Tessa exuberant with success, the marchioness so impressed she had invited Tessa to dine with her while the men dined at the Pavilion tonight, which thus necessitated another borrowed gown. Clara smiled, wondering if continued assistance might mean her wardrobe would be forever depleted, unless Lord Featherington finally summoned courage enough to make his wishes known to his sire. She knew Mattie held no objections to the match; she'd said as much yesterday. Apparently Lord Featherington had joined them for a meal on

Sunday after services, the subsequent interview among the men leaving them all convinced his intentions were as genuine as his faith, a faith that saw him forego gambling and intemperance for solicitude for others, revealed in the sizeable donation he'd made to the Sailors and Soldiers' Hostel.

Her smile faded. Would Mr. Kemsley ever speak to her father? Or would he think it more honorable to wait until things were settled with the Regent, and he could offer more than just his heart? Her spirits dipped. That is, if he still wished to make Clara an offer at all . . .

She bit her lip. Perhaps he had already spoken to her father. That might account for why Father had barely looked at her these past days, and every conversation between them had felt stilted and constrained. Her heart jolted. What if Father had not given his consent?

Her eyes burned; she willed away the tears. She would not spoil tonight. Besides, all this worry reflected lack of faith. She'd seen God answer even unspoken prayers; surely He knew and would intervene and cause her paths to straighten, as she trusted Him?

She closed her eyes, let out a sigh. *Help me trust You, Lord.*

A measure of peace lodged in her soul. She did not need to worry. Everything was organized, from tonight's meal and their transportation to the Pavilion, to Clara's music — Mozart's Piano Sonata Number 11 in A Major — and her attire tonight. Her red gown from London had been altered once again, with lace inserts on the sleeves and neckline to avoid immediate recognition, thus saving Father further expense, whilst still making her look elegant. She needed only to rest, to sleep, to not think. She'd done all she could do to ensure Tessa would be seen by the viscount's family in the best possible light, had done all she could to ensure Mr. Kemsley would have his case heard. All she could do now was hope, and pray, that the evening lived up to her wildest imaginings.

She squeezed closed her eyes. Relax. Trust. Believe. She breathed in. Released air slowly. Relax. Trust. Believe. God was in control. So relax. Trust. Believe —

A long, slow creak snapped her eyes open to the door. She gasped. "You!"

Her brother smiled his thick-lipped smile. "Hello, Clara. It's been a while."

"Not long enough," she muttered, pushing into a sitting position. "What are you doing here?"

411

"What reason do I need to see my family whom I love?"

"Love?" She snorted. "You do not love us. If you did, you would never have caused us so many problems," she said bluntly.

His eyes widened. "How can you say such things? My own dear, sweet sister." His gaze grew hard. "I hear you're going to the Pavilion tonight."

"How did you know?"

He shrugged. "I have my sources."

"Good news travels fast."

"News, anyway." His eyes seemed cold in the dim light of the room. The planes of his face shadowed as he glanced at his finger-nails. "I did not know you still associated with the upper echelons of society."

"I imagine there is quite a lot you do not know about me."

"I probably know more than what you realize," he said, in a tone that sent a chill up her spine.

She swung her legs off the bed, pulled on a wrapper. The day was warm but inside she felt more icy than a treat from Gunter's. "What is it you want?"

He sighed. "What is it anyone wants these days?"

"Money," she said flatly.

"You know me well."

The old indignation rose. "What's the matter? My dowry not enough?"

"I really wish you wouldn't harp on about such things."

"I'm sure you wish a lot of things." She shook her head. "We have so little. And you cannot barge in expecting Mother and Father to turn around and give you more. They cannot even speak of you without getting upset!"

"Still?"

"Still! You hurt us all immeasurably."

"Yes, well, some things cannot be helped."

"Of course they can," she said, eyeing him with dislike. "You chose to gamble, you chose to steal, you chose —"

"Goodness. You're beginning to sound as self-righteous as that chilly little cow I felt up for you at the Bathurst ball."

"For me?" She pushed to her feet, her fingers clenched. "How dared you treat her so? In attacking Lavinia you did me great disservice! I can never forgive you for such an act."

"No?" He took a pinch of snuff. "Decided to forget the earl, have we?"

"Yes. They are married, and happily so, I might add. What's more, I am glad!"

He chuckled nastily. "That I will believe when I see it."

413

"What do you mean?"

"Hawkesbury and his little farmhand wife are also going tonight."

"What?"

This time his chuckle had an even more unnerving quality. "You seem a little startled. Not quite what you hoped?"

"It makes no difference to me. I have no interest in that quarter."

"So I've heard, whereas I . . ."

She refused to bite. Refused to bite. Refused to — "What have you heard?"

He laughed. "I heard you have been spending an inordinate amount of time with a certain former captain of His Majesty's Navy."

"What of it?"

"Such low taste, my dear. Hardly what I would expect from you."

"People change. *You* proved that well enough."

His face darkened. "I see your propensity for nasty talk has not left you entirely."

"Only when it comes to people worthy of it," she murmured.

He loomed over her, his face mere inches from hers. But she refused to back away, refused to let him see her sudden fear. "I need you to do something for me, Clara."

She laughed in disbelief. "I think your

days of being able to demand my cooperation are long gone."

"You can think that all you like, but you will do what I say."

"You cannot make me."

"No?"

Before she knew it, he had her hand twisted behind her back and was pulling painfully, even more painfully. "Stop!"

He jerked harder. "You want me to stop? Then you must agree to what I say."

"How can I agree when I don't even know what it is you want?"

"Agree!"

Her arm felt like it would snap. How could she play tonight? She felt a shriek rise within. "Fine! Stop. What is it?"

He released the pressure slightly, and she yanked her arm away. "I want you to speak to Hawkesbury tonight."

"What? No."

"I want you to speak to him outside, while the fireworks are on. I want you to take him aside and let him see just what he's missing."

She stared at him in horror. "You want me to do what?"

"Kiss him, hold him, do whatever. I know you are not as virtuous as you'd like our dear parents to think."

"How dare you?"

"Did you think your sordid little tête-à-tête in the Regent's chambers would go unnoticed? I assure you, it did not."

Her senses began to swim. "Who told you?"

He laughed. "Who did not, you mean? You know your conduct is the talk of Brighton now."

"No. Nobody saw us, nobody knew." She tried to still herself, to listen to what she knew was true. Memories screamed at her instead.

London society eyeing her askance, sniggering behind raised fans. The *on dit* — oh, the poisonous gossip! — she knew only too well. Knew what they had said. Knew what they would say.

Richard laughed again, soft and pitilessly. "Surely you did not think such things would go unnoticed? The Regent built that monstrosity with the intention of keeping scandals secret, but they could never be kept secret from all his staff."

"Did Houghton —"

He smiled.

"I don't know what Houghton told you, but he lies."

"No matter. Enough smoke and people

are all too willing to believe there's been a fire."

She swallowed. "I cannot. I will not treat the earl that way."

He grabbed her hand, crushing her fingers mercilessly. "You will."

"Richard, stop!" Tears sprang to her eyes. "You're hurting me!"

"I know. I find I have a taste for it these days, and it proves most difficult to stop."

"Please, Richard, I don't think you really want to hurt them."

"You would be surprised." Blackness crossed his face. "I never thought I hated anyone until I met him. In abandoning you, he poisoned all my chances."

"No, you are wrong. He did not abandon me. He just did not love me."

"His reasons do not matter. It still amounted to the same. The loss of our good name, our prospects. Our financial security."

"But that was not the earl's fault! He did not steal Father's money and gamble it away." She eyed him steadily, saw him flush. "And my actions were not wise. I reveled too much in self-pity. I should have concealed my hurt rather than go along with Mother's schemes to win him back, but I was deluded into thinking myself more highly sought than I ever was."

"How can you defend him?" He muttered a curse. "After what he did?"

"I forgave him."

"Forgave him?" He looked at her incredulously, his grip loosing.

"Please, Richard," she snatched her hand away, rubbing uselessly at the pain. "What you are asking is against everything I believe."

"So you are like them now? I heard rumors that you'd gotten religious, that you even helped out at some pathetic sailors' shelter, but I could not in all my wildest imaginings credit that with any degree of truth."

"I have."

"And I bet Mother doesn't know, does she?"

She stared at him. Where had the sweet-natured little boy gone? The one she used to laugh and play with? "I do not like you."

"No, well you're not the only one." He glanced away, and for a moment she caught a glimpse of something that looked faintly like vulnerability. Her brother — the vile, invincible Richard — vulnerable?

Pity mixed with sorrow, renewing her resolve. "Richard, please. Please talk to Father. There has to be another way."

He shook his head. "There is not." His

gaze fell to her hands, then crawled back to her face. "You know I met a man called Johnson. He proved most illuminating."

"I do not care."

"No? He used to be Hawkesbury's agent at his little pile in Gloucestershire. He hates the man almost as much as I do."

"I do not care. I will not help you. You can break my fingers if you like, but it will only make me more sorry for you than ever."

Something flickered in his eyes. "You dare pity me?"

"I am not the one befriending unscrupulous men. I may not have an unblemished reputation, but I have done nothing illegal or immoral, despite what you may think."

He stared at her a long moment.

Lord, give me wisdom. "What is it you hope to achieve? Even if I did talk to Hawkesbury as you wished, what could that possibly accomplish?"

He shook his head. "You don't understand. I . . . I have gotten into trouble with some moneylenders and need to pay them back. Johnson still has some of Hawkesbury's money hidden, but he's promised me a portion if I can cause the earl another scandal."

"And you believe him?"

His eyes shadowed. "I have no choice."

"But you want me to play a part? That is so very wicked!"

"I need money. He promised, and you . . ." He shrugged. "Your infatuation is widely known, and Johnson is keen to do Hawkesbury a bad turn if he can."

"I will give you what I have. It isn't much, but —"

He looked oddly touched. "Your pittance will not cover the air I breathe." He shook his head, his mien hardening once more to what she'd become accustomed. "You *will* help me, dearest sister, else I'll make sure your little redheaded friend gets a visit from a viscount's son that she never wants to remember."

CHAPTER TWENTY-SIX

For a man deemed inadequate by a viscount, Ben found himself surprisingly at ease among his aristocratic dining companions, all of whom were titled and moneyed at a level far beyond him. Perhaps it was Lord Palmer's warm welcome, perhaps it was the fact he was seated at the opposite end to Clara's father, nearer the Marquess of Exeter and Lord Hawkesbury, men unaware of his dashed hopes, and with whom he did not need to pretend about such matters. He could not help notice Lord Winpoole refused to meet his gaze, which fired hope that perhaps Clara's father felt as uncomfortable as Ben. Regardless, the Prince Regent's stories were entertaining, resulting in much laughter, though that was probably helped along by the copious amounts of alcohol being consumed.

The earl, he noted, had barely touched his glass; Lord Featherington, too, seemed uninterested in following Lord Palmer's spirited attempts to match the Regent glass for glass. It was a slightly woozy company that finally stood when the gong was rung, but fortunately not by Lord Houghton, whom they had yet to see. Whether or not he had been dismissed, Ben did not know; he only hoped so, for Houghton should never hope to be retained.

He joined the others in the gallery beyond, a drawing room with rich blue drapery that provided relief from the excess of chinoiserie elsewhere. The Regent spouted on about his new designer, a certain Robert Jones, tasked with transforming the dining room into a feast for the eyes to stage such banquets as befit the future King. With talk of enormous chandeliers suspended from gigantic silver dragons, and rich decoration designed to put the other rooms in the shade, Ben couldn't help but wonder if the Regent had forgotten his promise to think upon his request. Perhaps Clara's father was correct and the Regent no sooner promised something before dismissing it from his mind. His fingers clenched, relaxed. He could not afford to think like that. He needed to trust God instead.

The conversation continued over port and cigars, from which he again refrained, having never acquired the taste — or the means — to indulge in them. Talk turned to war, and the final days of Napoleon's campaign before his final capture and removal to Elba. As someone who had served under Wellington in the Peninsular campaign, Lord Hawkesbury's opinion was sought, and it wasn't long afterwards that the earl turned to Ben and said, "But enough from me. I would like to hear again of your most marvelous miraculous escape."

The conversations elsewhere stilled. Ben caught the Regent's eye; was that a flash of guilt? The Prince looked away. Ben swallowed. "I would not wish to bore anyone, as I am sure most have heard the story not a few times."

"Nonsense. It's a tale of survival that never grows old," the earl said, with a steady look that made Ben suddenly wonder if he, too, knew of Ben's difficulties. He felt the heat rise up his neck. Was this an opportunity from God, after all?

He told his story briefly, unsurprised as he concluded to hear Lord Palmer's voice the loudest among the resounding cheers. He glanced briefly at the Regent, whose face held interest, but nothing more.

"Did you know this fine young man not only saved all those people, but then has spent a great deal of his prize money on helping those poor families whose husbands and fathers did not return?" the earl continued. "I think such manner of man most admirable and am so pleased to see him included in an evening like this."

"Hear, hear," the assembly cried. Still the Regent said nothing.

Ben glanced at Clara's father; he looked down.

"I thought you were to get some honor," Lord Palmer said, turning to Prinny. "Didn't you once say this man deserved rewarding?"

"I may have," the Regent allowed.

"You certainly did," the Marquess of Exeter said. "I recall now reading about it at the time." He shifted to face the Regent fully. "You said such an act deserved a knighthood at the least, with suggestion of financial reward, also."

"That does sound like something I *might* say . . ."

"Well? What of it?" Lord Palmer said. "You cannot say you have no funds when you were boasting just moments ago about all your fancy furbelows in yonder dining room."

The Regent frowned. "Are you daring to question my word?"

"Well, have you paid him?"

The Prince's face pinked. "I cannot say."

Lord Palmer turned to Ben. "Well, has he paid you?"

Through the course of his career, he'd been in some tight spots, but none so awkward as this. "Not as yet," he replied in a low voice.

"I wonder, Mr. Kemsley," the Earl of Hawkesbury said, "just how much of your prize money was spent on helping those poor sailors?"

All eyes swung back to him. His neckcloth grew uncomfortably snug. "I could not say."

"I think you should," Hawkesbury murmured, hazel eyes glinting.

"Spit it out, man. How much?" Lord Palmer reiterated.

Ben calculated rapidly. "Near two thousand pounds, I believe."

"So when that is added to the costs associated with his unfair dismissal from the Admiralty, it seems he'll require at least five thousand to make things square," the earl said.

"Five thousand?" The Prince looked aghast.

"Or do you intend to take a wife, Kemsley? If so, better make it ten," said Lord Palmer, the twinkle in his eye becoming more pronounced.

"Ten?" the Regent spluttered. "I am not made of money!"

"No." Lord Hawkesbury eyed the Prince across the top of his wine glass. "But surely it would be in your best interests, Your Highness, for the good people of England to see you reward one of their own, rather than knowing he was shortchanged because you preferred to festoon your summer palace with more dragons."

In the hush that followed, Ben could almost hear the Regent's thoughts ticking. Could his approval ratings, never high due to his well-reported profligate lifestyle, afford to be further damaged by refusing to keep his word? Ben's mouth dried, his heart thundered frantically, blood rushed in his ears. *Dear God, please look on me with favor . . .*

"I will think on it," the Regent said finally.

"Think on it? How much time do you need to think?" Lord Exeter frowned. "We've all heard Mr. Kemsley's story. His valor cannot be denied. Are you really going to continue to ignore him for the sake of a few pounds?"

Again, a strained silence stretched across the room.

The Regent finally turned to Ben, a look not wholly pleasant in his eye. "Did you put them up to saying this?"

"Put them — No, of course not."

"No one has put anyone up to anything," said Lord Exeter, "but I will say this. If you don't fulfill your word tonight, I shall make a point of stating such things the next time Parliament meets."

There was an inward hiss, as if the room's occupants had taken a collective gasp.

"You?" The Regent laughed, not with amusement. "You barely attend as it is, yet have the nerve to threaten me?"

"I attend sittings most regularly," said Lord Hawkesbury, his manner, his gaze intense as the soldier he'd once been. "And I will not be backward in promoting what this man is due."

"Quite right," muttered Lord Palmer. "Come on, Prinny. You do not want a revolution on your hands. Best give the man a knighthood and the rhino he deserves. Best not to be seen clutch-fisted, else the people may revolt."

The Regent's face flickered before he smiled genially at all. "Of course not. Such a thought is completely revolting!" He laughed at his own wit. "Mr. Kemsley" — protuberant blue eyes met Ben's — "please forgive my tardiness in this matter. I trust a knighthood will prove satisfactory?"

"Of course, sir."

"I am sure there are many officers from these wars who have distinguished themselves through eminent service and thus deserve high honor. Their names should be preserved for posterity, accompanied by such marks of distinction they have so nobly earned." The Regent looked around the table. "What say you all?"

"I say he needs more than a fancy medal or two," Lord Palmer said. "Give him the Garter at least. And don't forget the money. Man cannot live on promises alone."

"Of course not." The Regent offered Ben a tight smile. "For your illustrious valor, I trust you will think a sum of five thousand pounds reward enough?"

"Sir, I do not know what to say," Ben stammered.

"A thank-you shall suffice."

He wanted gratitude now? Ben did not care. "Thank you, sir."

"Still think it should be ten," grumbled Lord Palmer.

"One always thinks it should be more when it's not one's own money."

No one pointed out to the heir of the throne that the money he spent could scarcely be called his own. The Regent rose, his smile as gracious as if he'd not been strong-armed into finally rewarding Ben. "Shall we see if the ladies have arrived? I must confess to a hankering for their company and their music after such serious matters of state."

Hawkesbury rose, offered his hand to congratulate Ben, but his gaze was to the Regent. "I trust, sir, that we shall be informed of Kemsley's ceremony soon?"

The Regent coughed. "As soon as I am able. I need a new secretary, see."

"Oh?" Lord Palmer said. "Old Houghton finally left you?"

"He proved . . . rather less than satisfactory."

Lord Winpoole gave a decided nod before meeting Ben's gaze and flushing. Ben eyed him steadily, his good fortune still ringing in his ears. Five thousand pounds? Surely enough to buy a small holding, and if invested well, enough to live off for a number of years. But would it be enough to satisfy Lord Winpoole? A knighthood would make Clara a lady and would afford him a level of respect and honor even if he weren't inducted into the Order of the Garter.

Moments later, he was in the midst of a sea of congratulations, some of which seemed more about joy in squeezing money from the Regent than for any meritorious act of Ben's. But he would not complain, and with such illustrious personages as his witness, he felt reasonably certain that this would be a promise the Prince felt honor bound to keep.

They filtered through to the Yellow Drawing Room, where the ladies were arrayed. Ben's eyes searched hungrily for Miss DeLancey; she was sitting with her mother, near Lady Hawkesbury, as they listened to Lady Sefton speak in hushed tones about the Princess's latest trials.

Clara's father went to speak directly to his wife; she listened then looked straight at him. Ben offered a small bow, turning, as Lord Hawkesbury clapped a hand on his shoulder. "Well, I cannot say there have been many evenings with the Regent that have made me glad, but this has been one of them. Well done, Kemsley, well done."

He shook his head. "I think it more your doing, my lord, and that of Lord Exeter and Lord Palmer."

"Yes, but they would not have supported you if you weren't so unassuming. Nobody likes a proud man, and when your cause was so worthy . . ." He tilted his head. "Was there reason to wish for more? Lord Palmer hinted of a young lady?"

Ben's smile grew strained. "I had hoped

so, but cannot be certain. Her father deemed it impossible, but whether he continues to after this news, I cannot tell."

"What? Never tell me he is here! Tell me at once, and I'll give you a reference of the highest order." The earl's eyes gleamed. "Who is the lucky lady?"

"I . . . I do not wish to cause embarrassment, sir."

"Quite right. Go talk to her and her father, then, and if you need my help, just ask."

Ben muttered something of his obligation, and the earl strode to his wife, pointedly ignoring the lady whose name Ben had just refrained from saying.

He swallowed. What would happen when the earl learned who Ben wished to marry? Would he condemn him and withdraw his support? Or would the grace his wife extended to Clara be something Lord Hawkesbury could show one day, as well?

"Kemsley!" Lord Featherington shook his hand. "Have to say that was one of the more spectacular moments of my life. Don't think I've ever heard Father fired up about another man like that. Not even old Hartington got such praise." He grinned. "Between you and me, I think Father is softening to the idea of Tessa being the future marchioness. Mama thinks she's young enough that she can mold Tessa into her own pattern, said she's quite a pet — her words exactly, no word of a lie — and thinks settling down young might even be the making of me! I told her she's exactly right, and Mama likes it whenever she's told such things, so it wouldn't surprise me at all if she's told Father that he needs to be as supportive of you as possible. Can't hurt to have a naval hero in the family, and if he's got a title and some money — well, all the better."

So his good fortune might have more to do with others than he'd thought. Ben grinned, noting how Clara turned to him, her eyes huge in her white face.

His joy evaporated. Something was wrong. Now he watched her, he could see she was unnaturally still, had barely moved since they'd entered the room. Was it the memories of the last time she'd visited the Pavilion? Was it confusion over his intentions? He'd been too upset on Sunday to do much more than steal one glance. Had she misread that as lack of interest? Or was it something else?

He watched her carefully. Saw the way her eyes stole to the earl. Jealousy seared his chest. Did Clara still care for him?

A cleared throat brought Ben's attention

to her father. "Kemsley, I congratulate you. I did not think you'd be so honored."

Ben held his gaze squarely. "I know."

Lord Winpoole flushed. "I . . . I might have spoken too hastily before. I admit to not always being privy to the workings of my daughter's heart, but if you still wish to wed her, I shall not be opposed."

"Thank you," Ben said, working to keep the edge from his tone. "Your support is appreciated."

He glanced back to where Clara still surreptitiously peeked at the earl. But did he want to marry into a family more concerned with title than character? More importantly, did he want a wife who loved another?

Lord Winpoole held out a hand, which Ben shook blindly.

He glanced up and saw the Earl of Hawkesbury's sudden frown.

CHAPTER TWENTY-SEVEN

What was she to do?

The earl was close, so close she could smell his heady scent of bergamot and fresh linen. But how could she distract him? The idea he'd even listen to her was laughable; he'd made no secret of his contempt, turning away rather than looking at her. She fought a cringe. Thank God his wife was more forgiving, Lavinia making a point of inviting Clara to sit with her, asking her about her growth in God, before the ever chatty Lady Sefton had commanded attention in her gossip about poor Princess Charlotte.

But what could she do? She felt sick within; nerves straining so hard she could barely move a muscle. Then *he'd* entered, looking for all the world like he'd won the keys to a palace. She'd noticed how his eyes had instantly sought her out before several of the other men had distracted him with handshakes that looked awfully like congratulations. Her heart flickered. Had he managed to convince Prinny of his claim? She hoped so, for his sake as much as her own. But before contemplating matters further, she had to decide what should happen tonight.

Before leaving, Richard had assured her there would be someone watching — this mysterious Johnson fellow, perhaps? — someone to ensure the earl was embroiled in scandal more vicious than he'd ever known. Since his departure, she'd worried and prayed, while her hands and fingers throbbed. How could she be party to such a scandal? She could not hurt Lavinia so. God would not wish her to participate in such a wicked scheme. But what did He wish her to do? Her stomach heaved, and she placed two tender fingers to her mouth.

"Miss DeLancey?" Lavinia peered at her worriedly.

She shook her head, and Lady Sefton said, "It's the heat. It affects us all."

Clara smiled weakly as Mother retrieved a fan and began to wave it vigorously. Conscious she was fast becoming the center of attention, Clara lowered the fan. "Thank you, Mother, but truly it is not necessary."

"My dear, one minute you are flushed,

the next you're pale as a ghost. You are not well. Perhaps we should leave."

Leave? And escape the night's dilemma? But surely it would persist for another day.

The Prince called for attention before requesting Lavinia to perform, which she did to copious applause. Clara listened to the exquisite musicianship, certain her own efforts would not be so well executed. Another encore later, and the Prince turned to Clara.

"Miss DeLancey?"

She rose, rubbing her fingers in the hope the action might lend strength, and settled at the pianoforte. A quick glance up saw her parents smiling proudly, the Prince Regent looking expectant, and Mr. Kemsley's intense gaze wholly fixed upon her face. She could not let any of them down.

With a prayer muttered under her breath, she launched into the first movement, schooling her features to hide the pain as her muscles protested. Somehow she stumbled through, her only errors so small only an expert musician such as Lavinia might notice. Not that she minded; she'd long ago ceded aspirations to that lady's superior musicianship.

Applause was followed by a request for an encore; then she was released to listen to the Prince's efforts. But she could not concentrate, the musical performance merely the overture to the evening's hidden program. What could she do? How could she choose between the innocence of Tessa and hurting Lavinia, the former rival whom Richard had once assaulted?

"Excuse me, Miss DeLancey?"

Her breath caught. The music had ceased; conversations had resumed. She glanced up, met Mr. Kemsley's deep blue eyes. Heat flushed her throughout at the warmth she saw there.

"I enjoyed your performance very much."

"Thank you," she murmured.

"I wondered if you might care to take a stroll through the gardens. They are most lovely, and I'm sure it would be cooler."

"Go on," Father said, in a tone that left little room for question.

She swallowed, accepting Mr. Kemsley's hand. What would happen if she told him about Richard's threat? Would he be horrified? Would he help her? God forbid he not believe her! Her heart wrenched. Would it give him such disgust of her family he refused to have anything to do with them anymore?

He drew her hand through his, and she fought a wince. He seemed to notice, shooting her a quick look. "Miss DeLancey?"

She shook her head. Outside. If only she were outside and could breathe.

Within seconds they were outdoors, and she gulped in the cool, refreshing air.

"Miss DeLancey — Clara — forgive me, but your mother is right. You do not seem at all well."

She shook her head. "It is not that, sir. I am well, it's just . . ."

He led her to a seat, into which she sank gratefully. When next she looked up, his look of tenderness was gone, replaced by something rather cooler. "Is it Hawkesbury?"

She gasped. "What do you know?"

"Clara, he need not concern you. One day you will need to put these feelings aside."

"Oh, but —"

"I know you've cared for him in the past, but you cannot let it affect you forever."

"No, you don't understand. I do not care for him. Not that way. Not at all!"

He sat beside her, picked up her hand. "Then there is hope for me?"

"Oh, Mr. Kemsley." Her eyes blurred.

"My dearest, what is it?" He squeezed her hands gently.

Pain shot up her arm. She gasped.

"What is it? Have I hurt you?"

"No, but I am hurt." She swallowed the fear, prayed for courage. "My . . . my brother, Richard, came to see me today. He . . . twisted my fingers and bruised my wrists."

"What?"

"I would not do what he asked. He tried to force me —"

"My dearest!"

Before she knew it, she was being pulled into a close embrace, was inhaling his delectable scent, was once more hearing his steady heartbeat. Here, in his arms, she was safe. She closed her eyes, savoring the moment.

"What did he want from you?"

She told him the all, his arm around her, his breath stirring the tendrils of her hair.

"He threatened Tessa?"

"Yes."

"I cannot see how such a thing is possible. They scarcely know my family."

But obviously thought his regard well worth the risk. Her heart fluttered. His regard!

"And you say you think the man must be out here, watching?"

"It would appear so, yes."

She felt his chest move as he nodded, and she glanced up at him. "What should I do?"

He heaved in a breath as if sucking in the weight of the world. "There is only one thing we can do. We must tell Hawkesbury and somehow enlist his help."

Thoughts tipped and swayed, lurching through his head like a tiny sloop upon wild seas. What should he do? *God, give me wisdom.* He waited, listening for the still, small voice that so often guided his steps. A speck of an idea formed, then grew in strength and certainty.

"My dearest." He caught hold of Clara's hand, the one not damaged by that malicious brother. If he never saw Richard DeLancey it would be too soon. "Do you trust me?"

"Yes."

"You know I care for you, and I've no wish to see your brother hurt, but . . . but in order to protect you that may be a consequence."

Her sea-green eyes glimmered. "He has made his own choices."

"He has. But we will do what we can to ensure you are not adversely affected." He rose. "Come inside. If that man is somewhere watching, he will be expecting to see you with Hawkesbury, not me."

He gently pulled her to her feet, walking

440

beside her, but not too closely, in case any unseen witness even now observed how closely they'd sat before. His lips tightened. Of course, if they had spied his actions earlier the game would be up, as any woman who allowed a man to hold her in such a way could never be enamored of another. That is, unless they truly thought Clara a dishonorable woman.

His chest heated, and he strove for calm as he reentered the room and returned Clara to her mother. Faces turned to them, some expectant, some curious. A man did not wander in the dusky twilight with a lady unless he had a purpose such as to propose. But as he had not, he avoided answering their questions, instead asking Lord Winpoole, the earl, and Lord Featherington if they'd spare him a moment.

Clara looked up at him anxiously; he merely nodded. "I'll be back soon."

He took the men into the next chamber, briefly explaining the situation, right down to Clara's damaged hands. The earl looked thunderous; Lord Featherington pale; her father, ill.

"I cannot believe it," he muttered. "That boy, the bane of my existence these recent years."

"My lord, I cannot think it wise to waste

time in recriminations," Ben said, shifting his gaze to the earl. "I understand you may wish no part in this. Please believe I find these things anathema also."

"You wish to marry her."

Hawkesbury said it as a statement, yet underneath the bald fact Ben could still hear the question. "I do. I trust with this plan we'll find this scoundrel Johnson and see justice finally served."

The earl uttered a long, drawn-out sigh. "I do not like it. But if you are sure, then you may count on my support."

"I cannot be sure," Ben admitted. "But we are all praying men, are we not?" He glanced at Clara's father, the only one with whom his doubts lay. Lord Winpoole nodded. "Then let us trust that God will guide our paths, and protect us all from the enemy's snares."

"Amen," said Tessa's sweetheart.

"Amen," the earl said, with a ghost of a smile.

"Er, Amen," Lord Winpoole said, a puzzled look in his eye.

"So, Featherington, you shall make your excuses before the fireworks begin." Ben managed a smile. "I'm sure keeping an eye on Tessa won't be too onerous a burden. David is a stouthearted man, for all he is a man of the cloth. And even George, once you put him in way of the facts, will prove more brave than not." He hoped.

Ben turned to the earl. "While you are here, you are obviously Richard's target, which carries some element of danger, but I cannot think Richard would allow harm to come to his sister." He remembered the twisted fingers. "Let's pray not."

The earl looked grim. "My army days left me well versed in matters of defense, if necessary."

Ben continued outlining his plans, to the nods of the two younger men of the trio, and the obvious dismay of the man he most wished to impress.

Clara's father looked slightly gray. "I own I cannot like this. Why not simply give them money?"

"Because the demands will not stop. Perhaps it may for several months, but it will return. And I'm sorry, sir, but I'm simply not willing to take chances with my sister's safety."

"Of course not, no," Lord Winpoole muttered. "I just wish —" His words faltered to a stop as the door opened. "Clara?"

She moved inside, cheeks wan, gaze flitting from man to man. "I'm sorry for interrupting —"

"Is it true what Kemsley says?" her father barked. "Did Richard really hurt you?"

"You do not believe me?" Eyes pooling, she tugged down her white gloves. "Do you believe this?"

The others echoed Ben's gasp. Deep purple bruises ringed her forearms.

"Oh, my dear girl! I had no idea." Her father dashed at his eyes, his face seeming more aged than before. "Richard did that?"

She nodded, chin wobbling.

"But why did you say nothing?"

She gave a shuddering breath, which made Ben long to hold her again. Would that he had that right soon. "He told me not to tell anyone, else . . ."

"Else he'd hurt Tessa," he finished.

"Yes." As if she'd decided to take command of herself, she took an audible breath, her shoulders straightened, her chin tilted. "Which is why I cannot let Richard's recklessness continue. Not when I see it as my fault."

"Miss DeLancey —"

She stopped the earl with a lifted hand. "My lord, I have thought and prayed over this. I" — her cheeks flamed rosy-red before paling again — "I am sorry that my . . . prior behavior . . ." Her gaze fell, her long lashes fanning her cheeks. "I am sorry that my unchecked emotion led to all this."

The earl shook his head. "I am sorry, more sorry than you can ever know, that my conduct was not as it ought to have been. I do not see this as your fault, Miss DeLancey, but as my responsibility."

She peeked up at the earl, with a look Ben couldn't decipher, but which twisted his heart nonetheless. A wave of insecurity washed through him. Would she ever forgo feelings for the earl?

Ben swallowed his doubts, forcing his mind to the matter at hand. "Miss DeLancey, please trust us. We will do our utmost to ensure the safety of all parties, for both their persons and their reputations."

"But Richard's plan —"

Her father gave a grating laugh. "Surely you aren't going to follow that sapskull's plans now?"

She turned wide, worried eyes to Ben, but before he could reassure, movement outside signaled the commencement of the illuminations. He settled for giving her a smile and turning to his companions. "Godspeed, gentlemen. I pray we shall meet again soon."

Lord Winpoole harrumphed. "Meet at my house, if you please. The least I can do after all you're doing for my wretched family."

The others assented, there was a final clasp of hands, then Lord Winpoole escorted Clara from the room, each man departing to play his role, and to trust that God would bring justice.

CHAPTER TWENTY-EIGHT

Clara followed the others out to the terrace as if in a trance. She glanced at her father. Would it be best to follow Richard's instructions? Surely no good could come from ignoring him!

High above twinkled the first of the stars. The crowd ahead milled around several large flambeaux, the bright orange flames flickering color over the faces of the assembled crowd.

The Regent was talking, as were Lady Sefton and Lord Palmer, their voices louder, pitched higher above the others. Mother was listening avidly, evidently unaware both husband and daughter were elsewhere; if only she remained oblivious to all tonight would bring.

Lavinia leaned close to the earl as he murmured in her ear, her widening eyes telling of her shock. The countess finally turned to face Clara, the firelight revealing her pale cheeks, as she said in an under-voice, "Nicholas just told me. I cannot believe anyone could be so cruel!"

Wait. She did not believe her?

"You poor, poor thing." Lavinia drew near, eyes pooling with sympathy. "I never realized how difficult things have been."

Her compassion enlarged the already size-able lump in Clara's throat. "I am so sorry. I wish none of this had happened, nor needed to happen. Please believe I had no wish" — she swallowed — "no wish to involve your husband in any of this."

"I believe you." She patted Clara's twisted arm, forcing her to bite back a gasp.

The earl finally met Clara's gaze, his eyes inscrutable. "As I said inside, I do not see this as your fault, Miss DeLancey, but as the result of my poor behavior long ago." He considered her gravely a moment longer, before saying, "I ask your forgiveness."

She bit her lip to stop the tremble. "You . . . you had it long ago."

The handsome contours of his face that had once so charmed her fell into softer lines. "Captain Kemsley mentioned you have found faith."

She nodded. "I . . . I was challenged by many things. Not least of which was your wife's kindness to me at the Seftons' ball."

"Lavinia is a most excellent creature," he said, gazing fondly at his wife.

"You chose well and right, my lord."

He glanced at Clara, a smile curling his lips. "I agree."

A chuckle escaped. She remembered something she often used to say when she'd first tried to impress him. "In fact, she might even be described as wonderfully fine."

He chuckled, as Lavinia looked between them, the mock outrage in her raised brows revealed by her smile. "I am standing right here, you know."

Lord Hawkesbury swiftly kissed her. Clara turned away, not because the sight brought pain as it once would have, but because the passion they shared only fueled desire to do the same with her betrothed. Well, her *nearly* betrothed. Mr. Kemsley might not have spoken the words, but his actions made his intentions clear. Her heart thumped. She hoped it would not be very much longer until she, too, was finally a wife.

Somehow through the darkness she caught Mr. Kemsley's gaze. His eyes were shadowed, and she could not read his expression. Her heart twisted. Surely he did not think she remained enamored of the earl?

Clara swallowed and was about to move

to reassure him, when the first firework exploded above, drawing oohs and ahhs from the crowd. She paused and watched it like the others, head tilted back, her heart lifting momentarily. Fireworks still made her feel like a child.

She followed the golden drops as they fell to earth, peering through the smoke. There was Prinny, ever obvious in his raiment, center of attention as usual, oblivious to the deeper concerns hiding in the darkness. There were the marquess and marchioness; how she hoped Lord Featherington would be kept safe, for their sake, and for Tessa's. There was Mother, and Lady Sefton. But . . . she pushed to her toes, searching keenly. Her heart twisted. Mr. Kemsley had gone.

Something akin to feeling bereft swept her soul. Now that Richard wanted Clara to show affection to the man she'd always thought she'd loved, she realized how much she wished to be with another. Lord Hawkesbury was too tall, too hard, too cutting. He had never laughed with her, never gazed at her tenderly or protected her as Mr. Kemsley had. Tonight she need only pretend, but pretending to care had never been so challenging.

Movement nearby drew her attention back

to the Hawkesburys. Lavinia placed a hand on her midsection. "I promise not to worry, but will pray for your safety."

He nodded, his mouth pulled grim. "Don't stop praying. I suspect we'll need strength and wisdom before the night is out." The earl kissed Lavinia again, then escorted her to Lady Exeter before bowing and moving away.

Frustration roiled within. Had Mr. Kemsley not explained things clearly? Didn't the earl understand the role Richard wished him to play? That Tessa needed him to play? How would any person watching ever believe anything but the earl's deep love for his wife?

There was a thunderous boom of fireworks, reds and blues spattering drops of light across the ground. Clara watched the earl move to a section of garden farther away from the others, partly obscured by several large, potted ferns, the light spilling from the drawing room behind. Was she supposed to follow?

She moved to join him, when a hand grasped her good arm.

"Clara, no."

"But, Father —"

"Trust me, my dear. You do not need to follow him anymore."

"I know, but —"

"Clara," he muttered urgently, "if you will not trust me, at least trust that Kemsley fellow. He's got a surprisingly good head on him. Now," his grip firmed, "let's see if your mother is amenable to departing. I confess I have a great desire to return home."

"But the plan —"

"Now, Clara."

Forced to obey her parents' lead and murmur her farewells, Clara travelled home in a welter of confusion. How could leaving so meekly solve their dilemma?

Her father's brief explanation — once they had arrived home and were safely away from Mother's ears — left her with no greater assurance, but instead ensconced in a different bedchamber, struggling to sleep as troubling dreams chased fears that refused to be silenced by prayers.

Ben sneaked along the perimeter of the garden. Behind him, he could hear a stealthy rustle as one of Prinny's coachmen searched the grounds for an intruder. From this distance, Ben could just make out the figures on the lawn.

Clara had gone home. He was glad. Apart from the distraction she always proved, she was safe — he hoped — at home, and away from any taint of scandal as the remainder of the evening's events unfolded. But in other ways, ways that proved to take up a disconcertingly large proportion of his thoughts, her absence meant he had no way of resolving whether the envy tugged from him during her interactions with the earl was a mere figment of his green-eyed imagination or a portent of something true. He supposed it possible a lady could inflict such bruising herself . . .

Ben shook his head, as if to shake away the doubts. No. Choose to doubt and one might as well be a wave of the sea, blown and tossed about by the wind. He could not afford to listen to the nefarious winds of this world. He needed to trust the Clara whose character he knew, rather than be set adrift by fear and rumors from the past.

Refocused, he forced his attention to the bushes ahead. He could not see any of the other searchers; only trusted that they would keep their movements quiet as instructed. He sent up another prayer for Tessa's safety. While he trusted Featherington would make his case to guard and protect plain — and hoped the man lived up to his boast of shooting prowess at Manton's — he also hoped George would understand Ben's quickly scrawled message, though he felt sure Mattie and David would. They'd have locked all doors and windows and have surrounded her like lionesses around their cubs.

Another crack of colored lightning lit the sky.

He glanced back at the Pavilion. The earl's tall figure had detached from the group. Ben gritted his teeth. He did not like Hawkesbury making himself an obvious target, but he had agreed, and any subterfuge such as disguise would scarcely fool either Richard or Hawkesbury's former agent. What hold did Johnson have over Clara's brother? How could a viscount's son be inveigled in such a miserable business? And how could any man permit hatred to take hold to the degree that he was prepared to injure his sister?

His hands fisted, he shook his head. What a situation to be embroiled in, to embroil the man he would call father-in-law. Especially as it involved his son . . .

A third set of fireworks exploded, this time a set of three, one echoing after the other. More light spilled from heaven. More oohs and ahhs floated across the lawn.

Ben forced himself to sift the bushes and trees; these moments of light were the best chance to see the intruder. There was another crack, another wash of color. He blinked, forcing himself to watch closely. Was that —

No. He'd been mistaken. Just a branch.

The fireworks continued their relentless blooming in the skies. He examined the foliage carefully. What if Richard had lied? What if there was no other man, and all this was a set up to take aim at the earl? Nausea sloshed through him. Would a brother take such chances, even one as depraved as Richard obviously was?

There!

A glint of metal. On a cylindrical tube. A tube, pointed at the man separated from the others at the Pavilion.

There was another roar of fireworks, only this time followed immediately by a bang and spurt of fire. Amid screams from the Pavilion, he rushed to the man holding the weapon, saw the man's face, recognized the features, and hurtled towards him, even as the weapon was lifted once again.

Chapter Twenty-Nine

He was dead!

Clara's eyes flew open, and she sat upright in bed, dragging in frantic breaths. Darkness still filled the room, though a hint of the coming dawn seeped around the curtained windows. No. She placed a hand on her chest, willing her heartbeat to calm. It'd been a dream, a bad dream. That was all.

She sagged back onto the pillows, closing her eyes, but the images refused to leave. Mr. Kemsley, lying injured, helpless, and bloodied, as a faceless man took aim, and — No!

Her eyes cracked open. No. He was safe. He had to be! Surely they would have heard otherwise by now . . .

Lord, protect him.

A creak outside alerted her to someone's presence, just before the door opened silently. Her heart played *allegro* as she huddled against the headboard. Was it Richard? Johnson? What should she use as a weapon? She spied her Bible on the table beside the bed. Would God forgive her if she used her Bible for such a purpose?

A shaft of light traced Meg's features.

"Oh, it's you!" Relief made Clara chuckle at her misapprehension. "I thought —"

"The master wants you downstairs, miss."

"Father?" Clara glanced at the curtains, around which bled a thin, gray light. She rubbed her eyes, then studied the maid, who seemed abominably happy for the early hour. "What would Father want at such a time?"

The maid glanced down, cheeks flushing. "I couldn't say, miss."

No, Clara thought. Why would Father tell a servant of the plans? Her heart wrenched. He must have had news! Oh, how she hoped her dream wasn't a sign!

"Tell him I'll come right away."

Mind still half-fuzzy from lack of sleep, Clara shoved her feet into comfortable house slippers, then snatched up a thin robe, wrapping it around her as she descended the steps. Early morning chill ate through her shift and light nightgown. Normally she would never appear before Father dressed so *dishabille* but this was obviously important. She walked through the drawing room's opened door. A fire glowed in the grate. She moved directly to it, hands outstretched, hoping to ward off dawn's coolness.

"Hello, Clara."

She spun around. "Richard!"

Her heart beat *forte staccato* at the look in his eye. Meg moved from the room's shadowed recesses to stand beside him. He smiled down at her, and Meg gazed up at him.

Clara's insides gave a sudden heave. She recognized that look. It was one she'd worn too many times. "You . . . and Meg?"

He gave a grating laugh. "Why not? Meg is good and pliable enough. She's never minded helping me when I needed information, or a door left unlocked, especially in exchange for a few favors, shall we say?"

Meg ducked her head as Clara sent her a narrow look.

Bile filled her mouth as she returned her attention to her brother. Unlike his latest conquest, Richard's face wore no shame. "How could you?"

He shrugged. "I'm the son of a lord. This is what we do." He pinched Meg's rear, to her squeak of approval.

Clara shivered. Did her brother hold no compunctions? "I don't know how you had the nerve to come here again."

"After you told people, you mean?" He shot her a sardonic look. "Didn't you think I'd know you would? You've never been able to keep a secret, always thinking you know best, and look where that's got us."

"You blame me for your actions?"

"Of course! I never would've been in this mess if it wasn't for you and that fool Hawkesbury."

She bit back a hot retort at the familiar refrain, endeavoring for a calm tone when next she spoke. "So you saw Lord Hawkesbury at the Pavilion?"

"Kissing his wife, no less." He shook his head. "Seems he doesn't want you anymore, Clara."

She aimed for nonchalance as she shrugged. "I knew that long ago. Your plan was never going to work. Everybody knows how devoted they are to each other."

He muttered a curse. "Everyone but that fool Johnson. He insisted —"

"Where is he now?"

Another profanity. "Fool got spotted at the Pavilion and got caught. But not before he took out a few of your desperate helpers."

"What?" Her heart raced. Not Mr. Kemsley, not Mr. Kemsley!

He uttered a low laugh. "Yes, I'm afraid your sailor has sailed his final voyage."

"Mr. Kemsley?" She licked dry lips. "Is he —"

"Is that his name? Such a common, coarse-looking fellow. I cannot understand why my sister of all people should take a fancy to him." He smiled evilly. "No need to mind now."

She felt the room sway. "Is he dead?"

"Dead, or at least will be soon enough, judging from the amount of blood I saw."

She closed her eyes, hopelessness gnawing at her. *Dear God, please keep him alive . . .*

"She looks like she might faint, Master Richard."

"Hush yourself. She's only shamming."

Despair wove icy fingers through her soul, squeezing her heart until it seemed all hope had gone. He couldn't be gone. He couldn't be! She bit her bottom lip to stop the tremble, sucked in a huge gulp of air, and finally opened her eyes. Fainting would not help anyone.

"What do you want, Richard?"

"What I want is impossible. The past two years to be altered, to not be on the run, so desperate for money that I —" An odd light kindled his eyes. Was that regret shading them?

He shook himself. " 'What's done cannot be undone,' so Hamlet once said."

"Lady Macbeth," she murmured.

"What?"

A persistent throb of anger slowly intensified as she studied his once-handsome features, traces of the debonair youth he'd once been still faintly evident. "I think it more apropos to say that 'fair is foul, and foul is fair,' wouldn't you? How sad to learn those one thinks should be trustworthy cannot be trusted." She eyed the maid, who ducked her head again.

Richard's eyes slitted. "Just like a witch, aren't you, with your spiteful tongue? Well, come along."

Clara took another pace back. "I'm not leaving."

"Oh, yes you are." Quick as lightning, he dashed forward and grabbed her arm, wrapping a hand over her lips as she opened her mouth to scream. "And there'll be none of that, either. You might think you outsmarted me, putting those men to safeguard your precious little friend, but I still know where Hawkesbury lives, and I'll take great pleasure in finishing what I started with his countess so long ago."

She wriggled, but he twisted her arm

harder until she was sure it would nearly break.

"I saw you talking with her last night, acting so friendly, like you actually cared," he breathed in her ear. "If you actually do care, then you'll stop protesting. You're coming with me, and not a sound will you make."

His threat wormed into her heart and she ceased her useless struggle. No, he would not hurt Lavinia. She would die rather than let her brother hurt Lavinia again.

Maintaining his firm grip from behind, he forced her to walk to where Meg had the door opened. She was wrenched to one side as Richard gave Meg a loud smack of a kiss before he pushed Clara out into the hall.

Clara's thoughts raced frantically, nothing settling, nothing firming into purpose. At this early hour, the likelihood of encountering someone who could help her was virtually nil. And even if she screamed, Richard would run away, and doubtless fulfill his evil intentions against Lavinia. Her eyes pricked with tears as she was half dragged to the front door, Meg following close behind. She stumbled. If only Mr. Kemsley — a sob wrenched in her throat — No! She could not think like that! *Oh, Lord God, please help me!*

■ ■ ■ ■

Benjamin rubbed his eyes, gritty with lack of sleep. Beside him, Braithwaite mumbled something as they continued their vigil watching the Winpoole residence. He ignored him, just as he worked to ignore the stench of failure wafting in the predawn breeze. His bloodstained shirt stank of sweat and regret. How could everything have gone so wrong so quickly? One minute he'd held the wretch in his hands; the next he held nothing but a probable broken nose, and misery that his fool knee had given way just as his captive had wriggled free, escaping into darkness. Apart from an unexpected encounter with Braithwaite, who had offered his services the minute he saw Ben's distress, the only good outcome of the past three hours had been the capture of Johnson, who had admitted — under Hawkesbury's interrogation, and threats of the hangman's noose — to the whereabouts of the earl's missing money.

But money held little value when weighed against another's life. Especially the life of the woman Ben knew he loved. He loved her, with a gut-wrenching force equivalent to the most immense gale encountered at sea. But whether that love was enough —

"Look!"

Braithwaite's rum-soaked breath hissed through the murky dimness as a group of three individuals descended the stairs and made their way along the Crescent. Although sound might not travel quite as well as over water, the rough cobblestones and as-yet absence of early morning bustle would still make a whisper too loud. He tugged at his friend's arm, motioning him for silence, and they made their way closer, keeping low as they inched along the headland.

Why three?

Ben squinted, trying to make out the figure of the third. Had Lord Winpoole decided to forgo Ben's carefully laid out plans and determined a course of his own making? Did his wife and daughter accompany him?

No, he was being ridiculous. Ben shook his head at himself and crept closer.

Now he was nearer he could see just how ridiculous that thought was. The figures were all tall and slim, none having the viscount's rotundity. And he could not envisage Lord Winpoole holding another in such a cruel grasp. His mouth dried. That must be DeLancey, holding Clara!

A quiet clatter of hooves dragged his attention to where a carriage had drawn up at the corner of Marine Parade and Burlington, to where Clara was being slowly but surely hauled. But how could he save her? He had no weapon, nothing that could secure her release.

Long ago lessons of His Majesty's service resurfaced, mingling with verses read far more recently. Christians, like sea captains, did not sink under fear. He shook off his doubts and pushed to his full height. "Miss DeLancey!"

The figures turned. In the dawn's dim light, he saw Clara's widening eyes, saw the man shift in front of her, before hissing, "Leave us alone."

Ben rushed forward, eyes fixed on Clara. Her face wore traces of tears, her attire indicated she'd been rushed from the house without opportunity to change. "Clara?"

"How dare you address my sister so?" Richard DeLancey whipped out a small knife and held it to his sister's throat. "Get back."

Ben's heart drummed with fear. He stood his ground, maintaining DeLancey's gaze, even as the other lady climbed into the carriage. "Please release her. I don't care where you go, and I promise not to follow —"

"You think it's that simple? I've desperate men after me . . ." DeLancey swore a vile oath. "I'd rather swing than see a naval upstart have anything to do with my sister. She is a viscount's daughter, for goodness' sake!"

"And I am a baronet." Well, he would be soon. "A baronet who loves her."

The terror edging Clara's eyes softened as she gave a weak smile. Her brother blinked, before waving the blade wildly. "I do not care. Get away." He held the knife close to her throat, the sharp edge pressing into her skin.

Everything within wanted to pound the villain into oblivion. See him flogged with a cat o' nine tails before being strung from the yardarm of the nearest ship. Richard DeLancey was a traitor to his sister, his family, to gentlemen everywhere. Ben forced himself to remain still, yet poised for action, a lion readying for its prey. He would not see further harm come to Clara. He could *not* see her hurt anymore.

Richard gave a manic-tinged laugh. "Go away, Kemsley. I have business to complete."

What?

Before he realized what had happened, Clara was dragged inside, and DeLancey had leapt to the carriage front, pushing the coachman to the ground. The reins snapped, Ben was chasing the moving vehicle, then his knee buckled, and he toppled to join the coachman muttering curses on the ground.

He pushed up with his hands and lifted his head, as the vehicle tilted dangerously around a corner, then was lost from sight. And a wave of despair crashed over him.

CHAPTER THIRTY

Clara refused to cry, refused to show fear. How dare Meg betray her family in such a way? How dare Richard? The very fact that Mr. Kemsley was alive — alive! — instilled hope that somehow today would not end as wretchedly as it had started. But it seemed day's end was still so far away, even as the first rays of gold shafted light through the carriage.

She eyed her captor as the carriage careened wildly around another bend. Meg swayed, one hand gripping the strap, the other holding that venomous knife poised for use.

"I'm disappointed in you, Meg."

Her maid — or was that former maid? — sniffed. "I do not have to pretend to care about your disappointments anymore, miss."

Clara managed a raspy chuckle. "You never did a very good job of pretending to care. Although I'll grant you pretended very well to have no knowledge of Richard's whereabouts." She studied her. "How long have you been smitten with him?"

Meg lifted her chin. "I do not have to answer to you."

"No, but I should think you'd want to tell me. Because it's obvious you've cast a spell over my brother."

Clara offered a smile she hoped did not appear too false, but rather looked inviting of a confidence. Just as she'd hoped, Meg's face lit up. "You truly think so?"

Clara nodded. *Father, forgive me.* "I have never seen him so passionate as with you." She had heard whispers of his exploits, but — thank God — she'd never been witness to his carnal appetite until now. She swallowed, hoping to extract some kernel of information as to her plight. "I imagine he has plans to take you to France or Ireland once all this is over."

"Oh, not to France, because Richard says that's where Lord Houghton is taking —" She gave Clara a scared look and clamped her lips, refusing to look at her anymore.

She swallowed, fighting a wave of revulsion, as her father's words from the previous night sang softly in her mind. Just because her sapskull brother held evil plans did not mean she need acquiesce.

Clara looked through the small sliver of window not obscured by the red leather curtain. They had turned onto the Steyne and were drawing closer to the beach. Wherever she was headed, it seemed they would travel by boat. Nausea surged through her midsection. Suddenly she did not care what impact her actions might have on others. Let the earl take care of Lavinia; she had to take care of herself!

They careened around another corner. This time as Meg was thrown off-balance, Clara was ready, and she threw herself at the door, unlatching it at the same time. She fell onto the road, hitting her head so hard it seemed she bounced. She groaned, placed a hand to her head. Stared at the blood on her hand. What on earth —

Vaguely she became aware of the carriage stopping, of the thud of footsteps. Of a hand grabbing her, dragging her upright. Richard called her a foul name, then pushed her back into the carriage, whereupon she was violently sick. All over Meg's shoes.

Meg made a noise of disgust. She had at least put the knife away, not that Clara felt up for any more heroics. She huddled on the seat, pain heaving, her vision blurring in and out. If only she'd thought to be sick on

Richard, perhaps he'd be so disgusted he would wash his hands of inveigling her in any more of his wickedness. Her heart brightened. Perhaps such a method might work on others, too . . .

Finally the dreadful lurching of the carriage stopped, and she was half lifted, half dragged down. "Stand up, you silly chit."

She promptly collapsed on the ground.

"Clara, enough!" Richard seized her arm, jerking her higher. Pain shot up her arm, forcing her to release an almighty wail.

Slap!

A violent stinging sensation roared across her cheek. Her face swung round, her neck wrenching, as she saw the open palm come again, and woozily ducked from harm's way.

"Richard!"

"How dare you address me so?"

There was the sound of another slap — one not aimed at Clara — then a cry, and muffled whimpers. Perhaps Meg would not be travelling any farther, after all. Clara forced herself to her knees and glanced up to see two fishermen watching by a rowboat, their mouths agape. Mortification enveloped her more thoroughly than if she'd been dropped into the midst of the Channel. How humiliating!

She slowly rose, and stood, feet slipping

on the tiny stones, her knees trembling, but aiming to muster as much dignity as possible. She looked at her brother. "Why are you doing this?"

"I need money, Clara. What was I supposed to do?"

"You were supposed to behave as a *gentleman.*" She nearly spat the word.

"Haven't you heard? I appear to have lost any claim to that label right about the time you lost any right to be called an Honorable."

She refused to let the old wound sting. Time to change tack. "Where are you taking me?"

"You'll find out soon enough."

He yanked her forward, muttering curses as she tried to escape his grasp. Oh, if only the fishermen knew to rescue her! But how could they recognize her as anything but a strumpet, dressed as she was in a thin nightgown, with blood trickling down her face. Probably they'd not think anything of a finely dressed gentleman beating a woman or two. Surely no hope of help could be expected from them.

No, she'd have to keep praying those angels on guard on that wild night so many months ago knew to look on Brighton's beach this cool dawn. She stumbled, stones biting into her feet. About half a mile offshore she could see a small yacht waiting.

"Miss DeLancey." She froze. "I did not expect to find you quite so eager to meet me here."

Stomach curdling, she slowly turned to meet Lord Houghton's gaze. "What do you want?"

He smiled. "I'm here to make sure you end up married to the right man."

"And who might that be?"

"Why me, of course." He looked her over, the predatory glint in his eyes receding into a frown. "Although I did not expect to see you arrayed quite so . . . casually. Nor so bloodied."

Bile rose in her mouth. She swallowed. "I'm afraid you're mistaken."

One graying brow pushed high. "Not a situation I'm terribly familiar with, I admit. Tell me, my dear, how am I mistaken?"

"About the man who is right for me to marry."

"Clara," Richard said in a warning voice.

"It certainly isn't you! You are a vile, wicked man. I *despise* you."

"Clara!"

"In fact, your evil only makes my husband-to-be look all the more heroic! He may not have an old title or a great estate, but he loves me and wants what is best for — *ow!*" She rubbed her arm where Lord Houghton had pinched her.

"Don't hurt her," Richard muttered.

"That's rather rich, coming from somebody who already has," Lord Houghton sneered. "But then one might expect anything from a man willing to sell his sister."

Clara swiped at the trickling blood and eyed her brother. "You *sold* me?"

"He promised me money, Clara," he muttered, looking down. "I had no choice."

"You always have a choice." She sank onto the beach. If Lord Houghton wanted her, she would make that as difficult as possible for him. "See, Richard? A choice."

"Get up," Lord Houghton said.

Clara refused to move, sinking her fingers into the ground. She fisted her hands around large pebbles. Did stones still kill monsters today?

"Get up!" Lord Houghton yanked the arm Richard had hurt earlier, forcing her yelp of pain — and to release the rocks.

"Stop it!" Richard cried. "Clara, I know what you must think of me, but you must do what he says."

"It makes no difference now what she thinks," Lord Houghton said, putting his hand in his coat pocket. "You got her here as you said, and dressed quite appropriately I must say, considering what activities I have planned shortly."

Oh, dear God!

"Now all that remains is payment."

Richard's eyes gleamed with avarice, and he stretched out a hand.

The sound of a gunshot ricocheted off the streets of early morning Brighton, freezing Ben's steps. God forbid Clara was hurt! He could never live with himself —

"Come on!" Braithwaite tugged at Ben's arm, almost dragging him towards the shore. Thank God for his friend, whose presence offered a measure of reassurance. There was precious little to reassure otherwise.

He refused to let his mind wander over the exchange of looks between Clara and the earl. He refused to wonder whether she would accept Ben's suit.

The recriminations intensified one hundredfold. This was his faulty plan. His mistakes. How could he have lost Richard twice in one night?

They ascended a rise. Beyond, the sea glistened with the promise of daybreak. But there'd be no cleansing swim today. Ahead, he could see several fishermen gawking at the scene below on the beach. Nearby, a woman sprawled on the ground, her hysterical sobbing suggesting they should slow their steps.

Braithwaite moved beside her, helping her up to a more dignified position. "Miss?"

Clara's maid. The third figure from earlier. Ben fought the rising tide of panic. "Where are they?"

She pointed to the beach.

Ben gestured for Braithwaite to follow, and skirted the shore in reconnaissance. The beach was surprisingly deserted, save for three figures stopped halfway to a small rowboat where two men waited. Beyond, a small sloop, its sail trimmed for speed, bobbed in the water. It could only mean one thing: Clara was meant to sail to France.

His mouth dried. From here he could see the gleam of Lord Houghton's gun, could see Richard sprawled on the sand, and Clara bending over him, shoulders convulsing as if she were crying. No sounds reached him at this distance. Lord Houghton yanked at Clara to stand, but she shook her head.

What could he do? Although he could more than hold his own in a fist-fight, he was too far away to assist now. And he had no weapon. *Dear Lord, help us!*

"Kemsley."

He jumped. "Hawkesbury!"

The earl focused on the figures below. "Forgive the surprise. Apparently my army scouting training still proves its worth. Now, what do we know?"

"It appears working with Johnson wasn't enough for DeLancey, and he had another rig with Houghton. That old lecher appears to have shot him. Clara's behavior suggests it might be fatal."

"Might be the best thing for that family if that scoundrel — Forgive me, Kemsley. I should not speak ill —"

"I quite understand," Ben muttered. He'd never hated anyone with more intensity than he did Richard right now, though Houghton was coming a very close second. How he wished for a ship so he might keelhaul the pair of them. His hands fisted; he exhaled slowly. Such thoughts would not assist Clara. "What shall we do?"

"I borrowed a pair of pistols from our host last night. I thought you could have one —"

Ben shook his head. "I've never been a crack shot."

"Ah. I was considered something of a marksman on the Peninsular, but using another man's pistols means things are never guaranteed. And while you may think

477

I have no liking for Miss DeLancey, I certainly have no wish to put a bullet through her. But if I provide a distraction, perhaps you two" — he nodded to Braithwaite — "can somehow remove her from danger, and we can ensure Houghton does not continue in his perfidy."

Ben breathed in the salty air, as the first gleams of sunrise stole across the sea. Thoughts churned within before gradually settling into clarity, and he finally felt like he was on firm land. "God help us," he said aloud.

"Amen."

CHAPTER THIRTY-ONE

Tears obscured Clara's vision as she worked desperately to stem the blood blooming through Richard's shirt. *Dear God, help us.*

His mouth sagged, and he looked at Clara with something approaching disbelief. "I did not realize . . ."

She managed a weak smile, trying to communicate her forgiveness. "Honor among thieves is never really honor, is it?"

His face seemed suddenly forlorn, like a lost little boy. "I never meant things to turn out like this. I only wanted money. When I realized Johnson only wanted to kill Hawkesbury it was too late. Houghton offered money, and I —"

"Shhh, don't speak. You need your strength."

"You're nothing but a fool," Lord Houghton snarled. "As if I'd give you money."

"Houghton!"

The voice from the headland stole their

attention. Lord Hawkesbury.

Houghton swore and grasped her to himself. A muzzle pressed against her ear. She felt herself sway, but she would not faint. She would not! She had to help save —

"Let her go, Houghton," the earl called, lifting a pistol.

"Never!"

"Let her go," Richard's voice came weakly. "Clara —"

"Richard, I forgive you."

She was dragged away from her brother, along the beach to where a small rowboat sat. The two fishermen she'd noticed earlier were gone.

"Where are those fools?" Lord Houghton muttered.

"Perhaps they didn't like your method of payment."

He lifted the gun again. She flinched, and he laughed, eyes hard and cold. "Get in."

"I'd rather die here with my brother than go anywhere with you."

"That might still be arranged. Now get in." He wrenched her arm — why did they always choose her weakened left arm? — and forced her inside the small boat. She huddled in the rear, arms wrapped around herself to ward off the chill coming from the water as Lord Houghton tugged the boat to the water, his weapon still prominently displayed. She glanced over her shoulder. This position revealed the earl moving closer, pistol still raised, consternation on his face. No doubt he wished for a clear shot at Lord Houghton; how gratifying to know his resentment toward her was not so deep that he'd willingly risk her an injury.

With a few grunted pushes, they were in the water, and Houghton was rowing out to the small sailing boat. Waves were small, variously pulling them deeper, then pushing them back, but Lord Houghton persisted, with strength surprising for both his age and air of sophistication. She peered back at the shore. Lord Hawkesbury now seemed a speck; she could see figures clustered around Richard. Her heart cramped anew.

"Hawkesbury can't help you now," Houghton said. "Your stupid sailor is nowhere to be seen."

Her insides froze. She hadn't seen Mr. Kemsley in an age. Had he given up on her, too?

"Nobody is going to help you now, Miss DeLancey."

Except, that wasn't quite true, a small voice murmured.

Lord, what should I do?

481

A verse from a psalm read on Sunday surged to mind, something about how God was mightier than the mighty waves of the sea. She eyed the water. How deep was it? Could she swim? She wasn't bound. Once they reached the boat, she might not have another chance to escape. How she wished now she had tried swimming as she and Mattie had discussed so long ago!

"Do not get any ideas," Lord Houghton warned. "I will not fish you out."

"Is that a promise?"

"What?"

"As I said earlier, I'd rather die than spend any more time with you." She stood, rocking the small vessel wildly.

"Clara, no!"

But she ignored him, jumping from the boat to plunge into the stingingly chilled water.

Ben rubbed the seawater from his eyes, watching from the prow of the sloop as Clara vanished into the depths. No! He climbed up on the side. He couldn't lose her. Houghton was yelling, searching frantically, but the sea remained too dark, the water too murky. Houghton would never find her in time. So he dived in.

The water at once stung and sedated.

He'd forgotten until he'd dived the impact on his nose, and now struggled to breathe. He'd be lucky to even have a nose once this day was done.

With a gasp he broke the surface, then swam with clean, sure strokes, working to keep the terror at bay. God had proved faithful so far, giving Braithwaite and Ben strength to disable the two men Houghton had hired for the rowboat, then the ability to swim out to the sloop undetected by the ship's crew, who now lay bound or out cold, taken by surprise when they'd climbed aboard. Surely God would remain faithful now.

Eventually he reached the bobbing rowboat, where Houghton was swearing worse than any sailor Ben had ever heard.

Houghton turned. "About time! I hoped one of you would notice the wretched girl —" He peered at Ben more closely. "Wait! Aren't you —"

Ben duck-dived down, away from the yelled obscenities, ignoring the intense pain in his nose as he searched for a trace of white.

Memories surged, of another lady lost at sea, of another dangerous night and horrible adventure. A life he should have saved.

Gritting his teeth, he pushed aside water,

thrusting forward through choppy waves. There!

He pulled closer, closer. Clara was flailing, hair streaming behind her, white gown adhering to her body like some mythical Grecian sea-nymph.

He drew near, grasped her hands, and tugged her up to break the surface, where she coughed and spluttered, gasping as she released the seawater.

"Good girl." He hooked an arm around her torso, and kicked toward safety, allowing waves to propel them towards shore. Behind him, he could hear Houghton's screams. Ahead, past the whitecaps, he could see Hawkesbury's frantic pacing and figures huddled around Richard's body. His clutch firmed. He finally had Clara in his arms, able to prove himself again, to set to rest the failures of the past.

They reached the shallows, and he stumbled forward to collapse on the pebbled beach, Clara still in his arms. Her green eyes were wide with fright, she was muttering incoherencies, her hair tangled in her face. Ben smoothed away the dark strands from her eyes, from the bloodied graze on her forehead. "Hush, my love, you are safe now."

The moisture sheening her face was not only seawater. "You won't leave me?"

"Never," he promised.

She burrowed into his chest, clinging tight. He wrapped his arms around her, until her trembling ceased, and the heat stirring within bade him to remember he'd been born a gentleman, and she a viscount's daughter. He reluctantly released her, shifting away, conscious of onlookers, of feet hurrying toward —

"Kemsley! Look out!"

A shot blasted from behind. Beach pebbles scattered in an arc less than a foot from Clara's head. Ben hurled himself across her, spanning yet not touching her, the protectiveness surging within demanding he shield her from all danger.

"Ben!" Terror rimmed the green of her eyes, her shivering becoming marked.

"Stay still." He gritted out a reassuring smile, his knee throbbing as he maintained the awkward position, bracing himself with his elbows and feet to avoid contact. Heaven forbid her mother — or any of Brighton's infamous gossips — see them in such a shocking near embrace.

Another shot rang out. Behind him, he could hear a man's scream, then a thud.

Clara gasped, hers eyes widening even more. She was so close, he could see golden flecks in her eyes, feel her breath on his cheek, see her rosy lips tremble, inviting him to offer comfort the way he dreamed. Still he dared not move.

There was a crunch of boots on stones. He lifted his head as Hawkesbury neared, a gleaming pistol hanging loosely in his hand.

The earl offered a grim smile. "There's no need to worry now."

Ben pushed away and sat up, as the man Clara had once loved stripped off his coat and helped her into it. Jealousy flickered. He tamped it down, working to stem his insecurities by avoiding gazing at the pair murmuring together, choosing instead to focus on the small boat bobbing out at sea, the slumped figure of Houghton pitching with every shifting wave. A sharp breeze cut through his sodden clothes, reminding him of the need to find his coat and dry garments.

He drew in a ragged, painful breath, then forced himself to rise and walk unsteadily away.

CHAPTER THIRTY-TWO

The sickroom held the stench of death. Even in departing this world, Richard's calamitous influence held sway. The poison leaching through his body from the bullet wound had led to a fever that weakened him a little more each day. The doctor could do little for him; Clara could do nothing save pray and hope her oft-stated forgiveness eased his mind. He rambled about conquests and depravity, of which she tried hard not to hear. When he was really bad — describing his dealings with some of the light-skirts he'd encountered — the doctor or Father would insist she leave, and she would escape gratefully.

"Clara." Richard's over-bright eyes turned to her, the sheen on his brow evidence of burning sickness.

She sank a little lower in the chair, the better for him to see her face. "What is it?"

"I am dying."

Her eyes pricked, her throat clamped, forcing her to nod in answer.

"I . . . I didn't realize . . ." His voice trailed off, as had happened many times when he would either lose his thoughts or fall asleep.

"It does not matter now," she said.

Nothing much mattered now. In the past two weeks their world had shrunk to Richard, caring for him, then when assured it was a hopeless case, waiting for him to finally breathe his last. She barely had a chance to snatch news from the outside world. Mattie had been faithful in her visits, but she was one of the few. Tessa had been invited by Viscount Featherington's sister to spend some time in Lincolnshire, at Hartwell Abbey. They'd seized a moment for a brief consultation about Tessa's attire, all the time Tessa atwitter with the thought that she was going to stay at a duke's ancestral home.

"I'm told it has secret passages!" Tessa's blue eyes had grown wider than Clara recalled. "Hartwell Abbey is a very old and noble home."

Clara had nodded. "I'm sure the duchess will enjoy having someone to stay who will appreciate such things. Especially a bright, new face so willing to be pleased."

"I hope I do not embarrass myself or

Henry." She blushed. "I do so want to learn everything I ought."

As well she might. It seemed Lord Exeter must have given tacit approval for his son's engagement to encourage the connection.

"I'm sure you will succeed wonderfully well. You have a sweet and merry heart, and I'm sure Charlotte will appreciate such a thing at this time."

"Oh, yes. I forget sometimes that you know them."

"But barely."

"Well, I imagine I would welcome any diversion if I were confined, too."

Clara had smiled, in what felt like her first smile in an age. "That manner of plain speaking might be better left unsaid."

Her smile at the memory faded as she mopped Richard's brow again. It seemed hard to believe so much had happened; that so much remained unresolved. Her hands had healed now, the bruises faded. Sometimes when she watched over her brother, she was near inclined to adopt her mother's belief that Richard's behavior those past months was a momentary aberration. It still seemed impossible to reconcile the kindly brother of her youth with the abandoned-to-principle violent rake his delirium confirmed him to be. Regardless, his recent actions had not killed every vestige of her affection. Should she write him off for his bad choices in recent months? She could not. Forgiveness bade her not. Besides, her brother wasn't the only one who had made poor choices in his life.

Poor Richard. Her throat welled. She prayed he would find peace with God, for the alternative did not bear thinking about. Shivers rippled through her as she remembered a recent dream of a yawning chasm opening before Richard, into which he tumbled, falling, falling into an abyss of hopelessness and forever despair. God wanted Richard to find forgiveness, just as He wanted her to forgive her brother, to love the unlovely. She swallowed. There could be few better candidates than the man lying in her father's house that fit that category.

Remorse chased her uncharitable thought. It seemed the old Clara way of thinking might take a while longer to completely change. She murmured a prayer for forgiveness and returned her attention to the patient.

When the tall case clock struck half five, she was relieved by her father, whose care for his son now seemed in direct proportion to his lack of ability to show such attention in recent times due to Richard's prolonged absence. Mother could not bring herself to do so, claiming it hurt to see her son unwell, and she unable to do anything about it. It hurt Clara's heart to see her parents' pride slip into honest acknowledgment of Richard's failings, their remorse-tinged affection given when it was almost too late. How much better would it have been if Richard had never allowed pride to dictate his behavior. How much better would it have been if she had never allowed pride to dictate hers.

She plucked a shawl from the hook in the hall and moved outside, tasting a breath of fresh air. Ahead, the sun was dipping, slowly sinking into a pool of golden loveliness. Wrapping the shawl around her tightly, she moved past the sad statue of the Regent, and drew closer to the cliff.

The sunset played across the sky, twining streaks of pink and purple swirling into gold. That same golden shimmer of months ago, when she'd stood atop this same cliff, in this same spot, asking God to somehow set her free from the past, was again bathing the town in an almost mystical buttery light.

So much had happened since then. So much remained unresolved.

Her eyes pricked. She swallowed. A lonely gull cawed across the sky.

Clara huddled deeper into the shawl's protection. The ever-present breeze still found ways of piercing her silken armor, and she shivered.

Contrary to his word, Mr. Kemsley had left Brighton almost immediately. On one of her visits, Mattie had said it was something to do with the Admiralty, and Clara desperately wanted to believe it, but some days felt too hard to fight her doubts. The tiredness, the strain of weeks of caring left her vulnerable to those long-ago whispers that she was worthless, she was ugly, nobody would love her. She would fight them with God's Word, but sometimes, like now, the loneliness seemed to hold hands with rejection to beat her down. She wanted to think on good things, but . . .

Lord, help me.

As her prayer fluttered up to heaven, her thoughts shifted to that last day. She shuddered afresh. Thank God for Mr. Kemsley saving her from drowning. Thank God for the earl, who in shooting Houghton had saved them from certain peril. She even thanked God that such an incident had occurred so early in the day, before much of the town had a chance to be up and witness the events — and gossip. As it was, much of the gossip had been contained by the Prince Regent and Lord Hawkesbury, neither of whom wanted their names associated with the demise of Lord Houghton or Richard DeLancey. Eventually a rumor was put about — and adhered to most vehemently — that the ghost of his late wife had visited Houghton. She found a smile. She'd never thought she would be glad to be regarded as a ghost, but better that than people discover the true identity of the white-clad creature on the beach that morning.

Yes, so much had happened since the previous magical sunset. Yet so much remained unresolved.

Her heart caught. Why had Mr. Kemsley not visited? Was he ashamed of the connection, and now wished to withdraw from his near proposal, especially since she'd brought so much pain into his family's life? Mattie had tried to reassure, but the niggling doubts remained. Father had said he'd given his blessing, but surely an enamored suitor would wish to pay suit? Perhaps he did not love her any more.

Clara blinked. She could *not* think like that. She quickly sucked in another breath, releasing pain as she breathed out.

Think on good things, Mattie encouraged.

Good things, instead of listening to the tug of despair. Good things, like the fact she was not the same girl who'd once wondered about falling from a cliff. Instead, prayers and Bible reading kept her spirits — mostly — buoyant. She had friends now, genuine friends, people she could laugh with, even be a little silly with, who loved her despite her faults — despite those moments when she forgot she was a new creation and behaved like the old Clara again. She drew in a deep breath. Thank God for her friends.

Thank God for beautiful and lovely things, like the sunset before her, streaming its ribbons of gold across the sky. She drank in its beauty for another long moment.

Think on true things, like what the Bible said about her, that regardless of circumstance, God would never leave her or forsake her. Unlike some people . . . Her eyes filled. She blinked away the moisture.

Admirable things, such as the way Captain Braithwaite had helped Mr. Kemsley.

Praiseworthy things, such as — she frowned. Had she ever had the chance to thank Mr. Kemsley for once again saving her life? Father had been effusive in his praise, but in the aftermath, had she ever truly expressed her appreciation?

She swallowed. "Lord God, please help

him know. Be with him wherever he is, and bless him with his heart's desire."

The first of the stars came out. A wave of sadness rolled over her. How she wished to be of lighter spirits, someone who did not feel so deeply. Someone who could simply admire a sunset, then walk away, a smile in her heart. For while her lips might curve, it seemed her heart would never smile again.

She turned and made her way slowly back to the house, internally fortifying herself for the next stint of bedside vigil. She would be brave, as much for her parents' sake as for Richard's. Not for her the excesses of emotion anymore.

She veered into the Royal Crescent, traipsed past the silly statue, and stole a final look at the velvet sky.

"Excuse me."

She turned. Took a step back, her mouth drying. Words refused to form. Why was he here? Now? What did he want? Heat rushed up and down her skin at his intent look.

"Miss DeLancey?"

Ben studied the face that had haunted his dreams for weeks. How good to see her features — her eyes — up close once more. "Clara?"

"G-good evening."

He looked to the trailing remnants of the sunset. " 'Tis a pretty night."

"Yes."

Silence stretched between them, filled with the awkwardness of the unsaid. Regret gnawed his heart. How to explain what he'd been doing these past weeks, how to explain his absence, when her heart must have hurt so much. The dim lamplight revealed a sweep of color flooding her cheeks. Her astonishment was revealed in the way her eyes fixed on him, as if he were a figment of imagination and might disappear any moment. "I am sorry I left."

She lifted a shoulder in a half shrug that caused his heart to twist. Did she not care? "Mattie . . . explained."

God bless his sister, but she could not explain, not truly. The Admiralty had been his excuse until he'd known his way forward. But he knew now. Could only hope and pray Clara would understand. "I know my departure must have seemed abrupt. I tried explaining something of it to your father before I left."

"He did not mention it. He has been chiefly concerned with my brother."

Ben gestured back to the house. "I just called. I understand from the servant that Richard fights on."

"It is a futile fight. The doctor says the end comes any day now."

"I'm sorry." And in that moment, he was.

Head tilted, she seemed to take his words as genuine and nodded. "Would you care to come inside?"

He'd been inside too many grand houses lately. He had no wish to feel further confined. "I would rather —"

"Go for a walk?"

"Yes. But only if you'll accompany me."

She glanced at the door. "I . . . that is, they are expecting me —"

"I spoke to your father. He knows where we'll be."

He offered his arm, and she clasped it, but loosely, not the way a woman might cling to the arm of the man she loved. But still, tonight was about finding out the truth.

Ben led her along to the clifftop, noting the way her hand tightened as he led her to a vantage spot. From here, a few of Brighton's lights shone, the Pavilion among them. The breeze danced around them, alive and cool.

"Do you remember the first time we met here?"

He glanced quickly at her. They'd never had this conversation, the one about whether she really was that mysterious woman atop a cliff on a wild and windy night. "Yes."

"I . . . I was wretched."

"Were you? I'm afraid I cannot recall every detail of that night."

Although he could recall most. Like his feeling of terror when she slid towards the cliff edge. His immense relief when he'd managed to haul her to safety. That impression of warmth he'd had in those brief moments he'd held her.

"I . . ." She licked her bottom lip, an entrancing sight. "I don't know if I ever truly thanked you for saving me that night."

"You did. I remember that."

He studied her, and she did not look away. He searched her green eyes for the truth. "You never told me what you were doing up here that night."

Her hands, her gaze slid away. "I felt . . . unable to continue, carrying the shame . . ."

"Because of the rumors about you."

"The dishonorable Miss DeLancey." Her gaze returned to his, her lips curled slightly on one side. "I was amazed you didn't recognize me."

"I wondered if I'd seen you in a London ballroom years ago, but a humble sailor could never aspire to speak with a viscount's daughter. And then I was overseas . . ."

She nodded. Glanced down. "I am glad you did not know me then."

"Our past is finished, Clara. There is no sense in living there anymore."

"No." Her features lightened with a small smile. "I always appreciate your candor."

"Life is too precious to prevaricate." He grasped her hands, courage surging within to finally say —

"Thank you for saving me from Lord Houghton." A small shudder shook her frame. "I do not think I ever wish to go swimming again."

"I could teach you."

"What?" Her smile wisped. "That would only confirm my reputation."

"Then perhaps we should get married."

Her lips parted.

He swallowed. "Soon."

"You wish to marry me?"

"I still wish to marry only you."

"But Richard —"

"No, I don't wish to wed him."

Her laughter quickly faded. "No, but . . ."

He threaded his warm fingers through her cool hands. "When the time is right, and your parents are ready, then I wish us to be wed. I love you, Clara." His heart pounded, willing her to reciprocate.

"Oh!" Her cheeks glowed in the last traces

of sunset. "But you left."

Ben fought the twist of disappointment as he admitted, "I went to London to receive the monetary part of Prinny's reward. I also met Hawkesbury. Johnson's capture meant he was able to access his missing funds. Seems he wished to pay a small tribute —"

"Really?"

"I didn't want to accept, but when I visited my bank I found an anonymous donation had been made to that amount. Apparently an earl can override a mere mortal's wishes." He smiled wryly. "I did mention the matter to him, but he seemed somewhat distracted with Johnson's trial. I understand Hawkesbury wishes for him to be transported to the colonies rather than hanged."

"Johnson is fortunate the earl is so magnanimous."

Now came the difficult part. "You sound as though you admire the man now," he said carefully.

"Admire Lord Hawkesbury? Well, I suppose I do." Her head slanted, a slow smile crept across her face. "But while there is much to admire about Lord Hawkesbury, that is nothing in comparison to someone whom I adore."

"You adore?" His heart thudded fiercely.

She nodded, her gaze locked on his. "He is filled with buoyant spirits and courage and sweet consideration for others. How can I not adore — how can I not love — this man?"

Ben fought a grin as he nodded gravely. "Such a paragon deserves esteem, it is true. Even if such regard might not allow for the paragon to hold feet of clay."

"A quality that makes us all the more compatible."

Spirits soaring, Ben moved closer, lifting a hand to gently brush an ebony lock from her face. When he spoke, his voice was husky. "And who might be the privileged recipient of such favor?"

"I think we both know the answer to that, don't you?" Her mouth tilted in delightful invitation.

Heart throbbing in anticipation, Ben slid his hand to the back of her dusky curls, drawing her closer. He lowered his head, meeting the silken fire of her lips in a long, wondrous kiss that dispelled every doubt, ignited every dream, and made his body hunger for his wedding night.

Feeling a trifle dazed, he reluctantly pulled away. "I love you, Miss Clara DeLancey."

"And I love you." She smiled, pushing to

her toes to kiss him again. "You, and only you."

EPILOGUE

London
May 1816

Clara glanced around the ballroom, filled with the cream of the *ton,* young ladies just making their entrée into society, young bucks, preening parents, all gossiping over the latest news — for once, all wondrous and good. Tonight's ball was to honor the Prince Regent's daughter, Princess Charlotte, who had just married her prince — a love match — in a wedding that surpassed all others in style and expense. While the ceremony and public celebrations had certainly surpassed that of hers and Benjamin's nuptials last November, Clara was certain nothing could surpass this great love she had for her husband.

Benjamin was all that was good, all that was patient, all that was kind. She eyed him now, resplendent in a new suit and cravat, like he'd been born to the baronetcy rather than having it bestowed upon him only two weeks ago, in a ceremony marked as much by the Prince Regent's effusive commendations as it was for the lateness in its arriving. Ben was Sir Benjamin Kemsley now, invested with an Order of the Garter on St. George's day.

The reparation had been paid in full, which, along with an unexpected gift from the Marquess of Exeter, made their living more comfortable than she could have dreamed. A few weeks before his son's marriage in February, Lord Exeter had requested that Ben visit him at his earliest convenience. It seemed he'd remembered he possessed what he termed a little cottage not far away in West Sussex. A not-so-little cottage, it turned out, but a handsome manor that had belonged to a recently deceased cousin and had now reverted to Lord Exeter's stewardship. He hadn't wanted the bother, so he'd said, and offered it to Ben as a gift, saying it would benefit from having careful owners, who would soon be part of the wider family connection. Ben's surprise was equal to hers, and they delighted that their new home benefitted from a grand view of the Isle of Wight and close proximity to calm waters, where Ben had promised — or was it threatened?

— to teach her to swim.

"What is that smile for, Lady Kemsley?"

"Just happiness, Sir Benjamin."

Her husband's blue eyes twinkled as if he was thinking of their secret. "I do hope when we return home that the weather will clear sufficiently so those swimming lessons may begin."

"Benjamin!"

He shifted closer, twining his fingers through hers. "Surely you cannot begrudge my wish to spend time with you before we two are three?"

"Hush! Your siblings approach. I'd rather George not know yet."

She suspected George was none too happy to know his baronetcy ranked lower than Benjamin's honor — he had not seemed thrilled to learn of the gift of their estate. But George was rejoicing in Tessa's blissfully happy marriage to Lord Featherington, regarding the match proudly, as if taking credit for its devising — or so he boasted to his wife's relations whenever Ben and Clara were obliged to attend a family function at Chatham Hall.

Mattie and David were also expecting an addition, in early summer rather than mid autumn, thus necessitating their absence from London these past weeks.

Tessa drew near, enveloping Clara in a warm embrace. "It's so good to see you!"

"And you. How was Italy?"

"Oh, lovely! Charlotte said we would have the most marvelous time. Did I tell you she and Hartington visited there last year? Back before they knew she was expecting."

"And how are the twins?"

"Adorable!" She cast a look across the room at her husband, which made Clara wonder how long it would be until the baby of the Kemsley family was having her own babies. "Oh! Please extend my good wishes to your parents." Tessa's blue eyes rounded with concern. "I trust they are well after everything? I'm sure these past months have not been terribly easy."

They hadn't been. But Mother seemed to find some comfort in having had Richard restored to them for a brief time, if only to have held him before he died. "They are doing as well as can be expected, thank you."

Tessa nodded, eyes soft with sympathy. "And you?"

"I am very well, thank you."

"I thought I detected a certain glow." Her lips quirked to one side, her eyes dancing with merriment as she leaned forward.

"Twins do not run in our family, just so you know."

"Tessa!" Ben said with a laugh. "How you will ever attain the dignity of a marchioness, I'll never know."

"Good thing I only married a viscount, isn't it?" she said saucily, before moving off to join her husband, whose face lit at her approach.

Other guests obliged them to engage in social niceties for a few minutes more. When these further exchanges had been exhausted, they were finally released to find Lord and Lady Hawkesbury. Seated beside her was a brown drab of a girl, someone Clara felt sure she'd once been introduced to, but searching her memory, she could not recall . . .

"Ah, Clara, or should I say Lady Kemsley?" Lavinia held out a hand, gently squeezing Clara's outstretched one. "How are you?"

"Very well, thank you."

"I should think so, with your handsome husband, and your lovely manor house."

"Oh, and it is lovely, too," Clara nodded. "Not quite the cottage we were led to believe."

"I'm glad Lord Exeter found such worthy recipients."

"He is all that is generous. I trust you are in good health? You certainly are in good looks."

"She is, isn't she?" Lord Hawkesbury agreed. "But then, I am a little biased."

"Or a lot," Lavinia blushed, her gaze now on her husband.

Clara looked at the brown-haired girl beside the countess. She was somewhat plain, with a long nose, and large brown eyes. Now she remembered. "Miss Winthrop, is it not? Forgive me, I am sure you are married by now."

"I am n-not," Miss Winthrop said, with a blush every bit as rosy as the fire Clara could feel filling her face.

"My dear friend Catherine is here to spend some time with me before heading back to Gloucestershire," Lavinia said.

The brunette nodded, her gaze wary, shaded with something like sadness.

"I remember now. You enjoy riding."

The brown eyes lit. "Y-yes. Yes, I do. As do you, as I r-recall."

"I find I do not ride as much as I used to. My husband much prefers to sail than to ride."

"I im-imagine that proves inconvenient when one wishes to travel across land."

Clara laughed. Miss Winthrop had a nice

sense of humor.

They exchanged a few more pleasantries, before Ben drew her to one side, into a little alcove. "There. That wasn't too hard, was it?"

How well this man knew her. "You were right. But I assure you, I truly did not feel one sting." He lifted a brow. "Not one!" she asserted.

He chuckled, drawing her close once again. "I believe you."

Of course he did. And that was why she was the most fortunate of women. She had loved, and lost, then found new love. But this time her affection was returned — returned a hundredfold. She didn't deserve Benjamin, nor deserve to feel such heights of happiness, but she reveled in the love of a man who loved her just as she loved him: freely, without guilt or stain or blemish.

Ben's blue eyes darkened, his smile stretching. "Have we stayed long enough that we can make our excuses so I can take my wife home?"

"Take me home." She pushed to her toes and kissed him.

His breath caught. His grasp tightened. "How scandalous of you, my dearest."

"Not scandalous, simply necessary, seeing as you seem so unsure about my affections, my dearest, *only* love."

He laughed, the sound filling her heart with warmth, and tugged her from the shadows towards the door.

They would live, and not look back. The gloom of night had proved a mere interlude; now the light shone bright once more.

AUTHOR'S NOTE

I try to blend fiction with certain historical facts to help ground my stories. Here are some notes you may find interesting.

In April 1815 a catastrophic eruption of Mount Tambora in the Dutch East Indies (modern-day Indonesia) destroyed all vegetation on the island, produced a tsunami, and was responsible for over fifty thousand deaths in surrounding islands. The eruption column reached an altitude of over forty-three kilometers (twenty-seven miles), one of the most powerful volcanic eruptions in history. The ash and particles lingered in the atmosphere for months, producing brilliant sunsets witnessed in London in late June, early July, and September. These are the stunning sunsets Clara witnesses in this novel. This eruption is believed to have led to a global lowering of temperatures, which led to Europe and North America experiencing harvest failures in 1816, in what is known as "The Year Without a Summer" (which also led to mass migration, but that's another story . . .).

The wreck of the *Ansdruther* is based on the sinking of the *Arniston,* a British East Indiaman bound for England from Ceylon, carrying 378 passengers and crew, that was wrecked off the coast of South Africa in May 1815 with only six souls saved. These men survived for nearly a week, burying the bodies washed onto shore, until they were rescued by a farmer's son. It is generally believed that the lack of a marine chronometer — a piece of expensive navigational equipment used to determine longitude — was responsible for the wreck, as it meant the captain was unable to determine an accurate location due to the immense storm, and so he steered into a reef rather than towards the Cape of St. Helena as intended.

I could not kill so many people (even fictionally!) so I adjusted matters accordingly.

Fortuitously, in 2015 I was able to visit my sister, who was living in England at the time. A packed itinerary saw us visit Bath, Ireland, Derbyshire, Scotland, and London, and we even spent a day in Brighton. If you ever have the opportunity, visit the Royal Pavilion in Brighton. The Prince Regent's monument to excess (and questionable taste) is a wondrous building, filled with Chinese, Indian, and Moorish elements so fantastic it must be seen to be believed.

The wonderful staff at Brighton–Hove Pavilion — in particular, David Beevers, keeper of the Royal Pavilion — were extremely helpful in giving guidance as to the time frame of the Prince Regent's refurbishments. *The Making of the Royal Pavilion* by John Morley was invaluable in recreating period-precise detailings of the ornate décor. If you visit today, you may find the décor slightly different from what is described here, but that may be due to later refurbishments and, of course, creative licence.

The Prince Regent (later King George IV), after whom the Regency period is named, was by many contemporary accounts considered something of a hedonist, seeking pleasure in women, food, and appearances. For the style of his manners and address, I found *The Letters of King George 1812–1830,* edited by A. Aspinall, to be an excellent resource.

ACKNOWLEDGMENTS

Thank You, God, for giving this gift of creativity, and the amazing opportunity to express it. Thank You for teaching us how to love through the example of Your son, Jesus Christ.

Thank you, Joshua, for your love and encouragement. You are a rock.

Thank you, Caitlin, Jackson, Asher, and Tim, for understanding why Mummy spends so much time in imaginary worlds. I'm so thankful that God has blessed us with you in our lives.

To my family, church family, and friends: thank you for cheering me on. Big thanks to Roslyn and Jacqueline for being patient in reading through so many of my manuscripts and for helping me brainstorm the tricky bits.

Thank you, Tamela Hancock Murray, my agent, for helping this little Australian negotiate the big wide American market.

Thank you to the authors and bloggers in Australia and the United States who have endorsed, encouraged, and opened doors along the way. You are a blessing.

To the Ladies of Influence and Ladies Who Launch: your support and encouragement are gold!

To the great team at Kregel, thank you for making *Miss DeLancey* look pretty and read better.

Finally, thank you to my readers. I've really appreciated your messages of encouragement and kind reviews; your words are treasured. Thanks for helping spread the love for Miss Ellison and Lady Charlotte. I hope you enjoy reading Clara's story, too.

God bless you.

ABOUT THE AUTHOR

Carolyn Miller lives in the beautiful Southern Highlands of New South Wales, Australia. She is married, with four gorgeous children, who all love to read (and write!).

A longtime lover of Regency romance, Carolyn's novels have won a number of Romance Writers of American (RWA) and American Christian Fiction Writers (ACFW) contests. She is a member of American Christian Fiction Writers and Australasian Christian Writers. Her favourite authors arc classics like Jane Austen (of course!), Georgette Heyer, and Agatha Christie, but she also enjoys contemporary authors like Susan May Warren and Becky Wade.

Her stories are fun and witty, yet also deal with real issues, such as dealing with forgiveness, the nature of really loving versus 'true love', and other challenges we all face at different times.